Hidden Memories

Inside the elevator, Ramion pressed his body against Sage's and kissed her fully on the lips. His kisses grew in intensity with each passing floor. "Come home with me tonight," he said with a sensual smile.

Sage had to chase away thoughts of Ramion's rum-dark muscular body entwined with hers. She looked into his eyes shrouded by long, straight eyelashes and heavy black brows. His long, hawkish nose flared whenever he smiled; she could read his thoughts in that smile. She ran her hands across his cheek and said reluctantly, "I can't. I know I won't get any work done."

"I know," he said. He was disappointed, but that's what he loved about her: her commitment and compassion, her vitality and vision. From their first meeting, he had felt connected, drawn to her mesmerizing beauty—oval-shaped eyes, high cheekbones, and full lips. The huskiness of her voice had singed his soul when they first met and left an indelible imprint.

The elevator stopped on the ground floor, but Ramion pressed the stop button, preventing the doors from opening. "I love your passion for the campaign," he said, kissing her lips and unfastening the buttons on her dress. He worked his fingers inside her clothes and slid his hand into her bra. "Right now, I want to feel your passion for me."

"Ramion, what if the doors open?" she protested, feeling desire ignite.

"They won't."

Sage's resistance waned when Ramion massaged her nipples with his mouth, and by the time he wriggled his fingers into the waistband of her pantyhose to touch between her legs, she could no longer resist. She was on fire.

"Let me just feel you," Ramion said, dipping his fingers inside her. Sage moaned. She didn't want him to just feel her.

Advance Praise for *Hidden Memories*

"... A richly-textured contemporary story unfolds dramatically against the volatile world of high-stakes politics, tackling timely topics along the way. . . . A darn good read. Sure to reel you in."

Kate Ferguson, *Today's Black Woman*

"*Hidden Memories* is a soul-stirring novel with high-powered characters and an intriguing must-find-out-what-happens plot."

Sonia Alleyne, Editor-in-Chief, *Black Elegance*

"*Hidden Memories* is an intoxicating potpourri of stories about politics, love, sex, and family skillfully melded together into a climatic entanglement."

Women Looking Ahead

Hidden Memories

by Robin Hampton Allen

Genesis Press, Inc.
Columbus, Mississippi

Genesis Press, Inc.
406A 3rd Avenue North
Columbus, MS 39701-0101

HIDDEN MEMORIES

ISBN: 1-885478-16-X

Manufactured in the United States of America

First Edition

Dedicated in loving memory
to my brother,
William Edwin Hampton Jr.

**Visit our Web page for latest
releases and other information.**

http://www.colom.com/genesis

Acknowledgments

I am blessed to have two wonderful little girls, Cara Allen and Cassidy Allen, and the love and support of my husband, George Andre Allen.

My heartfelt appreciation goes to my parents, William and Julia Hampton. Daddy: Your unsinkable support has lifted by spirits on many occasions. Mommy: My strength and determination comes from you. I thank you for your prayers.

Much love to my Pittsburgh family: Lynn Manley, Tyrece Mitchell, Leah Stroman, Brandon Hampton, Karen Stroman, Jerome "Mann" Stroman, Jada Mitchell, Richie Mitchell, Tiara Hampton, and Javonta Stroman.

This book has gone through many revisions, and I thank my special friends for their words of encouragement: Yvonne Wells, Sharon Flake, and Marilyn Polite.

Special thanks to my editor, Donna Julian, for her patience and expertise.

To my brother's only son, Ramion Drew Hampton: Much love and happiness.

Chapter I

Sage Kennedy stared at the words on the computer screen, pondering the right spin on Cameron Hudson's gubernatorial speech to the New Generation Party. She wanted a different twist on their "The Dream Reborn" theme, an inspiring message that would rouse the young voters to help elect the first black governor of Georgia.

The unusual quietness of the campaign headquarters penetrated Sage's concentration as she looked around and realized she was the only person in the office. Sage glanced at the clock on the wall and, noticing that it was almost eight o'clock, decided to finish the speech at home. As she copied the speech file to a diskette, she reviewed her schedule for the next day, noting important priorities: finalize copy for campaign brochures; meet with production crew for television commercial; attend luncheon fund-raiser.

"Something told me I would find you here," a deep-timbered voice said.

"You know me too well," Sage said, without looking up. When Ramion Sandidge reached her desk, she raised her head to peer into his charcoal eyes. He returned her warm, familiar smile, revealing a showcase of white teeth and a cleft chin. "I was supposed to leave here an hour ago. I wanted to finish Cameron's speech, but I've run out of steam. I'll work on it at home."

1

"Cameron never sticks to the speech," Ramion said, shrugging his shoulders. "Why bother?" His wavy hair was trimmed neatly and precisely with a razor-sharp part on one side.

"You know why. If Cameron doesn't have a speech, he preaches."

Ramion laughed and bent down to kiss the most strikingly attractive woman he had ever seen. Sage was an exotic combination of amber skin, curly black hair, and olive green eyes. "You're probably right."

"How did the trial go?" she asked.

"They decided to settle out of court. My client is going to take money for silence. He'll get a healthy amount."

"Sounds like you got more than you expected."

"Yes, but let's get out of here, baby. You promised me you wouldn't be here late, especially after the threats Cameron's been getting."

"I know," she said, nodding. "Security is very tight now. Anywhere Cameron goes, they secure the building before he gets there. We even canceled some of his engagements because they were in open places that are hard to secure."

"Yeah, well, crazy people always find a way."

"At first, Ramion, I really wasn't frightened by those threats," Sage said, her heavy eyebrows drawn together in a worried expression. "But every time the media reports that Cameron is closing in on Baker's lead, the threats increase. And it's not just threats from known white hate groups," Sage continued. "We've gotten threats from people that just hate the idea of a black man being elected governor." Sage removed the speech diskette from the computer and tucked it inside her briefcase. "I don't know why I'm shocked by their deep-seated hatred, but I am."

"I'm not. That's why you have to be careful."

"You're right." Sage swept back her black hair, parted in the center of her oval face, and tucked it behind her ears. "I'm ready," she said, standing up and putting several file folders into her briefcase.

"Let's go," Ramion said, placing his arm around Sage's waist. He wasn't satisfied with merely touching her waist. He wanted to remove the black double-breasted dress, caress her curvaceous body, nibble on her bountiful breasts, and slide between her seductive hips.

They weaved their way through rows of desks and file cabinets. Campaign brochures were scattered around the room, envelopes and mailing labels piled on desks, and posters of Cameron Hudson for governor hung on the walls.

"You can lock up," Sage said to the burly security guard standing at the doorway of the campaign headquarters. "We're leaving."

"You got it," the guard said, pulling out a mass of keys. He announced into a handheld radio that he was "securing the eighth floor."

Inside the elevator, Ramion pressed his body against Sage's and kissed her fully on the lips. His kisses grew in intensity with each passing floor. "Come home with me tonight," he said with a sensual smile.

Sage had to chase away thoughts of Ramion's rum-dark muscular body entwined with hers. She looked into his eyes shrouded by long, straight eyelashes and heavy black brows. His long, hawkish nose flared whenever he smiled; she could read his thoughts in that smile. She ran her hands across his cheek and said reluctantly, "I can't. I know I won't get any work done."

"I know," he said. He was disappointed, but that's what he loved about her: her commitment and compassion, her vitality and vision. From their first meeting, he had felt connected, drawn to her mesmerizing beauty—oval-shaped eyes, high cheekbones, and full lips. The huskiness of her voice had singed his soul when they first met and left an indelible imprint.

The elevator stopped on the ground floor, but Ramion pressed the stop button, preventing the doors from opening. "I love your passion for the campaign," he said, kissing her lips and unfastening the buttons on her dress. He worked his fingers inside her clothes and slid his hand into her bra. "Right now, I want to feel your passion for me."

"Ramion, what if the doors open?" she protested, feeling desire ignite.

"They won't."

Sage's resistance waned when Ramion massaged her nipples with his mouth, and by the time he wriggled his fingers into the waistband of her pantyhose to touch between her legs, she could no longer resist. She was on fire.

"Let me just feel you," Ramion said, dipping his fingers inside her. Sage moaned. She didn't want him to just feel her.

* * * * * * * * * * * * *

When the elevator doors opened, Sage hoped no one was standing in front of the elevator. She quickly freshened up in the bathroom before walking through the lobby, past the security guards watching video surveillance cameras of the building.

"I hope there isn't a camera in the elevator," Sage ruefully said.

"Yeah, well," Ramion laughed, "might be the only action the guards will get."

They walked out of the building onto Peachtree Street, where the night air was unseasonably brisk for October. "Where are you parked?" Ramion asked.

"The parking lot across the street," she answered, pointing at the open parking lot between the convenience store and a restaurant.

"Tell me you wouldn't have walked there by yourself."

"Honey, if you weren't here, one of the security guards would have escorted me to my car."

As Ramion and Sage headed down the street to the traffic light at the corner, a loud crash sounded behind them like an unexpected boom of thunder and the ground trembled like an earthquake. With a cry of surprise, Sage lost her footing and tripped on the street curb. As she struggled to her feet, she was hit in the back of the neck and on her cheek by flying glass. When Ramion saw the glass blow out the windows of the building, he grabbed her hand, dragging her across the street and zigzagging through the steady stream of midtown traffic. Jagged splinters of wood and debris and particles of glass fell from the sky like a hailstorm. They ran, but not fast enough. The blast hurled a piece of wood that struck Sage's head. Ramion pushed the wood away and, in the next instant, the impact of the explosion sprayed their bodies like gravel shot from the barrel of a gun. Ramion pulled Sage into a convenience store and shouted at the shocked store clerk to call 911.

The last thing Sage heard before slipping into unconsciousness was the melodious sound of her father's voice—loud and boisterous and beckoning. She was terrified. It was a voice she hadn't heard in twenty-two years.

* * * * * * * * * * * *

Sage opened her eyes and saw a blurred image of a woman dressed in a white uniform. The nurse was saying something, but Sage couldn't make out the words. The ringing in her ears drowned out the sounds of emergency room drama, a cacophony of patient screams and moans, doctors yelling out orders, and nurses frantically running around administering to the hurt and wounded.

"My ears," Sage complained.

"The ringing will subside by tomorrow," the nurse said, a tall, thin white woman in her mid-thirties. "It's your head that we're concerned about."

"It's killing me." Sage winced as she attempted to sit up.

"We'll need to keep you for 24 hours just to make sure you don't have a concussion."

"What about my other injuries?"

"It took several stitches to close the wound on your neck. Everything else is minor. You were very lucky, considering," the nurse told her.

Ramion threw the curtain back and repeated the nurse's words. "Very lucky." He grasped Sage's hand, squeezing it tightly as he kissed her. Her fragile condition was the only thing that stopped him from taking her in his arms and cradling her in his embrace. "Baby, I'm so glad you're okay."

"What about you?" Sage asked, noticing the bandages on his forehead and wrapped around his left hand.

"Nothing serious. A few pieces of glass."

"You'll be moved to a room shortly," the nurse told Sage before leaving.

Ramion sat on the edge of the bed, his arms wrapped gingerly around her as Sage leaned into his chest. "I love you," he said, running his fingers through her hair.

"I love you, too," Sage said tenderly. As the reality of their brush with death descended upon her, tears rolled down her face. She didn't cry out loud; she just let the tears flow. When they stopped, she wiped her eyes. "I'm sorry."

"Oh, baby, don't apologize. You have every right to cry." He planted soft kisses on her forehead, realizing the depth of his love for her at the possibility of losing her. He was torn between wanting to prosecute the responsible parties and physically hurting them.

They were silent for several minutes, absorbed in the comfort and security of their love.

"Was anybody else hurt?" Sage asked.

5

"One of the security guards is in surgery now. Minor injuries for two guards."

"Any word on who planted the bomb?"

"Not yet."

* * * * * * * * * * * * * *

The first thing Sage noticed when she opened her eyes the next morning was that the ringing in her ears was gone. She could clearly hear hospital sounds: hurried footsteps pounding the floor, the whisking wheels of hospital beds, and rolling trays spinning against the floor.

A whiff of bacon turned her attention to the food on the bedside tray. She lifted the tray cover, but the scrambled eggs, toast, and greasy strips of bacon did not rouse her tastebuds. As she sipped the orange juice, she fumbled with the remote to turn on the television.

The door to her room suddenly swung open, and a security guard peeked inside. "Excuse me, this man says he's a relative." Casting the visitor a suspicious glare over his shoulder, the guard continued, "But he's carrying a press badge."

"He can come in," Sage said when she saw Drew Evans standing in the doorway. They'd met in a psychology class at Columbia University and become immediate friends. The campus rumor mill had tagged Sage and Drew a couple, but their relationship was platonic. Few had believed their "just friends" explanation, so by their junior year they'd stopped trying to explain their brother-sister bond.

Drew rushed over to Sage's bed and hugged her. "Are you okay?"

"I'm okay. Got a hell of a headache," she said, rubbing her hand across her forehead.

"I'm glad you weren't seriously hurt," he said, kissing her on the cheek. He settled on the edge of her bed. "When I heard about the explosion at the headquarters, I immediately thought about you. Then when I saw you on CNN being carried off in an ambulance, I almost lost it," he said, grabbing his stomach. "You know you're my heart, girl."

"I know," Sage said, smiling softly, feeling the genuine love that shone in his brown eyes. Drew hadn't changed much since college, except that his round, coffee-colored face had gotten rounder and his stocky, muscular build stockier. An extra large sweater and size 38

6

jeans covered his broad body, which was a little thick in the waist from drinking a six-pack of beer nightly. He still didn't shave, having inherited his father's baby-smooth complexion.

"Ah, you just wanted to make the front page," he teased, tapping her leg with the folded newspaper.

Drew could never stay serious or sentimental for long. She said with an understanding smile, "Of course I did."

He flipped open the morning newspaper with a picture of Sage lying on a gurney. "Voilà."

Sage quickly scanned the article. The explosion had been caused by a crude bomb made of dynamite wrapped together with gray duct tape, a detonating device, a timer, and a windup alarm clock. "Damn," she said when she finished reading the article.

"So tell me what happened," Drew said. "If you're up to it."

Sage inhaled deeply and nodded as the memories of the last twelve hours swirled in her mind. "Ramion was walking me to my car. We had just left the building, and were going to the light to cross the street. I heard this loud boom, then I felt the ground move . . . no, it rattled. I thought the world was coming to an end," she said, pausing to reflect on her words. "I stumbled a little, and that's when Ramion grabbed my hand and we started running. I don't know where we were going, but we were moving fast. It was raining glass and wood, and something hit me in the head. Ramion pulled me into the store." Her voice cracked. "I was bleeding. He was bleeding . . ."

"Sounds scary."

"Yes. What's really scary is to think that, if Ramion hadn't come when he did, I might have still been in the building."

"I knew I liked the brother," Drew teased. He lifted the tray covering her food and nibbled on a piece of bacon. "Mind?"

"Help yourself." Sage paused, struggling to maintain her composure. "I thought I'd lost Ramion, too. It hit me suddenly that all the men in my life have died. My father, Randy, Broderick." She closed her eyes and added softly, "I couldn't stand to lose Ramion."

"Nothing like that is going to happen," Drew said.

"I know, I know. I've got to stop thinking like that." Her mouth suddenly dry, she sipped her orange juice.

A columnist for the *Atlanta Times* newspaper, Drew said, "Anyway, you know the press is going to want to interview you."

"I hadn't thought about it, but I'm not going to grant any interviews. This campaign has already been sidetracked with the white supremacy threats and the mysterious FBI files. I'm not about to become another distraction. The election is four weeks away. Getting Cameron the governorship, that's what this is all about."

"Yeah, and that's precisely why you're in the hospital. They don't want Cameron to be governor. Whoever 'they' are."

"Whoever 'they' are may have just scared away the voters. If they can blow up campaign headquarters, what's to stop them from blowing up the polls?"

"You're right," Drew said, instantly hitting on the title for his editorial column in the Sunday edition of the newspaper: "Don't Let Fear Keep You Away from the Polls."

"Cameron's going to need every vote he can get," Sage said, finishing the glass of orange juice. "It's damage control time."

* * * * * * * * * * * * *

Her eyelids drooped while watching *Hawaii Five-O* and Sage drifted off to sleep, the episode about a hotel bombing too painfully familiar to watch. She didn't hear the light tap on the hospital door or the quiet entrance of two FBI agents. Her eyes flashed wide open when she suddenly heard her name. Sage sat up, still groggy from sleep, but the sight of two conservatively dressed men standing near the bottom of the hospital bed immediately awakened her. She stared at them suspiciously.

The two men, as if on cue, whipped out their badges. "Don't be alarmed, Ms. Kennedy. We're with the FBI," said the older agent, a black man in his early forties, sporting a grey-speckled, neatly trimmed afro. He stood over six feet tall.

Sage studied their identifications, making sure their faces matched the photo on the badge.

"He's put on some weight since then," the younger white agent said, referring to his partner's expanding girth. He was all-around average in height, weight, and looks. His bright red hair was his distinguishing feature.

Sage responded to their humor with a thin smile. "Have a seat, gentlemen."

"No thanks," the black agent said, stepping closer to the bed. "I'm Agent Jim Bennett and this is Agent Ron Davis."

Sage nodded. "You apparently know who I am."

"Yes, Ms. Kennedy, and we're sorry that you were hurt in the explosion. It can be a traumatic experience."

Sage nodded. "I'm okay. I'm going to be released tomorrow."

"We're trying to find the persons responsible, so we need to ask you some questions if you're up to it," Agent Bennett said, removing a notebook from his jacket pocket.

"Sure," Sage said, while adjusting the bed to an upright position.

"What time did you leave your office?" Bennett asked.

"We left about eight fifteen," Sage said, thinking about the ten-minute diversion in the elevator. She would never tell them about that.

"You left with Ramion Sandidge?"

"Yes."

"Did you see or hear anything as you were leaving?"

"Nothing out of the ordinary. Ramion came into the office and we talked for a few minutes. I was about to leave, but if Ramion hadn't come when he did . . ." she said, her voice dropping with the reality of her words. She paused briefly and said, "I might have stayed longer."

"When you walked down the hall to the elevator, did you notice anything?" Agent Bennett asked.

"I told the security guard that we were leaving. I heard him radio to somebody that he was securing the floor."

"Did you hear or smell anything unusual?" the younger officer interjected.

Her dark brows drawn together, Sage pondered the question for a minute. "No."

"What about in the elevator? Did you see or hear anything?" Agent Davis probed.

"No," Sage said.

Both FBI agents took notes as they questioned Sage. "We're aware of the threats Mr. Hudson has received since the campaign," Bennett said. "In recent days, have you received more threats or anything out of the ordinary?"

"No. We got a lot of threatening letters in the beginning, but then they tapered off. Every time the media reports that Cameron is narrowing the lead, we get a bunch of hate mail. A special security team has been assigned to protect Cameron during the campaign," Sage said. Suddenly thirsty, she reached for the pitcher of water on the bedside table and poured herself a cup.

"We know about them," Bennett said, nodding. "We'll be working with the security team and the ATF during this investigation."

"Can you tell me any details?" Sage asked.

"We don't have anything substantial," the black agent said. "We're following up on different leads."

"Even the ones that might not seem important," Agent Davis said.

"It's unbelievable what some people will do," Sage said, then took a sip of water.

"Believe me, we want to catch this person," Agent Davis said.

"Or persons," Bennett said.

"Persons?" Sage queried with a raised brow.

"Usually there's more than one person involved in something like this," Agent Bennett said. "We'll be in touch. Be careful, Ms. Kennedy."

* * * * * * * * * * * *

"Darling, I'm so glad you're all right," Cameron Hudson said as he entered Sage's house. He hugged his campaign manager, relieved to see for himself that Sage had recovered from her injuries. A large man with the massive body of a football player, Cameron's darkly chiseled features melted like chocolate as he smiled warmly at Sage.

They stood in the open two-story foyer of Sage's designer-styled house in an upscale Atlanta neighborhood. "Come in," Sage said, and led Cameron through her living room into the kitchen, passing Romaire Bearden and William Tolliver paintings that hung on the wall. Two of her father's paintings were displayed in the living room, and her favorite painting by him hung over her bed.

"Lady Day," Cameron said when he heard Billie Holiday's distinctive voice singing "Strange Fruit."

"She's one of my favorite singers, although this song isn't my favorite." Shrugging her shoulders Sage said, "Maybe it's my mood. Years ago they hung people on trees, now they blow people up."

"Billie Holiday knew what she was singing about. She couldn't get away from racism. She would perform in places that would let her entertain them on stage, but not allow her to sit in the audience."

10

"I know," Sage said, turning off the stereo. "Thanks for the beautiful flowers. As a matter of fact, they're on the table in the dining room."

"Sarah sends her love. Jessica and C.J. wanted to come see you, but they're in school."

"They're so sweet," Sage said, referring to Cameron's two children.

"I want you to know how grateful I am for all the hard work you've done on my campaign," Cameron said, sitting down at the kitchen table. "I credit you with making me a serious contender."

Sage had been at the press conference when Cameron declared his candidacy for governor of Georgia. She'd baited opponent U.S. Senator Baker into debating Cameron after mailing a fact sheet about the senator's questionable voting record. She'd steered the campaign back to the political issues when race became the divisive focus of the campaign. She'd garnered national attention with a massive voter registration drive, registering thousands of never-registered voters and reactivating nonvoting registrants. And, she'd managed to get key political support from local and national figures.

"I know," Sage smiled and, embarrassed, changed the subject. "I think Senator Baker is tired of denying responsibility for the bombing."

"I don't think he's responsible. That's not his style. He's too arrogant. He considers the governorship his birthright, and he doesn't believe for a second that he needs to scare people away from the polls to keep me from winning."

"I suppose," Sage said. "Anyway, I feel better knowing that the polling places will be secured, but you have to know the National Guard presence could deter voters."

"I can't take any chances. The FBI has several leads, but nothing concrete."

"I'm just glad they're treating this bombing seriously," Sage said, and took a seat across from Cameron. She opened up two folders. "Here's the information you need for your meeting with Rupert Williams, as well as your speech for the NAACP. Marika's working on your schedule."

"Doesn't sound like you're following doctor's orders," Cameron said.

"We're too close, Cam. If Baker agrees, we're going to reschedule the debate for next Sunday. The consultants will be here Tuesday to start coaching you."

* * * * * * * * * * * * *

Sage's telephone rang three times before rolling over to electronic voice mail. She didn't answer the phone. She didn't want to be disturbed. But whoever was calling was insistent. As soon as the phone stopped after the third ring, it started its insistent peal again. When it began ringing for the tenth time in less than ten minutes, Sage finally picked up the phone. "Hello," she said, irritation in her voice.

No one responded.

"Hello," Sage repeated. "Who is this?"

"Sage?" The voice was tentative and fragile; it was strange and unfamiliar. But Sage knew the voice. It was the same anxious voice, resonant with undertones of suppressed emotion that she'd heard the last time she saw her mother.

"Mama?" Sage asked. She hadn't expected to hear her voice. She hadn't spoken to her mother since she graduated from college.

"Thank goodness you're all right," Audra Hicks said, her voice high strung and nervous. "When I heard you were in the building that blew up, my heart stopped."

"I wasn't in the building. I was . . ."

"I've been so worried about you," Audra said, not hearing Sage. "I've been trying to reach you to make sure you're okay."

"I talked to Ava. She knows I was released from the hospital two days ago."

"She told me, but I had to hear your voice for myself."

"I'm fine, Mama," Sage said. "As a matter of fact, I'll be going back to work tomorrow."

"You be careful. It sounds so dangerous down there. Doesn't seem the South has changed much."

Sage wasn't in the mood for a new-South-still-the-old-South conversation. "I'll be fine."

"It's so good to hear your voice," Audra said, her own voice wrapped in deep emotions.

Sage didn't repeat her mother's words; she didn't share the sentiment. She struggled with long-buried feelings that now bubbled up and nearly choked her.

"I want to come see you," Audra said, hesitantly, nervously. "It's been so long. Too long since we've seen each other."

"This is not a good time," Sage said. Memories of the hollow, aching loneliness of her childhood flitted through her mind, memories that had begun when her father died. "I'll be very busy with the election."

"I'm coming to Atlanta for an assembly. I thought maybe we could have dinner." The words rolled out hurriedly, as if Audra needed to get them said before her nerve deserted her.

Sage searched for a reason to refuse her. She didn't want to dredge up old feelings. She'd worked too hard to keep them buried inside. She reached for her Day-Timer, flipping through the pages. "When are you going to be here?"

"Next Thursday through Sunday."

"I don't know," Sage said doubtfully, scanning her busy calendar.

"Please, Butterfly. It's been too long," Audra insisted.

Satchel Kennedy instantly flashed in Sage's mind and the warmest emotions filled her soul. She closed her eyes for a moment, picturing her father's warm smile. He'd called her Butterfly, sometimes Sweet Butterfly.

"We could have dinner on Friday," Sage said, her voice carefully nonchalant.

"Oh, that would be so wonderful," Audra said merrily. "I can't wait to see you."

"I'll see you next week, Mama," Sage said before hanging up the phone. She stared blankly at the papers spread out on the kitchen table, then got up from the table and walked into her bedroom. She stood in the doorway, staring at her father's painting hanging over her bed—a bright, colorful painting of butterflies flitting about a beautiful garden.

Chapter II

"It looks like people coming together, united by forces they don't understand," Sage said, peering up at the huge painting hanging on the wall of La Touissant Art Gallery.

"No, it's about an uprising. Maybe in a small country or island. See, their hoes and picks are their weapons, they're about to fight against their oppressors," Ramion said.

Sage narrowed her olive eyes at Ramion, amazed that his interpretation was so different from hers. "But the expressions on their faces are hopeful." Pointing, Sage said, "Look at that woman, the lady with her eyes closed. She's relieved that there's going to be peace. She's trying to connect with the force or something spiritual."

Ramion smiled slightly, enjoying their debate, a welcome change from courtroom arguments and statements. "I think she's scowling. She's tired and defeated," Ramion said, scrutinizing the texturized painting of islanders standing in a field with a majestic waterfall in the background. "Look at the picture on the other wall," Ramion said, indicating a similar painting on the other side of the spacious gallery. "It's by the same artist." Turning back to Sage, he said smugly, "Its theme is revolution."

"It's not a revolution. See, they're holding something in their hands." Chuckling, Sage said, "They're waving voter registration cards."

14

Ramion laughed and unconsciously rubbed Sage's arm with his hands.

Tawny Touissant, the owner of the art gallery, overheard Sage's remark. "Girl, you can't get your mind off the election, can you?"

"What can I say? The election is next week. I'm a bundle of nerves. I shouldn't even be here," Sage said. "It's been wicked."

"Relax, girlfriend. I'm just glad you weren't badly hurt by that bomb! Still no word on who did it?"

"Nothing," Sage said. "I try not to think about it too much."

"Well, Cameron is going to win in spite of the bombing," Tawny said with the earnest enthusiasm she showered on the artists she represented.

"Baker is holding a narrow lead," Sage said.

"So? It can change tomorrow. You know, politics is a lot like art. Everyone has his or her own perception. Think of yourself as an artist who painted Cameron's image. Election day will be the debut of your artist's work. The votes are the bids people make on the paintings. The person with the highest bid wins."

"That's an interesting analogy, Tawny," Ramion said.

"I never quite thought about it like that," Sage said, her voice husky with hope.

"What are you wearing?" Ramion asked Tawny. "You look like a . . ."

"Lamp post," Tawny said, giggling about her black jumpsuit and funky, high-top black and white hat. "I can't paint a damn thing, Ramion, so my creative expression comes through in my funky fashion style. I heard you all talking about Medu's painting. Believe me, it's not that deep . . . Ah, here he is now," Tawny said, waving her hand in a beckoning motion toward the man who'd just entered the room.

The artist approached with a friendly smile and a nod of greeting at Sage and Ramion.

"Medu, I'd like you to meet my friends, Sage Kennedy and Ramion Sandidge."

Medu shook Ramion's hand and turned to greet Sage. "Delighted," he said, his melodious accent revealing his Haitian heritage. "So you like this one?"

"They were just discussing it. They think it's about a revolution," Tawny said with a conspiratory laugh.

Medu joined Tawny's laughter, stroking his tightly curled beard that covered half his face. "It's a celebration . . . a holiday that we take midday."

"I certainly didn't see that," Ramion said, glancing at the painting with a new perspective.

"I don't think many people do. I love listening to people's interpretation of my work," Medu said. "I like tapping people's emotions."

"That's what I love about this business," Tawny said. "I'm not an artist, but it's fun to watch people's reactions." She hosted openings that went beyond the meet-the-artist-and-have-some-white-wine receptions. Located in the Virginia Highlands area in a turn-of-the-century house, her openings were real events bordering on theater or performance art.

"These two paintings always spark controversy. Either people see . . ." Medu's sentence was cut off when a pair of lips grazed his. He responded to the succulent pleasure of Edwinna Williamson's provocative kiss.

"Hello, baby," Edwinna purred to Medu. Her cinnamon-brown face glowed with regal pride that bordered on arrogance. Not a trace of embarrassment showed in her deep-set black eyes and sly smile.

"Hey," Medu said with an embarrassed smile. "Everyone, this is Edwinna Williamson."

"We all know each other," Edwinna said. "Hello, Tawny. Sage." With a provocative grin, she said, "I know Ramion very well," staring deeply into Ramion's dark eyes.

"Ah, *that* Ramion. I didn't make the connection. You two were once together. But we've changed partners. It's a good thing we're not friends, eh, Ramion?" Medu said, laughing lightly.

"Medu is most direct," Tawny said with an uncomfortable giggle.

"We're all adults," Medu said, casually shrugging his shoulders.

"Daddy tells me you're leaving us," Edwinna said to Ramion.

Surprised that Edwinna had learned so quickly of his conversation with her father only hours before, Ramion stepped closer to Sage as if to protect her from Edwinna's revelation. He saw the bewildered look pass through Sage's eyes, then disappear as it was replaced by an expression of curious interest.

"News travels fast," Ramion said, hoping that Sage wouldn't be angry that he hadn't told her about resigning from the law firm

16

founded by Edwinna's father. Under Edwin Williamson's tutelage, Ramion had gone from junior attorney to senior partner in five years. His resignation would take him from the empowered embrace of Edwin to the unchartered waters of a career with a new law firm. The prospect still unnerved him.

"I'm surprised. You never expressed interest in working for a bigger firm," Edwinna said, reprovingly.

"I just never shared that information with you," Ramion responded.

"I guess congratulations are in order," Tawny said, sensing the negative vibes in the air.

"Thanks, Tawny," Ramion said.

Noticing the crowd converging at the receptionist's desk, Tawny said, "Excuse me folks. I've got some people to greet." As she walked away, she added, "Help yourself to the food. Thanks for coming."

Medu filled the awkward silence that followed Tawny's departure. "Sage and Ramion were discussing this painting. Ramion thought it was about a political uprising, and Sage . . ."

Not interested in hearing Sage's opinions, Edwinna interrupted. "Ramion would think that. He's very focused. And politics are very much on his mind."

"Given that the election is next week, I think it's on a lot of people's minds," Sage said.

"And that explosion," Medu said. "You're very fortunate you weren't seriously hurt."

Edwinna ignored that and turned the topic back to Ramion. "Speaking of politics, Ramion has big plans to run for the state senate. Or have you changed your mind about that, too?" she asked, expressing remnants of anger for the way Ramion had ended their relationship. She'd always known that he didn't love her, but she'd intended to change his feelings. Edwinna despised Sage for robbing her of the opportunity to stake a claim on Ramion's heart.

"I wish you well," Medu said before Ramion could answer. "In my country, politics is *savoir faire*. My father was a government official. That's why some of my paintings have a political undertone, but in a much broader sense. I try to show how politics affect the common man."

"In some countries, that can be risky," Sage said.

"Indeed," Medu said. "That's why I say America is the greatest country on earth."

"I believe that's Don King's line," Ramion said.

"Well, then, I agree with him," Medu said. "But I must say, voting under the presence of the National Guard is reminiscent of something that would happen in my country."

"You're right. It's amazing what people will do to try and stop change," Ramion said.

"I still say America is a wonderful country," Medu said. "Look at what's being done to protect your rights."

"Come on, Medu. We've got reservations at the Abbey," Edwinna said, fastening her full-length mink coat over her purple dress. With three-inch purple pumps, the full-figured woman almost towered over Medu's medium frame. "By the way, Ramion, I've been thinking about running for the state senate, too."

"Ben Hill's seat?" Sage asked, assuming that Edwinna was referring to the senator's retirement. Ramion's political plans began with replacing the highly respected senator.

"Exactly," Edwinna said, lifting her waxed eyebrows in a taunting expression.

A scowl turned Ramion's dark eyes into narrow slits. "Since when have you become interested in politics?" Ramion snarled, knowing how little Edwinna cared about those less fortunate than herself. There weren't many blacks who had enjoyed Edwinna's privileged childhood—private schools, a fourteen-room mansion, first-class plane rides, unlimited shopping sprees, and a live-in maid.

"Hmm, I suppose I just never shared that with you," was Edwinna's parting repartee. She tucked her hand in Medu's bowed arm.

"Goodnight," Medu said.

When Edwinna and Medu were gone, Ramion said, "I can't believe she intends to run against me. She knows that seat is critical to my plans." The state senate was his launching point; the U.S. Senate his ultimate goal.

"And I can't believe you didn't tell me that you gave Edwin your resignation," Sage said.

"I was going to tell you tonight. I was planning to surprise you."

"But, you wouldn't have resigned unless you had another job."

"Of course not."

18

"You didn't tell me that either. I know you interviewed last month." She anchored both fists on her hips. "But you hadn't mentioned any more about it."

"You didn't ask," Ramion said in a clipped tone, more worried about how leaving Edwin's law firm would affect his political career than Sage's pique.

"I shouldn't have to."

"We've barely seen each other in the past two weeks," Ramion said impatiently. "You've been busy with the campaign, and I've been tied up with the Hughes trial."

"That's not the point. I shouldn't have to find out something that important from Edwinna."

"Look, Sage, they offered me the position two weeks ago, but there was no point in telling you until I had accepted the position."

"So now you have doubts about me," Sage said with a worried expression. Ramion's unwillingness to confide in her bothered Sage, but there was more at stake than his political career. Their relationship, once cloaked in darkness, was set free when he ended his relationship with his mentor's daughter. He was making these changes for Sage and for himself—to love Sage openly and to launch his political career without a debt card to Edwin. "About us."

"Of course not. This isn't about us. It's the risk. With Edwin's backing, my political career was practically guaranteed. Without him, the risk is much greater."

"Politics is always a gamble, Ramion. It's unpredictable," Sage said, the enthusiasm of her tone reflecting her love of politics. "There are never guarantees. Not even Edwin's backing could do that."

"I know, Sage. I want to win on my own. But if Edwinna runs . . ."

"Do you think Edwinna is serious?" Sage asked, incredulity sounding in her voice. She knew that if Edwinna ran against Ramion, the stakes were much higher.

"Of course. She doesn't care about winning. She just wants me to lose."

"Is she that vindictive?"

"She's used to getting what she wants," Ramion said. "Edwin has always indulged her."

"And she wants you. She doesn't hide it."

"That's over, Sage. You know that."

"But if you were with Edwinna she wouldn't be running against you."

"I have no doubts about us. I know I did the right thing." Ramion planted a soft kiss on Sage's mouth.

Sage's ringing cellular phone interrupted their kiss. She retrieved the phone from her purse. "This will be Cam or Marika. I'm going to take it in Tawny's office."

Ramion watched Sage walk away. She moved with the grace and elegance of a ballerina. He loved her more than he had ever imagined possible. So intelligent, so loving, so real. Those were the qualities he cherished in her.

Sage answered the phone as she rounded the corner to Tawny's office, the last picture on the wall catching her eye. As her assistant Marika told her about a car dealer reneging on his promise to provide vans for the Ride to the Polls program, Sage studied the painting.

Ten minutes later, Sage's gaze swept the gallery, searching for Ramion. She spotted him talking with mutual acquaintances. Starting in Ramion's direction, Sage bumped into Tawny.

"Sorry, I was lost in thought. I just had a phone call from Marika. One of the car dealers backed out of providing us with vans for tomorrow."

"I saw that on the news," Tawny said. "I was impressed that you were able to get car dealers to loan out their vans."

"Yes, well, that wasn't supposed to be made public," Sage said. "I don't know how the media found out about it. Sometimes I wonder if we don't have a spy in the office or a bug in our phones. Anyway, that dealer was only supplying five vans. We've got at least 30 vans and more drivers than we need."

"You're working it, girl. I like the way you stay on top of things."

"We've got to get going. Tomorrow is going to be crazy," Sage said. "But I meant to tell you, I love your haircut. It's very flattering."

"I love to be flattered," Tawny said in an exaggerated tone, batting her eyes for dramatic effect. She patted her high-fashion skull cap cut. "Very low maintenance. Just brush and go. You'd look good with your hair short."

"Not my style, especially not with this scar on my neck," Sage said. "By the way, you know that painting by your office?"

"The three women."

"That's the one. I like it." Sage and Tawny walked over to the painting. "It's a quirky blend of William Tolliver and Romaire Bearden, with an impressionist flavor."

"I knew you'd like that one," Tawny said. "There were originally two of them. I only got one. When Connie's gallery when out of business, I bought her inventory."

"Who's the artist?"

"I don't know a lot about him. He's from California, and he's . . ."

"How much is it?"

"You thinking about buying it?"

"I might," Sage said. "It kind of reminds me of my father's work."

"Oh, Sage, I'm sorry, it's not for sale. Connie asked me to return it. It wasn't supposed to be included with the inventory."

"Now I really want it," Sage teased.

"Want what?" Ramion asked when he joined them.

"That painting," Sage said nodding her head at the painting.

"Very nice," he said.

"I hope you don't see anything radical or political going on," Tawny laughed.

"Very funny," Ramion said. He placed his arm around Sage's waist and said, "Let's go, baby."

"Goodnight, Tawny," Sage said.

Tawny gave Sage a hug. "I'll see you at the victory party toasting the first black governor of Georgia."

* * * * * * * * * * * * *

Sage and Ramion stepped outside the gallery onto the wrap-around Victorian-styled porch. Sage buttoned her leather coat against the cool October air. Silently they stood side-by-side, neither wanting to leave with misunderstanding between them.

"Baby, I'm sorry I didn't tell you about the job offer," Ramion said.

Sage lifted her eyebrows expectantly, clearly expressing her need to hear more.

"And I should have told you that I resigned. I'm used to dealing with things on my own. I'm not very good at discussing my plans." He put his arms around Sage's shoulders and drew her close. "I'm going to have to work on it."

21

Sage said softly, "Okay," and rested her head against Ramion's chest.

Ramion tilted her head upward and kissed her lips, gently, then harder as lust surged from his lips to his loins. "I'll follow you home."

"Are you free on Friday night?"

"I'm always free for you."

"I'm meeting my mother for dinner. Maybe you can join us."

Surprised, Ramion said, "Your mother?" Sage rarely talked about her, although she'd often mention her father who died when she was a young girl.

"She called when she heard about the bombing. She was upset and pretty insistent about seeing me. I was reluctant . . ."

"Why? I don't understand why you're so angry with her."

"We can't change the past, Ramion. Why talk about it?"

* * * * * * * * * * * * *

Sage spotted her mother in the crowded hotel lobby. Audra Hicks looked as if she were posed for a still photo—her hands folded neatly on her lap, her legs demurely crossed at the ankles, and her face void of expression and unassuming. Only her eyes revealed her nervousness.

Sage stared at her for several minutes before approaching. A kaleidoscope of memories spun in her mind. Audra walking her to kindergarten and greeting her with a warm smile when she returned. Audra bent over the sewing machine making her clothes. Audra sprinkling cinnamon on the rolls before putting them in the oven.

Sage walked slowly, repressing the thought that each step closer to her mother was a step into the past. Sage swallowed the urge to cry, unsure whether the tears that threatened were tears of sorrow or joy. Her mother looked so very different, so much older than she remembered. She was a deeper shade of brown, still thin, and her wavy black hair was peppered with gray. Her features were the same, but there was a withered edge to them. She had a firmly planted picture of her mother in her mind. But suddenly, it was as if an artist had touched up the picture of her creation, adding strokes of living and pain.

"Hello, Mama," Sage said with a bittersweet smile.

Audra sprang up from her chair, coming to life like a resuscitated patient. "Sage, my daughter, you look so good, so beautiful," Audra said, and wrapped her arms around her daughter, hugging her tightly.

She saw her deceased husband's amber skin, green eyes, and soft smile in Sage's face.

Sage stiffened in her mother's embrace. It took several moments for Audra to realize that Sage was as cold and unyielding as a statue. Self-consciously, Audra drew back and stared into eyes she hadn't seen in ten years, eyes that she had hoped would offer forgiveness.

"I hope you didn't have a hard time finding the hotel," Sage said.

"I came over in a cab," Audra said, encouraged by the polite conversation. "You look so good, baby. Prettier than your pictures. Your father would have been so proud. You're successful. You're intelligent," she said, reaching up to stroke Sage's cheek. "You certainly have your father's spirit and determination."

"Thank you," Sage said awkwardly. She couldn't imagine how her father would feel about her. She often wondered how different their lives would have been if Satchel had lived. "I've invited Ramion to join us for dinner. We've been seeing . . ."

"I know who he is. Ava told me all about him."

"Good old Ava," Sage said, not surprised that her half-sister would share that information. "How does Aaron like pilot school?" Sage inquired about her half-brother.

"He's excited, but I worry. Flying is so dangerous. I was scared to death until the plane landed," Audra said, her face crunched into a worried frown.

"Sorry I'm late," Ramion suddenly interrupted.

"That's okay, honey," Sage said, glad to change the subject and introduce her mother to Ramion.

"Very good to meet you," Audra said with a generous smile. "I'm just so happy to be in Atlanta."

"Atlanta's glad to have you," Ramion said, turning on the charm. "Have you been anywhere special?"

"Just to the King Center. It was so inspiring."

"Excuse me," Aaron Hicks said, easing next to his wife. "Hello, everyone."

Sage's hand flew to her mouth. "What are you doing here?" she demanded, venom in her voice. She stared at her stepfather with hostile eyes, as she had never wanted to see him again.

"I was hoping to have dinner with you and your mother," Aaron said humbly.

"I didn't get a chance to tell her yet," Audra said, tugging on her husband's arm. "This might not be a good time."

"You're damn right it isn't," Sage said, her chest heaving with anger and outrage as she plunged on. "I'm not having dinner with him." She turned to her mother and said, "For that matter, I'm not having dinner with you."

"I want to talk to you," Audra said. "We've got to try and . . ."

"Try? You tricked me. You never once mentioned that Aaron was here with you!"

"Sage, please don't be upset," Audra said, nervously blinking her eyes. "I wasn't trying to trick you. When you were hurt in that explosion, I realized how much I miss you, how much . . ."

"As you can see, Mama, I'm just fine." Sage held her head erect.

"I just thought this would be a good time to resolve things between us," Audra said in a pleading tone. "I really . . ."

"This separation has been hard on your mother," Aaron said. "She talks about seeing you every day. I don't . . ."

"I don't give a damn what you want, Aaron. You can go to hell," Sage brutally said, staring menacingly at the man who had changed their lives. She paused and looked at her mother, concluding at once that very little had changed. "Mama, please don't call me again."

Sage spun around and marched away.

Ramion hesitated only a second before hurrying after her. Sage had always refused to talk about her mother and stepfather. Now he knew why.

* * * * * * * * * * * * *

Senator Nolan Baker looked like man out of a sepia photograph—tall and commanding, with an imperious air that conveyed inherited Southern wealth. His hair was silver, his mustache a mixture of black and gray. He had the hard eyes of a riverboat gambler, and even when he smiled, his gaze remained impersonal and cold. His hands were fine-boned with long, smooth fingers, the nails meticulously manicured and buffed.

Baker stood before a mixed audience—reporters, political analysts, and voters—at the Atlanta Press Club for the final election face-off. He listened intently as his opponent, Cameron Hudson, responded to the moderator's question about state taxes. He reached for the glass of water on the podium, mentally preparing his response.

He forced himself to breathe deeply and slowly at the resounding applause that Hudson drew. He smiled for the cameras and the voters, hoping the audience didn't detect his nervousness. He had never worked so hard to win an election. His family name had always been all that was needed to be elected as U.S. Senator three times. He always believed that Southern loyalties would inspire Southern voters to elect the grandson of a previous governor.

Gauging the audience's response to Cameron Hudson, Baker realized that this time his family name wasn't going to be enough to win. When his campaign manager had joked that the bombing would keep "new nigger voters" away, Baker had confidently replied that he didn't need the unwitting help of a white supremacist group to claim his birthright. He never would admit out loud how much he hoped his campaign manager was right.

When the debate was over, both Hudson and Baker claimed victory. Live news reports from both candidates' campaign headquarters showed a frenzy of excitement and nervous anticipation. Long after the camera crews were gone, the campaign headquarters—just blocks away from each other—still hummed with activity.

Escorted to her car by security guards, Sage left Hudson's new campaign headquarters at one o'clock in the morning. When she got home, she turned on the television to watch a repeat broadcast of the eleven o'clock news. She listened to the news as she removed her clothes and slipped into a nightgown. She turned up the volume on the television when she went into the bathroom, anxious to hear the final results of the news station's viewer response to the question, "Are you afraid to vote on Tuesday?"

At last, exhausted from a fifteen-hour day, Sage climbed into bed. She struggled against sleep, while waiting to hear the results of the poll. Only after she heard that the news poll showed that 85 percent of callers planned to vote (a 15 percent increase from the poll taken a week earlier) did Sage give in to sleep's magnetic pull.

Chapter III

Sage's telephone rang at five o'clock. "Good morning, baby," Ramion said when he heard Sage's voice.

"Good morning," Sage said, her voice still raspy with sleep though she'd just showered. She wrapped a towel around her wet body and removed the shower cap.

"You sound tired. If I had stayed the night, you'd be energized. Ready for victory."

"Right now I feel like crawling back under the covers and watching what happens on TV."

"You would go crazy. Seriously, no matter what happens today, you've done a hell of job. Cameron wouldn't have come this far without you. No matter who wins, be proud of yourself."

"Thank you," Sage said, his words boosting her more than she knew.

"Tell me what you have on."

"Nothing."

"Nothing? You slept in the nude?" He closed his eyes, and Sage's body flashed in his mind—the deep curve of her waist, her fleshy brown aureoles, and her triangular thatch of hair.

"I just got out of the shower."

"Oh, so you're all wet."

"Wet and slippery," Sage said in a suggestive voice.

"I could be there in 20 minutes."

"Uh huh, I got up early to get some work done," Sage chided.

"I want you, baby."

"I know, and after the election, I'm all yours."

"Can't wait."

"Every part of me," Sage teased before hanging up.

* * * * * * * * * * * * *

Sage arrived at Hudson's campaign headquarters to a host of activities: phones ringing, television sets blaring, voices clamoring, and printers, copiers, and fax machines running. It was as frenetic and hectic as she had expected.

"Good morning, Marika," Sage greeted her assistant as she walked through the maze of activities. A long, shapeless black dress hid Marika's thin body.

"Hey, Sage," Marika said. "I'm glad this day is finally here. I'm a nervous wreck. The anticipation is killing me, and it isn't even ten o'clock."

"I know exactly what you mean. My stomach has been fluttering all morning, and my heart . . ."

"Well, better tell your heart to calm down cause it's about to go into hyperdrive." She handed her boss a cup of hot cinnamon tea. "Sit down," Marika said in a weary tone. She pushed her long braids back from her chestnut-brown face. Flecks of dark brown freckles were scattered unevenly across her prominent cheekbones.

Sage leveled her eyes to Marika's anxious face. "Just tell me."

"Some of the vans have flat tires," Marika said.

"*What?*" Sage threw back her head with such force that her gold and ruby earrings swayed rhythmically.

"Yep, all the vans that were delivered last night to Reverend Powell's church have mysteriously turned up with flat tires," Marika said.

"How many?"

"Fifteen."

"How did that happen?" Sage said angrily. She put her hands on her hips and squared her shoulders. "It doesn't make sense. But the question isn't why—it's who. Who would do this?"

"You got it."

"This isn't the first time we've been sabotaged. This needs to be investigated. Did Reverend Powell call the police?"

"I believe so."

Sage inhaled deeply, forcing herself to calm down. "Well, that's not going to help us today. Are any of the vans drivable?"

"Two tires on every van have to be replaced."

"I've been worried about Baker's camp, but the enemy might be within." She sat down at her desk, and opened her briefcase. The folder marked "Acceptance Speech" caught her attention.

Marika raised one shoulder slightly as her lips turned down at the corners. "You really think somebody here did it?"

"I don't know," Sage said, shaking her head. "But I can't focus on that right now. It's bad enough that the National Guard has been dispatched to the polls. We registered thousands of new voters. I'm worried they're going to be too afraid to vote."

"When I voted this morning, it was real smooth. I saw the guards, but they were out of the way."

"Well, that's one bit of good news," Sage said, with a tight smile. "Find out how long it's going to take to replace or repair the tires. Notify the driving polls that there are going to be delays. Let's see if we can get people to volunteer their cars. We've got plenty of drivers."

"I'm on it," Marika said.

* * * * * * * * * * * * *

Three hours later, Drew showed up at Hudson's campaign headquarters. "What's up, girl?" Drew said to Sage when he reached her desk.

"Cameron's losing," Sage said, her attention on the television set. She listened intently to the news report about the election.

Leaning against the corner of her desk, Drew said, "I know. Morning turnout is poor in the areas where Cameron should be pulling in large numbers."

"Tell me something I didn't know," Sage said edgily, taking her eyes off the television.

"Baker was going to release some kind of statement early this afternoon. But he changed his mind."

"That would be foolish," Sage said. "It's too early for posturing."

"Did you know that the polls the news stations sample from aren't representative of the state?"

Sage raised her eyebrows. "Oh really?"

"We ran the stats last week and compared it to previous years. Basically they sample from areas that are predominantly white."

"So it skews the numbers and falsely builds momentum for a candidate," Sage said. "Which can discourage voters from voting if they think their candidate is losing."

"False perceptions turn into reality," Drew said, nodding. "Numbers can make a big difference."

"I knew the numbers were going to look bad this morning, but I didn't expect it to be this bad," Sage said and sipped on her tepid tea. "I know it's the late voters who are going to put us back into the race." She paused and added with a wry smile, "Hopefully."

"Black folks are always late."

"Uh huh, not to mention that they work and can't get to the polls until after five o'clock.

"Speaking of voting, I better get over there myself." He kissed Sage on the cheek. "Keep the faith."

* * * * * * * * * * * * *

Tears of joy shimmied down Sage Kennedy's face. "We won! We won! We won!" she rejoiced while watching the eleven o'clock news report that Cameron Hudson had been elected the new governor of Georgia. Surrounded by supporters waving "Hudson for Governor" flags, she watched the television monitors tuned to the Channel 5 news.

Anchorwoman Michelle Hoffman reported that Georgia had elected a black man governor: "With 90 percent of the polls reporting, Cameron Hudson has 58 percent of the vote. Mr. Hudson becomes the first black governor of Georgia."

The news station cameras cut to Senator Nolan Baker's campaign headquarters at the Ritz Carlton hotel. He bitterly acknowledged losing to his "formidable challenger." His words were short, bitter, and full of innuendo. "I'm sorry, folks, but we lost the election. It seems the majority of the people of Georgia, much to my surprise, believed in the dream rhetoric. Thanks for all your support and hard work. But remember the next election. We'll be ready to clean up the mess."

"What a gracious loser," Ramion said sarcastically. He wrapped his arms around Sage's waist and planted a soft kiss on her lips. His eyes beamed with pride and admiration at the beautiful woman he held in his arms, a woman he was proud to claim. Smart, successful, driven; she made him feel like the color of the sun—warm, vibrant, and happy. "Congratulations, baby. You pulled it off."

Sage smiled at his compliment. "The funny thing is, Baker probably wouldn't have lost if he hadn't made race such an issue."

"You're right," Ramion agreed, raising his voice to be heard over the throng of supporters demanding the just-elected governor's presence. The crowd shouted, "Governor Hudson! Governor Hudson! Governor Hudson!"

Feeling the crowd's energy, Sage felt a bolt of pleasure that coursed through her body at warp speed. She didn't know what to do with the intense feeling, but when she looked up at Ramion's beaming face, she was suddenly overwhelmed with strong feelings of love for him. It reminded her of when she first saw Ramion—an unexplainable rush of desire had pierced her heart and penetrated her soul.

"I better go get Cam. This crowd is going crazy."

Ramion kissed Sage again. "I love you," he whispered into her ear.

* * * * * * * * * * * * *

Sage moved through the crowd, stopping along the way to speak with local voters and national supporters. The crowd, converging at the Marriott Marquis hotel in the heart of downtown Atlanta, swelled to uncountable numbers. Additional ballrooms were opened to accommodate the unexpected throng of supporters, experiencing history in the making: the election of the first black governor of Georgia.

Sage rode the escalator to the hotel's main level. She was stopped by a reporter who wanted to interview her for an article about the election. She agreed to a brief interview, ending the conversation with the perfect sound bite: "Mr. Hudson was the best candidate for the job and that's why he won the election. Georgia will prosper under his wise leadership."

Ten minutes later, Sage entered Cameron's hospitality suite, where the roar of the crowd chanting "Governor Hudson" sounded like the rumble of distant thunder. Sarah Hudson embraced Sage, overwhelmed with relief that her husband was elected governor of Georgia. A bright

30

smile warmed Sarah's face, but Sage could see beyond the painted-on political smile. There was weariness in her dark eyes. The race for governor had been a rough and tumble course, and Sarah had felt every bump and bruise.

"Well, Sarah," Sage said, "you are now the first lady of Georgia."

"I guess I am," Sarah said, who now had seven weeks to prepare for her new role. Sarah's face was small and round. She wore her grey-streaked hair full on the top, tapered around her ears, and close-cropped in the back. The short hairstyle showed off her delicate facial features: almond-shaped eyes, a long narrow nose, and thin lips.

"Congratulations again, Governor Hudson," Sage said, hugging Cameron. "We did it, we won! I can't believe it, but we really won."

"Were there ever any doubts?" Cameron teased, recalling how uncharacteristically frantic Sage had been when the media reported him losing in the afternoon.

"I was afraid of a runoff," Sage said.

"Oh, no," Sarah said, her forehead folded into two deep creases above her brows. "I'd have to leave the state. I couldn't take the vicious campaigning. Or the threats."

"They're waiting for you to declare victory," Sage said with a twinge of urgency in her voice.

"I've been waiting for this moment," Cameron said, his round face full of joy.

Sarah straightened her husband's tie and adjusted the pocket square in his jacket. The yellow polka-dotted tie and pocket square gave his blue double-breasted pinstriped suit just the right touch of flare.

"Do you have the speech?" Sage asked. She had an extra copy in her briefcase.

"It's up here," Cameron said, pointing to his forehead.

Sage smiled, knowing that Cameron had memorized the speech she had written, replaying the campaign's theme "The Dream Reborn." She also knew that her words would be embellished. Some pollsters had accurately predicted that Cameron's oratory gift would lead him to victory, and with each debate Cameron had chipped away at Senator Baker's significant lead.

The door suddenly opened, bringing in the noisy sounds of the crowd demanding Cameron's presence. "It's time," he said, taking his wife's hand and heading toward the door.

31

"Come on, C.J. and Jessica. We need you to stand by your father," Sage said to the two Hudson children. C.J.—Cameron Jr.—and Jessica were replicas of their parents. Jessica was fair-skinned and petite like Sarah, while C.J. was big, broad, and chocolate-colored like his father.

The crowd's chants of "Governor Hudson! Governor Hudson!" grew louder and louder when Cameron entered the ballroom. Cameron shook hands and kissed cheeks as he made his way to the podium. Standing before the throng of supporters, reporters, and cameramen, he motioned with his hands, bringing the chanting to a halt.

"Governor Hudson. I do like the way that sounds. Has a ring to it, don't you think?" His round face broke into a broad smile, creasing the deep pencil lines layered in his fudge-brown face. Dark eyes gazed upon the sea of faces.

Supporters began clapping and the familiar chanting "Governor Hudson, Governor Hudson!" rose to a crescendo.

"First of all, I'd like to commend my campaign manager, Sage Kennedy; all the volunteers who went door-to-door to register voters; and the very dedicated folks who participated in the 'Ride to the Polls' drive. I appreciate everyone who, in some form or fashion, helped to make this moment possible. Above all, I especially want to thank the voters who did not let threats or fear stop them from exercising their constitutional rights. It is you, the voters, who deserve a round of applause," Cameron said, bringing his hands together.

It was several minutes before he could quiet the crowd and continue. "Georgia is the greatest state in the union, but its most significant resources remain largely uptapped. I'm talking about you—the people of Georgia. If we develop the minds, hearts, and bodies of our citizens, then we become even greater, rich with people and economic prosperity.

"People come to this state from near and far for economic opportunities. To find the American dream . . .

"As governor, I will help Georgians realize that dream. As an experienced government administrator and a human rights advocate, I will enact change to make the dream a reality for all Georgians.

"I've been elected governor because of *you*. *You* share my vision for the future, and with your continued support, we can make the vision a reality. We can again give birth to the dream."

Cameron's inspiring words drew an applause that sounded like the rush of Niagara Falls.

* * * * * * * * * * * *

As the last wave of supporters made their way to Cameron to congratulate him on winning the election, Sage sat down for the first time in hours. She looked at her watch. It was one-thirty in the morning. She leaned back in the chair and felt a wave of exhaustion wash over her from her head to her toes. Her long legs were stretched out in front of her as she watched the crowd dwindle, thankful they were finally leaving.

Sage closed her eyes and sighed deeply. Ramion stood behind her, massaging the tense muscles in her neck and shoulders. She was so relieved that the unpredictable, chaotic campaign had come to an end.

"I'm glad the election is over. Maybe now I can spend some time with my baby," Ramion said. "I've missed you."

Sage looked up at Ramion with a tender smile, thinking that, in the charcoal-grey pinstriped suit that draped his well-toned body, he looked like a model. He wore the multicolored vest and matching tie she had bought for his birthday four months ago. "I've missed you, too. How did it go today?"

"Very well," Ramion said, nodding his head. "I discredited the state's main witness. I think the jury is beginning to question the evidence."

"Score one for the defense," Sage said with a proud, approving smile.

"That's right. But I don't want to talk about work. I want to talk about us. No, I just want to be with you," Ramion said, with eyes of desire that conveyed more than words could.

"I've been meaning to tell you, the FBI came to my office last week to question me about the explosion."

"Do they have any clues or suspects?"

"I don't think so."

The music stopped, and quiet settled in the hotel ballroom. "It's finally over," Sage thought. In spite of her exhaustion, her mind moved to her next task. As Deputy Chief of Staff, there was plenty of work to be done—getting the family moved into the Governor's Mansion, preparing for the inaugural festivities, and selecting candidates for key appointments.

"How cozy!" Edwinna sniped, wishing it was her neck Ramion was rubbing. Edwinna stared at Ramion, baffled that she was still so attracted to him.

Sage's olive eyes flashed open, and she sat upright. She immediately became alert, feeling the animosity of Edwinna's hostile eyes.

"Hello, Edwinna," Ramion said coolly. "Enjoying the celebration?"

"With all those hip-hop kids here, it seemed like a concert, not a campaign party," Edwinna complained. "I hope I never have to hear or see 'Get Your Vote On' again," she said dramatically.

"You missed the point, Edwinna," Sage chided. "'Get Your Vote On' is one of the reasons why we won. It was targeted to the hip-hop crowd."

"That may be true," Edwinna acknowledged. "But some of these people, well, they seem like street people." Edwinna's face shifted into an exaggerated mask of disgust.

"Everyone isn't as fortunate as you, Edwinna," Ramion said. It was just such insensitive, arrogant comments that had chipped away his feelings. Most of the people Edwinna talked against weren't that different from him. Only his determination, education, and drive separated them.

"Don't even go there, Ramion. You wouldn't be as fortunate as you are if it weren't for my father," Edwinna said, putting her hand on her hip for emphasis.

"Edwinna, your father has nothing to do with this conversation," he retorted.

"He has everything to do with where you are," Edwinna snapped. "I guess you've forgotten that, now that you're with someone from your own humble beginnings."

"Edwinna, you don't know anything about me," Sage said coolly as she stood up.

"I know enough," Edwinna said, dismissing Sage and turning toward Ramion. "I predict that next year at this time, I'll be the one making a victory speech."

"You know I intend to run," Ramion said in a warning tone.

"Well, I intend to win," Edwinna baited, swinging the gold chain strap on her black Chanel bag.

"How many times have I heard you say that you would never go into politics? That you would hate to live under a microscope? I really can't believe you want to be a state senator," Ramion said.

"Obviously I changed my mind," Edwinna said. "Just like you changed your mind . . . about things." She cut her gaze toward Sage, her begrudging bitterness obvious.

Anger creeping into his voice, Ramion said, "You don't care about the people in that district. You know nothing about how they live and what they want."

"It doesn't matter," Edwinna said. "It's how you run the campaign and how much money you've got behind you." She released a nasty chuckle. "And my Daddy has plenty of it."

Medu joined them. "So we meet again?" he said. "Congratulations on Mr. Hudson's victory."

"Thank you," Sage said.

"I don't think Sage had anything to do with it," Edwinna said.

Medu flashed Edwinna a perplexed look. "That doesn't make any sense."

"People voted for Cameron, not Sage," Edwinna explained.

With a curious expression on his face, Medu asked, "Are you ready?"

Edwinna bobbed her head, although she wished she were going home with Ramion. She even thought of Ramion while in bed with Medu.

"It was a great victory party, Sage," Medu said.

"Thanks, Medu," Sage said, wondering how the mellow artist tolerated Edwinna's abrasive manner. "I'm just glad it's over."

"Let's go," Edwinna said, grabbing Medu's hand.

"Maybe she'll change her mind when it's time to actually declare her candidacy," Ramion said after Edwinna and Medu left the hotel ballroom.

"I don't think so, Ramion." Sage's intuition warned her that Edwinna could be dangerous. "She won't give up easily."

"That doesn't change anything for me," he said, running his hand down her arm. His voice lightened. "Are you still going to be my campaign manager?"

"You know it, honey," she said, grinning. "And we're going to win. Edwinna is just going to make it ugly. But after this election, I can't imagine an uglier campaign." Sage drank the last of her white wine. "I'm exhausted."

"So where do you want to stay tonight? Your place or mine?"

"I'm too tired to walk to the car and drive anywhere."

Ramion kissed her on the forehead. "Why don't we stay here? I'll rent us a room."

"Wonderful idea. I'll go say goodnight to Cam and meet you in the lobby."

* * * * * * * * * * * * *

Ramion kissed Sage like a thirsty man drinking water, drowning in the scent of her, the feel of her, the taste of her soft brown smooth skin. She kissed him back with equal hunger, pressing her nakedness against his hard muscled body. Their bodies twisted into a smoldering tangle of hungry flesh that neither wanted to unravel.

Ramion wrapped his hands around Sage's huge breasts, his hungry mouth covered her nipples. He sucked and moaned and buried his face in her breasts, his thumb flicking over her nipples, creating ricocheting bullets of heat and working their bodies into a frenzy. He massaged the soft skin of her thighs and buttocks, and Sage's pliant body shivered with his touch. Ramion eased himself above her, his throbbing sex at heaven's door.

"Ramion," she breathed, her eyes closed, her back arched, waiting for him to enter her.

Ramion kissed her on the lips, the sides of her neck and shoulders, his sex touching and teasing her to ecstasy.

Sage writhed with expectation. "Ramion," she moaned.

"Open your eyes," Ramion whispered. He stared into her eyes as his fingers stroked the inside of her thighs.

Sage shivered and writhed, anxious for Ramion to be inside.

"I love you," Ramion said and thrust himself into her. Sage closed her eyes and felt herself glide away like a cloud floating in the sky. Rocking and arching against him, her legs locked around his back. They rose together, higher and higher, until at last they touched heaven and then fell asleep before returning to earth.

* * * * * * * * * * * * *

When Sage woke the next morning, Ramion was not in bed beside her. She called out his name, but there was no answer. Her clothes were laying haphazardly on the chair across the room. Her black dress lay tangled along with her pantyhose on the floor. Her suede shoes weren't far away. She didn't have a change of clothes, toothbrush, comb, or curling iron. She didn't have to work today, but she didn't want to leave the hotel in the same clothes she'd come in.

Sage leaned back against the pillows and picked up the telephone. She started to check her messages, but changed her mind and returned the receiver to the cradle. She didn't feel like dealing with work. Instead, she pressed the power button on the TV remote and scanned the stations for the local news. She listened to CNN's report on the election.

She looked around the hotel room, decorated with expensive French pine furniture for a note from Ramion. She checked on the nightstands, the armoire, the desk and the rose-colored sofa and chair, but came up empty.

Sitting upright against the pillows on the king-sized bed, she half listened to the television. She closed her eyes. Her body, she realized, still tingled with passion. Her thoughts spiraled back to the first time she saw Ramion at the United Negro College Fund telethon.

He sat on the other side of the room taking phone calls from donators, while she sat across from him. She caught him staring at her several times. Smiling self-consciously, she hoped the cameras didn't catch them smiling and flirting with each other. After the telethon, Ramion introduced himself and they talked briefly, mostly about the college fund.

"It's a great cause," Sage said. "I'm glad to be a part of it."

"I do it every year," Ramion said. "UNCF helped get me through college."

"Oh, where did you go?" Sage asked politely, noticing the expensive cut of his suit, his polished manner, and his intoxicating smile.

"Howard University."

"Really? I'm from that area. Baltimore."

The conversation ended abruptly as they were interrupted by the volunteer chairman. Before walking away, Ramion tucked his business card into her hand.

Later that evening, when Tawny teased her about flirting on television with a "fine, fine brother," Sage admitted she couldn't help herself.

But Sage didn't call him. She believed that the man should make the first move, and she was afraid of the feelings he had evoked in their brief conversation.

She stared at his home number written on the back of his business card, but she wouldn't pick up the phone. If he's interested, she decided, he'll call me.

* * * * * * * * * * * * *

Sage heard Ramion's key in the door, rousing her from her stroll down memory lane. "Good morning, honey."

Ramion entered the hotel room carrying a Macy's shopping bag. Before Sage could ask about it, Ramion kissed her and said, "You slept late."

"You wore me out last night," Sage said with a coy smile.

"I thought it was the election," he rejoined.

Sage smiled at him. "Something for me in that bag?"

"I knew you wouldn't want to put on yesterday's clothes." He handed her the shopping bag.

Sage got out the bed, eager for a peek. There were several smaller bags inside. She pulled out a red pantsuit and black blouse from one bag and a bra and matching panties from another.

"They're all beautiful. You've got taste, baby."

His eyes traveling from Sage's large breasts to her long shapely legs, he said, "You got that right."

When she opened a third bag, she found a pair of flat red shoes and black stockings.

"Umm, you thought of everything," Sage said. "I love it, and would you believe I've been looking at this suit? Thank you so much." She gave Ramion a soft kiss on the cheek. "Order me some breakfast while I get dressed, okay?"

"I'm starving too," Ramion said. "Did you see Drew's editorial?"

"No, I haven't looked at the paper."

"He wrote a very interesting analysis of the election."

"I'll take a look after I get dressed."

* * * * * * * * * * * * *

Sage was a blur of red when she came out the bathroom. The single-breasted jacket hung past her hips, matching the pleated, cuffed pants. Her size-36D breasts threatened to spill out of the snug-fitting black blouse.

38

"You look delicious," Ramion said with a smile that not only created tremors in Sage, but also displayed the cleft in Ramion's chin. "Delectable," Ramion said, admiring her as she walked toward him.

"Well, red is my favorite color." She kissed him lightly on the lips. "Thank you, honey. I might have to hire you as my fashion consultant, you did such a good job picking everything."

"You know, come to think of it, red reminds me of candy apples." Ramion paused and moved closer, eyeing her like a piece of fruit. "I want to take a bite."

* * * * * * * * * * * * *

"I told you to kill him!" the old man screamed, his bony finger pointed at his son.

"Father, suspicion would have been directed at us in a heartbeat if I had him killed in the middle of the campaign."

"Like hell. Those people get killed every day. You could have paid some crack addict to shoot him, and he would have done it for chump change."

"Yeah, well, we just have to reexamine the situation," the son said.

"There'd be nothing to reexamine if you had listened to me. I should have never put you in charge. Resurfacing those FBI files certainly didn't work."

"Frankly, Father, I didn't believe Hudson could win the election. I didn't think he had a prayer of capturing the white vote."

"Traitors, that's what they are."

"I realize now, Father, that different measures are called for."

"Such as?"

"Just because Hudson is governor doesn't mean he has to stay governor."

"Okay, Son, now you're starting to think right. But we missed our window of opportunity. Getting rid of him now won't put Baker in the governor's office," the old man said. It'll just mean the lieutenant governor will take over. Ah well, he's not my choice, but at least he's white."

"So we're agreed, first we watch his family . . ."

"Uh huh, keep talking."

"And keep a close eye on people close to him." The younger man grinned and licked his lips. "I would love to get more than my eyes on his campaign manager, though."

"Don't get sidetracked, boy!"

"I wouldn't call focusing on her getting sidetracked. If it weren't for her, Senator Baker would be taking his rightful place."

"That's right, boy. And he would make a fine governor. I knew his grandfather when he was governor. He was one of the good old boys."

"Well, those days are long gone, Father. We have to concentrate on the present, which means figuring out the right time to take action. I've called a meeting for next Friday."

"All right! Now you're showing some spunk," the old man said.

Chapter IV

Sage Kennedy walked into the Fulton County North Annex government building carrying her purse, briefcase, and laptop computer. She struggled with her unwieldy baggage as she pressed the elevator button and then stepped back to wait for the elevator to arrive.

"Congratulations, Sage, on a job well done," said Roy, a friendly, older black man who supervised the building's cleaning crew. "You're one tough cookie," he added with a gold-toothed grin. "I was real sorry to hear about you getting hurt in that explosion. Me and my wife prayed for you."

"Thank you, Roy. I appreciate your concern. It means a lot."

"But, we got the last laugh, didn't we? We got us a black governor after all."

"You're right," she said, with a light chuckle. "But the battle has just begun."

"Yeah, but Mr. Hudson got a master plan," Roy said. "I know that's right."

The elevator doors opened and the old man stepped back. "Have a good one," he said.

Sage stepped off the elevator at the fifth floor and walked around the corner to the relocated campaign headquarters. The door was open, and she moved into the reception area. "Hudson for Governor" posters still hung on the walls, and campaign brochures remained scattered on the coffee table, sofa, and receptionist's desk.

"Good morning, Sage," Marika said. A large, contemporary painting in muted shades of mauve, blue, and green hung on the wall behind Marika, complimenting the mauve walls and carpet through the office suite. Holding up two fingers in *V* formation, she added, "Victory!"

"I'm just glad it's all over."

"Me, too," Marika agreed. "I thought it would be quiet today, but the phones haven't stopped ringing. Reporters are calling for interviews, and . . ."

"I'm not surprised. When is Cam coming in?" Sage asked.

"At eleven."

Sage looked at her gold watch. "Good, that gives me some time to get some work done."

Sage placed the laptop and briefcase on her desk and tucked her purse away in a drawer. Next, she looked through her mailbox, separating the mail into three piles—read, file, Cameron. She went through her briefcase and pulled out several file folders. For the next two hours, Sage worked at her computer, printing reports and documents for Cameron's review. When he arrived, she heard him talking to Marika before heading down the hall to his office, whistling a happy tune.

A half-hour later, she went around the corner to his office. He was on the phone when she entered, sipping coffee from his Mayor of Atlanta mug while listening to the other party. She placed several files in front of him and was turning around to leave when Cameron hung up the phone.

"That was some celebration," Cameron said. "No one wanted to leave."

"Folks were just so happy that you were elected."

"I'll tell you, Sage, I was sweating bullets all afternoon. It didn't look like we were going to win."

"So was I. All I have to say is thank goodness for the late voters."

"And the first-time voters."

"I was happy that the bombing didn't scare people away from the polls."

Cameron nodded. "That worried Sarah, too."

With a soft chuckle, Sage said, "Who knows, maybe it scared away the people who were going to vote for Baker."

"You just might be right about that."

"But now we get the pleasure of hiring your staff," she said, handing him a list of names for positions in his new administration.

"Some interesting names you have here," Cameron said, perusing the report through the reading glasses perched on his nose.

"I know you don't care much for Harry," Sage said, "but he's perfect for the job."

"True, he's just mean as hell."

"Well, it's not like we'll be dealing with him on a daily basis."

Cameron scribbled some notes on the report, crossing off names and adding others to consider for his staff. He wore a crisp white button-down shirt with his initials—CJH—embroidered on the cuff. The red and blue diamond-patterned tie matched the suspenders and pocket scarf in the custom-made suit jacket that hung on the back of the door.

"I'm also compiling a list of legislators who we may be able to influence on the vote for a new flag," Sage said.

The noisy chair squeaked as Cameron leaned his football-player frame back in the chair and focused on Sage. "That's why I hired you. You stay on top of things," he said, giving her an affectionate smile.

"If you want to change the flag in the next legislative session, we have to move quickly."

"Sister, I like your style."

"Thanks," she said with a light chuckle. "Well, tell me, has Sarah started packing?"

"She started talking about it last night."

"Are you going to sell the house?"

"I don't think so. Sarah wants to, but four years will fly by. Who knows if I'll be reelected. For now, I think we'll just rent it out."

"Excuse me, " Marika said. "These flowers arrived for you," she said, handing Sage a vase filled with a dozen white roses.

"Thanks," Sage said, admiring the beauty of the delicate flowers.

"Your mother is on the phone," Marika said in a curious tone. She had worked for Sage for three years and couldn't remember her mother ever calling. She noticed the warm smile on Sage's face transform into a frown.

"I'll take it in my office," Sage said as she walked out of Cameron's office.

Sage placed the vase on her desk. She opened the card and read the message: "Congratulations on winning! I'm so very proud of you. Love, Mama."

She walked around her desk and sat down. She glanced at the blinking button on the telephone and for a moment considered ignoring the call, surmising that her mother would eventually hang up. But the line continued to blink. Releasing a heavy sigh, Sage depressed the flashing button and picked up the receiver. "Hello," she said dryly.

"Oh, Sage," Audra said, relieved that Sage finally answered the phone. "I just wanted you to know I was thinking about you and how much . . ."

"Thank you for the flowers."

"I'm sorry about Aaron showing up like that. I told him not to come but he wouldn't listen. I wasn't trying to trick you. I just wanted you and . . ."

"Mama, I'm really busy right now."

"Did you hear me, Sage? I wasn't trying to trick you."

"It really doesn't matter. I have to go. Thanks for the flowers," Sage said and hung up the phone.

* * * * * * * * * * * * *

Ramion turned into his parent's subdivision, where all the streets were named after women—Mary Ellen Terrace, Susan Drive, Elizabeth Street, Anna Maria Way. It was an older development, built in the late 1960s, when carports and porches were the architectural rage. Most of the homes were ranch or split-level, featuring long driveways, wide picturesque windows, and lots of trees and shrubbery.

It was a picture-perfect Thanksgiving day—the leaves were orange and yellow, and the sun was bright and glowing.

"I can't believe I'm finally meeting your family," Sage said.

"You should have met them sooner, but . . ."

"I know," Sage said. "My schedule can be erratic. I was just thinking if I hadn't run into you at the mall, we might not be doing this."

"We were always running into each other," Ramion said, remembering the weekend that changed his life.

* * * * * * * * * * * * *

It happened like a summer shower, unexpectedly and unplanned. They ran into each other at Lenox Mall on a Saturday afternoon. Sage was riding the escalator up to the main level of the mall, and Ramion was riding down to the food court. Passing each other, they spoke, and Ramion impulsively asked her to wait for him at the top of the escalator. While riding back up, Ramion knew his life was about to change. He felt a magnetic pull every time he saw her and imagined touching her skin, tasting her lips. He wanted her and knew, from some voice within, that he needed her.

"You're not going to call me, are you?" Ramion asked when he met her at the top of the escalator.

"I was waiting for you to call me," Sage said with a teasing smile.

Over café au lait and beignets, talking and laughing, their long-simmering attraction beginning to bud. Saturday turned into Sunday and, before the weekend was over, their relationship was in full bloom.

* * * * * * * * * * * * *

Ramion pulled his black 750 BMW into his parents' driveway. "Eventually we were going to stop running from each other," he said.

"Oh, they're beautiful," Sage said, indicating the rows of flowers decorating the yard.

"Mama probably spends three to four hours a day in the yard."

"It shows," Sage said. She paused before continuing, "I'm a little nervous."

"My parents are going to love you. I promise you." Hearing the familiar squeak of the screen door opening, Ramion looked up to see his mother standing in the doorway, waving at them. "There's Mama," Ramion said. "See? They can't wait to meet you." Ramion stepped out of the car and walked around to the passenger side to open the door for Sage. After climbing out, she reached back inside to retrieve the rum cake she had baked for dessert.

They walked up the steps of the tidy red brick split-level ranch house with black shutters around the windows. "Hello, hello!" Linnell called, clapping her hands together in excited welcome.

"Hey, Mama!" Ramion said, as he hugged and kissed his mother on the cheek. Short and a bit stout, Linnell had to reach up to put her arms around her son's waist. Her nose was flat and broad, her black eyes deep-set, and her lips full and wide. Her hair was completely grey and softly fluffed around her chestnut-brown face. She never missed her weekly appointment with her beautician, who roller-set her hair. Linnell had been wearing the same hairstyle for more than 20 years.

Ramion introduced the two women.

"So good to meet you Sage," Linnell said. She took one of Sage's hands, and then changed her mind and impulsively hugged her.

"I'm happy to meet you, too," Sage said. "Ramion talks a lot about his family." Handing Linnell the Tupperware container, Sage said, "Here's a cake I made for dessert."

"Honey, you didn't have to do that."

"I wanted to," Sage said. "It's rum cake. I hope everyone will like it."

"Umm, smells delicious," Linnell said. "Come on in. Olivia and the kids are downstairs."

Ramion and Sage smelled collard greens and sweet potato pie as they entered the house. They followed Linnell down the narrow hall, passing the living room and dining room along the way. The large kitchen was bright and cheery, decorated in yellow and green wallpaper scripted with the names of herbs and spices. The yellow and white tiled floor complimented the yellow valances draping the windows.

Ramion peeked inside the porcelain pots on the stove. Some food was prepared, while other dishes were still cooking. He tasted a forkful of collard greens.

"Stay out of my pots, Ramey. You know better," Linnell chided.

"I had to taste the greens, Ma. They're just right."

"I know, boy. I been cooking greens longer than you been on this earth."

Raymond Sandidge came into the kitchen followed by his seven-year-old grandson, Richie. "Hey, son. About time you got here," he said, looking at his watch. Raymond Sandidge was narrow built and, unlike his wife, his body and hair had thinned over the years.

"Hi, Pops. This is Sage," Ramion said after a quick hug. Sage extended her hand, and Raymond reluctantly shook her hand. "I'm from the old school I'm afraid. Don't much like shaking ladies' hands, but it's good to meet you. Ramion has talked a lot about you."

Sage smiled her greeting at the deep-brown man wearing bifocal glasses. "How are you, Mr. Sandidge?"

"I'm doing fine. I've watched two football games, and I can't wait for the big game at eight."

"Hi, Uncle Ramey," Richie said.

"Hey, Richie, what's happening, little man?" Ramion asked peering down at his nephew who was tall for his age. Richie was caramel brown, and his black curly hair was cropped on the top and clipped close around his ears and the back of his head.

"Nothing much." Suddenly his black eyes lit up behind his brown-framed, square-lens glasses. "We don't have to go back to school until next week," he smiled, revealing the gap left by two missing front teeth.

"That's great. You deserve a break," Ramion said.

Richie looked at Sage and asked, "Are you Uncle Ramey's new girl-friend?"

"Yes, I suppose," Sage replied.

"I didn't like his other girlfriend," Richie said.

"Humph, neither did I," Raymond said. "Edwinna looked down on us. Miss High and Mighty."

"That's not polite," Linnell said.

"It's certainly something you've said yourself many times," Raymond said to his wife of thirty-seven years.

"Go on downstairs," she said, moving her hands in a shooing motion. "Out of my kitchen. No offense, Sage, but I'm trying to get dinner ready."

"I understand," Sage said, realizing full well that Linnell was trying to get out of an awkward moment.

Downstairs in the den, Sage met Ramion's sister, Olivia, and her four-year-old daughter, Courtney. Olivia was petite and wore her reddish-brown hair in an ear-length bob.

The den revealed a lot about the Sandidge family. From the comfortable, well-worn red and black plaid sofa and love seat and a lazy chair positioned diagonally from the forty-inch television, it was obviously a room where the family came together. From a bookcase brimming with VCR tapes, most of them old movies like *Casablanca, Duel in the Sun, Stormy Weather, Carmen, Imitation of Life,* and *The Count of Monte Cristo,* Sage learned that Ramion's parents appreciated quality.

Olivia motioned for Sage to sit next to her on the sofa while she pulled out the photo albums filled with family pictures chronicling their lives from childhood to the present. As they flipped through the album, Ramion commented or laughed about the pictures or pleaded with his sister to turn the page. Sage found herself enjoying the trek through Ramion's childhood.

The stroll down memory lane was interrupted when Linnell appeared on the steps, calling for them to come and eat.

Upstairs in the dining room, they sat down at the table, ready to devour the food before them. Linnell had prepared a virtual feast from turkey, ham, oyster and cornbread stuffing to yams, greens, green beans, macaroni and cheese, mashed potatoes, cranberry sauce, cornbread, and homemade rolls.

Before eating, the family held hands while Raymond began the grace, and each member added his or her individual blessing. Sage enjoyed the family's ritual of passing the food so each person could serve themself, then waiting until everyone's plate was filled before they began eating together. Sage was comfortable with Ramion's family, although observing the close family bond reminded her of the missing piece in the puzzle in her life.

It seemed like a lifetime ago since Sage had eaten dinner with her family. She remembered sitting at the kitchen table with her brother and sister, Ava and Aaron, her mother busy at the stove fixing their plates. Her stepfather worked the night shift at the car plant, so he wasn't home for dinners. Things were always better, Sage recalled, when her stepfather wasn't around to leer at her, his eyes hungry with desire.

Sage was drawn back to the present as Ramion's family talked about the election, the movies, and the latest trends in music. Linnell lamented that "rap music is ruining our kids," and the conversation invariably went back to politics.

"I'm glad you didn't let that bomb scare you away from the campaign," Raymond said.

"I thought about it for a split second."

"In that split second, I would have said, 'See ya, gotta go,'" Olivia said, laughing. She added, "Seriously, I would have been terrified."

"I'm just glad it all worked out," Linnell said.

"So what does the new governor plan to do about the flag?" Raymond asked. "There was a lot of talk about the flag for a while, and then it died down."

"Cameron is determined to change the flag," Sage said. "It's a priority of his."

"I don't think he would have been elected if he had made that an issue," Olivia said.

"That's why we avoided talking about it as much as possible," Sage explained.

"When Miller tried to change the flag, supporters of the old flag came out the woodwork. Those people will do anything to keep that old confederate flag," Raymond commented.

Olivia said, "They act like that flag is something to be proud of. I don't understand it. It's so racist."

"Well, times are a changing," Linnell said. "And some people will always be opposed to change."

"Which is why Governor Hudson will be risking his political career if he pursues this," Raymond said.

"He knows that," Sage said.

"Well, that man sure can give a speech. He just wows you with his words," Linnell said enthusiastically. Turning toward Sage, she moved the conversation closer to home. "I'm sure Ramion has told you about his plans to go into politics." With a soft chuckle, she said, "Maybe one day he'll run Mr. Hudson out of office. I always knew he would make a fine lawyer. When he was a little boy he used to argue with me about everything."

"We used to call him little Perry Mason," Raymond said. "He and Olivia would go at it. There wasn't anything they wouldn't debate. Sometimes I'd forget they were just kids."

"Smart kids. All my kids were good students, even Mackie," Linnell said. "Did Ramion tell you that he graduated from high school a year early?"

"No. I'm not surprised, though," Sage replied. "As a matter of fact, I graduated a year early, too."

"Ain't that something," Linnell said. "Ramion was the youngest to graduate from law school, too. Only 23! Graduated from Harvard Law School. That's the best school in the country. He tell you that?"

"Yes ma'am," Sage said. "I saw his degree at his office."

"I was so proud to frame his degrees. Did he tell you he was third . . ."

Ramion cleared his throat. "Mama, please. Enough."

"Well, I know you're not going to brag about your accomplishments, so I thought I'd fill her in."

"Actually, Ramion has told me a lot about himself and his family," Sage said.

"Well, I suppose I do go on," Linnell said. "I just can't help myself. I'm so proud of him. He worked so hard to put himself through school."

"Mama, I'm sure Sage knows all that stuff," Olivia said. "Besides, you take one look at my brother, and you know he's got it going on. And you know he knows it."

"All right, Olivia, you don't have to get in on it," Ramion said.

"Okay, I'll hush up," Linnell said, before sipping from her glass of iced tea.

When conversation turned to the youngest son, Mackie, Sage felt tension creep into the room. Raymond kept his eyes glued to his plate, as Linnell chattered on and on about Mackie's talents as a basketball player.

"Mackie just couldn't face the fact that his playing days were over when he hurt his leg," Olivia said, not putting much sympathy in her tone.

"You got to know when to give up," Raymond said. "There was no way he was going to make it to the NBA."

"You never give up on your child," Linnell said, chastising her husband with her eyes. Raymond looked away.

It was obvious that their young son was a source of great pain and disappointment. Sage wanted to say something soothing and comforting, but knew it wasn't her place to speak on family matters.

Looking over at Ramion, Olivia asked, "When was the last time you saw him?"

"Last Saturday. I took him some money and some new books," Ramion replied. "I hate it, though. It's not fair he got so much time."

Raymond said, "Son, it's not your fault."

"I can't bear to see him there. Locked up. Not my baby brother," Olivia said.

Silence fell thick and heavy on the room until Courtney suddenly asked, "What does Barney eat for Thanksgiving?"

Laugher erupted. Courtney's innocent question had the refreshing effect of a window thrown open.

"He eats rocks and grass," Richie explained authoritatively. "That's what dinosaurs eat. That's just the way it is."

Laughter filled the room again, and Sage looked around with an approving smile. Richie didn't know it, but he'd not only explained dinosaurs, he'd explained his family. They had known adversity and tragedy, but they would survive because that was part of living and loving. That's just the way it was.

* * * * * * * * * * * * *

After dessert and more family conversation, Ramion and Sage bid his family goodnight. Backing out of the driveway, Ramion pressed the button on the car's CD player, and the plaintive sounds of Babyface filled the air.

Sage leaned back against the plush leather seat and looked over at him. "I really like your family. I felt so at home with them."

"I knew you would fit right in."

"Can I call you Ramey too?" Sage said with a soft giggle.

"If you want to," he said with a light smile.

"It didn't sound like anyone cared for Edwinna but you."

"Past tense. I'm glad to be free of her and her father. Don't get me wrong. I like Edwin. He's done a lot for me. I learned a lot working for him. But he can be controlling."

Changing the subject, Sage asked, "What did your father mean when he said it's not your fault about your brother?"

Ramion's hands tightened visibly on the steering wheel. "I'll tell you about it one day."

"Okay," Sage said. "I'm really tired, honey. I don't feel like going to a jazz club."

"I know," Ramion said, turning out of the subdivision. "Drop you at your house or take you to mine?"

"My house."

"Good. I want to wake up beside you. You have this crazy habit of going home in the middle of the night." He kissed the back of her hand.

"I can't help it," Sage said.

* * * * * * * * * * * * *

Marika rushed into her boss' office. "Sage, come quick. Ramion's on TV."

51

"He is?" Sage questioned, as she leaped up and followed Marika into the conference room where a large television hung on the corner wall.

Television reporters and cameramen gathered around Ramion and his client, Sidney Royster, who had been charged with the murder of his ex-wife.

"Mr. Sandidge, why do you think the jury found your client not guilty?"

Ramion flashed a grin. "Because he is innocent. The evidence was circumstantial. The prosecution's case was based entirely on hearsay. And, finally, there was no concrete evidence linking my client with his ex-wife's death," Ramion said.

The cameras zoomed back to the street reporter, and Marika turned down the volume on the television. "Umh, umh, umh, Ramion is really making a reputation for himself. This is the fourth high-profile case he's won."

"You're right. And I'm going to treat him to dinner. Someplace special. Marika, call the Mansion and make reservations for two for tomorrow night."

* * * * * * * * * * * *

The Saturday after Thanksgiving, Sage was awakened by the ringing phone. It was three o'clock in the morning. It didn't ring two times before she picked up the receiver, her stomach nervously fluttering with anticipation of the voice on the other end. "Hello," she grumbled sleepily.

"Hi, Sage!" Ava said cheerfully. "Did I wake you?"

"What else would I be doing at three in the morning?" Sage growled.

"Maybe the wild thing," Ava teased. "Will you come get me?"

Ava was supposed to be at home in Baltimore, Maryland. Sage sat up in bed and turned on the light. "Where are you?"

"At the bus station."

"In Atlanta?"

"Hurry! The people here are creepy!"

"What are you doing here?" Sage asked.

"I'll tell you everything when you pick me up."

52

"Give me a half-hour."

Sage got out of bed and went into the bathroom. She quickly washed her face and brushed her teeth. She took off her blue satin nightshirt and slipped on a sweater and black jeans, then grabbed her purse and keys and went out the door after activating the security alarm.

A thousand questions turned in her mind as she drove to pick up her sister. She hadn't seen Ava since July when she came down with her twin brother, Aaron, for their annual summer visit.

An hour after being awakened, Sage pulled her red two-door 450 Mercedes Benz in front of the Greyhound bus station. She felt a little nervous getting out of her car, observing the street people lurking around the station. She passed several men passed out on the street, the stench of liquor in the air. An old toothless woman screamed at her, "Take me home, take me home." Another homeless woman spoke with her eyes, pleading for money with a tattered hat in her hand. Sage fished in her purse and tossed a $5 bill into the woman's tattered hat. "What about me, sister?" a shrill voice screamed as Sage opened the door of the bus station and went inside.

She spotted Ava at once, sitting on the largest of several pieces of luggage in the middle of the terminal munching on a large bag of pretzels. Seeing Sage coming toward her, Ava jumped to her feet. Despite the hour and surprise, Sage was happy to see her little sister, and the two women embraced warmly.

"What's with all the luggage?" Sage asked, staring at her sister

"I'm moving to Atlanta," Ava announced blithely.

"*What?*" Sage exclaimed, her heavy eyebrows arched in surprise as she gave her little sister a don't-play-with-me look.

"I'm serious, Sage. I want to live in Atlanta. I hate Baltimore."

"And when did you decide this?"

"Yesterday," Ava replied. "But you know, I've been thinking about it for a while."

"We were supposed to discuss it first," Sage scolded, picking up Ava's garment bag and suitcase.

"Well, I'm here," Ava replied happily, her high-energy attitude typical.

"Okay, come on," Sage said, picking up several suitcases and leading the way to the car. They loaded the trunk with Ava's mix of luggage—two garment bags, three suitcases, and an old trunk. The trunk reminded Sage of the months following her father's death in Vietnam when they'd moved in with her maternal grandparents. Sage treasured those memories, the time before her mother married Aaron Hicks, forever changing their relationship.

"Okay, what's going on?" Sage asked as she turned the corner onto Peachtree Street.

"Nothing much. I'm just tired of being at home. Ma and Daddy are driving me crazy. They bug me all the time." Ava scanned the radio stations until she heard a rap song she liked. She turned up the volume and leaned back in the plush leather seat, popping a pretzel in her mouth.

"I thought you were moving in with Jamilla."

"I was. Bought kitchen stuff, a bedroom set, everything. Then she up and changed her mind on me."

"I'm sorry, Ava," Sage said.

"Ma was so happy when I told her I wasn't moving. You should have seen her."

"I bet she was."

"But I can't afford to move into an apartment by myself. And I don't want to live with them anymore. I'm tired of going to the Hall, and they hassle me every day about not going."

"So what about your job?"

"I quit yesterday."

"I thought you liked working there."

"I did. But I don't want to be a secretary forever."

"So what do you want to do?"

"Design clothes—and everyone says Atlanta is the place to be."

"What do you know about being a fashion designer?" A memory of Ava making dresses for her baby dolls flashed in Sage's mind.

"I've been taking classes for a while. I never told Ma. She would have had a fit," Ava said, licking the salt off a pretzel.

"Is that why you left?"

"Why are you tripping, Sage? You left home when you were seventeen. At least I'm twenty-two."

"My reasons for leaving were very different."

"When are you going to tell me why you left?"

"I've told you why. I wanted to go to college, and they didn't want me to go."

"You still could have said goodbye to me and Aaron."

"Why are we talking about me? You're the one who just left."

"Maybe because you haven't told me everything."

Ignoring her innuendo, Sage said, "Well, I'm not surprised that you're tired of living at home or that you want to be a designer with the crazy way you dress, but I am surprised that you would leave Brandon."

Ava stopped munching on the pretzels.

Sage turned down the radio. Without looking at her, Sage had felt something change in Ava when Brandon's name was mentioned. "What about Brandon? I thought you two were serious," Sage persisted.

"So did I!" Ava said, as tears threatened to fall from her pretty brown eyes.

"What happened?" Sage asked gently.

"He broke up with me. He doesn't want to be tied down."

"I know it hurts, baby. Believe me, it will get better." Sage reached over and patted Ava's leg. "Men, they're so damn unpredictable."

"Yeah, well, I'm going to find a new boyfriend."

Sage turned into her driveway. She lived in a three-bedroom house with a two-car garage in the heart of Buckhead, one of Atlanta's upscale areas, just minutes from downtown. Sage had purchased the blush-colored, two-story brick house brand new and selected the fixtures, carpeting, wallpaper, and cabinetry. Sage pressed the garage door opener and pulled inside.

"I just love your house," Ava said, as they carried her luggage inside the house, up the spiral stairs to the second floor that had two bedrooms, a large bathroom, and a loft area with a view of the living room and dining room. They put Ava's luggage in the guest room where she always stayed.

"Everything looks the same," Ava said, when they walked down the stairs. "Oh, wait a minute," she said moving toward the curio cabinet in the foyer. "You have a new butterfly," she said, opening the glass door of the curio. Ava picked up a brass butterfly from an assortment of butterflies made of crystal, wax, glass, and brass on the four-shelved lighted curio. "I like the way the wings fold," Ava said. She returned the butterfly to its space on the crowded shelf. "You're running out of room."

"I know. I haven't bought one in a couple of years, but people keep giving them to me," Sage said. "That one was from a consultant who worked on the campaign."

"I can't believe you still have the one I made in high school," Ava said, spotting the ceramic butterfly she created years ago.

"That's my favorite one."

"Right!"

Sage yawned. "I'm going to bed. There's some food in the refrigerator if you're hungry. We can talk some more tomorrow."

It was 4:45 A.M. when Sage crawled back in the bed. In an hour, her alarm would ring to awaken her for another day.

* * * * * * * * * * * * *

"As soon as Drew gets here, we'll be leaving," Sage said. She sat at the dining room table, typing some letters on her laptop computer. Ramion was in the living room scanning the TV channels with the remote.

Hearing Drew's name, Ava ran down the steps. "You didn't tell me he was coming over."

"He has the tickets," Sage said.

"I love basketball," Ava said. "The Hawks have been hitting it."

"They're doing much better than last year," Ramion said.

When the doorbell rang, Ava rushed to the door, excited about seeing Drew. Her firm, five-foot-five frame was covered in black from head to toe—black jeans, black turtleneck, black boots. Silver necklace, long silver earrings, and an armful of silver bangles offered the only contrast. She opened the door flashing a toothpaste smile. "Hi, Drew!" she cried, throwing her arms around his neck.

"Ava," Drew exclaimed. "How are you, baby?"

"I'm great!"

"Sage didn't tell me you were here."

"I sort of surprised her," Ava said. "I just got here three days ago."

Drew went into the living room and walked over to greet Ramion, "Hey man, what's happening?"

"Ain't nothing going on, man! I'm just glad the election is over."

"I heard that!" Drew said. "You'd be amazed at how many people hate having a black governor. They don't mind writing to the newspaper and signing their name."

"I wouldn't be too surprised, especially after someone had the nerve to blow up his campaign headquarters." Changing subjects,

56

Ramion said, "I like those boots, man," indicating Drew's fancy black leather boots.

"Thanks. That's my thing. Boots."

"Drew's the only brother I know who wears cowboy boots," Sage said. "He even wore them when we were in school."

"We better get going or we're going to be late," Ramion said.

"Give me a sec," Sage said, turning off her laptop computer.

"Where's your date?" Ava asked.

"Kelly's meeting us there," Drew said.

"Do you have an extra ticket?" Sage asked. "Ava's been hinting."

"Yeah, you know I'm good friends with the sports editor."

"I'll get my coat," Ava said. "Are you serious about Kelly?"

"Baby, I don't believe in girlfriends," Drew said with a chuckle.

Chapter V

Within three days of her abrupt arrival in Atlanta, Ava had a job working in the office of the newly elected governor. Sitting at a desk across from Marika, Ava popped another piece of bubble gum into her mouth, chewing heartily on the cherry-flavored wad. She peeled off a mailing label and placed it on the front of the ivory, linen-textured envelope. She inserted a gold-lettered invitation into the envelope and sealed it closed.

"Marika, do you know Dr. Ralph Harris?" Ava asked, reading the name on the invitation. She placed the invitation on top of the stack of envelopes that she had prepared for mailing.

"Nope," Marika replied.

"Are you going to the party?"

"Are you kidding?" Marika replied saucily. "This is an exclusive inaugural party. It's going to be at the Governor's Mansion."

A quizzical expression covered Ava's face. "Have you been there?"

"Yeah, girl, and it's beautiful. Everything is real elegant and expensive. It's hard to describe because it's nothing like what you've seen before. You have to see it for yourself. You will when we set up offices over there. How long are you going to work with us?"

"I don't know," she answered, shrugging her shoulders. "I can't believe Sage got me a job so quickly. She said there's going to be an opening for an administrative assistant, but nothing's definite yet. It

58

would be cool to work here and find a way to go to design school at the same time."

Marika said, "I really like working for Sage."

"It feels a little weird to work for my big sister, but this is a chance to get to know her. I usually come down in the summer to visit for a couple weeks, but I've never spent a whole lot of time with her."

"How much older is she than you?"

"Eight years. But we have different fathers. Our mother remarried when Sage's father died. Anyway, when Sage graduated from high school, she left home to go to college, but never came back. I was only eight."

"Eight? How old was she when she graduated?"

"I think she was sixteen or something like that. She graduated from high school early. I remember her and Ma fighting all the time about college, but Sage was determined to go so she left." Her voice was suddenly tinged with sadness. "She left in the middle of the summer."

They were interrupted by the ringing telephone. Marika answered: "Cameron Hudson's office. May I help you?" After hanging up the phone a few minutes later, she said, "There's going to be another party. An everyday people party."

"What's that?"

"That's what I call it when they invite, you know, regular folks, working people, not the $500-a-plate contributors."

Sage came out of her office with a young white man. Dressed in a business navy, pin-striped suit, he extended his right hand to Sage. "Thanks again for the interview. If you have any more questions, please don't hesitate to call."

"I'll be in touch," Sage said.

After he walked out the office, Ava asked, "Who was that?"

"He was interviewing for the educational director position," Sage answered.

"Are you going to hire him?" Marika asked.

"Maybe, but I have two other people to interview first. He's definitely on my callback list for a second interview."

"He sure is a cute white boy," Ava said.

"And he knows it. He's kind of cocky, but he's got the right credentials." Sage noticed the pile of sealed invitations on both their desks. "You ladies have been busy."

"Yes, busy, busy, busy," Ava said. She grinned at Sage and placed headphones on her head. "This is my song. Salt-N-Pepa can jam!" She bobbed her head to the beat of the music.

"Let me know when that reporter gets here," Sage said, before returning to her office.

* * * * * * * * * * * * *

Callie Callison, a staff writer from *Atlanta* magazine, placed a tape recorder on the corner of Sage's desk. In her late twenties, Callie's curly bleached-blonde hair hung past her shoulders. Bright blue eyes blazed from behind black, square-rimmed glasses. She held her mouth tightly as she reviewed the list of questions she planned to ask Sage for her article tentatively titled, "Atlanta's Women Power Players."

Callie removed a yellow notebook and pen from her well-worn brown leather briefcase. While waiting for her host to end her telephone conversation, Callie wrote down several items in Sage's office—the personalized paperweight with Columbia University scripted on it, the pictures of Sage with former U.S. President and Georgia governor Jimmy Carter, former Atlanta mayor Maynard Jackson, Coretta Scott King, and Reverend Jessie Jackson, the abstract painting of a butterfly, and two framed poems by Maya Angelou: "Phenomenal Woman" and "On the Pulse of Morning."

When Sage hung up the phone, she apologized, "I'm sorry, Callie. I had to take that call. There won't be any more interruptions." She scribbled some notes in her Day-Timer, then glanced at her watch. "I can only talk to you for thirty minutes, and then I have to go to a meeting."

"That's fine," Callie said. "Perhaps later I can spend more time with you, maybe follow you around for a day."

"Hmm," Sage said, flipping through her calendar. "That may be difficult. I don't know what kind of deadline you're working under, but I won't be available for an entire day until mid-January."

"Maybe I'll get all I need today. Scott Denton, our photographer, will be calling you to schedule a photo shoot."

"That won't be a problem," Sage said. She opened her desk drawer and pulled out a microcassette tape recorder. "If you don't mind, I'd like to also record the interview."

Callie smiled wryly. "No problem." She flipped open her notebook and said, "Incidentally, congratulations on winning the election."

"Thank you. I'm relieved it's all over, and I'm thrilled we won. It was a battle down to the wire."

"How did the bombing affect your commitment to the campaign?"

"I was aware of the threats, and we beefed up security, but on some levels, I didn't believe the threats would become real. When I woke up in the hospital, it became very real. Of course, I wondered who had done it and why. Was it racially motivated? But I wasn't going to let it dampen my commitment to getting Cameron elected governor."

"Before getting into politics, you worked in public affairs at Coca-Cola. What prompted a move from the private sector into public service?"

"I've always had an interest in politics. I feel that working in government is a direct way to improve people's lives and to make a real contribution to society."

"I understand you did very well at Coca-Cola. Three promotions in four years," Callie said.

"Uh huh. You've been checking up on me," Sage said with a smile. Callie smiled back. "Of course."

"I'm proud of my accomplishments there. I started in the public relations department, moved to urban affairs, and then I was made director of community relations."

"All within four years."

"Four and a half years, actually, before I went to work for the City of Atlanta."

"How did that come about?"

"I met the mayor through my work at Coke. I'm sure you know that Coca-Cola sponsors a lot of civic and community functions, and I met the mayor at a fundraiser. Later, when Pat Hall resigned from his communications director post, I got several calls telling me I was being considered for the position. I interviewed, and Cameron offered me the job."

Sage shifted in the black high-back leather chair and continued, "It was a difficult decision to make because I really liked my job, but politics have always tugged at me. I suppose I believed I could accomplish more in public service. "

"Such as?"

"Help make things happen to improve people's lives, that's what matters most. Government is the epicenter of our nation. It's where the power and the money is. Even at the city level, people's lives are affected by government decisions. At the gubernatorial level, the power to influence is even greater. It's very exciting to know we can do a lot to help."

"What are some of the new governor's goals?"

"First and foremost, he intends to significantly improve the state's social service programs, especially for children and the elderly. We've always rank low in those areas."

"Are there any issues you and Mr. Hudson disagree on?"

"I think we are like-minded on the serious issues," Sage replied with a smile. "We sometimes differ on tactics or time tables."

Flipping to a new page in her notepad, Callie asked, "Why did Mr. Hudson pick you to run his campaign? Many expected him to hire a more seasoned person."

"He certainly could have. I think he chose me because I outlined a campaign plan and defined our strategies and tactics for winning very early, months before we started campaigning. Of course, we had outside counsel, locally and nationally."

"On a personal front, do you hope to marry and have children one day?"

"Absolutely. I want the whole dream. I look forward to being a wife and a mother."

"Are you seeing anybody seriously?"

"I'm involved, but that's all I'm going to say about it."

"Where did your ambition come from?"

Sage smiled. "Who could really answer that? Certainly not me."

"Well, what about strong role models in your life?"

"I suppose I'd have to credit my Aunt Maddie. She never married, but she was always career-minded. She's a teacher, and very well-traveled. She's always been very devoted to me." Her eyes softened as she talked about her father's sister. Aunt Maddie was the link to her father's family.

"My mother always wanted me to get married and have babies. The fact that I haven't married and had a family has disappointed her," Callie said. "What about your mother? Did she encourage you to go to college and have a career?"

"My mother is old-fashioned, too. Like your mother, she believes that women should be at home," Sage responded carefully, reflecting on her relationship with her mother. If she answered truthfully she would have to admit that there was no relationship. And maybe now, after their recent disastrous meeting, there never would be.

Callie shifted the questioning back to the present. "Is there any truth to the rumor that you had an affair with the mayor when you started working for him? Many people speculate that that's the reason he chose you to run his campaign."

Sage suppressed the urge to smile. That was one rumor that refused to die, and yet she'd never understood what had started the vicious gossip. Questions had been raised about her relationship with Cameron from the very beginning. But perhaps it was as simple as his reputation in private circles to be a womanizer. "No. We have never had a relationship other than a professional one."

"I understand that you have traveled together," Callie pressed.

"Of course," Sage said reproachfully, refusing to dignify the implication by defending their relationship any further.

"One more question," Callie said, checking her watch. "What three words would you use to describe yourself?"

Sage leaned back against the chair in thoughtful repose. "Confident, driven, and people-oriented."

"That's all for now," Callie said. "May I call you if I have more questions later?"

"Absolutely."

* * * * * * * * * * * * *

Ava was headed home for Christmas, even though she had only been in Atlanta for three weeks. Whether she would make the flight was still in question as Sage sped down the interstate, her speedometer registering eighty miles per hour. Ava's flight would be leaving in forty minutes.

"If there's no traffic and no red lights, we'll make it, Miss Last Minute," Sage said.

Sage hated rushing frantically and usually allowed herself plenty of time to get to the airport. Getting through the airport to the departing gate was a maze of checkpoints, ticket counters, trains, escalators, elevators, and terminals.

But Ava was different. Last minute with everything, she didn't start packing until they got home from work.

"I hope you don't get a ticket," Ava taunted, when Sage barely slowed in time to pass the police car without being stopped.

"You will pay for it if I do."

"Hey, you can handle it better than me," Ava said. "I've seen your bank statements."

"That's not the point," Sage said. "Why did you wait until the last minute to pack? We should have left an hour ago."

Ava covered her ears with her hands. "You said that already."

They rode in silence for a while, driving in the fast lane, on the lookout for patrol cars.

"Why don't you ever go home?" Ava suddenly asked.

"You know Ma and I don't get along."

"I have never understood why. You haven't been home since you left."

"Ava, why do you want to talk about that now? It's in the past."

"Because Christmas has always been lonely without you. I never got used to it."

"What's the big deal? We weren't supposed to celebrate Christmas anyway," Sage said, commenting on the Jehovah Witnesses' declaration against holidays. Hearing Prince's song "Little Red Corvette" blasting from the radio, Sage said, "Change the station. I hate that song."

Ava selected a different radio station, replacing the pulsing verse of "Baby you're much too fast" with Mariah Carey's octave voice. "You don't like Prince, do you?"

"Not really. The only song of his I like is 'Erotic City.'"

"I can't wait to see Aaron and Daddy," Ava said. She missed her twin brother and was very close to her father.

"I'd like to see Aaron, too. Maybe he'll come down for spring break."

"Mommy is going to hug me to death, and then she's going to yell and scream at me for leaving her. She just about died when I told her I wasn't coming back. She still hopes it's just a long visit."

"She'll adjust," Sage said.

"Guess who I met the other day," Ava said, fumbling through the box of CDs.

"Who?"

"Edwinna."

"How did you meet her?" Sage cast a sideways glance at her sister. "She came to the office with her father to see Mr. Hudson. I can't believe Ramion ever liked her. She's not even pretty."

"She's the boss's daughter," Sage explained. "And Ramion was Edwin's protégé. I don't think Ramion was ever in love with Edwinna, but she was crazy about him. I think Ramion got involved with her because of who she is, the people she knows, the whole bit. But she wanted to get serious, and he didn't. Ramion didn't want to owe Edwin for the rest of his career. Believe me, he didn't make the decision easily. He lost a lot of political connections when he left Edwin's firm. But he wants to make it on his own, without feeling like Edwin owns him."

"Whatever the reason, she's definitely Miss Attitude, and she's real upset that you stole her man. She looked at me like I was dirt when Marika told her I was your sister."

Sage laughed. "Yeah, that's what she gets for thinking she should get whatever she wants."

"I don't like her, Sage."

"Neither do I."

"She may be rich and well-educated and high society, but she's got a nasty personality," Ava observed.

"She's a bitch," Sage said. "She'll do anything to get what she wants."

Changing subjects, Ava asked, "So what are you going to do for the holidays?"

"I'm going to Ramion's family for Christmas dinner."

"What about New Year?"

"We're going to Cancun."

"Ooh, are you going to do it on the beach?"

"Ava!"

Sage pulled into the airport, adroitly maneuvering through the frenzy of cars driving in front of and pulling away from the airport's entrance.

"We made it!" Ava exclaimed.

"Girl, you have fifteen minutes to get to the gate. You're going to have to carry your luggage on the plane, so get to stepping."

Ava laughed. "So you do know some slang."

They got out of the car and retrieved Ava's luggage from the trunk. "Love you," Ava said, giving Sage a quick hug before dashing into the airport.

* * * * * * * * * * * * *

The day before leaving for Cancun, Mexico, Sage went on a shopping spree to buy clothes for her four-day vacation. Tawny went along.

Sage bought three swimsuits—a red one-piece suit and two bikinis for the beach—casual outfits to wear exploring the islands, and evening outfits for going to restaurants or clubs. On impulse, Sage stopped in Frederick's of Hollywood.

Holding an edible body suit, Tawny said, "How about this?"

"Now you know that's too wild for me." Sage held up a leopard print teddy with dangling garters and said, "This is borderline."

"Go for it," Tawny encouraged, her pretty brown face breaking into a friendly, gap-toothed smile. "No one will ever know."

Tawny and Sage had been friends since both women worked at Coca-Cola. They had been roommates until Tawny moved in with her boyfriend.

"I don't have the nerve," Sage admitted, putting the teddy back on the rack. "Let's get something to eat. I'm starving."

Their final stop after a four-hour shopping spree was at a restaurant.

"I knew you were going to come over here," Tawny said, looking at the Ruby Tuesday menu. "Let me guess, you're going to order the seafood gumbo and baked potato."

"Uh huh, and you're going to have the blackened chicken salad," Sage shot back.

"My favorite salad," Tawny said, laying the menu on the table. "You're glowing, girl. Ramion must be the one."

Sage smiled. "Boy, did we have to struggle to get this far."

"Yeah, but you're there now. You should feel really good about things. The man gave up a promising position with a prestigious firm for you."

"You act like he sacrificed his entire career when he's actually doing better and making more money."

"Sage, you know what I'm talking about. He left his big-time mentor, Mr. Williamson. Notice nobody calls him Ed or Edwin. It's always Mr. Williamson."

"So?"

"So, he's got clout. With Mr. Williamson backing him, Ramion was set. Breaking into politics would have been no problem. They would have laid out a welcome mat for Mr. Williamson's protégé."

"Are you implying that I ruined his career?"

"No. I'm just saying he did it for you. That should make you feel special," Tawny said.

"Don't be cute, Tawny. It wasn't just for me. Ramion wants to make it on his own."

"Are you in denial, girl? The only reason he left Mr. Man's law firm was because he knew he couldn't have a relationship with you after breaking up with Edwinna."

"Maybe," Sage said, shrugging her shoulders. "But it was over between them when we started going out."

"Not quite. And you know it. He probably wouldn't have broken up with her when he did if it weren't for you."

"Maybe."

"Sage, you know it's true. That's why Edwinna hates you so much."

"That's her problem," she said, tapping her finger against the menu.

A mini-skirted waitress approached their table. "Good afternoon, ladies. What can I get you?"

"A gag for my friend," Sage said to the waitress. "And I'll have the gumbo."

* * * * * * * * * * * *

When Ramion arrived to pick up Sage for their trip to Cancun, she was grinning with the glee of a child on Christmas morning. "I guess you're ready to go," Ramion said, noticing the three suitcases lined up by the door.

"I've been ready for hours," Sage admitted. "I can't wait till we get there."

"I can't believe I had to talk you into taking this trip," Ramion said, recalling her unenthusiastic reaction when he suggested a vacation for the New Year's holiday. Sage had been reluctant, explaining that she had a lot of work to do.

Ramion had been dauntless, placing travel brochures all over his house so that no matter where Sage went, an enticing brochure lay in arm's reach. The brochures were filled with pictures of coral beaches, the azure-blue ocean water, historic ruins, museums, elegant restaurants, uniquely architectured hotels, and shopping malls. It was the picture of the Cozumel ruins that finally captured her attention and tempted her to leave work behind for a few days.

Stretching up on her toes to peck his lips, Sage said, "I'm glad you convinced me."

Ramion loaded her luggage into his car and closed the trunk. Sage locked the front door of her house and came down the steps carrying her purse and computer.

"Baby, what kind of vacation are we going to have if you take that computer with you?" Ramion asked, his forehead creased in a frown.

"I can get some work done on the plane or lounging on the beach."

"You're not going to be able to relax if you bring that computer with you, baby. Leave it here, okay?"

Sage hesitated before turning around and going back inside her house. Minutes later, she came outside without the laptop.

"I was going to hide it in my suitcase," Sage said, grinning devilishly, as Ramion opened the car door for her.

"Let's leave work behind us. It's time for some fun!"

* * * * * * * * * * * *

Sage flipped through the current issue of *Vanity Fair* magazine as the airplane glided down the runway to position for takeoff. Seated comfortably in the first-class section of the jumbo jet, a glass of mimosa on the tray in front of her, Sage sighed with contentment. Ramion sat beside her reading a book. She heard the airplane's engines rev, and moments later they were on their way to Mexico.

Cancun greeted them with a light, misty rain. They went through customs, presented their passports to Mexican custom agents, and then retrieved their luggage. Outside the airport, they took a taxi to the hotel.

"Look at this place," Sage said, as the taxi driver drove through the resort zone, a mile-long stretch of hotels in all kinds of architectural styles and design.

"Tourism is the number one industry here," Ramion said. "So hotels are plentiful."

"Oh, that looks like a mall," she said pointing to a sprawling building with storefronts and restaurants. "We have to go there. I heard they have wonderful pieces of jewelry here."

"We can do that tomorrow if you like. But on Saturday, I want to go to a bullfight."

"Oh, Ramion, I can't believe they still do that."

"Believe it."

Sage and Ramion checked into a six-star resort that offered tennis courts, a golf course, a fully equipped fitness center, a sand-bottomed whirlpool, swimming pools fed by waterfalls, four restaurants, three bars, and aquatic activities. It was located on the beach and within walking distance of a shopping center.

The first thing Sage did after entering their room was walk out to the balcony. She didn't notice the entertainment center with the 40-inch TV, VCR, and stereo system. She gazed upon the crystal blue waters of the Caribbean coast and breathed in the salty ocean air.

"It's so beautiful," she gushed. "I guess I thought the pictures were too good to be true."

"It's real, baby," Ramion said.

"This is paradise," Sage said, peering over the balcony. White sails danced offshore in the distance and, closer inland, people swam in the turquoise water. The diamond-white shimmering beach, with its perfect sand, beckoned.

"I don't even want to unpack," she said. "I just want to get to that beach."

"Then let's change and hit it," Ramion said.

Under the sunny sky, Sage and Ramion walked along the beach holding hands. Removing her sandals, Sage let the silky sand ooze between her toes. They found a spot to sit under a tropical palm tree and savored the moment—the sultry sun, the silver-white sand, the turquoise ocean, and the cloudless sky. They had already fallen under Cancun's hypnotic spell.

Much later, they returned to their room, unpacked, and changed clothes for dinner.

Downstairs in the hotel lobby, they exchanged American dollars for Mexican pesos and caught a taxi to a downtown restaurant. They dined on lobster dinner while beautiful Mexican girls dressed in gypsy clothing performed a flamenco dance, their feet stomping and hips gyrating to a salsa-hot beat.

The waiter cleared the table, recommending flan for dessert.

"We'll pass on dessert," Ramion said, his gaze passionate and hungry as he stared at Sage.

"I'll be your dessert," she whispered, when the waiter walked away.

* * * * * * * * * * * * *

Dessert began on the balcony. Sage stood against the railing, the cool ocean breeze caressing her body. Ramion kissed the nape of her neck and tenderly massaged the muscles in her shoulders. She relaxed against him and closed her eyes, enjoying his soft, gentle kisses. He nibbled at her ear, his tongue delving inside, his teeth gently nipping at the lobe. He unbuttoned her blouse while licking the sides of her neck, slowly, then faster, faster.

Sage was quickly aroused and anxious. She wanted to kiss him back, felt an urgent need to run her tongue through the dense black hair on his chest. She wanted to feel his desire and touch his maleness. She tried to turn in his arms to face him, but Ramion held her tight.

He removed her silk blouse and the strapless bra and unzipped her skirt as he kissed her back. Restless with anticipation, Sage wrestled with him.

"Be still and patient," he whispered. "I'm going to love you."

He ran his hands up and down Sage's stocking-covered legs, loving the feel of silk against his hands. He rubbed the inside of her thighs before moving to the place between her legs to stroke her hot, wet center. She moaned encouragement when he pulled down her panties and stockings. She kicked them away impatiently.

"Don't turn around," he whispered, and sank to his knees. He caressed her soft buttocks, his hands moving in small circles, driving her senseless. She dug her fingers into his shoulders.

Ramion slowly moved higher, his hungry mouth kissing every inch of her flawless back until he was standing, then nibbled her shoulder.

Sage could not contain her passion. She turned and kissed his lips hard, her tongue determinedly probing the inside of his mouth.

She softly bit his bottom lip, and her slender fingers inched up and down his chest through the dark mat of hair and tugged at his nipples. Ramion then carried her from the balcony and gently laid her on the bed.

He quickly removed his clothes and unleashed a torrent of kisses on her breasts. His hot tongue began an encirclement on the fleshy tips of her breasts—around and around and around until her brown nipples were taut. His mouth covered her nipple, pulsating rapture through her body. He licked the fullness of her other breast, up and down, up and down, and when he finally took her nipple into his mouth, Sage trembled.

His hands began to explore the place between her thighs, and she writhed under his touch.

Ramion lowered himself so that his head was between her legs. He began licking her inner thighs to the vortex of her pulsing need. He opened her with his fingers, and his tongue plunged inside her lips to taste the sweet nectarine of her desire.

"Ramey, Ramey," Sage moaned.

When he raised up to meet her, she clasped her arms around his neck and bit into the deepness of his shoulders. Ramion spread her legs wide and entered her. Slowly, steadily, he moved inside her, deeper and deeper. Languidly. Sage arched to him and rocked with him. She opened her eyes and whispered, "Faster, faster."

Ramion looked into her flickering olive eyes. "I love you," he said.

"And I love you," she moaned.

He quickened his rhythm, controlled, sweeping.

Their passion exploded like the space shuttle blasting into orbit, and they collapsed into one another's arms.

* * * * * * * * * * * * *

Their days were spent leisurely wandering the streets of Cancun—shopping at the urbanlike malls, touring the ruins and museums, browsing through the flea markets, swimming and jet skiing in the ocean, and even attending a bullfight. At night, the restaurants and clubs were only a brief stop on the way to passion.

71

A party was planned for New Year's Eve at the hotel, their last night in Cancun. Before going to the party, Sage and Ramion took a walk along the beach. It was dusk, the sun on the crest of setting—suspended between the sea and sky.

They found a secluded spot on the beach, hidden away from the main area. They were sipping margaritas, Cancun style—tequila, vodka, and lime.

"Have you enjoyed yourself?" Ramion asked, breaking the silence.

"You know I have. It's so beautiful here. Atlanta seems so far away, another world. Almost wish I could stay here forever."

"You couldn't do it. Not for long," Ramion said. "I'm glad I convinced you to come, Sage. I had an ulterior motive for bringing you here."

"Uh huh, to keep me from leaving your bed in the middle of the night."

Ramion laughed. "Not exactly."

A seashell rested near Ramion's feet. He picked it up, examining its interior, and holding it out to her, said, "I think there's something inside."

Under the final rays of the sun, Sage peeked into the orange-colored striped shell with its delicate pearlescent tint. Something sparkled inside, just as he'd claimed. Her heart fluttering with excitement, she shook the seashell. A diamond ring fell out, its face winking up at her from its bed of sand. Sage held her breath as she picked up the ring that signified a promise of eternal love.

For a long moment, neither spoke a word. Ripples of laughter and rock music were carried to them on a breeze.

Ramion took the ring from Sage's hand. "May I?" he asked, before gliding the two-carat, pear-shaped diamond ring onto her finger.

Sage stared at the ring through tears. In the sun's twilight, the sand glistened and the ocean waters roared, sending its white foamy froth to the shore. When Sage peered up at Ramion, she was at once captured in the gleam of his onyx eyes.

He held his breath, waiting for her response.

Such a perfect moment, Sage thought: Ramion, the tropical paradise, and the ring. It was beautiful and exotic and erotic. She couldn't have imagined a happier moment; the joy bubbling inside her defied description. Soft tears fell from her face, wetting the sand.

"I didn't want you to cry," Ramion said. Her quiet response had surprised him, and now the tears. He'd imagined her ecstatic, screaming with delight.

"Oh, Ramion, these are tears of joy," Sage whispered.

With those words, Ramion gulped the air he'd been denying himself. Then he asked the only question left unanswered. "Sage, will you marry me?"

"Yes, baby, I will!"

Ramion touched her face and ran his fingers across her luscious lips. He looked deep into her eyes and felt himself being carried away in the green sea of her irises, swimming in the love shining at him. "I love you, and I want you to be my wife. I want to share my life with you." He spoke the words tenderly.

Sage wiped the tears from her face. "I love you, too, more than I can say. You make me feel complete. You filled the hole in my heart and the empty space in my soul."

Ramion pressed his lips against her face—kissing her forehead, her cheeks, and her lips. His kisses grew more intense as he ran his hands down her body, stroking her arms, her breasts, her legs.

A volcano of desire erupted inside her. It rumbled and roared and threatened to rip open her heart and spill out the lava of her love. She wanted to contain it, but it had a force of its own. Sage pushed him away gently. "People can see us," she said between ragged breaths.

"I don't care," Ramion said. He slipped a hand inside her blouse. "I don't care about anything except you."

Sage moaned, the wave of desire bubbling to the surface. She wanted to move, but she couldn't resist the wicked heat Ramion was creating with his touch.

"If you want me to stop I will," Ramion said in a voice husky with passion. "Who cares what anybody sees? I want you, right now, right here."

This was the man she'd just promised to marry, and suddenly she felt the way he did. She wanted him at this very moment, at this very spot. "Right here, right now," she agreed.

Chapter VI

Hung over and bleary-eyed from New Year's Eve parties, Edwinna opened her condo door, the blast of cold air jolting her awake. She quickly slammed the door shut and padded down the hall to the kitchen, where the aroma of brewing Kahlúa-flavored coffee filled the air. Edwinna poured herself a cup, stirring in heaping spoonfuls of sugar. The volume on the thirteen-inch television positioned on the black baker's rack was low.

She sat down at the kitchen table and casually flipped through the morning edition of the *Atlanta Times*. Beginning with the front page of the Living section, she turned to the second page to read "Peachtree Happenings," a gossip column about local figures and national celebrities.

Her eyes were immediately drawn to the three-sentence paragraph about Ramion Sandidge.

> Are wedding bells in the air for Sage Kennedy, Deputy Chief to the newly elected Governor Hudson? Kennedy and attorney Ramion Sandidge were spotted at the airport on their way home from a New Year's vacation in Cancun. A diamond ring glistened on Kennedy's left hand.

"Ooh, I hate her. That bitch!" Edwinna exclaimed furiously. She crumpled the newspaper and tossed it in the garbage.

* * * * * * * * * * * * *

Cameron raised his right hand and repeated the oath of office:

> I, Cameron Jamison Hudson, do solemnly swear or affirm that I will faithfully execute the office of the governor of the state of Georgia and will, to the best of my ability, preserve, protect, and defend the Constitution thereof and the Constitution of the United States.
> I do further swear that I am not the holder of any public money due the state, unaccounted for; that I am not the holder of any office of trust under the government of the United States, nor of either of the several states, nor of any foreign states in that I am otherwise qualified to hold said office, according to the Constitution and laws of Georgia, and that I will support the Constitution of the United States and of this state.

The small crowd of politicians, family, and supporters clapped as Cameron Hudson was sworn in as the eightieth governor of Georgia. A photographer captured Cameron being hugged by his family, the photo to appear on the front cover of the evening newspaper.

* * * * * * * * * * * * *

Several hours after Cameron was sworn in as governor, Sage and Ava entered the hotel ballroom filled with partygoers dressed in formal attire, gathered to celebrate the inauguration of the new governor.

"How do I look?" Ava asked Sage as they walked past the registration table.

"Beautiful! Gorgeous! How many times do I have to tell you that?"

"I've never been to a formal ball. It feels weird to be wearing a long evening gown." The black columnar gown elegantly showcased her lithe figure. "I can't wear these," Ava said, slipping off the elbow-length gloves and tucking them inside her purse.

"Suit yourself," Sage said. They stopped at the table where Cameron Hudson and his family were seated.

"Hi, Jewel," Sage said to the governor's eldest daughter, who was a freshman at Spelman College. "Where's everybody?"

"I don't know. I went to the bathroom, and they disappeared," Jewel replied. Rail-thin, her bored expression was as flat as her chest and in stark contrast to Ava's wide-eyed excitement.

"Hi," Ava said to Jewel. "I love your gown. Oh, this is all so thrilling."

"Thanks," Jewel said. "But I hate these affairs. They're boring." She stood up. "Excuse me, I'm going to look for my date."

Sage and Ava sat down at the table. Ava watched the crowd, blistering with excitement to be mingling among Atlanta's elite.

Black was the color of choice for most of the people attending the governor's formal dinner ball. Men wore black or grey tuxedos, and women were dressed in strapless, off-the-shoulder, and V-necked black dresses and gowns in varying lengths from below the calf to above the knee. There were the occasional rebels—women daring to wear red velvet dresses, slinky purple gowns, and turquoise tuxedo suits.

"Look, there's Edwinna!" Ava said, patting Sage's arm. "She keeps rolling her eyes at you."

"Ignore her. Don't even look her way."

"She's just mad that you're engaged to her man."

"*My* man," Sage corrected.

"Are you talking about me?" Ramion interrupted. Standing over Sage, he placed his hands on her shoulders. She tilted her head back, and he leaned down and kissed her on the lips. "You ladies look marvelous." His hands traveled down Sage's back, provocatively exposed in the halter-strap black gown.

"Thank you, honey," Sage said.

Cockily, Ava said, "We know we do!"

"No more compliments for you, Miss Thing," Ramion playfully said. "Sage, you look gorgeous as always. I'm surprised you don't have your hair up."

"Not with this scar," Sage said, self-consciously touching the back of her neck. Her curly hair hung loosely on her shoulders.

"It's barely noticeable," Ramion said, dressed in a black tuxedo. He kissed her neck and said, "You shouldn't let it bother you. I like it when wear your hair up."

"I'll remember that. I'll catch up with you guys later," Sage said, standing. She picked up her velvet evening bag. "I have some work to do."

"Remember our plans for later," Ramion said, a gleam in his eyes.

Her eyebrows arching upward, Sage answered with a sliver of a smile, "I haven't forgotten."

* * * * * * * * * * * * *

More than three hundred people attended the governor's inaugural celebration, participating in an event that would be remembered for many years. Cameron Hudson wasted no time in laying out his political agenda, setting an aggressive tone for his administration with his first speech as governor of Georgia:

> To give birth again to the dream, we must tackle some major problems, such as education, housing, and crime. Also on my agenda for this year is to change the state flag. The Confederate emblem on the flag represents Georgia's past. The star-studded Confederate cross was used as a symbol of defiance against court-ordered integration. I believe that many Georgians find this symbol offensive.
>
> We need a flag that is more representative of what Georgia is today, and what Georgia promises to be in the future. A state where all races can work, live, and play together. So I will sponsor legislation to make the flag in tune with our state's motto—wisdom, justice, and moderation.

The audience responded with a standing ovation as Cameron Hudson concluded his speech and left the stage. The tone of the evening changed from a sober political dinner to a festive party. Rhythm and blues, country, and pop singers entertained the melting pot of people who shared the new governor's dream.

The celebration was ending as Sage was freshening up her makeup in the bathroom mirror, when she heard one of the bathroom stalls open and an unfriendly voice. "Well, look who's here, the future Mrs. Sandidge." The words came out slow, slurred, and sarcastic.

Sage turned around and saw Edwinna sparkling like a firecracker in a sequined black gown and rhinestone earrings, choker, and necklace. It was late, and Sage was tired. She didn't feel like exchanging unpleasant words with Ramion's bitter ex-girlfriend, so she ignored her.

"I know you heard me," Edwinna said, when Sage turned her head back to the mirror. They made eye contact in the mirror—angry eyes stared into wary eyes. Edwinna's gaze traveled to Sage's left hand.

"Obviously, I don't want to talk to you," Sage said curtly.

"Obviously, I want to talk to you," Edwinna replied tartly.

Sage picked up her purse from the vanity counter. She moved toward the door.

"I see Ramion gave you a little diamond ring," Edwinna said. She squeezed her thumb and forefinger together to emphasize "little."

"I don't think a two-carat diamond is little."

Edwinna took a step to get a closer look at the ring. "I would have gone for something much bigger."

"Maybe that's why you don't have the man you still so obviously want," Sage said, moving toward the door.

"Just because you have him now doesn't mean you'll have him tomorrow. You're not married yet."

"We will be," Sage said acidly, and opened the door, releasing a taunting laugh while walking out of the bathroom. Sage heard Edwinna mumble an obscenity as the door closed behind her. She was tempted to go back into the bathroom and slap the other woman, but that wasn't her style.

* * * * * * * * * * * * *

It was Friday evening, and the chilly February rain rattled against the windows of Ramion's spacious and airy great room, with a nine-foot vaulted ceiling, skylights, and a green marble fireplace that crackled with firewood. Even with the sectional sofa and matching chair and ottoman, the 42-inch projection screen television, and the 50-gallon aquarium filled with saltwater fish, the room was not filled to capacity.

Several law books were piled in the corner of the sofa next to two videotapes.

"What about April?" Ramion asked, sitting on the edge of the dark green and white striped sofa in the middle of his great room. Sage sat on the floor on the opposite side of the forest green, rectangular-shaped cocktail table. Cartons of Chinese food were on the table, along with an open bottle of Zinfandel wine, its blush contents sparkling in two long-stemmed wine glasses.

"Too soon. That's not enough time to plan," Sage said, placing chopsticks between her index and middle fingers. "My, my, my! You are anxious to marry me."

"You said soon. Is May soon enough?"

"Maybe you think I'll change my mind," Sage teased, eating the Szechwan chicken that they had ordered from the China Wok restaurant.

Ramion gave Sage a sideways glance. "I know you won't," he said cockily, taking the last bite of the eggroll.

"You never know. I might change my mind on our wedding day. Have you standing in front of everyone, waiting nervously for me to come through the wide double doors and walk down the aisle," Sage teased, all the while knowing that nothing would prevent her from walking down the aisle to marry the man she loved more and more every day.

"Girl, you know you couldn't leave me like that."

"Wouldn't want to," Sage admitted.

"What about May?" Ramion asked, while closing up the cartons of Szechwan chicken, pork egg foo young, and shrimp fried rice.

Sage shook her head. "Still too early."

"June?"

"No."

"July or August?" Ramion asked.

"August," Sage said, having already determined that July or August would be the best months.

"We're making progress," Ramion said. "Where do you want to go for our honeymoon?"

"What about the Caribbean or Hawaii? I want to go somewhere hot and exotic."

"How about a cruise?"

"Ummh, sounds like fun."

"I'll take care of the trip," Ramion said.

"You get the fun stuff."

"And you're not having fun picking out your gown and planning for this and that?" he asked teasingly.

"I *am* enjoying myself," Sage admitted. "Cameron has agreed to give me away and said it's okay to get married at the Governor's Mansion."

"Ummh, I like that idea." He leaned back against the sofa, his hands clasped together behind his head. "Getting married in the Governor's Mansion. Mama and Pops will be in heaven."

"I don't belong to a church, and I might as well take advantage of my connections."

"Are we going to have a big wedding?" he asked, knowing that "big" probably wasn't quite apt. He had overheard Sage tell Ava that she would be inviting more than three hundred people.

"Yes, it's going to be big and beautiful and romantic. Everything I ever dreamed of and more. I don't plan on doing this again."

"Neither do I," Ramion agreed. "And while we're being serious, are you going to invite your mother?"

"You know how I feel about my mother, Ramion," Sage said. Her voice was reproachful. "Especially after she lied to me about my stepfather coming to dinner. She always puts him first."

"She apologized, didn't she?"

"Yeah, but sometimes apologies aren't enough."

"Sometimes you have to forgive and forget." Ramion said as he inserted one of the videotapes into the VCR.

"I can't forgive her," Sage said, with unsuppressed anger rippling in her bitter words. She paused and caught Ramion's inquisitive stare.

"She seemed sincere."

"It doesn't matter."

"I think you should let go of the anger."

"She told Ava that she wants to come to the wedding."

"Well, maybe it's time," Ramion said. He pressed the play button on the VCR remote.

"I wish Daddy were alive," Sage said wistfully, realizing that she had been thinking about him often lately. "I wish he could walk me down the aisle."

"I know, baby," Ramion said tenderly, rubbing Sage's arm. "Okay, let's let it go for now and watch the movie."

Sage stretched out on the sofa, her head resting on Ramion's lap. She sighed, wishing she could just let go of it so easily, wishing she could forgive her mother, wishing she could forget that awful night.

* * * * * * * * * * * *

The security alarm suddenly sounded, jolting Ava awake. She had just drifted to sleep after arriving home from partying at a popular nightclub. Ava loved the club scene in Atlanta; even though nightclubs frequently closed or changed names, there was always some place to party.

Ava waited for Sage to deactivate the alarm, but in her sleepy state, it seemed the piercing sound of the shrill alarm got louder. She reached under the bed for the long butcher knife she kept there if someone broke into the house, although she hoped never to need it. Ava quietly got out of the bed and eased down the hall, listening for footsteps or some sound to indicate a strange presence in the house.

Crouching low, her feet softly touching the stairs, she slowly crept down the stairs. She was halfway down the stairs when she heard the alarm being deactivated and saw that it was Sage.

"Sage!" she screamed. "What are you doing coming in at two in the morning? You scared me to death!" She could hear her heart pounding fearfully in her ears.

"It's my house. I can come home when I want," Sage retorted.

"But I thought you were over at Ramion's."

"I was."

"So what are you doing here?"

"I always come home."

"It's two o'clock in the morning!"

"I know what time it is. I like to wake up in my bed and get dressed in my house."

"Don't you like his house?" Ava asked. She walked down the remainder of the stairs. "Or did you all fight?"

"We didn't fight. And I love his house."

Suddenly suspicious about Ava's protests, Sage frowned and demanded, "Is there a man in your room?"

"I wish," Ava replied saucily. "But I still don't understand what you're doing here."

"Ava, I always come home. Ramion hates it, but I'm uncomfortable staying at a man's house all night, even if he is my fiancé."

"That's crazy!"

"Look, I like to get dressed in my own house. I don't like to pack clothes, curling iron, shoes, makeup, stockings. It's a hassle."

"This is the 90s, Sage. Get with the program."

"I'm going to bed, Miss 90s," Sage said as she walked through the foyer to her bedroom. "I've got my own program."

* * * * * * * * * * * *

Antioch Baptist Church—a sprawling, pale-red brick building with tall stained-glass windows—sat in the middle of run-down housing projects and abandoned homes. Major renovations were being made to improve the area, including a new stadium and new facades for storefronts.

The beautiful church bordered Atlanta's downtown area. Coca-Cola's corporate headquarters and the Georgia Technical Institute were nearby. The South's elite mecca of black educational institutions were around the corner—Morehouse College, Spelman College, Clark College, Morris Brown College, and Atlanta University. After a Saturday night of drinking and partying, many students would attend Antioch's popular Sunday morning services.

Ramion drove around the church, looking for a parking spot. The lots adjacent to the church were filled to capacity, cars squeezed together like sardines. He stopped at a red light. A family of five dressed in their Sunday best crossed the street, on their way to service.

"You can never find a parking spot if you get here after 11:15," Ramion said.

"I'm sorry, Ramion. I had to talk to that reporter," Sage said. She spotted a car leaving the parking lot. "Look, there's a space."

Ramion shifted gears and jetted around the corner. He turned into the parking lot and into the vacated space.

"A second later and that brother would have had the spot," Ramion said.

"You *did* jump in front of him."

"He was too slow."

Holding hands, Sage and Ramion walked toward the house of

worship, passing a flowing water fountain as they walked up the stairs to the front doors.

"It's a beautiful church," Sage said, taking in the stained-glass windows and eye-catching architecture. "It's huge."

"They spent a lot of money building it. It seats more than five hundred people, but still gets overcrowded."

Fierce clapping and thunderous organ chords barreled out when Ramion opened the doors. As they slid into a pew near the back, a few rows from Ramion's parents, the choir was boisterously singing the gospel song, "His Eye Is on the Sparrow."

The choir clapped and stomped each chorus with personal meaning, and the congregation grabbed the verse, breathing the words into their souls, absorbing its blanket of comfort. People stood up and waved their hands, praising God through music, the spiritual harmony of their soul and spirit.

The song ended with a huge expulsion of air, and the congregation sat down as one body.

An older woman with a colorful, high-pillared hat decorated with bright pieces of fruit that blended with the colors in her tropical-print dress went up to the pulpit to read the church's announcements.

"Good morning, Antioch," Sadie Morgan said with a red-lip-sticked smile.

"Good morning," the congregation responded.

The two thousand member congregation was a cross-mix of people from different backgrounds and lifestyles: doctors, lawyers, teachers, entrepreneurs, politicians, production workers, technicians, secretaries, and even the homeless. Mothers, fathers, husbands, wives, sisters, brothers, and children gathered at Antioch for spiritual nourishment and uplifting.

"It's a beautiful day, and I thank God for waking me this morning. We'd like to invite you to participate in some of our activities," Sadie said.

"But our first order of business is to recognize our visitors. Please stand up, visitors, so that we can acknowledge you and give you a membership packet."

Sage stood, along with other first-time visitors. Older women dressed in white blouses and black skirts passed out the packets.

"We welcome you to Antioch," Sadie said.

An assistant minister conducted the collection, inviting members to bring their tithes to the pulpit. After the tithers returned to their seats, the minister asked for general donations, and white-gloved deacons passed collection plates down the pews. The choir began a contemporary rendition of "Pass Me By," a gospel song with a stomping rhythm-and-blues beat. The stirring voices of the choir and the thumping music brought the congregation to its feet, clapping and singing along with the choir.

When quiet returned to the church, Reverend Benjamin DuBois approached the podium. Wrapped in a white robe, his tall, rotund body was an imposing figure. Pastor DuBois reigned supreme. This was his church, his congregation of the meek, the haughty, the tired, and the poor who came to hear him speak the word of God, seeking spiritual strength and solace. Those who could not hear would not be denied his message—a woman stood in front of the pulpit signing the service for the deaf.

"Good morning, Antioch," Reverend DuBois greeted, peering at his congregation from behind his glasses.

"Good morning," the congregation responded collectively.

"I'm glad you made it to church this morning. Tell the person in front of you, sitting next to you, and sitting behind you, 'Good morning, God bless you.'"

The organ intoned, as church members turned and twisted to greet people sitting near them. "Good morning, God bless you," rang out from the pews.

Pastor DuBois gazed upon the congregation. He had their full attention, and the congregation waited for him to wrap his voice around their souls and soothe them, to comfort their pain.

As the spiritual message about forgiveness poured from his mouth, people were moved to respond—some called out "Amen, Brother" and "Yes, Jesus," others jumped up from their seats when his words set fire from somewhere within. He pushed and pounded with clenched fists in order to be understood, and he dared not stop the rhythm of his voice until their replies had reached their fevered pitch of satisfaction. "Yes, Lord, free my son from addiction;" "Merciful Jesus, forgive my sins;" "Perfect Father, heal my mother."

Pastor DuBois's chest heaved in long spasms, and the sweat poured down his grey temples and rolled under his chin. His rich voice was now hoarse, and his raised arms waved dramatically like wands.

"God forgives us for our sins, our numerous sins. That's why he sent his only begotten Son, Jesus Christ. He sacrificed his Son, so that we would be saved. There's a lesson to be learned. We must learn to forgive each other for mistakes or misdeeds. We are imperfect creatures, and sometimes we expect too much from our brothers and sisters. Forgiveness is the way to peace of mind and soul. Forgiveness is the way of the Lord. And we must learn to forgive ourselves and others."

With the ending of his sermon, the congregation sat back, momentarily at peace. His words fortified their souls, giving them faith and strength. While still under the spell of his powerful message, their spirituality fully exposed, Pastor DuBois invited folks to become members of the church, where they could find peace, strength, and the protection of the Lord. With his invitation came the moving chords of the piano.

Sage was spiritually moved. She felt strange, as if the insides of her soul had been physically touched. She understood why so many people felt compelled to become members of Antioch. It satisfied a thirst she hadn't realized she had. She whispered into Ramion's ear, "He really knows how to touch your soul."

After the service, Ramion took Sage downstairs to meet the reverend. His family had been attending Antioch since he was a little boy, and he'd continued to claim Antioch as his church home after he moved from the area.

"Well, it sure is good to meet Ramion's fiancée. I've known this young man since he was a teenager. You got yourself a good man," Pastor DuBois said, patting Ramion on his back.

"He sure is," Sage said. She wore a wide-brimmed black hat and a black and white wool crepe suit. A pair of cameo earrings, engraved with the likeness of a black woman, adorned her ears.

"Have you set a date?" Reverend DuBois asked.

"Yes, August 15," Sage answered, observing that the pastor seemed even taller in person. Up close, his presence was awe-inspiring.

"Have you decided on a church?"

"Actually, Reverend DuBois, we're going to get married in the Governor's Mansion," Sage said.

"That's wonderful. That's a beautiful place. Beautiful," he said, patting his sweating brow with a folded white handkerchief. "I hope you're going to have a minister, a man of God marry you."

"That's why we're here," Ramion said. He was dressed in a single-breasted grey suit, silk vest, and yellow dress shirt. His tie matched the yellow, pink, and grey colors of the vest.

"What church do you belong to, Miss Kennedy?"

"I haven't joined a church in Atlanta."

"You haven't? I know you've been in Atlanta for a while."

"You do?" Sage said. Her face registered surprise.

Reverend DuBois gently touched her shoulder. "Yes, I know all about you. You know how Atlanta is. People sometimes know you before you know them. Now, do you believe in God? I wouldn't want to marry someone who doesn't believe in the Lord."

"Yes, I do," Sage said. "I just haven't found a church that makes me feel at home."

"Maybe you'll find our church is what you're looking for. We'd certainly love to have you as a member."

"I was definitely moved by your sermon," Sage said.

"Reverend DuBois, I'd like to know if you could marry us," Ramion asked.

"I'd be honored to. I'd love to marry a fine young couple like yourselves." Chuckling lightly, he said. "Especially in the Governor's Mansion. I surely would. I'll be sure to mark my calendar."

"I appreciate it," Ramion said.

"Sage, that campaign was outstanding work. Outstanding," Reverend DuBois said. "We definitely wanted to see a change in color."

Sage knew she must be blushing. "Thank you, Reverend DuBois."

As they walked to the car, Ramion asked, "So what did you think of the service?"

"It was very inspiring. I haven't been to church in a while. Baptist churches are so different from the Jehovah's Witness services I attended as a child. But I really liked it. I definitely want to go back."

* * * * * * * * * * * * *

Edwinna spotted Ramion getting on the elevator inside the Fulton County Courthouse. She stepped inside the elevator as the doors were closing. Ramion nodded in greeting and stared at the floor buttons. He got off at the fifth floor and was headed toward a courtroom when he heard Edwinna call him.

He stopped and turned around as she caught up to him.

"Is it true?" Edwinna asked.

"Is what true?"

"Your engagement to that witch!"

"Don't call her that," Ramion said forcefully.

"You did that to humiliate me," Edwinna accused.

"You had nothing to do with it. I want to marry Sage."

"You could have waited. We just broke up a few months ago."

"You know it's been longer than that."

"It doesn't matter. Everyone is going to think that you left me for her. And they're probably wondering why you didn't marry me." She reared back, her head bobbing back and forth dramatically with her words. "It would have made more sense, Ramion. You worked for my father. After all, he did so much for your career. You wouldn't be where you are if it weren't for Daddy. You're so ungrateful for all he did for you."

"First, you shouldn't care what people think. Second, our relationship had nothing to do with your father. Besides, we didn't have that kind of relationship."

"That's because you didn't want to be serious. I did, and you know it."

"I wasn't ready."

"And now you are. Just seven months later." She waved her hands in a dismissing fashion.

"Look Edwinna, we had a thing going. It didn't work out. End of story."

"I'm not some nobody you can simply dismiss. Sage is a nobody. She doesn't have the connections I have."

"You're free to think whatever you like," Ramion said impatiently.

"I'm not going to let you humiliate me like that, Ramion. You're not going to get away with it!"

"This isn't getting us anywhere," Ramion said, throwing his hands up in the air, wondering what he'd ever seen in her. Selfish and spoiled, she'd never inspired anything resembling love.

"When I win that seat in the state senate, you'll see what it feels like to have something taken away from you that you want."

"Edwinna, I can't stop you from running, but I can sure stop you from winning."

"You can try, Ramion. You can try. But you know I've got money behind me."

"It takes more than money to win an election," Ramion said. "I know things about you that you wouldn't want to become public knowledge."

Edwinna glared at him suspiciously. "What is that supposed to mean? Are you threatening to run a dirty campaign? Because don't forget I can dish up some dirt too."

"That's not my style, but I'm not going to lose the election just because you want to be vindictive."

"Don't flatter yourself. I've always wanted to get into politics."

"Since when? You only recently thought about it. We'll see what the public believes," Ramion said, as his beeper sounded. He checked the number and said, "I have to go."

Edwinna angrily narrowed her eyes at Ramion. As she watched him walk down the hall and open the door to a judge's office, she thought about how much she wanted him. She was furious that he didn't want to marry her. Only she didn't know who she was most angry with: Ramion for letting her go, or herself for not being able to let him go.

Chapter VII

Sage drove through the ornate iron gate entrance of Georgia's Governor's Mansion, up the sloping hill past the vast expanse of finely manicured lawn and hand-tended gardens. She normally drove around to the side entrance to the administrative offices but, accompanied by Ava, parked in front of the Governor's Mansion instead.

A fountain and pool, centered in the octagon turnaround featuring Georgia marble carved in Greek key design, graced the front of the twenty-four thousand square foot mansion located on eighteen acres of land. Located on West Paces Ferry, in one of Atlanta's most expensive real estate areas, the Governor's Mansion was nestled between elegant million-dollar estate homes.

Sprinkles of fountain water sprayed Sage and Ava as they got out the car. They buttoned their coats to ward off the wintry air.

The sisters went inside the stately red-bricked, two-story mansion surrounded by white-pillared columns bracing the elongated white roof. Their feet touched the bronze seal of the State of Georgia inlaid in the marble floor that dominated the foyer in the Governor's Mansion. Seeing the Governor's Mansion for the first time, Ava said, "Wow!"

Turning left, they entered the state dining room encompassed by a mahogany accordion-style extension table that seated eighteen.

"This is where the formal dinners will be held," Sage said.

"What kind of formal dinners?"

"Dinners for bill signings or to welcome politicians or foreign dignitaries."

"I guess I better check up on my table manners," Ava said, running her hands along the chairs, reproductions of originals found in the Telfair Academy in Savannah, Georgia.

"Like you're going to be invited," Sage teased.

"Fine with me. Sounds stuffy and boring," Ava said. "Oh, look at the silve.. It's beautiful."

"This silver is old. It's from a World War I battleship."

"It sure is shiny," Ava noticed. "They must have someone polishing and buffing it every day. I used to hate it when Mama brought out the silver. I had to stay in the house all day to get it to a shine."

"A live-in staff is employed to clean, cook, and maintain the gardens. Let's go into the drawing room," Sage said, stepping onto the Turkish carpet.

Mahogany Pembroke tables, square-back Grecian scroll-arm sofas, and matching card tables graced the drawing room. Classic Greek key design motif was reflected in the molded plaster work of cornices and the ceiling.

In the cherry-paneled library, Sage noticed books by Georgia authors such as Joel Chandler Harris, Erskine Caldine, and Flannery O'Connor. The shelves were filled with books about county histories and other works about Georgia.

"Who's this strange-looking man?" Ava asked, pointing to the engraved portrait of General James Oglethorpe on the Pembroke table near the antique scroll-arm sofa.

"He's the founder of Georgia."

"How do you know that?" Ava asked flippantly.

"I just finished worked on the new brochure we're putting together about the mansion."

"Oh, I thought you knew everything."

"I do," Sage said jokingly.

They moved into the circular hall, aptly named for the cascading stairs winding down from the second floor in a circular fashion. A daffodil-yellow chaise lounge blended tastefully with the yellow walls.

"Umh, umh, umh. Those stairs are bad," Ava said.

"I know. I was thinking about having the wedding in here."

"Yeah, you could walk down those steps, and take your vows over there," Ava said, pointing to the white-framed entranceway with two white pillars. "Or right here," Ava said, moving under the nineteenth-century gilt-wood chandelier on the other side of the circular stairs. "Either way, it would be live. I can't wait."

"You would think you're the one getting married," Sage said, her fingers gingerly touching the Benjamin Franklin vase—a rare French porcelain, the rarest piece in the Mansion.

"Sage, you should have heard Mama's voice when I told her you were getting married in the Governor's Mansion. She is so proud of you."

"I haven't made up my mind about having the wedding ceremony inside the mansion or outside in the gardens."

"Either way, I know it's going to be beautiful," Ava said.

"So did you notice anything missing here?"

"Like what?"

"The paintings, the artwork, the decor. Isn't something missing?" Sage asked.

"It's all very ritzy and elegant. Everything is so formal, how do you relax around here? If you just want to kick back and chill, those old ugly guys in the pictures will be staring at you."

"No, silly. The family's quarters are upstairs, and they've been redesigned to accommodate Cameron and his family."

"So what's missing?"

"Black art, black paintings, black sculptures. We need black art-work in here," Sage said.

"Oh, yeah!" Ava looked around at the estate paintings and the fine antiques. "Put some people on the walls that I can relate to." Ava started giggling. "But I have a funny feeling that might stir folks up. Like those rich old ladies with nothing to do but kick up a fuss."

"We just won't tell anybody," Sage said.

*　*　*　*　*　*　*　*　*　*　*　*

The power brokers convened around the mahogany table in Cameron Hudson's private conference room. It was after five o'clock, and Georgia's new governor and his advisors were discussing their legislative agenda. The meeting had begun three hours earlier and had survived interruptions for phone calls and faxes. For some, coffee and Coca-Cola would be replaced with scotch and whiskey.

For the first time since the Governor's Mansion was built in 1968, the power players sitting around the conference table did not fit the Southern political profile—white, male, and wealthy. This was a diverse group of men and women from different racial persuasions and economic backgrounds. There was Cameron Hudson, Sage Kennedy, Edwin Williamson, Lieutenant Governor Bradford Welch, Bill Shapely, and Alfreda Williams.

They had already discussed gubernatorial appointments to various state organizations and committees—board members for the Georgia Lottery Corporation, members for the State Board of Regents, open positions on the Governor's Commission on Effectiveness Economy, one position on the Public Service Commission, positions on the Health Strategies Council and the Judicial Nominating Commission, and an opening on the National Resources Board. They suggested people for these positions, examining candidates' experience and background and, most importantly, scrutinizing candidates' political alliances.

"Now, let's talk about the flag," Cameron said, making notes on the files in front of him.

"It's a can of worms," Bill Shapely said, a master behind-the-scenes strategist. "It's going to be difficult to get it passed."

"Difficult, but not impossible," Edwin Williamson said, chairman of the local democratic party. "Have you seen the editorial in the newspaper?" Edwin handed Bill the *Atlanta Times*, folded to the editorial section of the newspaper. "It will help us."

Bill took the newspaper and quickly scanned the editorial.

> *Atlanta Times*—January 29, 1998
> ## Will Governor Hudson Succeed in Changing the State Flag?
> *by Drew Evans, Staff Writer*
>
> The new governor proposes removing the Confederate emblem from the official banner of Georgia's state flag, carrying his predecessor's torch. I share his view that the red star-studded Confederate cross is a symbol of bigotry and racism . . . But, whether the legislature approves a new flag will represent the progress Georgia has made in race relations . . .

Bill Shapely shook his head. "Let's hope this editorial will influence the masses."

"It definitely will help our cause. Since it's not an election year, I think legislators will be more receptive to the idea," Sage said. "Polls show that businesses are favorable to changing the flag."

"I think the problem the last time around wasn't just that the governor wanted to change the flag, it was that he wanted to change the flag to another Confederate emblem. Too much negativity is associated with *any* Confederate symbol," Cameron said.

"That's why we had such a hard time getting support from some of the committees," said Alfreda Williams, a two-term legislative member of the Black Caucus.

"I suggest that we change the flag entirely. Nothing from the Confederacy. A new design altogether," Sage proposed.

"I agree," Cameron said.

"We can either legislate the new flag or hold a special election and ask voters to pick the flag they want. We give them two choices," Lieutenant Governor Welch said.

"Excellent, excellent," Bill Shapely said.

"We could probably get the House to pass on it if we let the voters decide on the design," Sage said.

"Yes, that way they won't lose as much politically," Bill Shapely said.

"If that works, then I won't have to give up control of the Public Safety Committee," Cameron said.

Nodding in agreement, the lieutenant governor said, "We just got that with the last session."

"I know, but I was going to trade off control of the Public Safety Committee for the flag. Now we need to come up with a new design that Georgians will accept."

* * * * * * * * * * * *

Butterflies were chasing her. They chased her through the thicket of trees, past the gazebo, and around the rose bushes. Sage turned and saw more butterflies descending upon her. She started running faster and faster, then suddenly could no longer feel the ground beneath her feet. She kicked her legs and felt herself rising into the air, flying with the butterflies.

Sage flashed open her eyes and was relieved to realize that she was lying in her bed. She closed her eyes, but couldn't go back to sleep. She got out of bed and went to the kitchen for a glass of water. Looking out the window, she noticed that Ava's black Toyota Celica was missing from the driveway. She opened the garage to see if Ava had parked the car inside. Her stomach dived when she saw the empty spot next to her car.

"Where is she?" Sage wondered aloud.

She sprinted up the stairs and opened the door to Ava's bedroom. There were signs of her hurry-scurry to get dressed: clothes and costume jewelry scattered on the bed and hanging out of drawers, and pairs of stockings and shoes lying on the carpet.

Ava had gone to a nightclub, Sage remembered, realizing that her sister went to clubs once or twice a week.

Grim news reports flashed in Sage's mind: woman snatched from the ATM, girl disappeared from her home, woman's unidentified body found in pond. Atlanta news stations were always reporting tragic news about women. Sage picked up the phone and dialed Ramion's number.

"Ava's not home," she said, her tone frantic when she heard Ramion's sleepy voice.

"Where did she go?"

"She went to some club with Marika, but it's after four. She should have been home by now."

"Some clubs stay open until six."

"On a weeknight?"

"Calm down, Sage. I'm sure she's fine. They probably went to get something to eat."

"What if the car broke down?"

"That's what I say when you insist on going home at three in the morning."

"Ramion, this is not the time to argue with me. I'm really worried that something's happened to her."

"Baby, nothing has happened to Ava. She's probably on her way home."

"I should put a phone in that car."

"Do you want me to come over there?"

"No, that's okay."

"Don't go out looking for her."

"I won't."

Sage hung up the phone and went into the kitchen. She made a pot of espresso and poured herself a cup. After a half-hour passed, she decided to call Drew because he knew the club scene. The phone rang fifteen times before he answered.

"Drew, sorry to wake you, but Ava's not home yet," she said in a rush, her voice cloaked in anxiety.

"That doesn't mean anything," he replied groggily. "Maybe she went home with a friend."

"She should have called me."

"I saw her at Club Escape. Some guy was buying her a drink."

"When was that?" Sage asked, her eyes veered to the clock on the wall.

"About 1:30."

"That was more than three hours ago."

"She's fine, Sage. She's out there having a good time, enjoying her freedom."

Sage heard a car pull into the driveway. "There she is now," Sage said with relief. "It's five o'clock. How is she going to go to work?"

"She's young. She can do it," Drew said before hanging up the phone.

Ava opened the door and was surprised that she didn't hear the chirp of the security alarm. She smelled the espresso brewing and realized that Sage was up.

"Ava, where have you been?" Sage demanded when Ava came rushing around the corner.

"I was hanging out!" she said, her words slipping out like blended ice.

"You had me worried."

"About what? I can take care of myself." Ava pulled off her shoes, placing them on the bottom of the stairs. She twirled around, gyrating her hips, dancing to the music in her head. "I was having fun. Big fun!"

"It's dangerous out there so late at night."

"Marika was with me. I saw Drew, and I met some new people."

"So I was worried for nothing," Sage said, sarcasm heavy in her tone.

"Chill out! We just went out to get something to eat."

Noticing her sister's saucer-wide eyes and high energy, Sage said, "Ava, I hope you're not doing drugs!"

"Stop bothering me. I'm finally having some fun in my life." Ava started up the stairs. "And don't worry, I'll make it to work."

* * * * * * * * * * * *

"How can I get Ramion back?" Edwinna asked. She was curled up in the corner of the high-backed sofa in her living room. The television and the radio were on, pop music and news competing for attention.

"Girl, you need to get Ramion off your mind and think about Medu," said Savannah, Edwinna's only girlfriend. They had become friends in boarding school, where they were the only black students in the all-girl school.

"Medu's lame."

"That's not what you told me the first time you went to bed with him," Savannah said, flipping her long black hair behind her shoulders. She was sitting on the floor, her long, thin legs crossed, leafing through the magazines beneath the coffee table.

"I didn't say he couldn't screw. That's all he's good for."

"Winna, you're cold, girl, and you're crazy. He's gonna have big money. His paintings are becoming very popular."

"So?"

"It's all about the dollars, baby! You know Ramion can't stack up against what Medu is going to make when his paintings hit big," Savannah said, raising her gray eyes from the latest copy of *Ebony* magazine that was spread across her lap.

"It doesn't matter. I want Ramion." Edwinna leaned over to pick up her glass of wine from the side table. "And I just hate it that he's engaged to her. She should have blown up in that explosion."

"Edwinna!"

"I don't care. I can't stand that green-eyed bitch!" She crunched her face into a deep frown. "If it wasn't for her, Ramion would still be with me."

"But he's not, girl. So get over it and move on."

"It's not that simple, Savvy," she said. "Now help me figure out how to get him back."

"Umh, umh, umh, you still love the brother." Savannah got up and turned off the radio, then turned up the volume on the television so she could hear the news. "Well, do you still have a key to his place?"

"He never gave me one, but I had a key made when he was over here."

Not surprised at her friend's stealthy behavior, Savannah laughed. "You were scheming then."

"So you think I should go over there one night, maybe one or two in the morning, when he'd be asleep?"

"Make sure she isn't there."

"I know that!"

"And just climb in the bed and show him what he's been missing," Savannah said, a wicked grin curling her thin lips.

Closing her eyes and recalling memories of a night with Ramion, Edwinna stomped her feet on the floor. "What I wouldn't do to be in bed with him," she said.

"Was he that damn good?"

"Girl, yes! Want to see?"

"What are you talking about?" Savannah asked.

"I taped us together one time."

"He didn't mind?"

"He didn't know."

"Ooh, girl, show me the tape!"

"But when I told him the camera was on, he made me turn it off. Just when we were getting to the good part," Edwinna said.

"I still want to see it."

"Okay, but let's get back to your idea. You think I should sneak into his house and climb in bed with him?"

"Uh huh, if you could arrange it so that she catches you in bed with him, then she'll call off the wedding."

"That would be so sweet." Edwinna's eyes glazed with hope.

"Don't get your hopes up too high," Savannah said, "He might screw you and leave you, like most men." She dipped a nacho in the hot salsa sauce before munching on it. Changing subjects, she asked, "So are you really going to run for the state senate?"

"If I get him back, I won't be bothered. If I don't, you can be sure I'm going to run against his black ass. Show him and his little nobody girlfriend that they can't mess with me."

* * * * * * * * * * * *

The sun filtered through the blinds in Ramion's corner office on the fifteenth floor. There was a beautiful view of the western corner of downtown Atlanta, although Ramion rarely stopped long enough to look out the window at the tall buildings—the Omni, Georgia

Congress Center, and Peachtree Center reaching toward the sky. Thick law books filled floor-to-ceiling bookcases on two walls. Ramion's undergraduate degree from Howard and his law degree from Harvard hung on a wall in gold frames that his mother had proudly chosen.

Ramion was so busy peering through a case book looking for a precedent-setting case on search and seizure law for a client that he didn't hear his father enter the office.

Raymond Sandidge quietly watched his son at work for several minutes before clearing his throat to get his attention. He admired his son's intelligence and accomplishments, and he'd always known that Ramion would succeed. Ramion had always been a dreamer and achiever, and law, in particular, had always fascinated him. Raymond remembered watching the Perry Mason television show with Ramion. Most often Ramion would solve the mystery long before he did, although Raymond would never admit it. Today, however, he couldn't stop himself from bragging about his son, especially to his new golfing buddies at the country club.

"Hey, son," Raymond said quietly when Ramion didn't seem to hear him.

Ramion jerked his head up. Surprise turned to pleasure when he saw his father standing there, looking dapper in green pants and a dark green sweater. "Hi, Pops," he said. "How are you?"

"I'm okay."

"Hungry? How about a cookie?" Ramion offered, indicating a basket of cookies decorated to resemble a dozen flowers. "Sage sent them."

Raymond glanced at the basket, noticing the words "Congratulations" scrawled on it. "Congratulations for what?"

"I won a case somewhat unexpectedly," he said. Observing his father's worried expression, he asked, "What's wrong?"

"Walter's in jail."

"Uncle Walter? What's he doing in jail?" Ramion asked, coming around his desk. "Sit down, Pops."

With a loud sigh, Raymond dropped into a chair across from Ramion's desk. "Hayley says he raped her."

"*What?*" Ramion exclaimed. He seldom saw his father's brother, but he'd attended his uncle's wedding to Flora Bell Cook two years ago. She had three beautiful teenage daughters: Hayley, Ashley, and Whitney. Sixteen-year-old Hayley was the oldest.

"What happened?"

"I don't know, son. No one will tell me anything. I went down to the jail, but they won't let me bail him out."

Ramion pulled out a fresh legal pad from the center drawer of his desk. "Let me get some information before I call down there. When was he arrested?"

"Early this morning."

"Who was the arresting officer?"

"I don't know." His father removed his brown fedora and placed it on the desk. Raymond never went anywhere without a hat.

"What is he charged with?"

"Sexual assault and resisting arrest." Raymond scratched the top of his bald head.

Stunned, Ramion shook his head. He couldn't imagine Uncle Walt defending himself, let alone raping someone. Ramion was very fond of his uncle, remembering the times Uncle Walt stayed with them when he was growing up. They'd stay up late, watching old movies. "I'm going to make some phone calls," Ramion said. "Don't worry, Pops, we'll get him out."

After calling the Fulton County Detention Center for his uncle's booking number and the exact charges, Ramion called the district attorney's office and spoke with the Kent Fitzpatrick, the assistant district attorney assigned to the case. Ramion learned that his uncle had been arraigned without bond and convinced the assistant district attorney to agree to a ten thousand dollar bond. The man also promised to quickly process the paperwork. Ramion made one more call to a bonding company, then drove his father over to the jail where they waited until Walter was released.

"Uncle Walt!" Ramion called out when he appeared, looking disoriented and angry. Walter stumbled toward his nephew and brother, cussing and mumbling.

"Thank y'all for getting me out," he said. Narrow, thin, and dark brown, Walter closely resembled his older brother Raymond, although he still had a full head of salt and pepper hair.

They walked out of the building to Ramion's car. "What happened?" his nephew asked as he drove out of the parking lot.

"I was sleeping when a knock at the door woke me up. Nobody was home but me, so I went downstairs and opened the door. Some damn police officer was standing there, looking mean and nasty. He said he had a warrant for my arrest."

Walter stopped to cough. "Got any cigarettes?" he asked Raymond.

"Man, you know I ain't smoked in a coon's age."

"Ramion, stop and get me some cigarettes," Walter demanded.

Through the rearview mirror, Ramion made eye contact with his uncle sitting in the back seat. "Okay. Now what happened when you talked to the cop?"

"Look, I was half asleep and half drunk. I told him he had the wrong man, and I just closed the door on him. That no-good cop kicked the door in, handcuffed me, and dragged me outta my own house like I was a murderer."

"Some of the police are crazy and crooked," Raymond said.

"Them womens, they about to drive me crazy," Walter complained.

Ramion stopped at a convenience store and waited while Walter went inside to buy cigarettes. Walter had already opened the pack of Marlboro cigarettes and lit a cigarette by the time he got back into the car. "You don't mind if I smoke, do you?"

"Go right ahead," Ramion said.

At Walter's split-level ranch house, he fumbled with his keys and opened the door. The house was empty except for a few pieces of stray furniture.

"Them damn women! They done cleaned me out! That's why they had me arrested."

"Uncle Walt, I have to ask, did you rape Hayley?"

"Hell no, I didn't rape that fast-ass girl. I tell you, they're some scheming women."

"What are you talking about, Walt? They're young girls!" Raymond said.

"They aren't innocent girls, Raymond. They were grown women who learned how to scheme and connive from their Mama. They were all going on thirty. Especially that Hayley."

"These are some serious charges, Uncle Walt."

"I know, boy, I know. I need you to help me. I done got mixed up with the wrong womens!"

Chapter VIII

Ava found Sage in the bathroom in the Jacuzzi garden tub, surrounded by bubbles. Her head pressed against a water-filled bath pillow, Sage's eyes were closed, and apricot facial scrub was smoothed over her face. Toni Braxton's smoky contralto voice floated softly from a CD player in the linen closet. A fragrance-scented candle burned with the pungent scent of jasmine.

"Sage!" Ava whispered.

Sage had relaxed in the swirling, warm water, drifting off into a hazy sleep. She vaguely heard Ava's anxious voice and slowly opened her eyes to see Ava standing over her. Tears shimmered in Ava's eyes, black mascara rimmed her eyes, and lipstick was smeared across her cheeks.

"What's wrong?" Sage sat up, immediately alert and concerned.

"Daddy's sick," Ava said, perched on the edge of the rose-colored tub. She hung her head low, her eyes reflecting her fear. "It's very serious, Sage."

A picture of Aaron Hicks flashed through Sage's mind—the man she remembered from her childhood, not the repentant man she'd seen a few months ago. Always a big man—tall, broad, and burly. When she had been eight years old, Sage had called him Mr. Giant and rubbed her face against his scratchy beard. But later, as she'd grown older and her body had begun to change, so had their relationship. Sage had quickly come to hate him for rubbing his face against hers. His beard no longer tickled. It had scratched her tender skin and induced tears she dared not shed. Hands probing places he shouldn't be touching, he would press a finger firmly against her lips, his eyes narrowed and glaring, warning her to keep quiet.

She had been powerless against the giant. She'd never forgiven him, but she'd learned to forget until a few months ago, when her mother had brought Aaron and all those memories back.

Sage shook her head, sending the ugly memories spiraling back to the hidden corner of her mind. She pressed the white button on top of the Jacuzzi tub to turn off the jet sprays swirling the water to a frothy roar.

"What's the matter with him?" Sage asked, careful to sound concerned.

"Mommy says he has cancer," Ava said in voice crackling with pain.

"I'm sorry, Ava," she said, chastising herself for the thought that it was nothing less than he deserved. "What kind of cancer?"

"Throat."

"Has it spread?" Sage wiped the cream off her face with a wet cloth.

"It's bad, Sage. I can tell in Mommy's voice that she's scared," Ava said. Her tone shifted from fear to confusion. "He was fine just a few months ago when I saw him at Christmas. I can't believe he's that sick." She was quiet for a few minutes. "Aaron's going home. He's dropping out of school."

Sage stood up in the garden tub. "When are you leaving?"

"As soon as possible."

"Hand me my towel, please."

Ava gave her sister the thick mauve and blue striped towel. Sage stepped from the tub and, after drying herself, wrapped the towel around her body. She sat on the vanity chair and poured Opium body lotion into her hand, then rubbed it over her arms and legs.

"Come home with me, Sage?"

"I can't, Ava. You know how busy it is at work."

"Just for a day or two."

"I can't, honey. I'm sorry."

102

"That scar on your arm still looks fresh," Ava said, momentarily distracted by the triangular-shaped scar on her sister's upper right arm. "How did you get it, anyway?"

"I don't want to talk about it," Sage irritably replied, a glimpse of the last night she spent at home flashing through her mind.

Too absorbed by her personal pain to notice the muted expression of anger on Sage's face, Ava released a long, loud sigh. "Sage, please come home with me."

"Ava, I can't, so stop asking me!"

"You mean you don't want to," Ava said, angry tears beginning to roll down her face. She stood up, yanked the door open, and announced, "I'm going to pack." She slammed the door behind her.

Sage slipped a nightgown over her shoulders and wrapped a robe around her. She sat down in front of the vanity mirror, picked up a brush, and began drawing it through her curly black hair. "You don't understand, Ava. Your father's a bastard, and I hate his guts."

* * * * * * * * * * * *

The scrabble board sat on the floor between them. It was partially filled with red-lettered square tiles, making words horizontally and vertically. The plastic bag of yet-to-be-played letters was near Sage's feet, next to the red Webster's dictionary. It was Sage's turn to make a word, and she pondered the seven letters she had drawn.

"You going to play today?" Ramion asked, dramatically pointing to his Movado sports watch.

"You in a hurry to lose?" Sage countered. She placed several letters on the board and scored double points for placing a letter on a starred square. "That's twenty-four points."

"So it is," Ramion said, writing the score down under her name on the pad. She was not only winning, she had made her play on the spot where he'd planned to place his letters. "Just because you're on the cover of *Atlanta* magazine, you think you got it going on."

"I do," she said, grinning from ear to ear. "And you must think so to have bought all those copies. You spent a small fortune on those magazines."

"Who else is going to buy them?" He played his letters and recorded the score. He was still ten points behind. "I took some out to

103

Mama and Pops, they were so proud. Mama wanted to know why my name wasn't mentioned. She said, 'What's that significant other stuff supposed to mean?'"

Sage laughed, as she had when Ramion brought fifteen copies of the March *Atlanta* magazine to her office at the Governor's Mansion.

"I told her that was me. She just laughed and said, 'That's why you need to go on and marry that girl.'"

"It was a great article," Sage said. "She didn't misquote me or take anything I said out of context."

"That's rare," Ramion said.

"I know. That's why I have such a hard time getting Cameron to agree to be interviewed," she said. "The photographer shot a nice photo, too. The behind-the-desk shot made me look professional, didn't it?"

"Made you look like you were running things," Ramion said.

"If Cameron heard you . . ."

"He'd admit there was some truth to it, and he'd be right. Besides, you deserve the favorable coverage, baby. Don't you doubt it for a minute. The only negative thing about you being on the cover is that people know who you are, they know what you look like."

"So what?"

"So the world is full of crazy people. Just be careful out there, especially at night."

"I always am, and I always win." Sage played the last letter, finishing the game and beating Ramion.

"Only in scrabble."

With both hands, Sage swept the letters from the scrabble board into a small plastic bag.

"How's Ava doing?"

"She's a mess. Doesn't even sound like herself. She'll probably come home later this week. Aaron's out of the hospital, but they've only given him a couple months."

"Is she going to move back home?"

"I don't know."

Ramion stood up and walked into his kitchen. He flipped the light switch on and opened the refrigerator door. "Want something to drink?" he asked, reaching for a can of beer.

"Bring me a Coke."

Ramion returned to the living room and handed her the cold soda.

She was curled up on the sofa, scanning the television channels with the remote.

"May I have the remote?"

"A man must have his remote," Sage laughed, tossing it to him.

"I want to catch the news. Want to see what's happening with the Bennet trial. I would have been defending him if I hadn't left." He leaned back against the sofa, swallowing some of his beer. "My father came by my office the other day."

"Oh, yeah? Did you go to lunch? "

"No. It's funny. Every time he sees me at work he says the same thing: 'Boy, I can't believe you're a lawyer.'"

"A big-time lawyer," Sage corrected.

"Anyway, he came by because my Uncle Walt had been arrested."

A brow raised, she said, "Really? Have I met him?"

"No, he wasn't at the family reunion. He's my father's baby brother. Used to be around a lot when I was little. Uncle Walt even lived with us for a while. I got him a bond and out of jail."

"What was he arrested for?"

Ramion hesitated only a moment. He was in the forbidden zone, that zone in her past she never would discuss. "Rape," he said in a quiet voice.

"Rape? My God, Ramion, who made the charges?"

"Hayley."

"Who is she?" Sage asked.

Ramion was getting deeper inside the forbidden zone.

"Who is she?" Sage repeated when Ramion didn't answer. She locked eyes with him, waiting for his response.

"His stepdaughter."

"Umph, umph, umph. I'm sorry, Ramion, I can't have much sympathy for a man who'd take advantage of an innocent girl. I hope you're not going to represent him."

Those words so vehemently uttered more than confirmed what Ramion had always suspected was at the root of her hatred of her own stepfather. "Sage," he said gently, "tell me what happened. Tell me about you and Aaron."

She set the can of Coke on the table with a loud thud. "Why? I don't want to remember it. I don't want to talk about the past." Her voice rising, she said, "It has nothing to do with today."

Silence settled between them as they quietly watched the news, neither of them really listening to the media report.

"Are you going to represent him?" she asked abruptly.

"He's my uncle. I have to help him."

"Did he do it?"

"I don't think so."

"And if he did? Think about Hayley. Think about what she's feeling. Or isn't that important?" She sat up from the sofa and put on her shoes.

"Are you going home?"

"Yes! I can't believe you're going to represent him."

"He's family. I'm an attorney, I don't have a choice."

"Of course you have a choice," Sage said, taking her leather coat from the hall closet.

"He's my uncle," Ramion said, his arms outstretched. "Don't you understand?"

"You always have a choice," Sage said again, her eyes as hard as granite stone.

* * * * * * * * * * * * *

"Damn! Her car is still there," Edwinna complained as she drove past Ramion's house. The digital clock on her dashboard read 1:10 A.M.

"I knew I shouldn't have come with you. We've been driving around the block for the last hour," Savannah grumbled.

Edwinna puffed on her cigarette. "She usually goes home. She doesn't stay all night. Even the weekends."

"She's crazy. You're crazy. And I'm crazy to be out here with you. Take me home, girl. I'm tired of this shit."

"All right, Savannah, but I'm not giving up yet."

* * * * * * * * * * * * *

Sage heard voices when she entered La Touissant Gallery, but she didn't see anyone. The receptionist area was empty, but there were signs of Tawny's presence: a lipstick-stained glass beside the phone, invitations stacked on the desk, and a sheet of labels in the typewriter.

Sage followed the voices and the hard-driving, thumping beat of a rap song. She recognized the song as one of Ava's favorite song-of-the-moments that she played often. Dr. Dre's gritty voice led her into the main gallery where she found Tawny climbing a fifteen-foot ladder with the aggressive assurance of a brakeman hopping a freight train about to roll down the track. The ladder teetered precariously as Tawny strained toward the ceiling, plugging and unplugging lighting cords.

"What are you doing?" Sage asked.

"What does it look like I'm doing?" Tawny replied as she unscrewed a lightbulb. "I'm changing the lights."

Sage looked up at the track of studio lights. No bulbs were burned out. "Why?"

"The lighting isn't strong enough for my opening tonight."

"Looks bright to me," Sage said.

"No, the photos have to pop, so we need higher wattage," Tawny said, scampering down the ladder to gauge the effect. "What do you guys think?" Tawny asked the receptionist and gallery intern who were helping with preparations for the opening.

"Much better," the receptionist said.

"Photos will definitely pop," the intern agreed, looking around the room at the black and white photos on the walls of the civil rights movement, taken by a famous photographer.

"Perfect," Sage said teasingly.

"Okay, Ms. Power Player," Tawny said. "You know how serious I am about my showings."

"I know, girl. That's why your gallery is the hottest place in town."

Dressed entirely in leather—black leather pants, black leather blouse, and a leather skull cap—Tawny said, "Uh huh, so how come I haven't got the cover of *Atlanta* magazine?"

"They just haven't called you yet," Sage said.

"Come into my office," Tawny said, taking quick steps. "I've only got a few hours to get ready, and I still have a lot to do."

Sage inquired about the painting she'd seen in November. "What did you find out about the painting of the three women?"

"Connie can't get in touch with the artist or the man's wife. So if you want it, it's yours."

"What a generous gift," Sage said in jest.

"Funny, Sage. I can let you have it for $1,000," Tawny said, as they entered her office. The painting was leaning against the wall, along with several others. "Excuse the mess, but I'm shuffling everything around."

Sage peered at the vibrant, colorful depiction of three women, with a twist of contemporary realism and abstract flare. "I'll take it," she said. "It's really an amazing piece. I almost believe I see them moving."

"Yeah," Tawny said, with a quick glance at the artwork. "By the way, I know someone who can help you find post-Civil War paintings by black artists. His name is Austin Gallagher. He knows that period like the back of his hand," Tawny said, handing Sage the man's business card.

"Thanks," Sage said.

"I think you need to get rid of all that pretentious stuff. Turn the Governor's Mansion into a gallery for black art," Tawny said, laughing. "Every painting, sculpture, picture, whatever, should have a black face in it and a black artist behind it."

Sage laughed. "Oh, yeah, we'll do that."

*   *   *   *   *   *   *   *   *   *   *   *   *

"I think you better see this," Marika said, handing Sage a letter and an envelope.

"What is it?" Sage asked.

"Another threat," Marika said in a worried tone.

Sage sat down at her desk and read the letter: "You change the flag, you die." The letter was computer-generated, every letter typed in a different type font, in large, bold headline letters.

"Has security seen this?" She asked, her eyebrows crinkled together.

Marika shook her head. "I don't think so."

"Did Cameron get one?"

"Yes," Marika replied. "He hasn't seen it yet."

"Same thing?"

"His was different. His letter said: "You change the flag, your family dies."

"This is serious. Call the FBI. Find the name of the agent who handled security for the campaign," Sage said, as a wave of fear washed through her. "I thought all these crazy threats had ended after the election."

Sage wasn't the only person to receive threats about the state flag as

Drew was targeted for his public support of the change-the-flag movement. Drew retrieved the draft of his editorial for Sunday's edition of the newspaper from the central printer. He read the copy while walking back to his desk, mentally noting what changes needed to be made.

Twenty days into the session, and lawmakers have adopted some major legislation. The House passed next year's fifteen billion dollar state budget and Governor Cameron Hudson's elimination of state tax on food. The cut in food tax sparked much controversy in the House, with several members giving emotional testimony about the state's responsibility to provide its citizens with the basic necessities of life. Both measures must now be approved by the Senate . . .

The governor's new state flag bill remains with a House committee, where it has been sitting since January. They are continuing negotiations on the controversial legislation proposing a new flag with a different emblem.

Back at his desk, Drew was hunched over the article marking changes in red ink, when he received an internal phone call. His editor, John Keyes, wanted an update on the police corruption story he was investigating. "I'll be there," Drew said, placing the receiver on the phone. He turned to his computer terminal and scrolled through the files, searching for the draft of the article that John wanted to review. He clicked on the computer mouse to access the file.

"Hey, Drew," said Martin Wilson, a skinny kid from the mail room with a crew top of dreadlocks. He dropped a pile of mail into Drew's mailbox. "How 'bout those Hawks, man?"

"It was a thriller of a game," Drew said.

"I'll catch you later, man," Martin said, putting the earphones from his Walkman over his ears once again. Bobbing his head to the music, Martin pushed the mail cart past Drew's desk.

Drew flipped through the stack of mail until a black envelope snagged his attention. He slit open the flap and pulled out a single sheet of paper. *"If the flag changes, you die."*

The cryptic message was the same as the previous three he had received since the publication of his editorial supporting the governor's efforts to change the flag.

Drew was used to receiving angry letters from readers who didn't agree with his pro-black perspective. People sometimes had extreme, even violent views, but he'd never received actual threats before. Drew decided to show the threatening letters to his editor.

Chapter IX

The bell tinkled when Sage pushed the door open and entered the plush offices of Weddings By Design. A stack of wedding invitations and hand-addressed envelopes were stacked on the receptionist's desk. Recent copies of *Modern Bride* and *Bride's* magazines were neatly placed on the cocktail table in front of an ivory-colored sofa. While waiting for the receptionist, Sage gravitated toward the wall splattered with pictures of wedding gowns and bridesmaid dresses in a variety of styles and colors.

"Ms. Kennedy?" a quiet voice suddenly spoke.

Slightly startled, Sage turned away from a picture of a wedding dress that she liked and made a mental note to ask about the dress. "Yes."

A tall, willowy, white woman with curly red hair approached Sage. "I'm Rebecca Redmond," she said, extending her hand. "My mother will be here shortly. She's running a little late this morning. You know how bad traffic can be. Anyway, can I offer you some coffee or tea?"

"Tea would be nice, thank you."

"Of course, follow me," the young woman said, motioning with her hand for Sage to follow her into a conference room that reminded Sage of a Victorian parlor. Sage took a seat at a cherry wood antique table and leafed through a brochure that described the company's services. Rebecca placed a gold-rimmed, fine bone china cup and saucer on the table in front of Sage. The rich aroma of cinnamon-flavored tea wafted through the air.

For the next ten minutes, Rebecca told Sage about the wedding she was working on for a wealthy client, describing in detail the gowns, the decorations, and the reception. "It's really going to be fabulous," Rebecca said.

The door opened, and an attractive woman came into the conference room. "Hello, Miss Kennedy," she said, extending her hand to Sage. "I'm Helena Redmond."

Sage accepted her hand. "It's nice to meet you," she said, noticing that Helena was an older version of her daughter, though with deeper blue eyes and a more refined manner.

The older Redmond woman wore a sapphire-blue wool crepe suit, the wide lapels of the stylish jacket trimmed in black and the waist fastened with a large black button that matched the knee-length skirt. Blue topaz earrings dangled from her ears.

"I apologize for being late. There was an accident on 285, and traffic was backed up," Helena said, placing her purse and briefcase on the table. "I see Rebecca has taken care of you. Is there anything else I can get for you?"

"No, thank you. I was just reading your brochure."

"Good. Good. Now I can give you the details." She sat down at the table across from Sage. Using a color slide presentation, Helena explained that Weddings By Design was five years old and that she had bought the company from a friend who'd left Atlanta after a bitter, nasty divorce. Helena went on to describe their range of services, from modest affairs for the budget conscious to the most elaborate wedding where cost is not a factor.

"Weddings by Design are very orchestrated events," Helena said. "They're major productions, much like the making of a movie. The end result can—and should—be as spectacular as an epic film."

Helena concluded her pitch with slides of past weddings coordinated by her company: weddings at churches, country clubs, mansions, gardens, and art galleries.

"We offer a broad range of services customized to fit our clients' needs," Helena said, before turning off the slide projector and then walking over to the doorway to turn on the lights.

"So have we convinced you to hire us?" Helena asked, her

bleached-white smile as dazzling as the large, emerald-shaped diamond on her right hand.

"It's all very impressive," Sage admitted, as she sipped from her Noritake teacup. "What I want to discuss is my wedding."

"Well, that's why we have a spec sheet for you to fill out. That way we can know what kind of wedding you want." Helena picked up a file folder with the name "Sage Kennedy" typed on the tab. She opened the folder containing several sheets of paper. "I was thrilled to see that you're getting married at the Governor's Mansion. Have you selected a date yet?"

"August 15."

"Wonderful. I don't have anything scheduled that day. I try not to do more than one wedding a Saturday, especially if it's an elaborate wedding."

"That's good to know."

"And how many people are you going to invite?"

"Approximately three hundred."

"Lovely. Do you wish to have the wedding inside or outside?"

"Inside, in the Circular Hall, if we can work it out logistically. If not, then outside in the gardens."

"Lovely, those gardens are absolutely beautiful. What tier of service have you selected?"

Sage looked at the page listing tiers from A to G in descending order of cost and services. "Definitely A," she answered.

"Lovely, lovely," Helena said with a pleased smile. "Now we can get down to details. While we do that, Becky can work on the contract."

"That's fine."

"I think the most exciting part of getting married is the bridal gown. It marks the event. After all, you are the star of the show. We can even select the gown for you if you like."

"No, I'll pick out my gown," Sage said. "I've been waiting all my life to do that."

* * * * * * * * * * * * *

The old man slammed down the phone so hard it fell off the desk, along with a pile of mail. "Winchester!" he yelled.

Hearing the loud thud, Winchester ran down the hall, afraid that his father had fallen out of his wheelchair. "What's the matter?" he asked, knowing that his father's thin-lipped expression meant he was angry about something.

"I told you to do something about that damned flag bill," Randolph snarled, his greenish-blue veins straining against the thin skin in his neck.

"I'm working on it."

"I just got off the phone with Russell Harper. He says the bill is going to be approved by the House."

"The Senate isn't going to pass it," Winchester said confidently.

"What makes you so sure?"

"With the swing vote, the bill can't be passed. I know for a fact that one of the senators whose vote is needed will hand in a nay. I happen to have some compromising pictures of the senator."

"Doing what?" the old man asked.

"Having sex with another man."

"Which senator?"

"Bridges."

"I can't believe it," the old man said.

"He hasn't made a public statement about his views. So he can go either way."

"You're positive?"

"Don't they say a picture is worth a thousand words? And, of course, I've kept the negatives," Winchester said with a sly grin.

"So we can count on him in the future?"

"I'm working on another senator."

"Who?"

"I don't want to say just yet. Give me a week."

"No more than a week," the old man warned.

"I don't anticipate any problems," Winchester said, noticing the scattered mail that had fallen on the floor. He bent over to pick it up. Sage's smiling face looked up at him from the cover of *Atlanta* magazine. "There she is. One of Atlanta's Women Power Players. Not for long," he promised, ripping off the cover page.

* * * * * * * * * * * * *

"Good news," Sage said, entering Cameron Hudson's office. "I just got off the phone with Bill Archer. He says the bill to cut food tax will get passed by the House, but they want it to be specific to staples, meats, bread, vegetables, dairy, and produce. Right now they're negotiating what food items will get taxed."

"I know the grocery chains are complaining that it will cause administrative problems," Cameron said. "But it can be overcome. What about the flag?"

"Bill says they'll probably hold it until last because of all the controversy. Sounds like they're open to the idea of a new design, though."

"Excellent," he said, nodding with a slight smile.

"Have you looked at the brochure?"

"Yes, I like it. Very colorful and friendly."

"The National Governor's Association wants you to be the keynote speaker at their convention," Sage said.

"When is it again?"

"In June."

"What's the topic?"

"Maximizing government funding."

"Just what I want to talk about," Cameron said sarcastically.

"I can get Benjamin Smith to write your speech. He does a lot of political speeches. He's very much in demand."

"Do that."

"I want to change some of the artwork in the mansion," Sage said, easing into a chair in front of Cameron's desk. "We need to add works by black artists and sculptors and include books by black writers in the library."

Cameron leveled his eyes at Sage, his round face an expression of bemusement. "Sage, are you *trying* to create more controversy? Our neighbors alone would be in an uproar, let alone those arts preservation committees."

"I know, but it's time the Governor's Mansion represented the people who live in this state, the people you have been elected to represent. After all, the mansion isn't a private home. It's on display, sort of like a museum. And museums change their art all the time."

"Good argument. So how do you suggest we go about it?"

"I think we should select artwork that goes with the decor and find a suitable location for the art that we're replacing. If we find other high-profile, prestigious venues for the pieces we remove, people won't have room for much complaint."

"Oh, they'll still complain. As a matter of fact, they'll scream to the high heavens, especially the preservationists."

"We can soften their cries of protests, especially if we find a suitable place for the outgoing pieces."

Cameron snapped his finger. "You know, Sarah would love to be involved in something like this. But let's be low key about it for now; let's get this flag bill approved first."

*   *   *   *   *   *   *   *   *   *   *   *

"You're back," Sage said, when she opened the door and found Ava lounging on the sofa in the living room. The television was on, the volume low, and Ava was lying on her back, arms flung across her face.

Ava raised up. "Hi," she said in a limp voice.

Sage greeted her little sister with an affectionate kiss and hug. Dark circles ringed Ava's eyes. "Honey, how are you?"

"Terrible."

"I can see that," Sage said and sat down next to her. "Talk to me." She grabbed her sister's hands and gently stroked them. She remembered the day her mother brought the twins home from the hospital. They had the smallest faces and tiniest hands; together they only weighed seven pounds at birth. She'd felt so protective of them even then. Little had changed in that way even after all these years, and it hurt her to see her baby sister in so much pain.

"He's going to die, Sage." Ava sobbed for the first time since she'd seen her father. Sage held and rocked her, gently rubbing Ava's face and hair. "Oh, God, it's terrible. You know how strong and big he's always been. A few months ago he weighed two hundred twenty-five pounds. Two days ago he was down to a hundred forty pounds.

"He's so small. Doesn't even look like himself," she said, her voice cracking with hurt. Wiping the tears from her eyes, she said, "I can't watch him die. I know it's selfish, but I can't do it, Sage. I just can't!" She looked at her sister. "Does that make me an awful person?"

Sage touched Ava's face and wiped away her tears. "No, you're not awful, honey. You have to know your limits. And I truly understand how you feel."

"I'm so glad, Sage. Mommy is furious. She wouldn't even go to the airport with me."

"Is Aaron still there?"

"Yeah, he's going to drop out for the semester."

"Aaron is strong," Sage said. "He can handle it, and he'll be able to help her a lot."

"I felt so guilty leaving them."

"Ava, you do what's best for you. It's all a shock. You need to prepare yourself. Maybe you can go back later, when you can handle it."

"Okay." Ava sniffled and wiped the tears rolling down her cheeks. "I want to get back to work tomorrow. Get my mind off things."

"You've got plenty of work waiting for you."

"Have you made any other plans for the wedding?"

"I hired a wedding consultant," Sage said, a tinge of excitement sounding in her voice.

"What about a gown?"

"I was saving that for me and you. We have to go shopping for my gown and the bridesmaid gown."

"No high-collared, fuddy-duddy stuff. The gowns have to be live."

Sage chuckled, pleased to see her sister smiling through her tears. "All the way live."

* * * * * * * * * * * * *

The Omni was filled to capacity with basketball fans. The Atlanta Hawks were playing against the Orlando Magic, and the air was filled with excitement and tension.

Sage, Ramion, Ava, and Drew sat in the pressbox with a full view of the court. It was an intense game, with the point spread between the teams just two points—a single basket. At the end of the second quarter, the game was tied. The screaming, high-strung Atlanta fans were almost as tired as the players from all the boisterous rooting: "Go Atlanta! Go Atlanta! Go Atlanta!"

"This game is wearing me out," Ramion said.

"Yeah, man," Drew agreed. "This game could give a guy a heart attack."

Ramion stood up. "I'm going to get something to eat. Anybody want anything?"

"Bring me back a hot dog," Sage said. "I'm starving."

117

"I'm straight, man. I'm trying to lay low on the beers." Drew patted his stomach. "I've got to get rid of this gut."

Ava stood up. "Let me go with you, Ramion. I want to walk around."

"You just want to get out there and parade around," Drew teased.

"Just like everybody else. It's time to see and be seen." Ava sashayed past Drew and followed Ramion up the stairs.

"Looks tight," Drew said, as he moved over two seats to sit next to Sage.

"It's hard to predict who's going to win."

"So how are the wedding plans going?"

"Great!" Sage released a long, contented sigh. "I'm so happy, Drew. My life is finally coming together."

"You deserve happiness, baby. Especially after Broderick's accident." Drew paused to stare after a tall, voluptuous tawny-brown woman walking down the row in front of them. She turned his way, giving him a seductive smile. Drew returned the flirty look with an equally suggestive smile. He cleared this throat and turned his attention back to Sage. "You know, you've ruined my chances of getting married."

"What are you talking about?" Sage asked absently as she fished through her purse and pulled out her checkbook.

"You know what I'm saying, Sage. Me and you. You and me."

"What me and you?" Sage asked. "You've always been my closet friend, my brother."

"Brother. Uh huh, I've wanted to be more than your brother. You just never noticed."

Sage stared down at her checkbook for a few seconds, before slowly looking up at Drew. She asked quietly, "What are you saying, Drew? No jokes. No BS."

"I've always had a thing for you, Sage, and you've always known it. You just don't want to admit it. When we first met in school, I knew it then, but you weren't ready. You were trying to adjust to school and going through all the changes with your family. I didn't want to do anything to hurt you. I knew with you I would have to come correct, and back then I was wild and out of control."

"Still are," she said.

"Yeah, maybe so. I never had any intention of getting serious with anyone while I was still in college. Then we graduated, you went to Atlanta and I went to D.C."

Sage smiled at a memory suddenly recaptured. "You know, I'll never forget something you said when we graduated. You said, 'It was time for school. Now it's time for a career. And then it'll be time for you.' I thought you were tripping."

"I meant it. But our timing has always been off. By the time I moved to Atlanta, you were engaged." His voice slipped a bit to a sadder note. "Then Broderick was killed."

"Drew, that was three years ago, and so much has happened since you called me that night. I remember exactly what I was doing when I found out. I was sitting on the sofa reading *The Firm*. I had just read the scene when he tells his wife that his firm is connected to the mob. I read it over and over again, hoping that I could somehow escape into the book and not have to face the reality that Broderick was dead. Then you were knocking at the door . . ."

"And you opened it, looking like a crazy woman."

"I was crazy," she said, reflecting on that turning point in her life. She hadn't thought about Broderick in a long time. He had been instantly killed when a car hit him head on. Even though it had been only three years, it felt like a lifetime ago. She had never been able to understand why he was taken away from her. In recent months, she'd wondered if fate had intervened because she had been destined to meet Ramion.

"If it wasn't for you, Drew, I don't know how I would have gotten through the funeral. You've always been such a friend, more than a friend."

"Don't say it, Sage. Don't say brother."

"Drew, you know you're my brother, my best friend, my family."

"Everything but your lover."

"When we were in college I thought you'd do something, make a pass, anything, but you never did. Not once."

"I always respected your feelings, your need for someone to lean on. I felt our friendship was more important than being lovers."

They were silent, thinking about what might have been if they'd shared their feelings years before.

Instead of letting the conversation drift into the regret zone, Sage tossed a dash of humor into the moment. "You couldn't have handled me as a lover, Drew. I'm telling you I would have blown your mind."

"You're probably right," he said, not even trying to joke.

"What about other women, Drew? I know you want children."

"One day. Right now, my career is my woman."

"Well, I know you've had your share of women, but it's dangerous out there. You don't want to catch something that won't let you go."

"I know, Sage. I read the reports. That's why I don't do anything without a hat. Believe me, I practice safe sex."

"I hope you find somebody special to love."

"I will, when I'm ready."

"Don't wait till you're 99," Sage teased, tapping him affectionately on the leg.

* * * * * * * * * * * *

Hayley Mitchell swaggered into Ramion's office, smelling like she'd sprayed on an entire bottle of Giorgio. The black lycra form-fitting dress was a showcase for her young, ripe body—breasts like melons, a bottle-neck waist, and curvy hips. Her movements were as exaggerated as the way she dressed and the way she talked.

When she sat in the chair across from Ramion's desk, she tilted her upper body forward, intentionally displaying her ample breasts in a low, V-cut bodice. She wriggled in the chair, struggling to pull down the hem of the dress that hung mid-thigh when she was standing.

"Uncle Ramion," she said, her voice soft and seductive, as if she were trying out for the lead role in a movie about Marilyn Monroe. "How are you?"

"The question is, how are you?" Ramion had only been around Hayley three times since his Uncle Walter married her mother, and each time he was amazed at how grown-up she acted. If he didn't know she was just sixteen, he would have guessed her to be twenty-three or twenty-four. It wasn't just her excessive makeup or seductive clothes, it was her eyes—eyes that had experienced things far beyond her years, eyes that knew the pain of life before she had the strength to bear it. Cold eyes wrapped around a wary, nothing-bothers-me attitude.

"I'm fine," Hayley answered. "Don't I look it?"

Ramion ignored her play for a compliment. "You've made some serious allegations against your stepfather."

"I know."

"Are they true?"

120

"Would I lie about something like that?"

"Perhaps it was a misunderstanding. I'd like to resolve this in the family."

"I didn't misunderstand what he wanted." She fished around her imitation Louis Vuitton doctor's bag and pulled out a pack of Salem 100's; a lighter was tucked inside the plastic wrapping. She looked around his desk and the nearby table for an ashtray while pulling a cigarette out of the pack. "Got an ashtray?"

"This is a nonsmoking building."

"Please!" Hayley said, waving her hand in the air. She spotted a Styrofoam cup in the wastebasket and sashayed around the desk to retrieve the cup from the garbage. She lit the cigarette and blew out circles of smoke. "What are they going to do? Arrest me?"

"Does your mother know you smoke?"

"Uncle Ramey, in case you haven't noticed, I'm not a baby," she said, slowly crossing her right leg over her left. "I do what I want to. Of course she knows I smoke. I've practically raised myself, anyway. She's always too busy either searching for a husband or getting rid of one. Walter is her fourth husband, you know, and he's practically history."

"Umh, let's get back to the subject at hand. Are you sure this wasn't just a misunderstanding?"

"Walter has been after me since he married my mother," Hayley said.

"Is that so? What has he done to make you think that?"

"He's very affectionate. He likes to hug and kiss me."

"What kind of kisses?"

"I know the difference between a peck and a kiss, especially French kissing," she smiled slyly, running her tongue around her lips.

"Did he kiss you like that in front of your mother?"

She rocked her crossed leg back and forth. "Please! He knows better than that."

"Did you like it when he kissed you?"

"Sometimes."

"Have you and Walter had sexual relations?"

Hayley looked down at the floor, at the black high-heeled platform pumps on her feet. She lifted her head and met Ramion's inquisitive stare. "Yes," she answered softly.

"I see. How many times?"

121

Hayley puffed on her cigarette and looked away. "Four, maybe five times."

"At your house?"

"Yes."

"When was this?"

"About four months ago," Hayley said, staring out the window.

"How come you didn't say anything before?"

"He didn't rape me those times."

"I see, and the last time he did. What happened that was different?"

"Uncle Ramey, I hope you don't think I'm a bad girl or anything like that," she said, her voice suddenly taking on all the nuances of innocence.

"I just want to know what happened, Hayley, so maybe we can find a way to work this out without things getting worse. So just tell me about that night."

"I really don't want to talk about it." With her legs crossed, she nervously kicked her leg back and forth, puffing on her cigarette, looking around the office.

"We have to, Hayley."

"I'm tired of talking about it."

"Your stepfather can go to jail. His life is at stake."

"I don't care," she said, shrugging her shoulders.

"You don't care if he goes to jail for something he didn't do?" Ramion asked impatiently.

Giving Ramion an exasperated stare, she said, "Oh, he did it all right."

"You just told me that you had sex with him four or five times and you didn't complain."

"Things were different then."

"What changed?"

Hayley paused before answering to puff on her cigarette, her expression angry. She met Ramion's probing stare, a betraying flicker of sadness in those seen-too-much-too-soon eyes. "He made me get an abortion."

Chapter X

The Georgia legislators convened at the state capitol to discuss the remaining bills to be decided upon during the last week of the three-month session. Sage sat near the press box, anxiously watching as the senators debated the issues surrounding changing the state flag.

Some senators made passionate pleas for the flag to remain unchanged.

"For historical significance."

"It doesn't offend the people in my district."

"It represents our Southern heritage."

"It's worked for us all these years, why change it?"

Others argued their reasons for changing the flag.

"It's a symbol of hatred."

"This isn't the 1800s. We're on the verge of a new century, and we should have a new flag."

"Why have a flag that offends people in this state, in this country, and in other parts of the world?"

Their statements drew strong reactions; voices were raised and fingers pointed. Several times the Speaker of the House had to bang his gavel to bring order to the diverse legislative body.

Sage focused on the senators she knew were going to cast the deciding votes. She watched them—gauging their faces, reading their body language—for a clue. She observed the undecided senators listening to their fellow legislators, trying to decide whether they seemed to be swayed by an argument.

After everyone had voiced his or her views, the floor leader called the bill to a vote.

When the votes were finally tallied, twenty-seven senators had voted to change the flag, and twenty-six senators against. Three senators were absent.

"Yes! Yes!" Sage cried when she heard the floor leader announce that the change-the-flag bill was approved.

She took her portable phone from her briefcase and called upstairs to the governor's capitol offices. "Hi Cindy, put me through to Cameron."

"It passed!" Sage announced, when she heard Cameron's voice. "Very, very close. It squeaked through by one vote."

"Excellent!" Cameron said. "Good work!"

"I'm on my way up. The media is everywhere. I'm going to set up some interviews for you. This is the perfect time for you to push the education program."

"Okay, Sage," he said, his voice reluctant. "But no more than three interviews."

"Will do."

As Sage approached the elevator to go up to the third floor to the governor's state capitol offices, she was surrounded by reporters and cameramen.

"How do you feel about changing the state flag?" a reporter asked.

"I'm very pleased that the bill has been approved. I believe it shows that legislators are listening to their constituents, and they realize the significance of the state's image."

"What about the voters? Do you think many voters will participate in the special election to select a new state flag."

"Absolutely, the voters have a voice and they want to be heard."

The elevator doors opened.

"I'm sorry, but I have to go," Sage said. "The governor will be available for interviews this afternoon."

Sage stepped inside the elevator and pressed the button to the third floor. Reporters called out questions until the elevator doors closed.

* * * * * * * * * * * * *

"Pops, have you talked to Uncle Walt about Hayley?" Ramion asked while driving the golf cart to the driving range on the eighteen-hole golf course.

"He won't talk to me. He just mumbles, 'Them womens done cleaned me out.' He's still very upset about it," Raymond said.

"Those charges aren't going to go away. Did he tell you that he had been having sex with Hayley?"

"Yeah, but he claims she seduced him."

"She might have, she's a hot little girl. But it doesn't matter because she's underage." Ramion parked the cart, jumped off, and went around to the back to pull out the bag of clubs. "Flora Bell won't return my calls."

"Says she's too upset. She keeps calling Linnell, crying about not being able to pay the bills."

"Why did she move out like that?"

"She said she had to protect her daughter. But if you listen to Walter, he's the one who needed protecting. He knew it was wrong, but he says he couldn't help himself. She just threw herself at him."

"Where were the other girls when this was going on?"

"At school."

"What about Flora? Where was she?" Ramion asked. He swung at the golf ball and watched the ball roll near the hole.

"At work. She's a nurse and works odd hours, sometimes at night."

"Leaving Uncle Walter with three beautiful girls," Ramion said, lightly tapping the golf ball and successfully knocking it into the hole.

Raymond and Ramion strolled over to the next hole. The sky was overcast, threatening rain.

"He won't say much about what happened," Raymond said.

"Neither will Hayley. What does Flora say? I really need to talk to her. I may have to pay her a surprise visit."

"I think she regrets acting so hastily. She was trying to keep Hayley away from Walter. She still wants to keep them apart," Raymond said.

"Oh, really."

"And Hayley is supposed to be moving back to Chicago to live with Flora's sister."

"This is crazy, Pops. What about Uncle Walt?"

Raymond reached into his bag for a shorter golf club. He putted on the green. "He says if Flora forgives him, he'll go back to her."

Shaking his head, Ramion said, "I would think Flora would be concerned about the other girls. They're just as pretty."

"You think Walter would mess with them?"

"Pops, I don't know what to think. It sounds like a volatile situation."

"I don't understand why he won't talk to me about, you know, the rape," Raymond said.

"Because he didn't rape her, Pops. They were having sex, and Hayley got pregnant. Uncle Walt made her get an abortion."

Raymond dropped his golf club. "I told Walter to stay away from that woman. And he's thinking about getting back with her. He's out of his mind," Raymond said. "So what happens if Hayley leaves? Will she drop the charges?"

"It doesn't matter, because the state will pursue it. He's facing three to ten."

"Son, I know Walter was in the wrong, but he needs you to stand by him. He's family. You've got to help him."

* * * * * * * * * * * * *

Bennigan's was loud and noisy—bursts of laughter, excited voices, rock music playing, dishes clanging, television blasting. Sage and Ramion waited at the bar for a table in the popular restaurant. A young, happy-go-lucky waiter, an earring in his right ear, took their drink orders. Ramion ordered scotch and soda, and Sage a Grand Marnier on the rocks.

"Your hair looks good like that," Ramion said.

Sage touched her hair; it was blow-dried straight and hung past her shoulders. "I thought I'd do something different. Miguel was surprised that I didn't want it set." She was dressed in a silk aqua pantsuit, the tunic-styled jacket accented with shimmering embroidery.

"So what do the security people think about these threats you've been receiving?" Ramion asked.

"They're trying to trace the letters. In the meantime, they've beefed up security again. After the explosion, they're treating all threats pretty seriously, which makes me feel better."

"You still have to be careful, Sage," he said, his voice filled with concern. "I don't want anything to happen to you."

"I'm very careful."

"I know Cameron is excited about the flag bill."

"It was so close. And it was a strange coincidence that Senator Davis committed suicide when he should have been voting."

"What's the connection?"

"We didn't know how he was going to vote. He could have swung it the other way."

"Surely he wasn't the only senator absent."

"No. It's just strange that he committed suicide. He had a wife and two kids, and a bright future in politics."

"Who knows?" Ramion said, shrugging his shoulders. "By the way, I talked to Hayley."

"What did she say?"

"She wouldn't talk about it. But she's something else. She sashays into my office in a slinky dress and heavy makeup. She acts like she's twenty-five."

"Don't defend your uncle. He knows she's just a teenager."

"It's more complicated than that."

"How so? I admire her mother for taking the girls out of there, protecting her daughters from a horny old man." She popped some peanuts into her mouth. "Many women wouldn't do that. They would ignore the situation, pretend they don't see, or blame the daughter, the victim."

"There's more to it. This family is strange. I don't know how to explain it. Flora Bell acts like she's trying to protect her daughters, but I'm beginning to think she may have done it for herself."

"What are you talking about?"

The waiter returned with their drinks and a fresh basket of peanuts.

Ramion took a long sip from his glass. "Uncle Walt was having sex with Hayley."

Her eyebrows raised in surprise, Sage's face was a mixture of disbelief and dismay. "*He admitted it?*"

"Hayley did, and I believe her."

"Just how long has he been raping her?"

"That's just it. It wasn't rape."

The blond hostess approached and escorted them to their table. Sage and Ramion followed the hostess, who chattered about the crowd and the unusually cold Atlanta weather. They slid into opposite sides of a booth.

"What do you mean?" Sage asked. Away from the front door and the bar, it was much quieter.

"It was consensual. Hayley's no innocent girl. She's young and hot, and flaunts her body like an invitation."

"Wait a minute!" Sage said, gesturing with her hand. "Are you saying that she seduced him?"

"I don't know who seduced whom, but they've been having sex, and Hayley has been a willing partner."

"She's still underage."

The blond hostess interrupted. "I'm so sorry. I forgot to give you menus," she said, handing them large, plastic-coated menus. "Your waitress, Jane, will be right with you."

"That's where Uncle Walt is going to have legal problems."

"He should. Even if they've been having consensual sex, she's still a minor, and he's guilty of statutory rape."

"True, but she enjoyed it. Besides, it was her way of getting revenge against her mother."

"Ramion, I hope you're not trying to justify what your uncle did," Sage said, frowning deeply from behind the wide menu.

"Flora Bell is the kind of woman who can't keep a husband. She's been married three times, and Uncle Walter is her fourth husband. I get the feeling that she's more into finding a man than raising her kids." He paused to sip his drink as did Sage. "I know my mother never liked her much, always said she was a loose woman."

"Even if all that is true, Walter was dead wrong to have sex with a girl," Sage said hotly.

"I agree, but this is about revenge. Uncle Walt got Haley pregnant and made her have an abortion. I think this is her way of getting even. I don't know if she wanted the baby or . . ."

Sage stopped listening to what Ramion was saying. In her mind, she traveled back to the one and only time she'd thought she might be pregnant. She was living with Aunt Maddie, who had picked her up the night her stepfather raped her, the night her mother had thrown her out of her home.

Sage had waited for Aunt Maddie on the front porch. She huddled against the corner of the glider, her mind and body in turmoil.

Audra was inside the house on the phone, waiting for Maddie to answer. With the phone ringing in her ear, she was trying to decide who to call if Maddie didn't answer. Audra didn't want anyone in her family to know what her daughter had done, and was relieved that Ava and Aaron weren't home to witness Sage's betrayal. She was thinking about calling Sage's grandmother when Maddie finally answered the phone.

"Come get your niece," Audra said in a strange voice that Maddie barely recognized. She hung up before Maddie could ask questions.

Maddie knew Sage felt uneasy around her stepfather. Sage had told her she would never stay alone in the house with Aaron. She didn't feel safe. Knowing intuitively what happened, Maddie immediately got back in her car and drove to Audra's house.

Sage sat on the glider, wrapped in a blood-stained sheet, shivering even in the warmth of the summer night. The sky was filled with twinkling stars and a glowing full moon.

"What happened, baby?" Aunt Maddie asked, as she rushed up the porch stairs.

Sage was too ashamed to look at her aunt. She couldn't find the words to describe what happened to her, nor the emotions to convey how she felt. They were caught in the hurricane that was swirling inside her, strangling her and choking off her voice.

Maddie touched her niece's face and threw her arms around her in a protective embrace. "It's going to be all right, darlin'. It's going to be all right," she soothed, gently rubbing Sage's face and kissing her forehead.

As Maddie reached for the suitcases that were sitting near the front door, she heard Audra slowly open the front door. Maddie spun around to confront Sage's mother. "Audra, what the hell happened?"

Audra stared at both of them, then bent her head in shame.

"Audra, what happened to Sage? She's been hurt. Look at those bruises and that ugly burn on her arm!"

"Take her," Audra said softly, her voice sounding strange and unfamiliar to Sage.

Sage stood up from the glider and walked weakly toward the edge of the porch. Suddenly sure she was going to faint, Sage grabbed the porch's railing for support. Her eyes locked with her mother's. But they weren't her mother's eyes. Those eyes were wide and bewildered—they were the eyes of a stranger. "Mama, I didn't do anything wrong! Please, Mama. Please believe me," she pleaded.

Audra slammed the door so hard, the porch shook.

It took Sage many years to close the door to the past, to bury the memory, to escape the pain. But it was finding its way back into her life.

Now, sitting in the noisy restaurant, she remembered the pain, the agony, the confusion, the despair. She remembered waiting for her period to come, counting the days when it didn't. She remembered running to the bathroom every time she thought her period would show, and the engulfing fear she felt when she didn't see red.

Sage couldn't speak, wouldn't talk, and didn't utter any words until at last her period made its presence known, and she knew that there were no traces of her stepfather inside her.

When she finally spoke to Aunt Maddie, who had taken off work for two weeks to stay with her, she said, "I'm not pregnant. I don't have to carry him inside me."

Maddie's face reflected joy and relief when she heard Sage's voice, gritty with pain and anguish. Tears poured from Maddie's eyes, and she embraced her niece, holding her tightly. "I love you, Sage. Release it, baby. Don't carry it inside your soul. Free yourself from the pain. Banish it from your memory!"

"Sage!" Ramion said, waving his hand in her face. "Sage," he repeated.

Those memories burned inside her, fresh as new snow, and when Sage looked over at Ramion, she saw the shadow of her stepfather.

"I don't think you should represent him. He's scum. What kind of man has sex with his stepdaughter? I don't care if she paraded around the house nude. She's underage, and he should go to jail for that." Peering at the menu, she realized her appetite had suddenly vanished.

"You're overreacting," Ramion said.

"No, I'm not. He got her pregnant and made her have an abortion. That's traumatic for a grown woman, let alone a teenager."

"You think she should have had the baby?" Ramion asked.

"Ready to order?" their perky waitress, Jane, inquired while placing a basket of warm bread and butter on the table.

Ramion ordered pasta primavera, and Sage selected the mesquite grilled chicken salad.

As the waitress walked away, Sage leaned in and said furiously, "No she shouldn't have had the baby, but if he hadn't been sleeping with her, she wouldn't have gotten pregnant!"

"I agree with you. He was wrong. But he's my uncle, and he can't afford an attorney." He smoothed soft honey butter on his wheat roll.

Her voice rising angrily, she said, "I can't believe you're going to represent him!" She picked up the cloth napkin wrapped around the place setting and it fell to the floor. She made no effort to pick up the utensils.

"It won't be the first time I represented somebody that was guilty. He's entitled to due process, and his legal rights must be protected."

"Tell him to get a court-appointed attorney."

"I'm sorry Sage, but I can't do that. I promised my father I would help Uncle Walt. He's family."

"What about the rights of a child to remain a child!" she shouted. Realizing how loud she was, she lowered her voice. Clenching her teeth, she said angrily, "And the rights of a teenager. Just because you have the body of a woman doesn't mean you are a woman," she said, banging her fist on the table. Glaring at Ramion, she stood up. "It's obvious you know nothing about women and respect."

"Baby, calm down. You're taking this personally."

"You're damned right I am," she said. "I'm not hungry! I'm going to take a cab home!" Sage grabbed her purse and stormed out of the restaurant.

* * * * * * * * * * * * *

It was after nine o'clock when Ramion left his office, and within thirty minutes of non-rush-hour traffic, he was pulling into his garage. His plans for the evening were to grab a bite to eat, read the mail, and go to bed.

He unlocked the door and went into the kitchen. Flipping on the light switch, he placed his briefcase and jacket on the kitchen chair and opened the refrigerator. Three minutes later, he was swigging from a can of beer and munching on two-day-old pizza heated in the microwave.

He sorted through the mail on the way to his bedroom, where he absently pressed the switch plate to turn on the lights. He looked up, coming to a dead stop when he saw Edwinna lying on his waterbed, stretched out like a lion, wearing a leopard-printed teddy with garters and black stockings.

"Hello, baby," she said with a devilish grin.

"Edwinna! What the hell are you doing here?"

"I wanted to see you." Slinking over to the edge of the bed, she said, "Remember how much fun we used to have?" She spread her legs wide and slowly moved her hands to her breasts.

"I don't remember it that way," he said, his anger rising along with his manhood, which made him even angrier. "How did you get in here?"

"I had a key made a long time ago so that I could surprise you whenever I took a notion."

"Nothing you do surprises me," he said with a contemptuous scowl.

Edwinna raised up from the bed and pressed her perfume-scented body against his. "Oh, I think I've got a few tricks up my sleeve that could still surprise you." She rubbed her hands against his thighs and pressed her hips against his crotch. She could feel his erection.

Ramion pushed her away. She fell back against the bed, her over-sized breasts popping out of the tight teddy. "I'm not interested," he said, his jaw clenched.

"You know you don't mean that. You know you want me to do you. I can lick you till you come." She stuck her tongue out of her mouth. "You're getting hard just thinking about my lips on you, sucking you. I'll do anything you want, anything baby, if it feels good." She pressed her body against his, sensually moving her hips. "Umm, you know you want me. No one will know." She pressed a finger against her lips. "It will be our little secret."

Ramion grabbed her face and kissed her hard. He fondled her breasts, pressing them together, and then pushed her down on the bed. Glaring at her, he couldn't believe that she had the nerve to sneak into his house. I don't want you, he thought, but you're going to learn to leave me alone.

"Is this what you want, Edwinna?"

"Yes," she said, reaching up to unzip his pants.

"You want me to fuck you?" he asked, his eyes disguising his disgust.

"Yes, baby, yes!" she muttered, her eyes closed.

He stroked her legs, heating up her body as his hands moved between her thighs. He then abruptly stopped. "Now get out!"

"*What!*" Her eyes flashed open.

"Get out, Edwinna! I don't want you."

"Yes you do, baby. I can see it in your eyes." She arched her back upward and spread her legs.

"No!"

"Oh, yeah, you're excited!"

"Get out of my house, Edwinna. Understand me? I don't want you." He resisted the urge to yank her off the bed and physically throw her out of his house.

In a haze of shock and disappointment, she regained her senses, her face sinking into a frown. Edwinna reached for her fur coat, lying on the floor next to the bed. As she put it on, she frantically tried to think of something she could do or say that would make him change his mind. "I'll tell Sage that we had sex, that I was in your bed."

"Tell her anything you want, Edwinna. But get the hell out of my house! I'm going to change the locks so you can't get back in here."

"So you think you're going to play me like that?" Edwinna asked, moving quickly down the hall.

"You played yourself. I never lied to you or misled you."

"You're going to regret this, Ramion. I swear it," she threatened before opening the front door.

She ran down the stairs, down the driveway, and around the corner to her car. Fumbling for her keys, she finally got the door open and climbed inside. She put the keys in the ignition, turned on the car, and drove off. She picked up her cellular phone and dialed Savannah's number.

"He put me out, Savvy. He started to make love to me, but he never intended to finish it. He just wanted to humiliate me," Edwinna sobbed.

"I told you to leave him alone," Savannah said.

"I need you."

"Come on over. I'll take care of you."

Fifteen minutes later, Edwinna was ringing Savannah's doorbell. Savannah opened the door wearing silk pajamas. Her silky black hair hung loosely down the middle of her back.

133

"I'm so hurt. One minute he was kissing me, and then he stopped. He played me, Savvy. He humiliated me," she said bitterly.

Savannah pulled Edwinna into her arms, gently hugging her, and then wiped the tears from her face. She helped Edwinna take off her coat, tossed it on the sofa, and led Edwinna down the hall into her bedroom. "I told you, men ain't shit. All they do is bring you pain."

Edwinna sat down on the bed, her head hung low.

Savannah stood in front of her and slowly ran her fingers down the sides of her neck and her shoulders. She cupped Edwinna's chin with her hand and kissed her on the lips. "I know what you need," she whispered.

Savannah stroked Edwinna's breasts and then took a breast in her mouth, licking her nipples until the sensation singed the both of them. Edwinna leaned back on the bed, moaning, "Savvy, Savvy."

Chapter XI

Ramion rang the doorbell at Sage's house, hoping she would immediately answer the door because it was an usually cold night for Atlanta, with temperatures dipping into the teens. He'd left his heavy coat in the car and stood at the door with only his suit jacket on.

He impatiently rang the doorbell a third time, wondering if Sage was intentionally ignoring the peal of the bell. He was turning to leave when Ava opened the door.

"It's about time," he said, embracing the warmth of the foyer as he went inside.

"Hey, Ramion," Ava greeted him with a mud mask plastered all over her face.

Ramion stepped back, feigning fear. "A monster!"

"This is how I stay beautiful!" Ava said. "I'm surprised Sage didn't hear the doorbell. She must be asleep."

"Well, I'll go wake her up."

"The flowers you sent her were beautiful. All the girls in the office were raving." With one foot on the stair, she asked, "So what did you do, Ramion?"

"What do you mean?"

"Men usually send flowers when they do something wrong. Since it wasn't her birthday or Valentine's Day, you must have done something wrong."

"When did you become such an expert on men?"

"I wasn't the only one to think that."

"You clucking hens need to mind your own business."

"I know something's wrong. Sage has been so grouchy."

"I know," Ramion said. "She's got a lot on her mind."

"I knew I was right," Ava said. "I'll leave you to go kiss and make up," she taunted before hopping up the stairs. "Goodnight."

"Goodnight," Ramion said, heading toward Sage's bedroom.

Ramion found Sage asleep on the bed, coiled in a fetal position with the comforter tossed across her body. The hunter green paisley-printed comforter coordinated with the toga valances hanging from the windows and the fabric covering the nightstands. Her laptop computer, several file folders, and loose papers were scattered across the king-sized bed. She held an ink pen in her hand, almost touching her face.

Ramion was struck by her beauty, just as drawn to her inner loveliness as her physical appearance. He swept away the hair covering her face and softly kissed her cheek.

She stirred slightly, her eyelids flickering open. "Ramion," she whispered, when she saw him looking down at her. Feeling tired and disoriented, she closed her eyes again.

"Hi, baby," Ramion said.

His deep voice always struck a chord inside her, and whenever he said "baby," it played a melody inside her heart. She opened her eyes again and gave Ramion a soft, sleepy smile. "You woke me up."

He raised the comforter and teasingly asked, "Do you always sleep with your clothes on?"

"I fell asleep."

"I can see that," Ramion said. "You work too hard."

"I'm guilty," Sage said with a yawn, stretching out her legs before raising up from the bed. She gathered the files and papers scattered on the bed and closed her laptop computer, placing them on the desk. "The flowers were lovely, Ramion."

He sat on the chaise lounge across from the bed and removed his jacket and shoes. "You didn't call me to let me know that you got them."

"I didn't want to talk to you."

"I waited for your call."

"Don't even try it, Ramion. You were in court all day." She gave him a piercing stare. "I didn't call because I was mad at you. Still am."

"I know you are. That's why I'm here. We can't resolve anything not talking to each other."

Sage reached inside a dresser drawer and pulled out a knee-length purple sleep shirt. "What is there to talk about? You know how I feel and you know why I feel the way I do, yet you still are going to represent your slimy uncle." She went into the bathroom and slammed the door behind her.

Ramion stood at the bathroom door. "I really don't know what happened. Parts of your past are closed, sealed tight like a steel drum. You won't talk about it." When he heard water running, he moved away from the door.

Ramion stripped down to his underwear and climbed into the bed. He scanned through the channels, looking for local news, not realizing how late it was until the Tonight Show appeared on the screen. Checking his watch, he saw that it was 11:45 P.M.

He hoped she would understand his desire to help his uncle. He had given his father his word that he would help Walter, and he couldn't go back on his word.

Sage came out the bathroom smelling of toothpaste and musk-scented perfume. Arching her eyebrows dramatically, she asked, "Who invited you to stay?"

"Sage, don't be like that."

"It's my bed."

"Well, if you want me to leave, just say the word," he said in a defensive tone.

She glared at him for several seconds, then reluctantly said, "That's okay," sliding into the bed beside him. "So how are we going to work this out?"

"I don't know exactly why you feel the way you do."

Pressing her arm against his shoulder, she said, "Yes, you do, you just don't know the details." She looked away from him and was silent for a long time.

Ramion turned down the volume on the television.

"You know my stepfather raped me," she said, meeting his curious gaze. "You know it hurt me deeply. It was the most devastating thing to ever happen to me. I've buried it inside because that was the only way I could survive. I guess you could say that I even tried to hide the memory from myself. I buried it real deep, and I don't want to dig it up."

"But it's coming up anyway, isn't it? When we were at the restaurant, you had this sad faraway look in your eyes like you were remembering something."

"Yes, I thought I had this tight lid on my memories. But now the lid's come loose, and it's all starting to leak out."

"Baby, you know I don't want to cause you pain. I don't want to do anything to hurt you." He stroked her arms and entwined his feet with hers.

"I know. At least part of me knows. The intellectual side of me understands that you have to help your family and, in a way, that's what hurts me the most. My mother didn't help me."

"What do you mean?"

"She took my stepfather's side." Her voice was rigid. "She believed I seduced Aaron. And I felt betrayed. I *was* betrayed." Passionate emotions strangled her voice. "I'm her daughter, her flesh and blood," she said, patting her chest with her hand. A painful lump had lodged in her throat. "But she believed him over me."

"What else, baby? I know something else happened."

She bolted up from the pillow and leaned over Ramion. "Don't you think her betrayal was enough? She threw me out. I was only seventeen. If it weren't for Aunt Maddie, I would have had no one."

"I have a feeling there's more to the story."

Sage touched her right shoulder, where the ugly iron mark was hidden beneath the short-sleeved gown. "I don't want to discuss it," she whispered. "I can't talk about it."

Ramion gently stroked Sage's cheeks and tenderly kissed her forehead and lips. "Okay, but I'm here for you, baby, whenever you want to talk about it."

"He's dying, Ramion. He's dying, and I'm glad. I feel so guilty, especially when I think about Ava. She's going to be crushed when he dies. So will Aaron. And I want to rejoice with happiness."

"Ava doesn't know, does she?"

"No, she doesn't know what her beloved father did to me." She paused. "My Daddy used to call me butterfly, and after he was gone I used to wish I was a butterfly so I could fly away from Aaron."

"How old were you when your mother married him?"

"Nine. He was okay for a long time. He didn't start looking at me that way until I was twelve. When I started to develop, that's when everything changed. He stopped looking at me as a daughter and began staring at me like a woman. I didn't feel comfortable around him anymore."

"Nobody noticed?"

"Oh, yes, my mother did, but she pretended she didn't." She sighed and leaned her head in the crook of Ramion's shoulders. "What he did ruined everything. Even my memory of my father."

"I don't understand."

"Aaron made me angry with Daddy for dying, for leaving me. If Daddy hadn't been killed, then Aaron would have never touched me."

* * * * * * * * * * * * *

"I'm exhausted," Ava complained wearily to Tawny. They stood by the food court of the Georgia World Congress Center surrounded by soon-to-be brides and grooms attending the Bridal Expo. They'd spent the last three hours following Sage through the maze of booth exhibits of wedding gowns, bridesmaids gowns, shoes, and veils, along with wedding invitations, registry services, catering services, and exotic honeymoon packages.

"So am I," Tawny said, eyeing the tables in the food court for a place to sit down.

"Oh, let's grab those seats," Ava said, pointing to an unoccupied table in the crowded food court, already off to grab the seats before someone else did.

"We'll be here all day with Sage talking to everybody," Tawny said.

"They see that huge rock on her finger and dollar signs appear. Everybody wants a piece of the wedding."

"At first I thought she was crazy to hire a wedding consultant. An expensive one, I might add," Tawny said. "But there's so much to do, I understand why she wanted help."

"Yeah, and she can't make up her mind about her gown," Ava

said, with an elbow on the table, she leaned her head against the palm of her hand. "I swear we've already looked at a zillion."

"She'll probably look at a zillion more before she decides," Tawny said.

"We've got five more months of this madness."

"So do you really think we can surprise her with a bridal shower? You know how nosy she is. She'll know we're up to something." She slipped out of her black and red suede jacket, and said, "I'm burning up in here. I feel like coming out of this sweater," she said complaining about the green appliquéd sweater.

"I hear ya, " Ava said, as she removed her black leather coat, revealing a blue jean jumpsuit with silver studs dotting the collar and bodice. Silver earrings and bracelets dangled from her ears and arms. "We'll just trick her. Tell Miss Planner what day we're going to have the shower, but give it the week before."

"That should work if she doesn't go out of town or anything."

"I checked her calendar, and the thirteenth is wide open," Ava said. "That's three Saturdays before her wedding."

"We'll have it at my house," Tawny offered.

"She'll expect that. What about Elise's?"

"I'm sure she won't mind. I'll ask her."

"But how do we get her there?" Ava asked.

Tawny shrugged her shoulders. "We'll think of something. Maybe we can get Ramion to help."

"You know we got to have a stripper, girl," Ava said, her eyes gleaming. "Somebody fine, with a hard body."

"A friend of mine knows some strippers. I'll find out how much they charge."

"Make sure they know to climb all over Sage. She'll be so embarrassed, I can't wait to see her face." She paused, her face lighting up with a devilish grin. "Ooh, ooh, we have to get it on tape."

"She'll die," Tawny said, laughing heartily.

"I'll get the invitations. We're talking about twenty-five people, right?"

"Uh huh, I'll give you names and addresses."

"What about food?" Ava asked.

"Shrimp, wings, some kind of casserole, daiquiris . . ."

"Margaritas," Ava added to the list.

"Margaritas?" Sage inquired as she slid into the chair next to Ava. "They serve alcohol here?"

"No, I just got a taste for one," Ava said, shifting her feet and fanning her face with her hands. "This place is crazy, it's a zoo."

"I know. I'm dying of thirst from talking to everyone," Sage said.

"I see you have two bags of goodies," Tawny said, noticing the shopping bags filled with samples and promotional items.

"Everybody has something to give away or something to entice you to their booth. Talk about hard sells, they wanted to set up appointments," Sage said, fanning herself with a brochure.

"Trying to get you while they can. Did you see anything, or did you just get more confused?" Tawny asked Sage.

Sage giggled. "Yes to both. I know what china I want, and I narrowed down the invitations."

"Well, that's progress," Tawny said.

"What about your gown?" Ava asked.

An impish grin curled Sage's lips. "I found out about another store that sells gowns. It's in Gwinnett." She flicked her wrist to look at her watch. "It's only two o'clock, ladies. We can be there in an hour."

Ava and Tawny exchanged exasperated looks.

"Girl, I'm not used to all this shopping," Tawny complained. "Stan couldn't believe that I was up and dressed by 10:30."

"Yes, but you were supposed to be ready at ten o'clock," Sage chided.

Ava thought about protesting, but she didn't have anything else to do. Besides, she wanted to make sure Sage didn't pick a gown that was too traditional, hideous, or plain, her words of warning when they'd begun this search for the perfect wedding gown. Ava sighed. "At least feed us."

"Okay," Sage said. "We have fifteen minutes."

* * * * * * * * * * * *

The alarm sounded as Sage opened the kitchen door, her arms ladened with her purse, briefcase, and grocery bags. With thirty seconds to deactivate the alarm, she quickly set the bags on the kitchen counter top and turned it off.

"Ava," she called from the bottom of the stairs. Concerned about

Ava's mood swings lately, Sage decided to surprise her with her favorite meal—lasagna. She planned to prepare the meal herself but, after a late meeting at the state capitol, she'd made a quick stop at Harry's Farmer's market and bought some ready-made lasagna and groceries.

After putting the groceries into the refrigerator and cabinets, Sage transferred the lasagna from the plastic container to a casserole dish and put it in the microwave. She placed two geometric-patterned plates, salad bowls, silverware, and wine glasses on the table, then mixed up a salad of romaine lettuce, tomatoes, eggs, croutons, bacon bits, and shredded cheddar cheese.

Setting the timer on the microwave to ten minutes, she left the kitchen. Before going through the living room to her bedroom, she called up the stairs, "Ava, come eat."

Sage took off her olive pantsuit, hung it in the closet, and slipped into her silk lounging pajamas. She washed her face and hands before returning to the kitchen, expecting to see Ava pinching on the food. Her eyes veered to the clock, noting that it was only eight o'clock, too early for Ava to be sleeping. Ah, she thought, snapping her fingers. Time for Ava's favorite television show, "Martin."

A strong offensive odor whiffed at Sage's nose when she reached the top of the stairs. The skunk-like smell grew stronger as she neared her sister's bedroom. She knocked on Ava's door several times. Assuming that Ava couldn't hear her because of the blaring television, Sage opened the door. What she saw sent a sharp pain to her stomach: Ava inhaling a joint clenched between her teeth. "Ava, what the hell are you doing?"

"Shit!" Ava mumbled as she quickly snuffed out the joint in an ashtray. Ava looked guiltily at her sister, feeling like a kid caught with her hand in the cookie jar. Ava opened her mouth to explain, but she couldn't lie or deny what she'd been doing.

Sage was dumbfounded. "Ava, I don't believe you're doing drugs! Marijuana! I just don't believe it!" She grabbed the television remote and pressed the mute button.

"Sage, don't trip. Please don't trip," she pleaded with her sister. "I get high every now and then. It's not an everyday thing." Ava removed the top from a can of air freshener and began spraying the room.

"It doesn't matter how often. You shouldn't be getting high at all. You never did it before, so why now?"

Ava sat back on the bed, thinking about the reasons she indulged in the pleasure principle. That's what she called it. Marijuana made her feel good. But she knew Sage would never understand that kind of feeling. You had to feel it, be under its awesome influence, to understand the pleasure that could be derived from inhaling the toxic weed. "I do it because it feels good. Isn't that why most people get high?"

"We're not talking about other people. We're talking about you!" Sage screamed, pointing her finger at Ava.

"Maybe I do it to escape reality. I don't like to think about my father dying from that horrible disease."

Sage stared at her sister, her eyes devoid of empathy. "I know it hurts, Ava. But that is no reason to do drugs. How would Aaron feel if he knew?"

"He'd freak out."

"And Mama?"

"She'd freak out big time."

"I can tell you not to do this because it would hurt them. But this is about you. How you deal with life. How you deal with hurt. Life can be very painful, but you have to face up to whatever happens and deal with it. Rise above it. Developing an addiction to escape pain only creates more pain."

Ava put up her hands. "It's just reefer," she said, shrugging her shoulders.

"I don't like you doing drugs. Period," Sage said. Shifting from anger to concern, she added, "I don't want anything to happen to you."

"It's not like I get high every day," Ava defended herself weakly.

"Where'd you get it?"

"Why, Sage? Nobody you know. Everybody gets high in Atlanta."

Sage shook her head. "That's bullshit, Ava."

"Some of the people I hang out with do."

"Marika?" Sage asked, although she would be truly shocked if Ava answered affirmatively.

"No way," Ava said flippantly. "Kelly and some of the girls I hang with from the sports club."

Sage nodded her head, remembering their brief introduction months ago. "Maybe you shouldn't hang out with them."

"It's not like I have a whole lot of friends here."

"Give yourself some time."

"Look, Sage, I'm not strung out. I don't smoke every day. Mostly when I go out. I'm a recreational user, so you don't have to worry about putting me in some kind of rehab program."

"Maybe this is recreation for you today. But what about tomorrow? Once you get started, you crave it more and more. Or you move on to more addictive drugs."

Ava rolled her eyes. "Don't play the commercials for me. I know the deal," she said, and slid off the bed. "I'm in control of this."

"You're not in control if you have to use drugs." She inched over to Ava and stood directly in front of her. "The point is, I don't want you to stay in control, I want you to stop! Just say no. Just stop."

"Please, Sage. Don't give me that 'just say no' crap."

"I'm serious, Ava. I care about you. You're my sister, and I love you. I don't want anything to happen to you because what you're doing is dangerous."

"I hear you loud and clear," Ava turned away and moved over to the dresser. She pushed some of the open drawers closed. "But I'm grown, and I'm going to do what I want."

Sage glared at her sister, fighting the temptation to grab her by the shoulders and shake some sense into her. "What more can I do?" she thought. "She's grown. I can't run her life, but neither can I let her destroy it."

Ava could see the struggle her sister was waging with her thoughts and feelings. She'd never wanted her to know she was using. More than anything, Ava didn't want to hurt her.

"I will tell you this one time only," Sage said. "Don't do drugs in my house or anywhere around me. I'm not going to tolerate it!"

Ava stared at her sister, uncertain how to respond to her righteous anger. She couldn't remember the last time she'd seen Sage this upset. Suddenly she was ashamed. "I'm sorry."

Sage nodded, hoping Ava was sincere. More than anything, she wished Ava wouldn't use drugs again.

"What did you come busting in here for anyway?" Ava asked, changing the conversation.

"To tell you that dinner was ready. I bought lasagna."

"Thanks, sis. You are so good to me," Ava said, rubbing Sage's shoulders.

"Don't try to sweet-talk me. You need to stay away from those drugs. It's that simple."

Ava released a weary I-thought-this-conversation-was-over sigh. "You never indulged?"

Sage hesitated. "When I was in college, a couple of times."

The revelation sparked Ava's attention. "I knew it. You're too cool to have always been so straight."

"I smoked a little reefer to be sociable. I can count on my hands the number of times I did. I could never even roll a joint."

"Want me to teach you?" Ava joked.

"That's not funny, Ava."

"I don't know how either," Ava said. "I was just trying to make you laugh."

"Let me put it to you in terms you can understand. Don't go there. You may not find your way back. Do you feel me?"

"I hear you," Ava said sheepishly, her eyes cast downward. She felt like a chastised parishioner.

"I sincerely hope you do, girl. "

"I'm okay, Sage, really."

Sage raised both hands in an end-of-conversation gesture. "I've said what I had to say. Now it's up to you."

* * * * * * * * * * * * *

The camera zoomed in on Sage as she nervously clasped her hands in her lap. For her television appearance on the "Good Morning Atlanta" talk show, she was dressed in a short-waisted bolero-cut purple jacket and matching calf-length skirt with a knee-high split. Her hair was full and curly, draping her shoulders.

Erica Jayes, host of the morning talk show, gave Sage a reassuring smile. "Remember to look at the camera," Erica said.

Sage crossed her legs at the ankles as the production assistant signaled "action" with the tilt of her fingers. The cameras were rolling.

"Good morning, Sage," said Erica, a slender, black woman with a tapered haircut. "Thank you for joining us this morning."

"It's great to be here," Sage responded with a warm smile. "Especially to talk about the new flag."

145

"The flag has been controversial for a long time, but that's all behind us now because voters can vote for the flag of their choice."

"That's right, Erica. Voters have a unique opportunity to vote for the design of their choice. This will be the first time in Georgia history that citizens can decide what the state flag will look like."

"Well, it certainly has gotten us a lot of national attention," Erica said with a friendly chuckle.

"It certainly has."

"So tell us about the new designs," Erica prompted.

"There are two designs. And I brought both samples with me." She waved the two miniature flags. "As you can see, the stars on flag A run diagonally across the stripes and, on flag B, the stars create a circle."

"Which one do you prefer?"

Sage tilted her head to the side and said, "I haven't decided. But what's important is that voters get out there and vote for the flag *they* like."

Erica nodded. "Polls show that only forty percent of registered voters plan to get out to the polls."

"We're hoping to increase those numbers. That's why we're launching a campaign to encourage voter participation. We hope people respond to 'It's a New Flag Day.'"

"The new administration certainly has been busy during its first quarter."

"Yes, it has."

"So tell us more about the special election," Erica said.

"The special election to vote on a new flag will be held in June. Voters can go to their regular polls or, as always, if they're going to be out of town, can vote by absentee ballot," Sage explained.

"Sounds like a regular election."

"Everything about the election is the same, including the voting polls and the tabulation process."

"When will the new flag go into effect?"

"Some companies have already stopped flying the existing state flag. But the new flag will become the official flag of Georgia next year on July 1, the beginning of the fiscal year. That gives everybody a little more than a year to get the new flags made and distributed."

"Thanks for joining us, Sage. I can't wait to see which flag will be selected."

"Neither can I," Sage said, smiling warmly into the camera. "We'll find out in three weeks."

* * * * * * * * * * * * *

The two men watching the "Good Morning Atlanta" show in a rural Georgia town fifty miles south of Atlanta were not smiling.

"I can't rely on you for anything," the father complained.

"How was I supposed to know the senator would kill himself?" the son said.

"It's too late now. First you didn't stop the black bastard from getting elected, and then you couldn't even stop the legislators from passing a simple bill." Randolph stared at his son with unveiled disgust.

"I tried, Father. The people I hired weren't reliable."

"You hired outsiders? Who? You're not to discuss what we do with anyone but the team."

"Sometimes the team can't do what needs to be done," Winchester explained heatedly.

"You haven't done what you were supposed to do. Tom wants to elect a new leader."

The younger man knocked a kitchen chair to the floor. "I'm in charge, Father!"

"Maybe not for long."

Winchester stared at Sage on the television screen. "I'm going to get you, bitch," he mumbled to himself.

"What's that?" Randolph asked.

"Nothing," his son answered and walked out of the room.

Chapter XII

The 100 Black Women of Atlanta, a high-profile organization of successful, professional black women, hosted quarterly lunches as well as an annual conference that drew people from all over the country. Sage had relinquished her position as vice president of the local chapter, but was still active in the organization. Today, as mistress of ceremony for the "Rising Above the Corporate Ladder" luncheon held at the Omni hotel, Sage introduced the featured speaker, Georgette Frazier, who drew the audience to their feet with her keen observations and funny quips about corporate life.

When the luncheon was over, Sage spoke with several members, chatting about the speaker's presentation and local events. She heard some of the rumors circulating through town about a city council member who was being investigated for taking kickbacks.

The hotel ballroom was almost empty by two o'clock as the women returned to their offices, newly motivated to reach for the next rung on the slippery corporate ladder.

Sage waved goodbye to the president of the organization as they were leaving the ballroom. "See you at next month's meeting." Remembering that she'd left her cellular phone at the office, Sage headed toward the bank of telephones to call Marika. She dropped a quarter in the pay phone and was dialing the number to her office when Edwinna tapped Sage on the shoulder.

"I need to speak to you," Edwinna said.

"I'm on the phone," Sage said with an unfriendly glare, turning her back on the other woman.

"I have something to tell you," Edwinna insisted. "Something you should know."

Ignoring her, Sage finished her conversation with Marika, who reminded her of her appointment with a real estate agent later that evening. She hung up the phone, then headed toward the parking garage elevators. Sage rounded the corner and almost bumped into Edwinna.

"I need to talk to you," Edwinna said, standing in front of the elevators.

Sage eyed her suspiciously. "I'm not interested in anything you have to say."

"On the contrary," Edwinna insisted smugly. "I think you'll be very interested."

"Look, Edwinna, I don't have time for your games," Sage said in the crisp warning tone mothers use before disciplining their child. The elevator door opened and Sage stepped inside.

"Ramion must have told you about our evening together last week," Edwinna said, her hands planted on her hips. Her voice was loud and emphatic, a clear broadcast to anyone standing near.

Sage swung back around to face her nemesis. "What are you talking about?" She stepped off the elevator just as the doors closed.

"I spent the evening at Ramion's last week." Her lips twisted into a predatory smile. She laughed, dramatically touching her chest. "We really enjoyed ourselves. You know what I mean," she said, her implication clear.

Sage moved closer to Edwinna; their faces were only inches apart. She could smell the woman's perfume. "*If* you spent the evening with Ramion, it hasn't changed anything between us. We're still getting married."

"I don't care about you marrying Ramion. I don't mind sharing him. After all, I had him first. We've always enjoyed a satisfying relationship." She swiveled her hips and tossed her head to the side. "Let me rephrase that. We enjoyed a very erotic sexual relationship. And it's obvious you don't know how to please him, Miss Prim and Proper. That's why he still needs me."

Her eyes unwavering, Sage said, "Apparently I satisfy him enough for him to marry me. Hmm, just think about it a minute. You're Edwin Williamson's daughter. One would think Ramion would marry you." Sage turned away and walked over to the elevators, pressed the call button once again. "Instead he's marrying me. Don't you wonder why? Or could it be you already know it's because you're a whore?"

"Bitch!"

"No, no, you're the bitch, Edwinna, which is precisely why Ramion doesn't want you. And just between us, I don't believe your lie about Ramion. You're too pathetic to believe."

The elevator doors opened and Sage stepped inside, hoping that Edwinna didn't follow her. She scowled at her as the doors closed.

Sage put the key in her car door with trembling hands. She didn't want to believe Edwinna, but the thought of Ramion, naked, making love and enjoying Edwinna's body felt like a knife in her heart. Gripping the steering wheel, she closed her eyes and fought the tears that threatened to fall. "How could he betray me like that?" she asked out loud.

She drove to the Governor's Mansion with jumbled thoughts and emotions. She vacillated in thinking Edwinna was a liar and Ramion a traitor.

The first thing Sage did when she got to her office was call Ramion's office number, ignoring her stack of messages. She silently cursed when his secretary told her he was in court. If he slept with her, that sleazy whore, I'm not going to marry him, she thought. But that's exactly what Edwinna wants. Are you going to let her win? I have to talk to Ramion.

Sage spent the afternoon working, although she really wasn't able to concentrate, Edwinna's words ringing through her mind. She tried to reach Ramion several times, but he was out of the office all afternoon. She was on a conference call when he called her back and left a message that he would meet her at the real estate agent's office.

On her way to meet Ramion at the real estate agent's office, Sage ran into evening rush-hour traffic. Driving at a frustrating ten miles per hour on Georgia 400, Sage looked at the clock on her dashboard and realized that she was going to be late. She called Ramion's cellular phone, but there was no answer. She then dialed the real estate office and left a message for the agent that she was going to be late.

She turned up the radio, the stop-and-go pace of the traffic increasing her agitation. Suddenly she heard the unmistakable whine of Prince singing, "Little Red Corvette." "Not that damn song," she said out loud, and then pushed a tape into the cassette player. David Sanborn's searing sax filled the air.

Ramion and the real estate agent were looking at a large, picture map of the metro Atlanta area when Sage arrived at the New Homes Center. Multicolored stickpins representing new subdivisions dotted the color-coded map.

"Ramion," Sage said in a flat, emotionless voice when she approached them.

Several brochures clasped in his hand, Ramion turned, smiling broadly at Sage. He grabbed her hands and kissed her on the cheek. "Sage, this is Fran, our real estate agent."

"Hello," Sage said, shaking the agent's hand.

"It's good to finally meet you," said Fran, a red-haired, freckled-faced white woman. Her soft-spoken voice didn't hide her deep Southern drawl. She appeared to be in her early thirties.

"I'm sorry we had to cancel on you so many times," Sage said.

"Don't worry about it. I'm just glad to show you some of the wonderful homes we have. I've already shown your fiancé some of the new developments in the area you're interested in." She pointed to the map, indicating the yellow stickpins that marked subdivisions in the price range they were looking for in the northern portion of Atlanta.

"Look at all the subdivisions under construction," Ramion said, pointing to the purple stickpins dotting northern Gwinnett, Fulton, and Forsyth counties.

"There are some beautiful properties out there. Many of them have golf courses, swimming pools, tennis courts, and private lakes. You get more for your money out there."

"But we prefer to live in the city. We both work downtown," Sage explained.

"A lot of people who live out here commute. Some even take the subway. Atlanta has become quite a commuter town. If you want to take a look at some of the homes in the Alpharetta area, I'd be glad to show you. In fact, a lot of celebrities live out there. There are plenty of communities to choose from."

"As I told you on the phone, we're not interested in living in the

151

suburbs," Sage said in the impatient, clipped tone of voice of a remedial teacher talking to a simple-brained student. She was tired of real estate agents who tried to steer them away from the city. Every real estate agent she talked to gave the same more-for-your-money, less-taxes-in-the-suburbs speech. She didn't care; suburban living was not conducive to their lifestyle. Besides, at the moment, she wasn't sure she even wanted to marry Ramion.

"It's not worth the inconvenience and aggravation," Ramion explained. He pointed to the homes in the Vinings area. "That's a perfect location for us. It's near the Governor's Mansion where Sage works, and getting to the courthouse won't be a major obstacle for me."

Fran smiled and apologized. "I'm sorry if I'm giving you the wonderful suburban life song. It's such a habit. I know there are beautiful homes in the areas you like, especially in your price range. I'm sure we can find something that you'll love."

"I hope so," Sage said, her enthusiasm sinking rapidly to the level of a sunken ship.

"It's easier if I drive you around, or if you prefer we can take separate cars."

"We're yours for the next couple of hours," Sage said.

"Great! I've already given Ramion some of the brochures from the builders we represent." Fran showed them additional brochures, pointing out some of the unique architectural features of each builder.

* * * * * * * * * * * * *

Two hours later, Fran parked in front of the New Homes Center, her tour completed.

"That pink stucco house in Vinings was fabulous, " Fran said, pulling up the brake on her Saab. "There was plenty of closet space, and the sunken living room and spiral staircase would certainly impress even your most important guests."

"Yes, I liked that one the best," Sage agreed.

"We didn't cover much in Buckhead and Chastain," Fran said. "When would you be available to go out again?"

"In a couple of weeks," Sage said, opening the car door and getting out. "I'll call you when I know for sure."

"Do you want to be moved in before the wedding?"

"We'd like to be," Sage said, "but it depends on the house."

"Thanks for your time," Ramion said, shutting the car door.

"What's wrong with you?" Ramion asked after Fran drove off. He couldn't understand why Sage had said so little to him. They stood in front of Ramion's car; Sage's car was parked around the side of the building. "You were so cold. No, correction, you were rude."

"Why didn't you tell me you slept with Edwinna?" Sage asked, glaring angrily into Ramion's face, unveiling the feelings she had barely contained for the last two hours.

Ramion hesitated before answering, searching for the right words to explain Edwinna's duplicity.

Sage perceived Ramion's hesitation as a sign of guilt and turned away, rushing over to her car.

"I didn't sleep with her. I came home, and she was in the house."

Sage spun around, her green eyes narrowed and her mouth wide open. "She has a key?"

"I didn't give her a key if that's what you're implying. She had one made without my knowledge. Nothing happened. I threw her out. We did *not* sleep together!"

"So why didn't you tell me?"

"Because nothing happened," he explained, gesturing emphatically, his arms extended, his palms face-up. "I didn't want to upset you."

"The fact that you didn't tell me upsets me." She rubbed her forehead with her hand, feeling a headache coming on. "At first I thought Edwinna was lying, but apparently you and she did spend the evening together."

"She sneaked into my house and tried to seduce me. I wasn't interested. I put her lying, conniving ass out," Ramion said. "I didn't feel it was necessary to tell you because I didn't sleep with her." He walked toward her, but Sage stepped back. "You must believe me, I did not go to bed with Edwinna." A loud, shrill noise sounded, momentarily distracting them. "My beeper," he said, almost apologetically. He checked the number.

"I have to go. It's Judge Watkins. She wants me in chambers now."

"At seven-thirty?"

"You know how those judges are. They say jump, you say how high."

153

"Are you sure it's a judge? Maybe it's another important client who raped his stepdaughter and needs you to come to the rescue. Or maybe it's Edwinna calling."

"Sage, that's not fair."

"Fair? First you betray me by representing your sleazy uncle, and now you sleep with your old girlfriend, and you're talking fair!" She walked away from Ramion, taking quick steps to her car.

Catching up with her, he said, "Sage, you're mixing everything up. Don't let Edwinna do this. You know what a liar she is. I've done nothing wrong. After I meet with the judge, I'll come over so we can talk this through."

"I don't want to talk to you, Ramion. Just leave me alone." She opened the car door, slid behind the wheel, and slammed the door. "Don't call me. Don't come over."

She turned on the ignition and put the car in drive. "I mean it," she said, then sped out of the parking lot.

* * * * * * * * * * * * *

Sage couldn't fall asleep. She kept thinking about Edwinna's version of the story, very different than Ramion's. The telephone rang again. It was after eleven o'clock, and she hesitated before answering the phone. Ramion had called several times in the past hour, and every time she had refused to talk to him. Whoever it was this time wasn't giving up. Sage snatched the receiver off the hook; a whispered "hello" responded to her disgruntled greeting. The voice was coated with sadness.

"Mama?" Sage queried. Sitting up, she swung her legs over the edge of the bed. She anticipated her mother's next words, thinking immediately of Ava and dreading how she would react.

"It's me," Audra said. She sighed loudly into the phone, a swishing sound that echoed in their ears. "I called to tell Ava that her father has gotten worse." Audra paused as if drawing courage before relaying the next part of the message. "The doctors don't think he has much longer. She needs to come home right away." Audra paused, and her voice took on a pleading tone. "Right away. He keeps asking for her."

"Ava's not home, but I'll tell her as soon as she gets in. She'll probably leave sometime tomorrow."

154

"Okay," Audra said, her disappointment evident. She'd wanted to talk to Ava, to hear her promise to come right away.

"Is Aaron there?" Sage asked, as a picture of her brother loomed in her mind. Aaron had always been quiet and serious while his twin sister had been bubbly and happy-go-lucky.

"Yes, thank goodness! He's been with me through everything. His father can't do anything for himself, and Aaron's helped me take care of him. "

"So, how's Aaron holding up?"

"He's strong. He's been my rock," Audra said, pride ringing in her voice.

There was an awkward silence; neither knowing what to say next.

Suddenly, Audra said, "Sage, I really didn't intend for your stepfather to surprise you . . ."

"Mama, don't worry about that now," Sage said, thinking that this wasn't the time for *that* discussion. "Anyway, I have to go. I'll tell Ava you called. She'll call and let you know when she's coming."

"Thank you, Sage. Take care of yourself." In a quiet voice that longed to say more, Audra said, "Goodnight."

Sage stared at the phone for several minutes, her mind in a daze. She started calling Ramion, but hung up before she finished dialing his number. She was still upset with him, and was in no mood to discuss Edwinna.

Sage turned over on her stomach and closed her eyes, needing to rest her mind from confused thoughts. Before falling asleep, she thought, Aaron is finally getting what he deserves. She drifted to sleep, slipping into a deep slumber, swirling to an unforgettable past.

* * * * * * * * * * * *

Sage was in her room on the third floor packing her suitcases for a two-week visit to her grandmother's house. She was ironing a pair of blue jeans when she heard footsteps on the stairs. She remembered locking the front and back doors; and it was too early for her mother and the twins to be home from the Kingdom Hall. She looked at her watch. Her stepfather wasn't scheduled to be home from work for two more hours. She turned down the radio, listening for the creaking noise on the stairs, and eased closer to the closet door to hide.

When she heard the noise again, this time much closer, she knew someone was definitely in the hall. She opened the closet door, shutting it softly behind her. She slipped to the back of the closet and crouched behind boxes of clothes and junk, hoping the intruder didn't hear her movements.

"Sage," a familiar voice called out.

It sounds like Aaron, Sage thought.

"Sage," the voice called again.

"Aaron," she said, relieved that it wasn't a burglar. She opened the closet door and came out of hiding. "I was scared. I thought you were a burglar. You know some guys broke into Mrs. Murphy's house."

"I know," he said, lumbering over to the bed. His red-rimmed eyes roamed Sage's body, from her long, lean legs to her curly black hair that flowed to the middle of her back.

Embarrassed at the way he was staring at her, Sage was suddenly self-conscious about the white shorts and sleeveless white midriff shirt she wore. She couldn't meet his leering gaze and turned away. Fear returned to the pit of her stomach.

"Mama and the twins will be home any minute now, and I want to finish packing," Sage said, standing in front of the ironing board, her hand curled around the handle of the iron.

"Oh, they won't be back for at least an hour," Aaron said, as he hobbled over to Sage. "Anyway, there's something I've been meaning to say to you. You're the prettiest young thing I've ever seen. Prettier even than your Mama."

Sage was immediately sickened by the smell of alcohol on his breath. Aaron didn't drink often, but when he did, he was meaner and nastier. Sage stepped around him. "You shouldn't talk to me like that."

"I'm just speaking the truth."

"Mama doesn't like it when you drink." She stood by the bed and resumed packing her suitcases, hoping Aaron would leave. She didn't want him in her room. "The elders say you should drink in moderation."

"I just had a few beers with some of my buddies."

"Aaron, I need to pack," Sage said with urgency. Hearing "Little Red Corvette" playing on the radio, she turned up the volume, hoping the music would drive him out. When he didn't move, she said, "Please, Aaron, would you go downstairs?"

He was standing so close behind her she could feel his hot, foul breath on her neck. She felt him softly finger her hair. She jerked her head away. "Stop, Aaron," she cried, stepping away from him.

"Hold on there, girl. You know I'm not going to hurt you. I've been taking care of you since you were a little girl—and my, my, my, you get prettier every year."

Sage backed away from him, inching her way to the door.

Aaron saw where she was headed and moved to the doorway. He closed the door behind him.

"Aaron, let me out of here!"

"No, little girl, you're not going anywhere."

"I'm not a little girl, and you better not touch me," she screamed defiantly.

She backed away from him, but he was steering her toward the bed with a menacing stare.

"You're right, you're not a little girl. You're a woman, a fine young woman. How many boys have you been with?"

"Aaron, please leave me alone," she pleaded, leaning against the edge of the bed, trying not to lose her balance and fall on top of the bed.

"I want to know. How many boys have you been with?"

Tears filled her eyes and began to pour down her cheeks. "No one."

"You're lying. As pretty as you are and all those boys in school. What about Stephen? He's always coming over here."

"I don't like Stephen that way." She felt the fear of a soldier caught in enemy territory.

"Well, who do you like?"

"Nobody!" she cried, putting her arms across her chest.

"I know one of those boys done had their way with you."

She shook her head. "Please, Aaron, please, don't touch me," she begged. Her eyes glued to the floor, she added, "I'm a virgin."

"You're lying, but don't matter none to me. I'm going to show you what it's like to be with a man."

He pushed her down on the bed with one arm, knocking the suitcases on the floor with the other hand. The radio tumbled after the luggage, its volume increasing when it hit the floor. The song "Little Red Corvette" by Prince blasted from the radio.

"Get off me," Sage screamed as she kicked at his legs. "Get off me!"

Holding her down, he loosened his belt and unzipped his pants. He pulled his pants and shorts down to his knees. "Now that's what a man looks like."

His erect penis was throbbing. It was long, ugly, and putrid. Sage closed her eyes, refusing to look at it.

"Hey, that's okay, it don't matter if you look. You're going to find out what it feels like. That's what counts."

Sage tried to wriggle away from him, but he tightened his grip on her arm.

"Take your clothes off!" he demanded.

"No!"

"Damn it, take your clothes off."

"No! No! No!"

"I said take your clothes off. Now!" he shouted, releasing his grip on her. Sage bolted from the bed and headed toward the door.

Aaron grabbed her arm and swung her back around. With a vicious yank, he ripped off her blouse, the buttons popping as the material gave way. He tore off her bra, exposing her breasts. "Oh, they're beautiful," he said, pawing at her breasts with his huge hands. Sage tried to pull away as he dragged her toward the bed, but he was too strong.

He shoved her down on the bed, pinning her with his knee. Sage kicked at him, but he was unfazed by her struggle. He sucked her breasts, mumbling with sordid pleasure, ignoring her cries, "Please stop, please stop!"

She fought, but Aaron only lifted himself far enough to pull down her pants. She used the opportunity to kick viciously, and struck him in the stomach.

"Aaron please stop. You're hurting me," she pleaded, tears running down her face. "You're hurting me!"

Aaron held her down with one hand while he put his penis between her legs with the other. He pushed himself inside her, but he couldn't enter all the way.

"Stop moving around so much. Relax. You'll enjoy it."

With a fierce grunt, he drove himself inside her. A searing pain penetrated her pelvis. She screamed as he plunged deeper and deeper, grunting and pushing, oblivious to her agony.

She tried to escape from the moment, to distance herself mentally from the violent assault on her body and soul. But the only thing she heard was the voice on the radio crooning, "Little Red Corvette, baby you're much too fast."

It had felt like hours, but he finished quickly, plopping his full weight on her.

"Get off me. I hate you, Aaron. I hate you. I hate you!"

Aaron raised himself from atop her and slowly pulled his flaccid penis out of her. He looked between her legs and saw blood.

His gaze moved to her face, and for the first time shame and fear shone in his eyes. "You a virgin?"

"I was!" she screamed, kicking at him, with all her force and power. She kicked his face and arms, and when he raised up, she punched him as hard as she could.

The door suddenly swung open and Audra entered. She saw her daughter—her blouse torn off, her naked breasts, her shorts around her ankles.

"What have you done? Sage? Aaron?" Audra picked up the iron.

"She came downstairs and opened her blouse in front of me," Aaron said, stumbling around, looking for his pants. "She lured me up here. She . . ."

"No, Mama, he's lying," Sage cried, running to her mother. "He raped me!" She put her arms around Audra.

Audra stepped back, pushing Sage away from her. "Don't touch me! You—you—Jezebel!"

* * * * * * * * * * * *

The ringing telephone woke Sage from a nightmare she hadn't invited, a memory that she never wanted to relive. For weeks the nightmare had been coming back to her in bits and pieces. It came in snatches—a flash of Aaron coming into the room, a flash of Aaron leering at her, a flash of Aaron tearing off her clothes, a verse of "Little Red Corvette" ringing in her ear. But tonight she'd relived it all—the rape, the pain, her mother's betrayal.

She was grateful for the ringing phone.

"Hello," she said, tears clogging in her throat.

"Sage, what's wrong?" Ramion asked.

159

"I had a bad dream. A nightmare."

"What did you dream about?"

"My stepfather. What he did to me," she said, her tone hushed, as if she couldn't bear to hear the words spoken out loud.

"Baby, I'm sorry you had to relive that. I wish I was there. I'd hold you in my arms and kiss away the pain. I would rock you back to sleep with the comfort of my love."

"I dreamed about everything," she sighed wearily. "Almost everything. It's so hard because I stopped having those dreams in college. I though I had put it all behind me."

"Sage, do you want me to come over? I can be there in a half-hour."

Sage looked at the clock. The digital dial displayed 3:36 A.M. Yes, she wanted him to come over, but she couldn't admit it. "That's okay. I'll be all right in a bit." She sighed loudly, a revealing sad sigh. "I just have to stop thinking about it. I've trained myself to forget."

"I'm going to come over."

"No, I'll be fine," she said, turning over on her back. "What made you call?"

"I don't know. I woke up with you on my mind. Couldn't go back to sleep without calling you."

"Well, I'm glad you did. You saved me from going through the whole nightmare. I just hope it doesn't continue when I go back to sleep."

"What do you think made it come back?"

"My mother called."

"Did your stepfather die?"

"No, but the bastard's barely alive. She wants Ava to come home right away."

"How did Ava take the news?"

"I haven't told her. She wasn't home. I'll tell her in the morning. She'll probably leave right away."

"Are you going with her?"

"No." Yawning, she added, "I hadn't even considered it."

"Maybe you should."

"I'll go to the funeral. But that's it."

"I know this isn't the time to go into it, but I swear to you, I didn't sleep with Edwinna. I don't want any other woman but you. I love you, baby, with all my heart and soul."

160

Silence.

"Sage, do you believe me?"

"I believe you," Sage said, knowing in the deepest corner of her heart that Ramion wouldn't betray her like that. But it was hard to trust. She was afraid of being made a fool. She didn't want to be betrayed the way Aaron had betrayed her mother.

"I love you, baby," Ramion said. "As soon as I finish this trial, I'll spend more time with you. I'll fly up for the funeral."

"Okay. Goodnight, Ramion." Sage smiled and burrowed into the bed covers. She was suddenly content, the memories of the past already dissipating. She sighed. No, she would never have to worry about Ramion.

* * * * * * * * * * * * *

Several hours later, though, Sage woke up feeling tired and restless from a dreamless sleep. She took a long, leisurely shower, luxuriating in the hot, pulsating water. She dried herself, absently putting on lotion, facial moisturizer, deodorant, and powder. She selected a red single-breasted coat dress with velvet collar and cuffs, then brushed her hair into a ponytail clasped in place with a black velvet bow.

Ready to greet the day, she went into the kitchen and turned on the coffee pot and the television. She moved around the kitchen, preparing a light breakfast—toast, cereal, and fruit—half listening to the "Good Morning America" show. She could hear Ava moving around upstairs, the radio blasting as usual.

A few minutes later, Ava bounced happily down the steps. "Good morning, Sage!"

"Good morning," Sage said. She couldn't help noticing her sister had a special glow about her.

"Guess what?"

"What?"

"I met the most gorgeous man last night. Brother man is fine, you hear me? And he asked *me* out. He spent all his time with *me* last night." She closed her eyes and faked a shudder. "I get chills just thinking about him."

"What's his name?"

"Brent Summers. He's a sales rep for Proctor & Gamble. Been living

161

in Atlanta about six or seven months. He's twenty-six. And the best part is we're going on a date tonight. Can I borrow your black jumpsuit? I want to look sophisticated." She removed her hot cup of tea from the microwave.

"Ava, I have something to tell you."

She stood at the kitchen counter. "What's up?" she asked while pouring sugar into her tea.

"Your father's taken a turn for the worse. He doesn't have much longer."

Her face transformed from joy to sadness in seconds. Ava stopped what she was doing, moved to the kitchen table, and sat down across from Sage. Sipping her tea, the hot steam swirling around her face, Ava stared out at nothing, a quiet, sad look in her eyes.

"Ava," Sage said gently.

Ava didn't respond.

Sage walked around the table and put her arms around her sister's shoulders. Ava leaned against her, eyes closed, still silent. "Be strong, okay?" Sage encouraged.

"I don't want to go home. I don't want to see him like that," Ava said.

Sage was shocked. She'd thought Ava would want to go home immediately. She bent down and kissed the girl's forehead.

"I know it's going to be hard, Ava. But you need to go home. You have to say goodbye."

"He doesn't look like himself. He's withered and shriveled and old looking." Her voice faltered. "He's scary looking."

"That's what cancer does. It's a cruel disease. Don't you be cruel by not going to see him. Go to him, Ava. Hold your favorite memories of him in your mind. And remember, you need to do this, too. How are you going to feel later if you don't see him? Can you live with that?"

"I think I could, Sage. But Daddy wouldn't understand. Neither would Mama. It would hurt him to know I didn't want to see him." She sipped her tea. "I can't do that to him."

"Then go. You can leave this afternoon. I'll make the reservation."

"Would you go with me?"

"I can't leave today, but I'll come in the next day or so. I don't want you to wait on me."

"Are you really going to come home?"

"Yes, I'll be there. I promise."

Sage thought about the last time she'd stood on her mother's porch, waiting for Aunt Maddie, feeling afraid and abandoned. She hated her stepfather for brutally taking her virginity and destroying her relationship with her mother. For years she'd wanted to seek revenge, to cost him something precious. But in the end, she'd settled on disappearing from their lives. She had hoped her disappearance would come between Aaron and Audra, that her mother would come to hate him for what he'd done to them. But Audra had remained loyal to her husband, and now he was about to die.

Sage didn't feel anything for her stepfather, not sadness, not pity, not sympathy. She thought his death was a late punishment for a cruel crime. But mixed in those feelings of dispassion was guilt. His death was going to be devastating for her brother and sister. They were the reason she hadn't filed charges against him. She would never hurt them by revealing the truth.

Chapter XIII

Five days after Audra's late night call, Sage plodded up the four steps of her mother's porch. The three-story brick house looked different. It was a deeper shade of red than she remembered, and the wood shutters were now black instead of blue. A green and pink flower-patterned glider had replaced the blue and white striped glider.

She rang the doorbell, telling herself not to think about the last time she'd stood outside this door. Not to remember the moonlit summer night, the fear and hurt and the ache between her legs. But the anguish in her heart was there again all the same—along with the memory of her mother's angry, reproachful eyes and the sound of "Little Red Corvette" blasting from the radio.

Her brother swung open the door, a slight smile softening his somber expression when he saw Sage.

"Hey, big sis," he said, throwing his arms around her. Sage hugged him back affectionately. "It's good to see you, Aaron," she said. "In spite of the circumstances," she added, looking him over. He had lost weight since she'd last seen him the summer before. His blue corduroy pants and a tweed navy blue sweater hung loosely on his tall, lanky frame. Round gold-rimmed Benjamin Franklin-style glasses covered his small dark brown eyes, the focal point on a long cinnamon-brown face with an angular, thin nose and wide mouth.

164

Sage suddenly remembered when she bought Aaron and Ava their first pair of contact lenses. The twins were high school juniors, and Ava constantly complained that her thick glasses were interfering with her dating. Ava took to the contacts like a fish in water, but Aaron fumbled around with the cleaning and disinfecting and enzymatic solutions like one of the Three Stooges. Ava never wore her glasses and, after two months, Aaron never wore his contact lenses.

Touching his chin, "A beard?" Sage said, rubbing her hand against the heavy stubble. "It looks good on you."

"I've been too busy to shave," Aaron said matter-of-factly. He looked around the front porch. "Where's your luggage?"

"It's at the hotel."

"Sage, you didn't have to go to a hotel. You could have stayed here," Aaron chided, his brows creased.

"I wanted to stay in a hotel. Besides, I knew your Dad's relatives would be coming into town, so it just made it easier."

"Well, let's not stand in the doorway forever. Come on in and see everybody. Dad's brothers are here, and Aunt Bertha and Aunt Cora."

"Where's Ava?"

"She went grocery shopping with Mama."

"How's she doing? She was reluctant to come," she said, trailing behind Aaron through the wide hallway.

"She's a basket case. That's why I'm glad you're here. She became hysterical the first night she saw him. The doctor gave her Valium."

Sage batted her eyes. "Valium?"

Noticing the disapproving expression on Sage's face, Aaron said, "I don't like her taking them either. But she needed something to calm her down."

"Ava doesn't need to be taking any drugs," Sage said with a protective fierceness in her voice.

"The doctor prescribed them," Aaron explained casually.

Shaking her head, Sage said, "I know, but . . ."

"Sage, darling, how you doin'?" her Uncle Cedric interrupted, as he stepped out of the bathroom, shutting the door behind him. "You sure have changed. I haven't seen you in years. The last time I seen you was probably sixteen or seventeen, just graduated from high school."

"That's right, Uncle Cedric," Sage said. His big round face and grin reminded Sage immediately of her stepfather. She had forgotten how much the brothers resembled each other. Both had been big and burly but, unlike Aaron, Cedric had the personality of a teddy bear. As a young girl, Sage often wished it had been Cedric her mother had married.

"Sugga, you gotta give me a hug. It's been too long." Cedric put his arms around Sage's shoulders, embracing her warmly. "You looking good, girl. Even prettier than I remembered," Cedric said.

"Thank you," she replied coolly. "You look pretty good yourself." They walked down the hall, passing the front stairs, the living room, and the dining room. Voices grew louder as they approached the kitchen.

"Hey, everybody, Sage is here," Cedric announced when they entered the huge kitchen. The dark brown kitchen cabinets, she noticed, had been replaced by pecan and white cabinets. The green and white checkered tile floor and the tier gingham curtains hanging on the windows were also new.

Sage found herself surrounded by a host of steprelatives, greeting her with kisses and smiles and introductions to cousins, nieces, and nephews. Most of the men sat around the kitchen table, while the women were busy at the sink, stove, or countertops, chopping, dicing, cleaning, or cooking. Bottles of whiskey, vodka, and rum sat open on the table.

"Here, let me take your coat," her brother offered. "I'll hang it in the closet."

Sage unbuttoned her black leather coat with fur trimming the collar and sleeves. She was dressed in a purple two-piece pantsuit, a button-down tunic top with matching pants.

She offered to help with the food, but the women wouldn't hear of it.

"You go take a seat over there. Buster, get on up now! Let Sage sit down. Let her rest a spell before she gets mixed up in this madness," Aunt Essie, Cedric's wife, said.

Buster, Cedric's nineteen-year-old son, stood up reluctantly, offering Sage his chair. She took the seat at the end of the rectangular oak table that matched the corner hutch brimming with dishes and knick-knacks. The kitchen was always her favorite room, where she'd spent most of her time with her family.

Sage found herself the center of attention, as if she were on trial with all the questions they fired at her.

"What's the governor of Georgia really like?"

"Oh, I heard you live in a mansion."

"Ava says you drive a Mercedes Benz, is that true?"

"I'm glad you didn't get hurt bad by that bomb. Do they know who did it?"

"Have you really met the President of the United States?"

Sage answered their questions, surprised that they all knew so much about her. She'd assumed her mother wouldn't talk about her except to complain that she'd gone to college, then gotten a big-time job in Atlanta, and forgotten all about her family. Now she didn't know what to think about her mother's apparent pride in her success.

Chatting with her steprelatives, Sage learned how devastating Aaron's death was to his family. Aaron's family depicted him as a wonderful, giving, and generous man. If only they knew the truth, Sage thought. It was amazing how a man could be both revered and hated, with the same degree of passion.

For just an instant, Sage wished she had come home before Aaron died to confront him about the rape. She had made arrangements to fly to Baltimore two days earlier, but had to reschedule because of an unexpected business meeting. She'd actually been relieved when Cameron asked her to attend the meeting on his behalf. She hadn't really wanted to see Aaron on his deathbed. Seeing him frail and helpless and ravaged by cancer might have lessened her anger and bitterness, made her want to forgive him. And that was one thing she never wanted. She didn't ever want to forgive him.

"Excuse me," Sage said, glancing at the cuckoo clock on the wall over the stove. The old clock brought a soft smile to her mouth, triggering a memory of the time seven-year-old Aaron Jr. had taken it off the wall to let the bird out. She had put it back a few minutes before their mother came into the kitchen. "I need to use the phone."

"Use the one in my room," Aaron suggested. "It's much quieter."

"Okay," Sage said, rising from the chair. She bent to retrieve her briefcase leaning against the kitchen counter.

"Are you going to call the governor?" asked a cute little girl with long ponytails. Sage couldn't remember whose daughter she was.

"Not right now," Sage answered, returning the child's sweet smile. She walked up the back stairs to the second floor and their voices faded away, replaced by an eerie quiet.

Sage stopped at her mother's room. Peeking in the doorway, she realized the room was virtually unchanged. The next room was her sister's. It was typically Ava—bed unmade, drawers half opened, clothes strewn on the floor, and bottles scattered on the dresser. She continued to Aaron's room. Smiling as she eased down on the bed, Sage remembered how different the twins were. Aaron's room had always been neat and orderly, Ava's room a disaster zone. As a teenager, Sage had often asked her mother, "They're so different. Are you sure they're twins?"

She picked up the telephone and called Marika. After talking on the phone with her assistant, she took a chance and called Ramion at his office, smiling when he answered.

"I thought you'd be in court," she said.

"The judge ordered a recess until three o'clock," Ramion said. "How are you, baby?"

She sighed into the phone. "I'm okay."

"You don't sound okay."

"I am. Really. It's just being surrounded by Aaron's relatives. They drilled me about my life in Atlanta, and I guess they know more about me than I expected."

"What about your mother? How did it go with her? How did she act?"

"I haven't seen her yet. She and Ava went grocery shopping. But part of me wants to leave, go back to the hotel, and wait to see her tomorrow. The only trouble is the other part of me knows I'm just trying to avoid the unavoidable."

"Listen to the first part, baby. Get it over with."

"I wish you were here."

"I'll be there tomorrow night."

"I know. I know." She heard the shrill sound of his beeper. "You gotta go?"

"Yes," Ramion said. "I'll talk to you tonight. Love you, bye."

Sage leaned back against the bed and closed her eyes for a few minutes. She thought about the attic where she'd slept—where she'd been raped. Struck with the urge to go up there, she crossed the hall to the attic door. She turned the doorknob, but the door wouldn't open. She tried again, but realized that the door was locked.

She heard the floor creaking and turned toward the back stairs.

"That door has been locked for years. Mama closed off the attic after you left," her brother explained as he walked over to Sage. A wry smile spread across his face. "No one ever goes up there. After you left, Ava thought there had to be a ghost up there."

"She told me," Sage said.

168

"I came up to tell you that Mama and Ava are home," Aaron said.

"I'll be down in a minute."

"Okay," he said, before turning around and heading toward the stairs.

Ten minutes later, Sage walked down the back stairs that led into the kitchen.

"Oh, Sage, Sage, Sage," Audra said, when she saw her daughter emerge from the stairs. She ran to Sage, hugging her tightly. Sage felt the eyes of everyone on them, and slowly, reluctantly responded to her mother's overpowering embrace.

"Hello, Mama," Sage said, backing away and staring into her mother's face. The woman she'd seen just a few months ago looked different. It was in the eyes, Sage decided—the bright, vibrant eyes that were now dull, weary.

"You look so good, so beautiful," her mother said. "I'm so glad to see you."

"Don't hug her forever," Aaron said, watching them hug and wondering why Sage had never come home before now.

"I could," Audra said, releasing her tight grip around Sage's waist. "It's been so long since I've seen her."

"You saw her in October," Aaron reminded his mother.

"I know, but it wasn't long enough."

An awkward silence filled the space between mother and daughter until Ava broke the spell. "Don't I get a hug?"

"Ava," Sage said, grabbing her younger sister. "Are you holding up?"

Ava tilted her head to the side and released a somber, Mona Lisa smile. "I'm okay."

"Enough with the hugs and kisses," Aaron said. "Let's get the groceries out of the car so we can eat."

"Amen," Cedric said, twirling the glass of rum and coke in his hand. "I'm starving."

* * * * * * * * * * * * *

Sage didn't shed a tear at her stepfather's funeral. When she spotted her Aunt Maddie sitting across the church aisle, an understanding gaze passed between their eyes. They both knew that the praises the minister bestowed upon Aaron Hicks were not entire truths, but distorted by the prism of permanent passing. Sage wanted to stand up and shout the truth about the man lying dead in the coffin. But she knew no one would have believed her.

Sheets of rain poured from the sky as the funeral procession made its way to the cemetery. Sage and Ramion headed in the opposite direction, toward the Hicks home, where family members would all gather after the funeral services.

"Aunt Maddie! I didn't expect to see you here." Sage jumped up from the couch and embraced her aunt when she entered the living room crowded with relatives.

"I came to see *you*," Aunt Maddie said, putting emphasis on the last word. Lowering her voice, she whispered into Sage's ear. "I certainly didn't come to pay my respects to Aaron. That funeral was too good for him. That minister made him out to be a saint. But we know better."

"We sure do," Sage said, and then noticed the expensive fur coat. "You look fabulous." Her aunt had always managed to dress like a wealthy woman despite the teacher's income she'd always lived on.

"Thank you, dear. And you're as pretty as ever. Satchel would be so proud of you." She smiled, making deep impressions on both sides of her round face. "Well, aren't you going to introduce me to your fiancé? He's the real reason why I came to old Aaron Hick's funeral."

Ramion was in deep conversation with Cedric about sports.

Sage tapped his shoulder. "Excuse me, Cedric. I want Ramion to meet my aunt."

"Yes, yes," her uncle said, getting up from the sofa. "I need to fix another drink."

Ramion stood up as well.

"Honey, this is my aunt. Aunt Maddie, I'd like you to meet my fiancé, Ramion Sandidge."

Ramion extended his hand, but Aunt Maddie ignored the offer. "We're going to be relatives. You're marrying my very favorite niece. I think a hug is more appropriate." Aunt Maddie gave him a quick warm embrace.

"It's a pleasure to meet you, Miss Kennedy," Ramion said, flashing a warm smile at the tall, big-boned, light-skinned woman.

"Oh no, call me Aunt Maddie." She tucked her arm into Ramion's elbow. "Come walk with me. I want to get to know you."

"Remember, Aunt Maddie, he's a lawyer. He knows how to duck and dodge questions."

"Good, because I'm pretty good myself. I'm really going to enjoy this," Aunt Maddie said, steering Ramion into the dining room. "Now tell me how you met my niece."

* * * * * * * * * * * * *

While Ramion became acquainted with Aunt Maddie, Sage and her mother traveled down memory lane to the fork in their past that sent them down separate paths. Audra longed to cut through the tangled vines of their memories.

"Sage, I really need to talk to you," Audra said, her fragile voice unusually insistent.

"Yes, Mama?" Sage said, leaning against the kitchen counter, nibbling on the last piece of coconut cake.

"I heard you telling Aaron that you're leaving tomorrow." She paused, carefully choosing her next words. "I want to talk with you privately. With you leaving so soon, I might not get another chance."

Sage nodded. She'd dreaded this moment, although she'd known it was inevitable. All day, she'd felt her mother watching her, practically stalking her with her eyes. Even at the funeral when Audra should have been focused on her grief, Sage had caught her mother staring at her with pleading eyes.

"Come upstairs. We'll have some privacy in my room."

Sage followed her mother up the stairs, noticing the familiar creak and squeak of the floorboards. The third step from the top would squeal, and the step at the top of the stairs had always creaked the loudest. As Sage entered her mother's bedroom, she immediately felt Aaron's presence—his smell was there, still lingering.

"So, Mama, I see you haven't changed much in your room. Same furniture, arranged the same way. Exact same pictures on the wall. Nothing's different."

"Yes there is," Audra said, closing the door before easing onto the queen-sized bed. "You're here. You're standing in my bedroom."

"True," Sage said, as she perched on the edge of the vanity bench. She turned around and peered into the mirror, seeing the reflection of herself as a young girl, instead of the image of the woman she now was. She remembered how she played with her mother's makeup, creating an unrecognizable face—black eyeliner dotting her eyelids, blush smeared all over her cheeks, and more lipstick on her chin than her lips. Audra

171

would catch her and lightly chide, "Don't rush your childhood. Once it's gone, you can never get it back."

Sage turned around and found her mother staring at her, as if she were suddenly going to disappear before her eyes.

Sage glanced away, fixing her gaze on the mantelpiece that accented the gas-burning fireplace. "Ah ha, I see where some of my pictures have disappeared to," Sage said, noticing recent photos of herself neatly lined on the mantelpiece. There were more pictures of Sage than the twins. "I knew Ava was swiping my pictures."

"That's not all," Audra said, as she stood up and walked over to the tall mahogany armoire. Sliding open the top drawer, Audra removed a photo album. She handed it to Sage.

With a curious expression, Sage opened the album. Unable to contain her surprise, Sage cried, "Mama, I don't believe this." It was all there. Her life organized on the pages of this leather book—an invitation to her college graduation, report cards, pictures, and newspaper and magazine articles.

"I don't remember these photographs of me and Daddy," Sage said, peering at a strip of black and white snapshots of her at seven with her father at an amusement park. There were four pictures: Sage kissing her daddy on the cheek, Satchel kissing her, she and Satchel smiling, and Satchel covering Sage's eyes.

"Please let me take these pictures and have them copied."

"Okay," Audra said hesitantly.

Sage continued to leaf through the album. A picture of Billie Holiday surrounded by a group of children fell out. Sage picked it up and gave her mother a questioning gaze.

"That's the time your father met Billie Holiday. He was always crazy about her."

"I remember," Sage said, smiling tenderly at her father who appeared to be twelve or thirteen in the picture.

"I sent that article about you in *Essence* to everybody. I know they get tired of me boasting about you."

Sage smiled. "So that's why Ava came to live with me."

"Ava admires you a great deal. Every time she comes back from Atlanta, she talks nonstop about you. She tells me everything in detail. I was disappointed when she moved to Atlanta, but I always knew she would one day. She wanted to be with her big sister."

"I'm glad she came down. I love having her around."

"Your Ramion is such a nice young man. He's quite handsome and smart."

"Yes, he is. He's a brilliant attorney. He's going to run for the Georgia legislature."

"I see," Audra said, searching for something to say. "You really like politics."

"Uhm hum. I always have."

"Yes, I remember."

There was an uncomfortable silence. The moment of truth had arrived, the moment to unfurl the silence of the past.

Audra folded her arms nervously across her chest and stared at the floor. As the silence grew heavy between them, she began rubbing her arms as if preparing for the gust of cold air that was certain to come.

"Sage, I want you to know how sorry I am for Aaron, for what he did to you." She spoke quietly, and every word was filled with remorse.

Sage stared into her mother's eyes. Bitter eyes met guilt-ridden ones. "He *raped* me," Sage said, challenging her mother to say the ugly word, to acknowledge out loud the assault on her body, the devastation to her mind.

Audra bowed her head and tightly closed her eyes. "Yes, he . . . he . . . he hurt you."

"No, Mama," Sage's voice rose mightily and angrily. "He *raped* me!"

Audra was quiet for several minutes. She raised her eyes from the floor and met her daughter's unwavering gaze. "I'm sorry . . . I'm sorry that he raped you," Audra said haltingly, stumbling over her words. She released a deep sigh. "I'm very sorry that I didn't stop him."

"You knew, Mama. You knew about Aaron's lecherous desires. You saw the way he watched me." When Audra turned away, Sage leaped up from the vanity bench and stepped over to the bed. She stood beside her mother, both hands on her hips, poised for battle. Audra raised her head and stared into green daggers of bitterness and betrayal. "I did nothing wrong, Mama, but you blamed me. You acted like *I* enticed *him*," Sage uttered angrily. "I was a virgin, Mama. A *virgin!*"

Audra rubbed her forehead and ran her hands through her hair, tugging at a grey-streaked chunk. "I know you were innocent. But I didn't want to believe he would touch you without provocation. He was an elder in the congregation. I thought that would help him control his desires. But it didn't." She heaved a weary sigh. "Believe me, deep in my heart I never forgave him, and he knew it. Before he died he asked me to forgive him."

It never occurred to Sage that the rape had affected her mother's relationship with Aaron. Somehow she'd always assumed that their lives had gone unmarred by Aaron's uncontrollable lust.

With her head cocked to the side, Sage asked, "Did you?" in a you-better-not-have tone of voice.

"Yes, I forgave him." Seeing the flash of anger in Sage's eyes, Audra raised her hands. "Don't be angry, Sage," she said in a defeated, weary tone. "The damage was done. What he did to you stood between us. Believe me, our relationship was never the same. I didn't want him to die with the space between us."

"That space wasn't wide enough for you to get out, to leave him, was it? You should have, Mama." Sage sat down on the bed next to Audra. "Most mothers would."

"I couldn't."

"Why not, Mama? Why didn't you protect me from him?"

"I don't know. I suppose I was too weak to fight him. If I had confronted him, if I had said out loud, 'I know you desire my daughter,' it would have been the end. I was afraid he would leave me. Then how would I take care of you and the twins? When your father died, I didn't know what I was going to do. I couldn't go through that again."

"So you sacrificed my virginity for food, clothing, and shelter." A cryptic, sarcastic laugh escaped Sage's lips. "What a trade-off."

Audra shook her head vigorously. "No, Sage, I didn't see it that way. God help me, I loved him. Even with his faults and weaknesses, he wasn't all bad."

Those words were like a lit match hovering over a can of gasoline. Sage jumped from the bed, the anger for too many years suppressed rising to the surface. "Tell that to a seventeen-year-old girl who was thrown out of her house for something she didn't do! I was the victim!" Pointing at herself, she said, "I wasn't bad, Mama. I didn't deserve what he did, what you did." Sage brushed away the tears flooding her eyes. She hadn't intended to cry, but she couldn't contain the tears.

"I was wrong, Sage. I was wrong. Please forgive me."

Sage didn't respond. She sat down on the vanity bench across from her mother.

Heavy silence loomed between them.

Audra broke the silence before it became an unpenetrable force. "In my own twisted way, I was trying to keep my family together, to protect Ava and Aaron."

"How could you be sure he wouldn't have raped Ava?"

Audra gasped and covered her mouth with her hand. "Ava's his daughter!" she cried indignantly. "He wouldn't have touched her."

"Oh God, Mama, are you really so naive? Don't you watch Oprah or Montel or Sally or the news? Don't you hear how twisted the world has become?"

"He would never have hurt Ava," Audra said stubbornly. "He's her father."

"It wasn't immoral to rape me?" Sage asked indignantly.

"Aaron was wrong, Sage." Audra pressed her fingers against her temple. "I was wrong too. I don't know what else to say."

"You know, Mama, I understand that I wasn't related to him, so in his mind it wasn't incestuous. But your reaction hurt me more than the physical pain he inflicted on me." She was silent for a long time, struggling with her thoughts and feelings, trying desperately to submerge those memories. But those memories were crowding her heart, thumping inside, ready to escape.

"Sage?" Audra said, but received no reply.

Suddenly, she asked, "And you were my mother, so what about this, Mama?" She pushed aside her blouse to reveal the ugly triangular scar on her shoulder.

Sage expected her mother to look ashamed or sad, but instead Audra's expression was confused. "You burned me with the iron!" Sage screamed.

"Oh no, Sage," Audra cried, as a stream of tears flowed down her cheeks. She jumped up and went over to her first-born child. She slowly raised her hand and tenderly touched the burn mark on Sage's shoulder, a raised ugly scar. She looked into her daughter's eyes and, for the first time, understood her bitterness. She understood why Sage had hated her all these years.

"I didn't know," Audra said. Her head hung low, she whispered, "I didn't know."

"Mama, how can that be?" Sage asked, wondering if her mother would lie to win her forgiveness. In an incredulous, suspicious tone she said, "You picked up the iron."

"I don't know. I suppose I blocked it out of my mind. I tried to forget that night ever happened." She paused, as the long-hidden memory of seeing Aaron standing over her daughter forced its way into her consciousness. She closed her eyes and in a hushed tone said, "I remember. I remember picking up the iron. I was going to hit Aaron with the cord, and I didn't realize it was still hot. Then everything happened so fast. You ran over to me, and the iron fell . . ."

"You pushed me away!" Sage cried.

"I never knew I'd burned you. You ran out of the room screaming, but I didn't know the iron had fallen on you." She sighed wearily. "I swear to you, I didn't know."

Sage met her mother's gaze. She looked away, averting her eyes to the floor, realizing for the first time that it was possible her mother truly may not have known. I buried the memory all these years so I could go on. Maybe Mama truly never knew, she thought to herself.

The silence grew as time ticked away minute by minute. Each waited for the other's next move, wondering whether the conversation was going to end with their feelings still tangled in the past.

"Sage, I can't undo the past. I wish I could, because I would take back that night. I would change so much. You will never know how sorry I am for losing you." A tear slipped over her lashes. "My firstborn child who I love with all my heart. I may not be the strongest woman in this world, but I do know that living in the shadow of yesterday is torture."

Audra touched her daughter's face, tracing the trail of tears. "I hope you will forgive me, because I don't want to spend the rest of my days without you. Can you forgive me?"

Sage stared into her mother's eyes, and there was something in the chocolate-brown circles that tugged at her. It wasn't the swirling anguish and sorrow. What she saw shining in her mother's eyes was the same longing she felt in her heart—the need to heal, a mutual need to heal from yesterday's wounds.

"Will you forgive me?" her mother asked again.

How can I heal if I don't forgive, Sage thought. How can I heal without releasing the past? The tears were gone when Sage whispered into her mother's ear. "I'll try."

* * * * * * * * * * * *

The day after her stepfather's funeral, Sage met Aunt Maddie for lunch before catching a plane back to Atlanta. After spending a restless night dreaming about the past, she was ready to return to the reality of the present.

"So, darling, tell me how you really are," Aunt Maddie asked Sage after the waiter placed a plate of broiled salmon, new potatoes, and broccoli in front of her.

"I'm confused," Sage admitted. She picked up the miniature bottle of honey mustard dressing and began pouring it over her fried chicken salad.

"Confused about what?"

"I thought I would hate my mother forever. But seeing her looking older, I realized one day she'll die too."

"And you don't want her to die knowing that you hate her."

"I don't want to keep hating her. It's an awful feeling. It suffocates you." Sage stuck her fork into a piece of chicken and put it into her mouth.

"But," prompted Aunt Maddie, raising her eyebrows as she spoke.

"She wants to be a part of my life. But I don't know if I'm ready. She tried after I was hurt in the explosion, but Aaron blew it." She leaned back in her chair and frowned. "Part of me feels like it's too convenient. Now that Aaron's gone, she can claim me again."

"I understand what you mean. Maybe it's just a little too soon. Give it some time. But, I think it will be good for you to renew your relationship with your mother."

"I hated her all these years for being weak, for not standing up to Aaron, for not protecting me," Sage said, sipping Zinfandel wine. "And now, I see that she couldn't. Some women can stand their ground against a big overpowering brute, but some women just can't."

"I've always known that about your mother," Aunt Maddie said in a matter-of-fact tone. "She's the type of woman who falls apart easily. She went to pieces when Satchel died." She tasted the salmon.

"I remember Mama crying all the time. I tried not to cry because it always made her cry," Sage said, suddenly remembering how sad and empty she'd felt when her father died. She'd felt as if the sun had set in her world and would never rise again.

"That's Audra. She can't help herself."

"And I'm supposed to forgive her like that," Sage said flippantly, snapping her fingers. "Like nothing happened, like my feelings don't count."

"No, darling, you forgive her because you're stronger than she is. It's as simple as that."

Those words struck a chord in Sage's heart. "It doesn't feel simple," she said, wiping the dressing from her mouth with the linen napkin.

"You want to forgive her. It would be a big weight off your shoulders. You've carried that albatross for too long, haven't you?" Aunt Maddie said gently.

Tears shone in Sage's eyes. "Yes, it feels heavy and burdensome. For some reason it suddenly feels heavier than it has in years."

"That's because it's time you got rid of it," she advised.

Sage reached for her glass. "I'm almost there. Almost," she said, and sipped the blush-colored wine.

"Dry your eyes, darling. There's something I want to tell you. Something you need to know."

"I'm not crying," Sage said defiantly, even as she wiped the spring of tears pooling in her eyes. She placed the wine glass back on the table. "What is it?" she asked, noticing that her salad bowl was still quite full.

"It's about your father."

"What about him?"

"I think you should have this." Aunt Maddie pulled a velvet rectangular box from her large pocketbook and handed it to her niece.

Expecting jewelry, a cry of glee escaped Sage's mouth when she found an official army medal instead. Sage touched the medal, dangling from the red, white, and blue ribbon.

"I never knew Daddy won a medal for bravery," Sage said, staring at the medal. In the twilight of night, when her thoughts and feelings were safely tucked away, she sometimes thought she could faintly hear his big, hearty laugh.

"Audra gave it to our Mama after she married Aaron. I always thought you should have it."

"I definitely want it," Sage said fervently. A picture of her father loomed in her mind. He was sitting at the kitchen table eating a plate of barbecue ribs. Barbecue sauce covered his mouth and hands. "I'll always treasure it," Sage said softly, fingering the medal like a precious jewel.

"There's something else you should know."

Catching the tone in Aunt Maddie's voice, Sage looked up at her aunt. "What's that?"

"Your father's body was never found."

"What do you mean?" Sage asked, as a crease crept between her eyebrows. "They said he was dead. I remember it so vividly. Those two scary-looking men ringing the doorbell and asking to see Mama. They said they found his dog tags."

"Yes, they'd found his dog tags, but they never found his body. He was presumed dead because the village he was in was razed by bombs."

"You mean his body wasn't in the coffin?" Sage asked, thinking about the closed-casket funeral. She could still see her mother clinging to the casket, weeping hysterically.

Aunt Maddie shook her head.

"And even after all these years, they've never resolved his MIA status?"

"I don't know, Sage. Once he was officially declared dead, they probably stopped looking for him. You know how the government is."

"What do you mean?"

"Vietnam was a very unpopular war. When cases were closed, they usually stayed close." Tossing her head lightly, Aunt Maddie said, "Think about it this way—if he were alive, he had many, many years to come back to his family."

"What if he's a prisoner of war?"

"They claim they know which soldiers were captured. And if he had been taken, he would have been released by now."

"What if he were stranded over there?"

"It's unlikely. Highly unlikely."

Her eyes gleaming with hope, Sage asked, "Aunt Maddie, what if he's alive?"

"Sage, please, I didn't tell you this to give you false hope. I don't think he's alive." Aunt Maddie placed her hand against her chest. "I would know in my heart if my brother were alive. Too many years have gone by. I just wanted you to know the truth. That's all."

Chapter XIV

The scent of musk from a single burning candle wafted in the air of the darkened room. Wearing thigh-high stockings, red panties, and a sheer red bra, Sage lay in the middle of her bed. Her eyes were closed, but she wasn't asleep. Nor was she alone.

"Are you ready?" Ramion whispered into her ear.

"Ready for what?" Sage asked, her body tingling with expectation.

"To forget," he said, nibbling softly on her ear, shoulders, and neck. He slipped his fingers between her legs, touching her center, so soft and wet, so velvety smooth.

Waves of pleasure pulsed through Sage. She quivered with anticipation.

"I think you're ready," Ramion whispered, his fingers lingering inside her moistened folds. His tender kisses become insistent, probing, demanding. Sage returned them with equal intensity.

Ramion moved his mouth from her swollen lips. "I'm going to love you from the bottom to the top."

He opened her legs, spreading them wide. He massaged and licked the bottom of her feet and very tenderly kissed the inside of her legs, from her calf to her knee to her thighs. He licked the insides of her legs, stroking and caressing the softness of her inner thighs.

He placed his mouth between her legs and tasted her liquid gold, his tongue circling, exploring. A rush of pleasure spiraled through her.

"Please don't stop," she groaned, wanting him to continue the exploration of pleasure.

Ramion was ready to probe deeper and laid supine beside her. He plunged inside her, probing deep inside her cavern. The presence of his probe inside her vibrated her body as Sage arched her hips upward and he moved deeper inside her. They flowed together, rocking back and forth in a fluid motion, flowing freely, intensely until ecstasy spun them free.

"Water, please," her hoarse voice crackled in ragged breaths.

Ramion lifted up from the bed, sweat glistening on his naked body, and said, "I'll be back."

He returned a few minutes later with two ice-filled glasses of water. Sage took a glass from him and drank the water in quick gulps. Handing Ramion the empty glass, she leaned back against the pillows and pulled the sheet up to her chest.

Closing her eyes with a satiated smile and feeling better than she had in weeks, Sage uttered happily, "I forgot everything."

Ramion stretched out against her body. "I could tell," he said, smiling with pride and satisfaction.

"Oh, what's that supposed to mean?"

"Baby, a lot has happened to you in the past week. Going to your stepfather's funeral, talking to your mother after all these years. You needed to forget, if only for a moment."

"Make me forget again," Sage said.

Ramion tenderly kissed her on the lips. "I understand the range of emotions you feel, everything from anger to excitement, from joy to sadness."

"You're right." Sage rubbed her hands against her face and through her tangled mass of curls and released a long sigh. "And everything is so mixed up together that I still don't know how I feel."

"Maybe you just need to give yourself time to figure out which feelings are temporary and which ones are permanent." Ramion put his arms around Sage's shoulders.

"I feel relieved about seeing Mama, in a bittersweet kind of way."

Twirling her hair around his fingers, he asked, "Is it going to end there? I mean, are you going to spend time with her? Let her visit . . ."

"You mean let her back in my life?" She sighed before continuing. "Probably. It's going to take time, but I think we can begin again. I want to get to know her. I can't believe it myself, but I want to reestablish a relationship with her. Does that sound strange?"

"No, baby, we all need our mothers, no matter how grown we are."

Shaking her head, Sage said, "It feels like I closed one door, only to open another."

"What do you mean?"

"I'm talking about my father."

"There's no mystery, Sage. You know something you didn't know before. It doesn't change anything."

Sage raised up and leaned over Ramion, her expression puzzled. "It changes everything. What if he didn't die? What if he's alive?"

"If he were alive, you would know. He hasn't been in touch with his mother, his sister, you, or your mother." Ramion softened his tone and affectionately stroked Sage's cheek. "You resolved the issue with your mother, it's time to move on. Get out from under the dark cloud of the past."

Sage sunk back into the bed, the truth of his words getting through. "Maybe you're right."

Ramion placed his hands on her cheeks, drew her face toward his, and kissed her on the forehead. "I don't want you to be hurt or disappointed."

Sage settled into his arms, leaning her head in the crook of his shoulder. They were quiet, savoring the moment, as the embers of their passion died down.

Sage was almost asleep when Ramion asked, "Do you want to go away? Maybe next weekend or the weekend after that? A quick trip to Florida or South Carolina?"

Yawning, Sage said, "Sounds wonderful, but remember we're going to D.C. next month."

"Oh, yes, the governor's conference."

"Dinner with the President," she said, her voice laced with excitement.

"I'm looking forward to it," Ramion said. "I have something for you."

"What?" Sage said, leaning her head on her elbow.

He reached under the bed and removed a small gift-wrapped box. "For you, baby."

"You are so sweet." She unwrapped the gift and opened the jewelry box. "It's beautiful," she said, staring at a gold pin shaped like a butterfly. Diamonds bordered the wings.

"For your collection."

Tears filled her eyes.

"Why do you cry when I'm trying to make you smile?"

She laughed softly. "It's just so beautiful, so thoughtful, so sweet."

"But there's something else. Keep going."

"My mother said that Daddy started painting again after I was born. He tried to make it as an artist, but he got discouraged and started working for a factory. After I was born he found his muse. She said he called me butterfly because I had inspired him to try again to be an artist."

"I don't doubt it," Ramion said.

"When he was painting, he would play Billie Holiday over and over. One time, Mama bought him a new album. She was sick of hearing Billie Holiday. I can't remember who it was, Sarah Vaughn, Esther Phillips, Nancy Wilson, somebody like that. She played the album and Daddy got very upset. He wouldn't paint without it."

"Maybe he couldn't paint unless he heard Billie Holiday's voice."

"Maybe," Sage said.

* * * * * * * * * * * * *

At the Governor's Mansion, Sage stepped onto the terrace, feeling the soft spring winds gust around her, blowing her hair and stirring the aroma of blooming flowers. She looked up at the cloudless powder blue sky and thought, what a beautiful day to take off work.

A glass of orange juice and a plate filled with croissants rested on the cocktail table centered in front of the antique wrought-iron furniture. Looking for the governor's wife, Sage walked over to the window and spotted Sarah kneeling beside a row of flowers.

Sage opened the terrace door leading to the gardens and went down the steps. She smelled the freshly cut grass as she walked across the lawn. "Good morning," she said when she reached Sarah.

"Hi, Sage," Sarah said. She was kneeling beside a bed of annuals, smoothing dirt around them. "I'm finished here. I was about to come up."

"They're beautiful," Sage said, also admiring the rows of perennials that Sarah had planted. "What are they?"

"Oh, they're day lilies. They grow well in the shade. The soil here is so rich and fertile, my plants are really thriving."

"I thought the gardeners took care of the flowers."

"Poo! They have their job. But I love gardening, and I wasn't about to give that up because I live in the Governor's Mansion." She took off her gloves and started back toward the terrace.

"Ah, this is your private garden," Sage said.

"Yes, and I'm very proud of it. I spend hours out here. This is the best time of year to plant . . ." She stopped and then said, "You didn't come to hear about gardening."

Sage and Sarah walked up the stairs and entered the terrace. Sage sat down on the chaise lounge.

"So how do you like being the first lady of Georgia?" Sage asked.

Sarah stood in front of the wrought-iron tea cart. She picked up a glass pitcher filled with iced tea, the color of honey, and poured herself a glass. "Would you like some?" she offered, gesturing with the pitcher.

"Sure."

"I absolutely love it," Sarah admitted, as she poured another glass of tea. "People treat us like royalty. I was always given special attention as the mayor's wife, but well, being the first lady of Georgia, it's a whole different ball game. I've attended several functions—lunches, teas, social clubs—where I'm the only woman of color, but nobody makes a big deal of it." She handed Sage the glass of tea and sat down on the black and white striped sofa.

"What about the kids?" Sage asked. "How are they adjusting?"

"Jessica and C.J. are doing fine. They complain sometimes that they don't have the freedom to play like they used to, but they're getting used to it. Now Jewel, she's always hated being in the spotlight, so I'm sure she never tells anyone that she's the governor's daughter. Jewel has always been contrary. I thought college would make her appreciate the advantages of being a politician's daughter, but it seems to have made her more resentful.

"Enough about the kids," Sarah continued. "Let's talk about our project. I'm very excited about it." She reached across the table, picking up a red file folder. "I've gone through the Mansion and come up with a list of items I want to replace," she said, handing Sage the folder.

Reading the list, Sage arched her brows. "Is this all?"

"I'm not crazy about the Federal period. It's too formal and conservative, but the artwork compliments the decor. The goal shouldn't be to drastically change the Mansion, but to enhance it, to reflect the artistic contribution of blacks in this state."

"I agree." Chuckling, Sage said, "Imagine if we completely renovated the Mansion and furnished it with nothing but black art."

"Whoa! That wouldn't just be controversial, that'd be tantamount to blasphemy. They'd throw us out of here."

"Or burn the place down."

"Exactly. There are a lot of people who wouldn't be amused."

Sage sipped her iced tea. "What about the library? There aren't any black books on the shelves."

"That's why I want to devote a whole section to black literature. I'm going to be meeting with several ladies from the Black Librarians Association on Tuesday. Hopefully they can make recommendations or refer me to other organizations."

Sage snapped her fingers. "I just got a great idea. If we can track down some of the families of the authors and painters when we officially announce the new additions, we can invite them and local artists to the Mansion for the opening reception."

"Reception?"

"I want to present this positively. So when we add the new artwork, I think a reception would be the appropriate forum, an unveiling of sorts."

"I like that," Sarah said, nodding.

"We need to be prepared to counter the negative fallout. When it becomes public that we're adding art and literature by black artists, a lot of people and organizations are going to be upset."

"Try furious," Sarah said. "I've met some of the grand ladies of Georgia. Believe me, they don't believe in cultural diversity."

"I've got a list of black art galleries we can check out. My girlfriend, Tawny, is looking for me. As a matter of fact, there's going to be a showing at the Hammonds House next week. Would you like to go?"

"Sure."

"It's Tuesday night at seven o'clock."

"Okay, I'll meet you there."

* * * * * * * * * * * * *

Shrimp and scallops sizzled in the wok, mixed with mushrooms, bamboo shoots, snap peas, and Oriental vegetables. Ramion poured soy sauce into the mixture and stirred the food around.

"Smells good," Sage said, peeking over his shoulder.

"Hmm," Ramion said, spearing a scallop with a fork. "Taste it."

"Ummh, delicious."

"It's not too soft, is it?"

"No, it's ready. Let's eat." Sage picked up a plate from the counter and handed it to Ramion. He loaded the dish with his teriyaki stir-fried meal. He turned off the wok, then went to the table.

"We have to start working on my campaign," Ramion said, tasting his food. "Pass me the soy sauce."

Sage handed him the bottle. "You read my mind. I've been thinking about it, and you're right, it is time to start working on it."

"I don't have to declare my candidacy until August 1," Ramion said.

"But you have to start laying the foundation. The earlier the better. That is, if you really want to win." Sage stuck her fork into the salad.

"Of course I want to win. Why else would I run?"

Sage shrugged. "Oh, I don't know. Publicity, name recognition, to attract new clients for your practice."

"Where is this coming from?"

"You're getting a lot of media attention. You could run for district attorney. That's a very powerful position."

"True. But that's not what I want."

"Okay, Ramion. I just want to make sure there isn't a hidden agenda that you haven't let me in on."

"No hidden agendas, baby. I'm going for the state senate seat. From there, I want to go to Congress."

"You're serious about Washington?"

"In four years."

"First you've got to get the state seat."

"Yeah, and I'm a little worried about losing key supporters. Paul Gates backed out of chairing my fund-raising committee."

"Why didn't you tell me?"

"It just never seemed the right time," Ramion said.

"I'm sorry."

"It's not your fault."

"If you were still with Edwin's law firm, you'd have Paul's support."

"That's a moot point."

"Edwinna isn't," Sage said.

"She's just blowing smoke."

"Uh huh, and where there's smoke, there's often fire."

"She's going to have to run as an independent, and she can't win on an independent ticket. The Republican candidate, Roosevelt Hartman, is retiring, and the party doesn't have anybody strong. That's why I decided to run this year instead of waiting a couple more years."

"Ramion, there isn't anything in your past that could hurt you, is there?"

"You mean, are there any skeletons in my closet?"

"Exactly, and if there are we need to have a contingency plan in case skeletons start talking." Sage had been teasing for the most part, but she noticed the troubled look on Ramion's face that had replaced the confident smile and expectant gleam in his eyes.

She laid her fork on the table, unconsciously bracing herself for the worst. "What is it?" she asked softly.

"It's about Mackie."

Sage had only seen pictures of Ramion's brother in family photo albums, and most of the pictures were of Ramion and Mackie together. But Mackie had been in jail for the past five years. How could anything to do with him hurt Ramion's future? Perplexed, she asked, "What about Mackie?"

"I represented him. He was my first case."

Sage suddenly felt her stomach knot.

"I didn't want to represent him, but Pops insisted, and Mackie didn't want anybody but me. It was a drug charge, a simple possession case, and it was the first time Mackie had ever been arrested. He should have gotten probation."

The nervous feeling in Sage's stomach intensified.

"The DA lied to me about the evidence, completely blindsiding me. I told Mackie to plead guilty, promised him he would get probation, but he wanted a trial. He was confident he'd be exonerated. So we went to court, and the undercover detective lied on the witness stand. He said the police report was wrong, that Mackie had more drugs on him, and that he had sold his niece some bad drugs that had caused her death."

"You knew nothing about this?" Sage said, disbelief in her voice.

"There was nothing in the police report, and when I talked to both of them, I took them at their word. The DA added new charges. Believe me, I learned all about cops and glory-hung prosecutors."

"What happened?"

He drank some of his soda. "The jurors were sympathetic to the detective and bought into the story about his niece. The jury found Mackie guilty, and the judge handed down a sentence more fitting for a mass murderer." Ramion blotted his mouth with a paper napkin, then crumbled it in his hand.

Sage stood up and walked around the table. She stood behind him and placed her arms around his neck, squeezing tight. "I'm sorry, honey. That had to be hard to deal with." She massaged his shoulders and then said, "But that shouldn't destroy your campaign."

Ramion tilted his head back and looked up at Sage. "Sit down, baby. That's not the end of the story."

She kissed him on the forehead before returning to her chair. "Plenty of lawyers lose cases and still get elected."

"Do they beat up the star witness?"

"What?!" Sage asked, dropping her fork on her plate with a loud bang.

"I followed the detective, Danny Gibson, and when I caught him alone in an alley, I beat the shit out of him."

Sage covered her face with her hands. "Ramion! You didn't!"

"He took my brother's life away in so many ways and because of a woman."

Confused, Sage said, "What woman?"

"He did have a niece who died from an overdose. But she OD'd on speed, not cocaine, and there was no connection between her and Mackie. The detective had a mistress, though, and when Mackie started messing with the girl, she ended her relationship with the detective. The jerk was very upset."

"Mackie was dating his girlfriend?" Sage asked, incredulous. Confused, she shook her head, "You said she was his mistress. Was the detective married?"

"Yes, but he claimed to be in love with the girl he had on the side, and then Mackie comes along. She dumps the detective for Mackie, and that's when all the trouble starts. The detective framed Mackie, and . . ."

"You beat him up?" Sage asked, finding it hard to believe that her mild-mannered fiancé could be violent. He'd once told her he used to argue his way out of fights when he was in high school.

"I kicked his ass, and I'm sorry to say it, but the bastard deserved it. As a man I was right as rain, but as an attorney, I was dead wrong."

"Did he press charges against you?"

"No, but only because I knew about some of his dirty dealings. I knew about some of the other officers in his department, too. I watched him for a week before I did anything, and I learned a lot."

"So nothing happened?"

"No, he didn't do anything, because I had the power to destroy him. But what I'm worried about is the present. He's been suspended from the police force, and he's having financial problems. He had to sell his home, and then his wife left him," Ramion said, before standing up. "With problems like his, you can never be sure what a person like him will do. That's the only snake in the closet that may come out to bite me."

* * * * * * * * * * * *

The wedding was four months away, and Sage still hadn't selected a gown. She had searched through catalogs and racks of gowns at bridal boutiques, but she wasn't satisfied with her choices. She was considering a custom gown and hoped that the designer she was about to hire would have the creativity, talent, and time to make the wedding gown she envisioned.

"Excuse me, excuse me," Sage said to a Hispanic woman bent over a sewing machine, guiding the sleeve of a wedding dress under the needle in a precise, straight line. The dark-haired woman looked up at Sage, her eyes darting about nervously. "I'm looking for the designer Xavier Xandu," Sage said, carrying her Day-Timer and an envelope stuffed with pictures of wedding gowns.

"No speak English," the woman said, pointing to the stairs at the back of the building.

Sage walked past several rows of sewing machines and bolts of fabric, heading toward the staircase. Along the way, she stopped several times to ask for directions before finally finding Xavier's office.

"I thought I'd never find you," Sage said, when she marched into Xavier Xandu's office. She towered over the fashion designer, who reminded her of one of the Keebler elves. He had a round brown face and a long fluffy beard. He was extremely short, four feet nine inches. A frayed measuring tape hung around his neck, and a pin cushion wristband was fastened on his wrist.

"Ah, Miss Kennedy," Xavier said. "I'm sorry about the miscommunication. My secretary stepped away from the office. Otherwise she would have paged me," he explained while removing bolts of fabric from a chair. "Have a seat."

Sage sat in the only chair in the crammed office.

"It's been a hectic morning," he said apologetically, closing the door to drown out the sounds of the throbbing sewing machines. "I just got a very special order. It's supposed to be confidential, but I have to tell someone. You must swear to keep it a secret," Xavier said, placing his index finger over his mouth. "Calvin Klein wants to use my designs for his spring collection."

"How wonderful," she said, wondering whether to be impressed or skeptical. "That will certainly get you some recognition."

"Big time." He spun around and raised his arms in the air, sputtering "Oh thank you, God! Thank you!" He caught Sage's bemused expression. "Excuse me, I'm just beside myself with joy." Xavier reached for the half-filled cup of coffee sitting on the edge of his cluttered desk. "Now back to reality," he said, giving Sage an assessing stare over the reading glasses perched atop his nose. "You were referred by a very good friend of mine."

"Daphine Struthers. I attended her wedding last year, and her gown was absolutely beautiful," Sage said, as her eyes traveled to the montage of pictures hanging on the walls. There were pictures and sketches of wedding gowns, evening gowns, and cocktail dresses.

"Thank you, dear. I see that you have good taste. That's a Donna Karan outfit you're wearing. Nice touch," he complimented, pointing to the butterfly diamond pin on the collar of her black and white houndstooth pantsuit.

190

"Are all those pictures your designs?"

"Yes, I won't display other people's work."

"My little sister wants to be a fashion designer," Sage said. "She'd find this place exciting."

"Bring her down. I'd love to show her around and give her tips about the big, bad fashion industry." He took a sip of coffee and made an ugly face. "Ugh, this is cold." He moved to the lone file cabinet in the corner of his small office where a coffee pot sat. "Do you want some coffee?"

"No, thank you," Sage replied. "I've been looking for a wedding gown, and I haven't found the right one. I've seen some I like. The style or the cut is right, but there's always something about them that turns me off. So here I am."

"Do you have a picture in your mind?"

"Yes, something elegant and glamorous, but not too frilly or too weddingish, if you know what I mean. I don't want traditional. I want something with some funk, some style. A gown so unique and stunning it leaves me breathless."

"Ummh," Xavier said, rubbing his beard thoughtfully. "Want kind of neckline do you like? High-collared . . ."

"Oh, don't cover me up!"

"You want cleavage," Xavier teased.

With a rueful smile, Sage said, "I brought some pictures of gowns I like." Sage opened the envelope and removed several pictures of wedding gowns torn from different bridal magazines. "I like the cut of this gown, the detailing on this one, the train on this one." She spread the pictures on his desk, pushing aside stacks of fabric samples and patterns. "Can you somehow put all of this together into one gorgeous wedding gown?"

"Let me see," Xavier said, his lips pursed together. Pointing to the floor-length sheath, he said, "I like this one. The pearls are exquisite. It looks hand sewn. How much time are we talking?"

"The wedding is in August."

"That gives me four months. I can work with that. First I'll do some sketches, and then, once we agree on the design, we'll pick out the fabric."

"How much?" Sage asked, knowing that the soon-to-be-famous Xavier was not going to be inexpensive. But she didn't care; she had to have a gown that she loved.

"That's going to depend on the fabric and the amount of hand work. I'll give you an estimate when we agree on a sketch."

"When can you have the sketches ready?"

"How about late next week?"

Sage flipped open her Day-Timer. "Okay, I'll put you down for Friday afternoon."

"That'll work. Now let me walk you out of here."

* * * * * * * * * * * * *

A foreign, acrid smell assailed Sage's nose as she entered Cameron's library. The walls were paneled in dark wood, the furniture massive— huge tufted leather chairs and dark oil paintings of wealthy families from the eighteenth century, their faces stern and unfriendly. She took a deep breath, identifying the distinctive odor of a Havana cigar and, at the same moment, she remembered the last time she had smelled the pungent scent—the day Cameron was elected governor of Georgia.

"What are we celebrating?" Sage asked as she approached the governor, sitting in front of the burning fireplace. Cameron puffed on a long brown cigar, his face reflecting contentment.

He cocked his head to the side and twisted his mouth into a relaxed smile. "I'm celebrating a moment. A rare, personal moment."

"I can come back later, Cam."

Placing the cigar in the ashtray on the end table, Cameron shook his head. "I've had my moment."

Sage eased into the leather chair next to the end table. "Are you happy with your speech?"

"Benjamin is impossible to work with. He insists on writing the damn thing."

She gave him an incredulous look. "That's what I hired him to do."

"I like to use my own words."

"I know. You can speak from the heart and sermonize when you're campaigning, but this is a different audience. You're going to be speaking to governors. Heads of states. So the speech has to be strong and powerful, creative and polished."

"What are you implying, Sage?"

"Your national image is at stake. It's an honor that you've been asked to be the keynote speaker, but you have to talk about the issues that are of concern to other governors. It can't be full of rhetoric or sound like a Sunday sermon."

"You sound like Benjamin. He's working on the draft. We agreed on the theme and the key points."

"Cameron, the conference is in three weeks," Sage chided. "You should be working on the final draft."

"Don't worry. I'll ad lib."

"That's what I'm worried about," she said, chuckling softly. "I'll talk to Benjamin tomorrow."

Cameron leaned back against the chair and picked up the cigar. "What else is going on?"

"There's a problem with Nona Corporation."

Cameron's demeanor changed from relaxed to worried. "I thought it was a done deal."

"It was, until South Carolina countered the bid."

"They've got to bring that plant here. That's a possible two hundred additional jobs in an area of the state desperate for jobs. I've told some of the community leaders that the manufacturing facility was a go. I'll look like a fool."

"Clark Anderson has arranged another meeting with Nona's president and the board of directors," Sage said. "But he doesn't want to go in empty-handed. He wants to know if you would authorize tapping into the building funds to float them a forgivable loan."

"I hate to do that, Sage. I know I'm going to need that money to entice other companies."

She rested her chin on the palm of her hand. "We may not have any other choice."

"If all else fails, tell Clark to negotiate on the price of the land," Cameron said. He put the cigar in his mouth and inhaled the bitter tobacco. "We'll give them a loan, if they provide two hundred jobs over a three-year period. But they have to give us a guarantee."

Chapter XV

It was early evening when Sage drove out of the heavy rain into her garage. As the garage door descended to the ground, she heard the door to her house open. Peering through the windshield, she saw Ava motioning for her to hurry. Sage reached across the seat to retrieve her briefcase and shopping bags, opened the car door, and climbed out.

"Come on, Sage," Ava urged. "Hurry up."

Oh, no, something was terribly wrong, Sage thought, assuming the worse. "What's the matter?"

"Something came for you. Come into the living room."

Sage placed her briefcase and shopping bags on the kitchen table and followed her sister into the living room. A large package wrapped in heavy brown paper leaned against the sofa.

"That woman from next door brought it over. She said they left it on the porch. She's a nosy woman. I always see her peeking out the window," Ava said.

"That's Ms. Odom. I guess she doesn't have anything else to do." She picked up the rectangular-shaped package. "It's from Aunt Maddie," Sage said, glancing at the return address.

"Open it," Ava urged.

"Girl, you scared me. I thought something was wrong," Sage said, tearing away the wrapping with the excitement of a child opening a Christmas present.

"Let me help," Ava volunteered, ripping away the brown paper.

They were momentarily speechless when they saw what was hidden under the brown packaging—a spectacular, gold-framed painting, an abstract depiction of a man, woman, and child connected by a heart.

"Wow," Ava said.

"It's beautiful!" Sage gushed, her eyes beaming with admiration and pride. "This is my father's work. Look at the bold lines and vivid colors."

"There's a note on the back," Ava said, removing the envelope and handing it to her sister.

Sage recognized her aunt's large expressive handwriting. The note read,

> This painting was stored along with several others in Mama's attic. Since we're moving her to a nursing home, we have to get rid of some of her belongings. Satchel painted this shortly before he went to Vietnam. I thought you should have it.

"This is a wonderful surprise," Sage said, stepping back for a fuller view of the painting. "I always wondered if Daddy had done more paintings. Mama said that he painted a lot when they first met, and then he stopped. She said she begged him to keep painting, but he was discouraged, complaining that no one would buy his work. When I was born, he started painting again."

"He was talented, that's for sure," Ava said, plopping down on the chair.

Sage ran her fingers over the painting, imagining the brush strokes. Her thoughts swirled along with the painting's circular strokes, swimming back to a past of turpentine, paint, and musk, remembering her father standing in front of an easel with a faraway look on his face and paint smeared on his face, hands, and clothes. A Billie Holiday album would be spinning on the record player, her distinctive voice filling the air. "Turn it over, Sage," he would say when the last song on the album ended. It took many tries and several scratched records before Sage learned to position the needle on the beginning edge of the 33⅓-vinyl record.

"It reminds me of Gauguin," Sage said distractedly, memories spinning in her head. "You know, if he had lived, Daddy might have been another Jacob Lawrence or Romaire Bearden."

"Or William Tolliver," Ava said, giggling mischievously.

Sage turned toward Ava, her eyebrows lifted in surprise.

"He's the only artist I know," Ava said, pointing at a Tolliver print hanging over the sofa.

"I know it's crazy, but this reminds me of the painting I bought from Tawny," Sage said. An inexplicable, eerie feeling washing through her.

"I don't think so," Ava said, shaking her head emphatically. "Let's go see." She raised up from the sofa and went into the hall.

Sage followed behind, her curiosity fully aroused.

They stood in front of the picture of three women in motion, dancing to a drum beat.

"It's the colors. The color palette is the same," Sage said. "The bright reds, greens, and purples."

"I guess," Ava said, shrugging her shoulders nonchalantly.

"So where are you going to hang it?"

"Over the sofa."

Talking to the lone figure sitting on the bench in the William Tolliver lithograph, Ava said, "Well, old man, it looks like you're going to have to find somewhere else to hang around."

Chuckling, Sage glanced at the picture. "By the way, you had another message from Kelly. She's been trying to reach you."

"I know. But I've been trying to stay away from her."

"Really?"

"All she wants to do is get high. Every day. All day. I've decided that's not what I want to do."

"I'm glad to hear that. I've been worried about you since the funeral. I've noticed that you haven't been going out much."

"I haven't felt like partying," Ava said, taking a few steps up the staircase. She stopped and then turned back around. "To tell you the truth, the last time I went out with Kelly, she took me somewhere." Ava paused, and a trace of fear glazed in her eyes. "She said it would help me forget Daddy. It was real scary, Sage. Everybody was high. I didn't like it. I made her take me out of there."

Sage noticed the fear in Ava's eyes, and wondered what her sister had seen that had frightened her. For a brief moment, she thought about asking Ava about the place, but decided she didn't want to know. "That's good."

"I miss Daddy a whole lot. I think about him every day," Ava said somberly. Leaning against the railing, she continued, "It hurts to think about him, but I don't want to forget him. But even though he's not here, I wouldn't want to do anything that would hurt him. Anyway, I've decided to go to school."

"Atlanta School of Arts?"

"Yep, I really want to be a fashion designer. Mommy is sending my sewing machine."

"I'm proud of you, girl," Sage said.

* * * * * * * * * * * * *

Ramion reached for Sage's hand as they walked out of the lobby of the historic landmark Fox Theater, where Broadway plays and musicals were staged and singers, dancers, and comedians performed. Ramion steered her through the crowd of people dressed in fancy suits and cocktail dresses.

"Didn't you just love it?" Sage asked.

"Yes, it was very powerful, very moving."

"August Wilson's plays are always so deep and spiritual. You know, the next time he has a play in New York, I'd like to go."

"Let's plan on it."

"Ramion," a squeaky voice called out.

Ramion and Sage stopped in front of the ticket counter.

"Ramion," the voice repeated. An attractive, petite brown-skinned woman with long flowing hair emerged from the crowd. "How are you?"

"I'm fine, Selena. How about you?"

"Great!" she answered with a flirtatious smile.

"I'd like you to meet my fiancée, Sage Kennedy," Ramion said. "Sage, this is Selena Tucker. She used to work at Edwin's law firm."

Selena flashed Sage a cold look. "Hello," she said, turning her eyes immediately back to Ramion. "I didn't know you were getting married."

"We're getting married in August," Ramion said. "I heard you finished law school. Where are you working?"

"Ah, I work for an attorney," Selena said, her expression carefully blank. "Umh, in Gwinnett."

"Is that right? What firm are you with?" Ramion asked. "I know a few attorneys out that way."

"Ah, there's my date," Selena said. "Gotta go." She disappeared into the crowd.

"That was strange," Sage said.

"What do you mean?"

"Didn't you see how nervous she got when you asked her who she's working for?" Sage spotted Edwinna rushing in their direction. "That damn Edwinna is coming."

With a scowl on his face, he said, "She can't possibly believe I want to talk to her."

"Ramion, Sage!" Edwinna said.

Sage refused to speak to her, communicating her disdain with hostile eyes and a tight mouth.

"Edwinna," Ramion said, his voice as warm as an icicle. I must have been crazy to date her just because she's Edwin's daughter, Ramion thought.

"I'm really getting into this election. In fact, I've discovered being a state representative has a lot of perks," Edwinna said. "Becoming an elected official is appealing to me more and more."

"Edwinna, do whatever you please," Ramion said, shrugging his shoulders. "It makes no difference to me."

"We'll see if you feel that way on election night," Edwinna taunted. Turning toward Sage, she said, "To be or not to be. I'm talking about the wedding, of course. It was just in the news that twenty percent of planned weddings end up being cancelled. Sometimes it's the bride, but most of the time the groom gets cold feet."

"That won't happen," Ramion said firmly.

"You just never know. You can find out something about the other person that you can't live with."

"Don't count on it," Sage said.

"Stranger things have happened."

Rolling her eyes at her nemesis, Sage said, "Obsession does not become you. Maybe you should see a psychiatrist."

"Let's go, baby," Ramion said, turning away from Edwinna.

"It's very rare that I don't like a person," Sage said, as they moved through the crowd milling around the entrance to the Fox. "But I can't stand that woman. She's a bitch. I don't know how you tolerated her."

Ramion squeezed Sage's hand as he said, "Neither do I. Don't let her ruin this evening. Do you still want to get something to eat?"

"I'm starving. I've got a taste for some wings."

Ramion and Sage walked from under the Fox Theater's marquee onto Peachtree Street, hand in hand. A full moon glowed brightly in the dark clear sky.

"I had to go to court for my uncle today," Ramion said.

Sage was silent.

"I understand you didn't want me to represent him because of what your stepfather did to you, but I had no choice. And by helping him, I wasn't condoning what he did."

"I know," Sage said. At her stepfather's funeral she'd realized that she was angry at Ramion for doing the very thing she wished her mother had done—stand by her.

"He's my uncle," Ramion said, stopping to gaze into Sage's eyes. "I promised my father I would defend him."

"I understand," Sage said, with no trace of anger or resentment in her eyes. "What happened?"

"They dropped the charges," Ramion said, walking down Atlanta's most famous Peachtree Street, as there were many streets tagged after the peach, Georgia's official fruit. "Hayley admitted that she lied. The D.A. still wanted to charge Uncle Walt with statutory rape, but when Hayley showed up wearing a tight dress, breasts hanging out, and heavy makeup, the judge dismissed the charges."

"Oh, Ramion, your family must be so relieved. Especially your uncle."

They walked in silence for a few minutes, listening to the street sounds—loud music from car radios, honking horns, snatches of conversations, bursts of laughter.

"I just wish I could have gotten my brother's charges dropped, or at least negotiated a shorter sentence."

"You did the best you could, honey," Sage said, squeezing Ramion's hand. "Don't keep beating yourself up."

"I feel responsible."

"You're not," Sage said. They stopped at the red light. "You played by the rules."

"That taught me the real rules."

"Mackie doesn't blame you, does he?"

"No."

"Then don't blame yourself."

* * * * * * * * * * * *

"Hi, Daddy," Edwinna said, as she planted a kiss on the top of Edwin Williamson's bald head. A founding partner in the law firm, his richly furnished corner office was decorated with expensive antiques. Flashing neon lights shone through two large picture windows. The office was spacious, but sagging bookshelves on every wall and stacks of files on the floor made the largest office in the law firm seem small.

Edwin jerked his head back. "You startled me, Winna." Spinning the tall black leather chair around, he peered at the clock on the wall. "It's late. What are you doing here? "

"I was working on a brief. Last-minute thing."

"I taught you better than that. You only do things last minute if it's strategic or at the client's request."

"I know, Daddy. I've been preoccupied."

"With what?" he said, closing a file folder. Edwin was a peculiar-looking man with small eyes, a broad nose, and a wide mouth. His most attractive feature was his voice, strong and commanding like Sidney Poitier. He spread his hands wide. "You've got my full attention."

"I want to run for the state senate."

"Winna, since when have you been interested in politics?"

Edwinna shrugged her shoulders and positioned herself on the corner of her father's desk. She wore an ankle length button-down brown dress, dark hose, and brown pumps. "Change of heart. Change in career direction."

"Okay, but what's being a state senator going to do for you? Except get you in the newspaper if you do something wrong."

Edwinna gave her father a sheepish look, knowing he would soon figure out her motives. She swung her feet back and forth, something she did as child when visiting her father at work.

"What district?" he asked, impatiently drumming his fingers on the desk.

"District 11."

"Okay, now I get it. This has nothing to do with your career. You're going after Ramion," he grinned. "Better step fast, girl, 'cause he's got a head start."

Edwinna perked up. "What do you mean?"

"He's been busy getting his campaign contributors lined up. Have you forgotten I'm head of the political action committee?"

"No, but Daddy, what organization aren't you connected with?" She leaned back, her weight resting on the palms of her hands. "Is he getting a lot of support?"

"Well, yes. He was campaigning behind the scenes early. He lost a lot of support when he resigned, but he's working hard to make up for it."

Edwinna reared her head back and rolled her eyes. "I betcha that damn Sage is behind this."

"She knows how to run a campaign."

"Well, Ramion won't have your help," Edwinna said in the retaliatory tone of a child rubbing something in.

"I do know something that will put you ahead of the game," Edwin said.

"Ooh, Daddy, what's that?"

"Roosevelt doesn't plan on running again."

"Really?"

"He's been ill, and his doctors have advised him to resign. He could have another heart attack."

"I betcha Ramion was counting on that. He knows that if Roosevelt retires and there's no strong candidate to take Roosevelt's place, he'll be elected hands down."

Edwin placed his long fingers tip to tip and smiled encouragingly. "Umh umh."

"That means," she said slowly, "I can go Republican."

"You should think carefully about that. You won't be the first to switch parties, but sometimes it can hurt you both politically and in business."

"In this case," Edwinna said, rubbing her hands together, "switching parties could mean a chance to win the election." She grinned. "I can beat Ramion."

201

Edwin patted his daughter's knee affectionately. "I'll vote for you, baby, but I'm not going to become a Republican."

* * * * * * * * * * * * *

Ramion steered his car into a new subdivision consisting of two cul-de-sacs. Signs of construction were evident in the houses in various stages of completion—some houses were shells of foundation and frame, while other houses were finished with freshly painted shutters and manicured lawns.

"The Elan," Sage said, reading the sign posted in front of the model home. There was a "be back" clock hanging in the window, its hands set at four o'clock. "Looks like the real estate agent won't be back for a while," Sage observed.

"See if there is a brochure in the mailbox," Ramion said, pointing to the black and white mailbox, designed in a trendy replication of a cow.

With an impish grin, Sage said, "Let's guess what the price range is. I say, between $200,000 and $250,000."

Ramion leaned back against the car seat and peered through the windshield at the houses. "No, these are $300,000 homes. Brick on all sides, sodded lawns . . ."

"Yes, but this subdivision is further from the highway."

"I'll bet you lunch."

"You're on," Sage said, as she opened the car door and got out of the car. She reached in the mailbox, pulled out a brochure, and shouted, "Ah ha, I was right." She climbed back inside the car and handed it to Ramion.

He scanned the brochure and shook his head. "Okay, so where do you want to eat?" Ramion reached for the zipper on Sage's blue jean jumpsuit and zipped it up a few notches to the base of her neck.

"How about the Horseradish Grill? We passed it earlier."

"Yeah, the restaurant by the park," Ramion said, and put the car in drive. He pressed his foot on the gas pedal and slowly took off. "The houses on the other end are just about done. Let's drive down there."

Ramion cruised through the upscale neighborhood, driving less than fifteen miles an hour. "Looks like they're using different builders," Ramion said, noticing the disparate architectural styles: ranch and two-story, contemporary and traditional, brick and stucco.

"I like that," Sage said. "I don't want the exact same house as my

202

neighbors." Peering through the tinted windshield, she said, "Let's look at that one," directing Ramion to a red brick house in the middle of the cul-de-sac.

"I thought you wanted stucco."

"I prefer stucco, but I like that entrance. Look at the way it curves. It's so dramatic."

Ramion parked in front of the house and removed the car keys from the ignition. The driveway was blocked off with a wet cement sign, so they walked across the grass. Ramion pushed open the slightly ajar door, and they entered the two-story foyer that featured a spiral staircase, marble floor, and a multi-tiered crystal chandelier.

"Look at this kitchen," Sage said, admiring the tall white cabinets and fruit-decorated ceramic tile that matched the wallpaper. "It's enormous. I've never seen a kitchen this big! And so many cabinets! I wonder if the bedroom closet is spacious. I need more closet space for my clothes than kitchen cabinets."

"And it has an island. Just what you wanted."

"Uh huh," Sage said, opening some of the cabinets. She tilted her head back and said, "There's a skylight over it."

"You know, I really like this open floor plan," Ramion said, as he stepped into the great room with its nine-foot vaulted ceiling and white marble-faced wood-burning fireplace with decorative mantle and gas log starter, and French doors that opened onto a deck.

"I do, too. At first I wanted separate rooms, but the more I see of this floor plan, the more I like it," Sage said.

"There's a bar in here, too."

"I didn't even see that," Sage said, moving into the bar area that included a small sink, refrigerator, and cabinets.

"What's that room?" Ramion said, pointing to the opening over the bar area of the family room. "It looks like a loft."

"Let's go find out," Sage said, following Ramion into the formal living and dining room.

Ramion pointed to the key-shaped molding that trimmed the ceiling. "I like that. It makes the room look elegant."

"Bay windows," Sage said, nodding her head as she walked through the living room into the foyer. Waving her hand, she said, "Come on, let's go upstairs." She ran her hands along the wood railing as she jetted up the spiral staircase. "I love it."

Standing at the top of the stairs, she peered through the two-story paladian window that showcased both the upstairs and downstairs halls. "Can't run around naked," Sage observed.

"Just put up some blinds," Ramion said, as he reached the top of the stairs.

"Right, Ramion. These beautiful windows were not meant to be covered up," Sage chided.

Sage turned to the right, moving down the long hall, which featured three bedrooms and a full bath. "Guest rooms and an office," Sage decided quickly as she looked in the rooms.

"Let's go see the master bedroom," Ramion said, spinning around and heading in the opposite direction.

"Wow," Sage said, as she entered the bedroom. "This is beautiful." Her attention going immediately to the tray ceiling and window seat.

"Look in here," Ramion said, swinging open the bathroom door, complete with separate garden tub and shower, his and hers marbled vanities, and gold-plated fixtures.

"Now this is a bathroom," Sage said, moving around the room and touching the fixtures. She stopped in front of a door. "I wonder what's in here." Her eyes gleamed with approval at the spacious walk-in closet with separate shelving for sweaters and blouses, skirts and pants, lingerie, long dresses, and suits. "Well, there's plenty of room for my clothes." She teased, "By the way, this is my closet."

"Maybe they have his and hers closets," he said, opening another door that revealed a toilet. "I guess we'll have to share."

"I don't mind sharing with you."

They went back into the bedroom and noticed a door on the far side of the bedroom. "Maybe this is a closet," Ramion said, reaching for the doorknob. He almost stumbled down two steps into an adjacent room.

"By the way, I'm sorry I can't make the governor's conference. This trial is going longer than I expected," Ramion said.

"That's all right. I'll tell the President you were too busy," she teased.

"This must be the room we saw from downstairs," Ramion said, looking down at the family room and kitchen below.

Sage flipped through the brochure to the page describing the house they were in. "According to the layout, this is the nursery. But I suppose you could use it as an office or something."

"A nursery is fine," Ramion said, returning to the master bedroom. "We can make babies in here."

"Babies?" Sage asked, her hands on her hips. "As in more than one?"

He gave Sage a thoughtful stare. "That's something we haven't talked about. Children."

Sage shook her head. "I'm not ready."

"Wait a minute," Ramion said, placing an arm around her shoulders. "Maybe I should be asking, do you want kids?"

"Yes, I want kids," she said in a tone that suggested the question was absurd. "I just don't want them now. I have other things I want to do first."

Ramion gave his fiancée a curious stare. "Like what?"

"Maybe start a consulting business."

He tilted his head to the side. "Oh, being Mrs. Ramion Sandidge isn't enough for you?"

"You know me better than that."

"I thought you would quit your job and stay home."

"And make cookies and have your dinner waiting when you come home," she said, an impudent look on her face.

Ramion touched the tip of her nose. "I'm joking, Sage. I used to want someone like that. Someone like my mother."

"I'm not putting your mother down, but that wouldn't work for me."

"I know, baby. It's a different generation. A different world, for that matter."

"I'll be ready to have a baby in a couple of years," Sage said, unable to imagine herself as a mother.

"I'm in no hurry either," Ramion admitted. He engulfed Sage in his arms and leisurely pressed his lips against hers. "This would be a great room to make a baby. Don't you feel it?" He tightened his embrace and kissed her again, letting his lips linger.

She smiled at him, wondering what kind of mother she would be.

"Let's try it out." With an arm around her waist, he pulled the zipper on her jumpsuit down to her waist. He circled his fingers around her breast, stroking the tips of her nipples.

"What if someone comes in?"

He kicked the door shut with his foot.

205

"If someone comes in the house, we'll hear them. We'll stop."

"You don't like to stop."

"Neither do you," Ramion said, easing Sage to the floor as his mouth covered her breast.

* * * * * * * * * * * * *

"Ramion, I've got some ideas for your campaign," Sage said, pulling a notebook from her briefcase. "Everybody always uses the promise of creating jobs or fighting crime to draw voter interest, but I think you should push the environment. Black folks may not seem to care about the environment, but if they knew that most landfills are in black neighborhoods, they might feel differently."

"That's interesting," Ramion said distractedly, not really paying attention to Sage or the basketball game playing loudly on the television in Sage's living room.

"Another thing. Your platform should center around your commitment to the community. Instead of making campaign promises, which everyone is tired of hearing, make campaign commitments. We have to come up with five major commitments that voters . . ." Sage said, stopping in mid-sentence. "Ramion, you're not listening."

Ramion finished his beer. "As usual, Sage, you have good ideas, but they may not matter much. Running for the senate may not be such a good idea. At least not at this time." He stood up and went into the kitchen.

"What do you mean?" Sage asked when he returned to the living room.

"I mean I might have to put the campaign on hold for now," he said nonchalantly. "Maybe I'll run in two years." He popped the top of another can of beer.

Sage arched a brow. She couldn't remember a time she'd seen him drink so heavily. She sat beside him on the sofa and turned down the volume on the television. "What are you talking about?"

"Remember Thomas Madison?"

"Of course, he's one of the major contributors to your campaign. He even helped solicit funds from other sources."

"Not anymore," Ramion said and took a swig of beer.

"What happened?"

"Last year Edwin and I met with him. He was one hundred percent in my corner. Now he's pulled his support."

"Why?"

Ramion didn't respond. Instead, he guzzled the rest of his beer.

"Why?" Sage repeated.

"It doesn't matter why. The point is, he's out. Changed his mind."

"It's because you're no longer with Edwin's law firm, isn't it?"

"It never crossed my mind that leaving the law firm would be the biggest mistake of my career." He crushed the can with his hand.

"Oh, so I'm a mistake," Sage said indignantly.

"I didn't say that."

"That's what you meant, Ramion. I know how important your career is to you."

"Of course it is," Ramion said defensively. "I had everything all planned and mapped out. The Georgia Legislature, the U.S. Congress. But things change."

"You know what? It's not too late," Sage said, rising to her feet. "I'm sure Edwin would welcome you back to his band of lawyers, and we know Edwinna wouldn't hesitate to take you back into her bed." She paused, unable to hide the hurt in her voice. "Is that what you want?"

Ramion hesitated. He didn't want to admit that, in fact, he regretted his decision and wished he had waited until he was elected to change law firms.

He hesitated just long enough to break Sage's heart. "Go home, Ramion," she said angrily. "And go back to her, if that's what you want!"

Chapter XVI

Sitting at her desk in the kitchen, Sage opened the bottom drawer where she stored her mail. She sorted the one-week stack of mail into several piles: bills, magazines, invitations, letters, and other. She opened her checkbook and wrote checks for various bills, then read through the rest of her mail, noting in her Day-Timer events she wanted to attend.

While putting the mail into various file folders, Sage noticed a large envelope at the bottom of the drawer. She didn't see a return address, but the handwriting on the envelope was vaguely familiar. She opened the envelope and removed a videotape.

Why isn't there a label or anything to identify the tape? Sage wondered.

She went into the living room and inserted the tape into the VCR. The images that appeared on the screen were grainy and fuzzy, but she immediately recognized the people. Ramion was kissing Edwinna, who was barely clad in a provocative negligee, his mouth covering her lips, his hands fondling her breasts.

Sage closed her eyes and grabbed her stomach. She felt as if Mike Tyson had punched her in the stomach with a knockout left hook. When Sage opened her eyes, Edwinna had unzipped his pants and taken his penis into her mouth. Sage suffered another Mike Tyson right jab in her stomach—so brutal and painful it reverberated to her heart.

The shocking video immobilized her—she was too stunned to move, too hurt to feel the tears rolling down her cheeks. She forced herself to look at the date stamp, irrefutable proof of Ramion's infidelity. Anger and despair rose bitterly to the back of her throat. She pressed the stop button on the VCR and grabbed her car keys.

* * * * * * * * * * * * *

Sage repeatedly rang Ramion's doorbell, her anger building with each passing second. When Ramion opened the door, she brushed past him. "You couldn't stand the thought of losing the election, so you went for the sure thing?"

"What are you talking about?" Ramion asked, trailing behind Sage, wondering why she was so upset.

"You haven't changed. You still reek of ambition," she fumed, standing in the middle of his great room. She pointed her index finger at Ramion. "Your career comes first—always has and always will."

"Sage, what the hell are you talking about?"

"What better way to make sure Edwinna doesn't run against you, than to go to bed with her." Sage popped herself in the head. "Gee, why didn't I think of that!"

"I haven't slept with Edwinna," he said in a clipped tone, wondering how Edwinna convinced Sage to believe her lies.

"Just answer one thing for me. Are you screwing her so she won't run against you, or are you screwing her because you want her back? Maybe you're going to go back and work for her father. Did you forget to tell me that, too?" Sage screamed.

Ramion was stunned. What the hell was she talking about? Ramion rubbed his hand across the stubble of a beard that had begun to show on his face. "I have no idea what you're talking about, Sage. I'm not going back to work for Edwin, and I definitely have not slept with Edwinna."

"You would do anything for your almighty career. You just told me two weeks ago that you regretted leaving Edwin's political connections for me."

"I never said that." He took a step toward Sage, but she backed away from him. "I was drinking that night. I apologized for what I said."

"So the apology was the real lie," Sage said.

"I have no interest in her."

"Stop lying! If you get back with Edwinna you win the election. Your career plans stay on target. Isn't that what you want?"

"No! But, I'm really getting tired of this line of questioning," Ramion said impatiently.

"Oh, so now you want to play lawyer on me. Okay, I'll make it easy for you. Go back to the security of Edwin and his daughter."

"I don't want her."

Sage's anger flared out of control. "Then why were you fucking her two weeks ago?"

Ramion looked at Sage as if she were an alien that had landed in the middle of his backyard. "I haven't touched her. If she told you that, she was lying."

"People might lie. Cameras don't."

With his jaws clenched, Ramion said, "I don't know what the hell you're talking about! I have not slept with her, and I'm getting damned sick and tired of telling you that."

"Counselor, here's exhibit one," Sage said, waving the videotape in the air. "Let the record show a videotape of your sexual liaison with Edwinna two weeks ago."

Sage threw the videotape at Ramion, almost hitting him in the face.

Blinking back tears, she tried to muffle her sobs with the back of her hand. With tears shimmering in her eyes, she said, "Let the record further show that the wedding between Sage Kennedy and Ramion Sandidge is off."

She spun around and ran out the door.

* * * * * * * * * * * *

"Excuse me," Sage said impatiently for the third time to the two clerks huddled together at a desk. She stood at the counter at the local offices of the Veterans Administration. "Can I get some service, please?" Her words were clear, her tone insistent and indignant.

"Just a minute," one of the clerks responded without looking up. Laughing sharply, the dark-skinned woman with wide hips stood up, holding a paperback book in her hand. "Whoa, girl, this stuff gets me heated up," she said, fanning herself. She shook her head, reluctantly placing the book on the table. "I'm gonna go eat my lunch."

"You better be back here at one o'clock. I got some business to take care of," said the bleached-blond, twenty-year-old black clerk.

The first woman waddled down the aisle and, without looking back said, "LaKeisha, you tripping!"

"Excuse me," Sage said, her voice sharp and haughty.

"I'm coming," the clerk said as she sauntered over to the counter. Her blond braided hair was wrapped around her head like a beehive. "What can I do for you?"

"Finally. I tried calling, but I was either put on indefinite hold or connected to a computer that couldn't give me any information."

"I'm sorry about that, but that's the way it is around here. What were you calling for?"

"I was trying to get some information about my father. He was in the Vietnam War."

"I'm sorry lady, but if you want to know about benefits, you're in the wrong place. This department doesn't handle stuff like that."

Sage gave the clerk an imperious look. "I want to know what happened to him."

"What do you mean?" the clerk asked, blowing a big bubble.

"Here's his Social Security number," Sage said, handing the clerk a piece of paper. "Tell me what's in the files. What happened to him."

"You trying to find him, huh? I never knew where my Daddy went either."

The clerk walked over to a row of computers. After trying several computers, she found one that worked. She entered her access code and keyed in a series of numbers and letters. She entered Satchel Kennedy's Social Security number and waited a few minutes for the computer to retrieve the file. She then read the information. After a few minutes, she said loudly, "I'm sorry Miss, but the computer says he dead. He was killed in the Vietnam War." The clerk paused for a minute and said, "They didn't tell your Mama?"

Sage ignored the clerk's inquisitive comment. "What's the date on the report? Were you able to access the whole file?"

"No, it just gives you certain information. If you want, I can run a search and the system will retrieve all his files."

"Yes," Sage said, nodding her head. "Run a search."

"It takes a couple of weeks. You should get something in the mail."

"Thank you," Sage said, and turned away from the counter and headed toward the door. Face it, Sage thought. He was killed in Vietnam. You just wanted to believe he was alive. Give up on your fifteen seconds of hope.

* * * * * * * * * * * * *

Sage impatiently tapped her foot as she waited in the lobby of the Waldorf Hotel for a limousine to take her back to her hotel. Awake since five o'clock, Sage's day had been extremely busy—the governor's conference, dinner at the White House, and a cocktail party.

But she was glad to be busy, glad to get away from Ramion's phone calls and claims of denial for a few days. She dreaded tomorrow, when she would return to Atlanta and face her crumbling life.

Glancing at her watch, she eased over to the concierge's desk. "Excuse me," she said, "Can you find out if the limo for Kennedy is on its way?"

The young concierge, attired in a maroon uniform and hat, said, "There's been an accident on the freeway, so he might be stuck in traffic. But I'll call and see what I can find out."

"Thank you." Pointing to the sofa across from the hotel bar, she said, "I'll be sitting over there." She held onto the railing as she trotted down the stairs.

A man spoke to her when she reached the bottom of the steps. "Hello. I'm Enrique Lopez. I work for . . ."

"Ambassador Lopez from Puerto Rico," Sage said, gazing into the blackest eyes she had ever seen, eyes that elicited a smile from her. His hair was jet black, a striking compliment to his olive complexion.

Sage extended her arm, expecting a handshake, but Enrique took Sage's hand, leaned over, and kissed it. Flattered, Sage's smile widened and she said, "I'm Sage . . ."

"Kennedy," he said, finishing her sentence. "You work for Governor Hudson."

"It's a pleasure meeting you."

"I've been waiting for this moment," he said, his grin flirtatious, "when I could meet you." He spoke with the smooth, seductive accent of South American aristocracy.

Suddenly Sage forgot how tired she was. "I guess you're glad this conference is over so you can go back home."

"Actually, it saddens me that it is over. For me, it means only that I won't be able to see you." He exuded a foreign, exotic charm.

You're a dangerous flirt, Sage thought, deciding not to fuel the situation by responding. "The conference was very informative."

"Yes, it was. Governor Hudson gave a dynamic speech."

"Yes, he did," Sage said. She glanced away, searching for the concierge, yet not finding him.

"Actually, my colleague was supposed to come, but his wife went into labor and he couldn't leave. So being single, unattached, and without family obligations, it was decided that I could come in his place." His eyes lingering on hers, Enrique added, "Lucky for me."

"Of course. How often does a person get to dine with the President of the United States?"

"Perhaps only once in a lifetime. Just like this meeting with you. Maybe it was destiny."

Sage cocked her eyebrows. "Destiny?" she repeated incredulously.

"Perhaps my colleague's bambino timed his arrival with this journey because I was destined to meet you."

"Or maybe it is simply coincidence," Sage said. His crazy logic made her wonder about the tape of Edwinna and Ramion.

"You don't believe in destiny? How unromantic. How un-American."

"How dare I be un-American?" Sage said with a teasing smile, thinking, this man could make me forget my name, maybe even Ramion.

"I don't want to rely on destiny or coincidence to see you again."

"What did you say?"

"I'd like to see you again. I don't want to leave it up to the gods of fate and chance."

"I'm flattered, Enrique," she said. "But I don't think so." To herself she thought, I'd follow you back to Puerto Rico if I thought it would help me forget Ramion.

He nodded. "I noticed the ring. You are engaged."

Pain knifed through her as she followed his gaze to her engagement ring, remembering the romantic moment when Ramion had slipped it on her finger. She still wasn't ready to face the reality of his betrayal. The past few days had been a much-needed distraction.

"Actually, I *was* engaged," Sage said, feeling a mixture of strange emotions to hear those words out loud.

"Ah, past tense. Then this *is* destiny," Enrique said with a seductive smile. "You are a single woman. From the look on your face, this breakup has been recent."

"Yes," Sage said, as images of Ramion kissing Edwinna flashed through her mind. She remembered the suffocating sensation she'd felt around her chest that had threatened to steal her heartbeat. It hovered there still.

"Let me help you forget," he said, edging closer to Sage. "I too am single, and I would very much love to have your company."

She could smell his cologne—a musky, sexy scent. I wonder if you look as good without your clothes, Sage thought. "I can't," she said, trying to deny her attraction to Enrique.

"Ah, you think you're not ready. But I've been watching you, and I know you've been watching me."

"That's because you were looking at me. It's a natural reaction."

"You were looking because you felt the same thing."

Sage would never admit he was right.

"He doesn't know how lucky he is," Enrique said. "Or how lucky he was."

Sage noticed the concierge at the hotel entrance waving at her. "My limo's here."

"Are you sure I can't change your mind? We can go anywhere you like. I have a plane at my disposal."

You know how to tempt a girl, Sage thought. "I can't," she said.

"I think you want to."

Sage didn't respond. She gazed into his dreamy eyes. She felt hypnotized by his charm.

Enrique kissed the back of her slender hand. "Let's just go into the bar over there. We'll have just one drink."

"One drink," Sage said.

Chapter XVII

A mob of reporters and cameramen swarmed around Sage like a hive of bees as she emerged from the state capitol building. Sage greeted the reporters she knew and agreed to three brief interviews. Tamara Banks, a popular reporter from the Fox network, stepped forward and signaled to the camera crew to start filming. Speaking into the microphone, Tamara asked Sage, "Do you have a statement about today's election?"

Attired in a hunter green business suit, Sage turned on her media face: head held upward, bright smile, and warm, friendly eyes. "We're happy that so many people went to the polls. Special elections don't usually draw the masses, but we appreciate the fact that people are taking time out of their busy day to vote for a new flag."

Tamara moved the microphone away from Sage and spoke into it. "The state flag has been such a controversial issue, why do you think so many voters went to the polls?"

"I believe people realize they can't stop the winds of change. So they decided to be a part of the process. We wanted our citizens to be involved. That's why we held a special election, so Georgians can be part of this history-making event."

"Are you surprised that flag B was chosen?"

"I think both designs are beautiful and special. Flag B is similar to the national flag, which is probably why it's getting the most votes."

Sage held up her hands, indicating that she wasn't going to answer any more questions. "I'm sorry, but that's all I have to say at this time."

* * * * * * * * * * * * *

Ramion spotted the license plate on the black 500 Mercedes Benz— EDWINA. He closed his eyes, as if pressing his lids tightly would erase the memory of going car shopping with Edwinna when she purchased it. He stealthily studied her movements, like an undercover detective, watching her park the car, get out with a Gucci handbag dangling from her shoulder, and reach inside the trunk to retrieve several shopping bags. He never knew a woman who could shop so much. If Edwinna wasn't bringing bags home from boutiques or department stores, she was opening boxes shipped to her condo by catalog companies.

With the coolness of a cop about to catch a thief, Ramion stepped from the shadows of the trees. "Edwinna," he said, his voice as cold as a polar bear's toenails.

"Oooh," Edwinna shrieked, her bags tumbling to the concrete. She backed away a few steps before the voice registered. "You frightened me, Ramion!"

This was the moment she had been waiting for, when he would return to her. She just wasn't sure how long she would let him think all was forgiven before she ended the relationship. That was the way it was supposed to be: Edwinna deciding the outcome of the relationship.

"Why did you send Sage that tape?" Ramion asked, his tone so hostile that Edwinna stepped back from him.

"What are you talking about?" she said, stooping down to pick up the bags she had dropped. She was reaching for the last bag, the Neiman Marcus bag that contained an Armani suit, when Ramion pressed his foot against the bag.

"You know exactly what I'm talking about."

Edwinna looked up at Ramion, her hand clasped around the handle of the bag. Ramion's foot was clearly in the way. With a sinister smile, she asked, "Did it turn her on?"

"You bitch!" he bellowed, his voice registering the suppressed rage of a caged animal. He fought the urge to kick her, to release the anguish of his anger. He breathed deeply, then slowly moved his foot from the bag.

"It hurt her little feelings to see you with me? To seeing us having a good time?" she taunted while standing up. "You remember, don't you? That's why you're here."

"Why Edwinna? Why would you do that to her?" His face was a mixture of confusion and anger. He was truly baffled by her Machiavellian ways.

"She stole you from me just when we were getting serious."

"I don't know where you got the idea that our relationship was serious. I never lied to you, Edwinna," he said impatiently. "I never told you that I love you. I never told you that we had a future together."

"You just didn't realize it. Think about it, if we were together and you still worked for Daddy, you wouldn't have to hustle to win the state senate. You would win hands down."

"That's not what we're talking about. That's not why you sent Sage a tape you had altered. That was vicious and mean, and you wonder why I ended our relationship."

"She canceled the wedding, didn't she?" she asked with a snide smile.

"It's not going to work."

"I already know that the wedding is off. She doesn't want to have anything to do with you. So tell me, without Daddy's backing and the bitch's campaign know-how, how the hell are you going to win the election?"

"I don't care about the election. I care about Sage," he said. He knew that Sage's feelings didn't mean anything to her, but her father's did. He paused, and then added. "I can't imagine that Edwin would approve of what you've done. He would be very disappointed."

"I can't imagine that you would run and tell him," she retorted, her expression changing from unconcern to worry for a few seconds.

"I don't know you at all," Ramion said disgustedly. "You're an evil, conniving woman, and I can't believe that I ever went to bed with you."

"You loved what's between my thighs, baby. That's why you're here now."

"No, I'm here to tell you to leave Sage alone. Take out your twisted hatred on me, but don't mess with Sage."

She leaned forward and said, "I'm not some little nobody that you should think you can intimidate."

"Let me tell you something, Edwinna. I don't believe in hitting

217

people, especially women. But if you bother Sage again, I will break every bone in your body." He leaned forward, pressing Edwinna against the wall. "I'm tempted to now . . . but I won't."

The venom in his voice and the viciousness in his eyes unnerved Edwinna. But she wasn't going to let him know that he had frightened her. "I got what I want," Edwinna snapped back. "I don't have you, but neither does she."

"Don't bet on it," Ramion said, before turning away.

* * * * * * * * * * * * *

Sage sorted through her CD collection, searching for something to soothe the restlessness of her spirit, the sadness in her heart. Her fingers glided down the CDs neatly stacked in a storage tower, flipping past Babyface, Kenny G, The Winans, Angela Bofill, Anita Baker, and Toni Braxton. Stopping at a TLC CD, she smiled and reminded herself to return Ava's favorite CD. Ava's taste in music was rubbing off on her, she was loathe to admit.

None of the CDs appealed to her feelings at the moment, so Sage returned to her old favorite. Billie Holiday could lift her spirit with the sassiness of the music or drain her soul with the realism of her lyrics. Billie could be an upper or a downer, depending on her emotional state. Billie Holiday's voice was familiar and was always there.

She pressed the first song on the "Best of Billie Holiday" album that was already in the disc player. Billie's sultry, sexy voice and lazy inflections in the song "Strange Fruit" filled the room.

The melody wafted through the air, the haunting lyrics scattering like dust particles in the air, present but unseen. Sage didn't hear the words, but the music seeped into her soul.

Sage turned on her computer and, while waiting for the system to boot up, searched through her briefcase for several file folders. She glanced through the folders and selected the project she wanted to work on for the evening. As she clicked the mail icon on her computer screen, she wondered if something was burning. Sage went into the kitchen and checked the stove. The burners were off, and the oven was off, too. Nothing was burning, so she decided to get something to drink before returning to her bedroom. Opening the refrigerator door, she heard Ava upstairs walking down the hall.

"Something's burning, Sage. You got something in the oven?" Ava questioned as she bounced down the stairs. When she reached the bottom of the stairs, she saw flames raging in front of the living room window. "Oh my God! The house is on fire! We're on fire!"

Sage slammed the refrigerator door closed and peeked around the corner. She saw flames billowing through the curtains. "Oh, no!" she screamed. "Let's get out of here!"

They ran into the kitchen. Ava opened the door that led to the garage and pressed the button on the garage door opener. Sage grabbed the cordless phone and ran through the garage door.

Sage dialed 911. "My house is on fire. I need the fire department!" she screamed into the phone.

"Ma'am, they're already on the way," an annoyed voice said.

Sage took a few steps to the front yard. She saw the source of the fire. It wasn't her house in flames, but a flag on a pole, burning on her front lawn.

"I don't believe this," Sage said, fear pulsing through her veins. She heard the piercing wail of sirens in the near distance.

Ava's mouth hung open. "Neither do I."

Several of their neighbors approached them. "Are you all right?" Ms. Odom, from across the street, asked.

"We're okay," Sage answered.

"No, we're scared," Ava said.

Sage didn't correct her sister, silently agreeing with Ava. The song "Strange Fruit" about black bodies hanging from Southern trees suddenly rang loudly in her ears like a clash of cymbals. She shivered as if she were caught in the middle of a snowstorm.

A fire truck and two police cars pulled in front of Sage's house. Two firefighters jumped off the truck, quickly removed the hose from the truck, and sprayed water on the burning flag. The flames were out within minutes from the powerful force of water bursting from the hose.

A uniformed police officer approached the small crowd watching the firefighters spray down the fire. "Is the owner of the house here?"

"I am," Sage said, stepping away from the crowd.

"Is anyone hurt or in need of medical assistance?" the officer asked in a strong Southern drawl.

"My sister and I were the only ones in the house," Sage said. "We weren't hurt."

"We were just scared to death," Ava said.

"I understand," the police officer said. Removing a notebook from his shirt pocket, he asked, "What is your name?"

"I'm Sage Kennedy, and this is my sister, Ava Hicks."

The stocky, red-haired, freckle-faced officer wrote their names in his small notebook. "I'm Officer Douglas. I just need to get some information."

Sage nodded. "Okay."

"Ma'am, did you see anything?"

"Just the flag burning at my window. From inside my kitchen, I thought my house was on fire."

"Did you see anybody suspicious lurking around?"

"I didn't even think to look," Sage said, noticing that her entire neighborhood seemed to be gathered in front of her house. She then saw a satellite dish perched on top of a white van driving toward them. "I see something I don't want to see."

The officer looked up and nodded. "I hate the media." He turned to Ava. "What about you? Did you see anything?"

"No," Ava said, shaking her head. "Nothing."

"Three people called in the fire. I need to talk to them," the officer said, peering into the crowd.

"I did," Ms. Odom said, moving toward the officer.

"So did I," Mrs. Peterson said.

The crowd in front of Sage's house grew as reporters and camera crews arrived on the scene. As quickly as the flames were doused, the camera crews prepared their equipment and the reporters positioned microphones to capture the moment. The reporters fired questions at Sage and Ava.

"Were you or anyone else hurt?"

"Have you received threats?"

"Who did it?"

"What flag did they burn?"

"Did they leave a note or some type of message?"

Sage didn't respond to individual questions, but made a brief statement. "I'm fine. I wasn't hurt, nor was my sister. But I'm angry and shocked that someone would come to my home and do something like this. Things have changed around us, but what some people feel in their hearts has not. That frightens me." She stopped before fully expressing her outrage. "That's all I have to say at this time."

The fire trucks and media vans were driving away when Ramion pulled into her driveway. He was relieved to see Sage standing near her front door, but when he saw the ashes and the singed remnants of the new flag, he felt the indignant, righteous anger he had felt when his brother was unfairly sentenced. He wanted to physically hurt whoever had violated Sage's sense of security.

"Baby, are you all right?" he asked, putting his arms around her.

"I'm fine," she said, stepping back from his embrace. "I wasn't hurt, so please leave."

Her curt response surprised him. "I'm not leaving until I know you're okay."

"I said I'm fine, Ramion. I'm not your responsibility. You don't have to worry about me. I'm just fine."

"You look upset," he said, seeing through her facade of indifference.

"Of course I'm upset. I'm angry and tired, and right now I just want to be left alone."

"Do they know who did this?"

"I don't know," Sage said, shaking her head. "I don't think so. I heard them say they were going to canvas the neighborhood to see if anybody saw or heard anything."

Ramion noticed a police officer talking to a woman who lived several doors down from Sage's house. "Did you tell them about the threats you've been getting?"

"I didn't bring it up, but the FBI knows about it."

"They need to treat this more seriously. You do, too."

"I'm not laughing," she said reproachfully, feeling the dull pain of a headache. She wanted to take a pain reliever to prevent the dull ache from turning into a throbbing migraine.

"I'm going to talk to the officers and . . ."

"No," Sage said, stepping in front of him. "I don't want you involved. This doesn't concern you."

Ramion looked at her strangely, unable to believe that she could so easily cut him out of her life. "I care what happens to you, Sage. I love you, baby. I don't want anything to happen to you."

"I can take care of myself, Ramion. I told you before, I don't want to see you. Don't call me, don't . . ."

He placed his hand on her shoulder and said, "I did not sleep with Edwinna."

She stared at him for a moment, the sincerity of his words penetrating her resistance, but she would not let down her defenses. "I know what I saw, and I don't want to discuss it. You made your decision to work for Edwin. You're certainly not going to have us both. Now leave me alone," she said. The words that escaped from her lips were not spoken from her heart.

"What are you talking about?"

"I saw you talking to Edwin a couple of weeks ago. Then the tape with Edwinna."

"I'm not going back to work for him. Sage, we need to talk—I mean really talk."

"There's nothing to talk about. Our relationship is over. The wedding is off. So please leave me alone." She turned away and headed to her front door.

Ramion followed behind her. "I'm not leaving until I know you're safe."

"Ava's here."

"No, you need protection from . . ."

Officer Douglas interrupted them. "Excuse me, Ms. Kennedy."

"Yes?"

"I've just spoken with the captain. He's assigning an officer to stay with you and your sister for the night."

Sage peered at Ramion, her head throbbing mercilessly. "So now you don't have to worry about us."

"What about tomorrow?" Ramion asked. "Until the perp is caught, she needs to be protected."

"The captain is looking into twenty-four hour protection. He's got to make some scheduling changes."

"Now will you leave?" Sage asked impatiently.

Ramion stared into Sage's eyes. He saw the anger in her eyes, sensed the fear in her mind, and felt the pain in her heart. He wanted to hold her, make love to her, erase all her fears and doubts.

"All right," he said. "But not without telling you that I love you." He leaned down and lightly pressed his lips against hers. He didn't care that the officer heard him.

Ramion turned around and slowly walked to his car. Leaving was the last thing he wanted to do. Sage needed him, but a door of deception stood between them, thanks to Edwinna's wicked machinations. While driving away, he regretted that he hadn't slapped Edwinna for creating the tormented, untrusting look swirling in Sage's eyes. His mind replayed the earlier confrontation with Edwinna, his anger escalating while driving on the interstate. He pressed down on the gas, accelerating his speed to eighty miles per hour. He was tempted to return to Edwinna's house. His hands gripped the steering wheel tightly, his mind wishing the steering wheel was Edwinna's neck. He slowed as he neared the exit that would lead to Edwinna's house and steered into the exit lane.

But the consequences of his actions prevailed. He passed her exit, breathing a sigh of relief. Ramion knew if he had confronted Edwinna at that moment, she would have felt the full impact of his fury against her and whoever had burned the flag in Sage's yard. He would have ended up behind bars.

* * * * * * * * * * * * *

A butler greeted Sage as she stepped into a foyer that was five times the size of her house. "Good evening, Miss Kennedy. I'll tell Mr. Lincoln you are here." The expressionless butler pointed to a settee with his white-gloved hand. Sage sat down, awed by the richness of her surroundings: marble floor, carved beams, gilded chandeliers of ecclesiastical design, and antique furnishings. The grey-haired, elderly butler reminded Sage of the ushers in a church, with his white gloves, shuffling walk, and humble demeanor.

Twenty minutes had passed when Sage flicked her wrist to check the time. She'd begun to wonder whether the mysterious invitation to Mr. Lincoln's home was some sort of hoax.

"Mr. Lincoln will see you now," the butler announced gravely.

Sage stood up and followed the butler through a pair of heavy carved wooden doors, like those of a cathedral, and through a series of rooms, each one larger and more elaborately furnished than the one before. Sage had a confused impression of rich Oriental carpets, marble fireplaces, gold-framed paintings, tapestries, fresh flowers, and antique furniture. This house should be a museum, Sage thought.

The butler escorted Sage into the bedroom of Oliver Lincoln. The first thing she noticed about the room was the smell—the pervading odor of body fluids, medication, and disinfectant hung in the air like a cloud.

The frail old man sat upright in bed, propped up by pillows. A nurse sat nearby, her expression gloomy and stern.

"Hello, Miss Kennedy," Mr. Lincoln spoke in ragged breaths as if he had just completed the Peachtree Road Race. A warm toothless smile traced the edges of his mouth, and his eighty-year-old eyes sparkled. The once-handsome face had sunken in; the only indication of his youth was the fire in his eyes. Time had taken his color, darkening his skin from the tan brown of his youth to the mahogany brown of his declining years.

"Hello, sir," Sage said softly, unnerved by the man's slight body and sickly appearance, a stark contrast to his reputation as a powerful and influential man who wielded his wealth like a Greek god. From the time Sage arrived in Atlanta she had heard the name Mr. Lincoln, always spoken reverently. He had founded a life insurance company in the 1940s, and his business prowess grew as he expanded into peanut farming and timberland. He was a reclusive man who had used his wealth and power to help elect Atlanta's first black mayor. But as his health weakened, so had his behind-the-scenes stakehold in Atlanta's business and political scene.

"I'm honored to meet you," Sage said.

"I can't hear you," Mr. Lincoln said weakly, his thin arms beckoning her closer.

Sage edged nearer, but Oliver Lincoln continued to wave his bony hand until she stood right next to the bed. "It's beautiful," Sage said, remarking on the hand-carved, four-poster mahogany bed. She couldn't resist the urge to touch the figures of African warriors, animals, and masks engraved on the solid wood headboard.

"I know you're not talking about me," Oliver said, his sarcastic laughter a strain on his voice. "I had it custom made. Years ago. As you can see, I'm a collector of fine art."

"I see," Sage said, peering at the paintings hanging on the wall in expensive gold frames. She didn't have to stand in front of the paintings to know that they were all original works.

"That's my favorite," Lincoln said, pointing to a Henry Ossawa Tanner painting.

"My father was a painter. He painted abstracts like Hale Woodruff." Sage paused for moment. "But he was killed in Vietnam."

Mr. Lincoln acknowledged her comment with a slight nod of his head. "I had my favorite paintings brought in here," he said, sputtering his words with a raspy cough. "So I can look at them from this bed. I can't get around much." His coughing caused him to wheeze and gulp for air.

The nurse shot Sage a piercing, reprimanding glare and stepped over to the bed to place an oxygen mask over her patient's nose and mouth. Oliver Lincoln stared into Sage's face, his eyes blistering with pride and anger over his condition.

Sage turned away, focusing on the numerous paintings. She noticed the French doors that opened onto a small, glassed-in terrace, full of bright abstract paintings and flowers.

"You're a beautiful young lady," Oliver Lincoln said suddenly, bolding raking her body with his eyes. The tight-fitting knit dress displayed Sage's figure much like a gilt frame on a beautiful painting.

"Thank you, sir," Sage said, with a reticent smile.

He stared at her for several minutes, as if a young beautiful woman were a rare sight for his weary eyes. "If I were thirty years younger."

Tilting her head, she gave Mr. Lincoln a lingering gaze. "No, but if I were thirty years older."

"Imagine that. Ha! Ha! Ha! Of course, that's all I can do is imagine. That's all I got working for me—my imagination." He coughed again and then said, "On a more serious note, you were on television a couple of days ago. Somebody burned a flag in your front yard."

"Yes," Sage said.

"Do they have any idea who did it?"

"I haven't been told if they do," Sage said. She paused a moment before adding, "Both Cameron and I have received threats about the flag. Security has been increased. I have a bodyguard until they find out about the flag."

"What about the bombing of Hudson's headquarters? Do they have any leads?"

"No. They seem to think they'll be able to find out who burned the flag before they know who planted the bomb." With a wry smile, she said, "You really follow the news."

"That's all I have to do. But that's not why I wanted to see you,

225

Sage. I asked you to come because I heard you were looking for black paintings for the Governor's Mansion."

Sage cocked her eyebrows. "How did you hear that?"

"Just because I'm a sick old man don't mean I'm completely in the dark. I don't keep up with business or politics anymore; it's bad for my health. I let my son run my businesses. I hope he don't run them into the ground." He stopped, his eyes a little confused, as if he'd forgotten what he wanted to say. "But art is my passion," he said, unable to keep his eyes off Sage's cleavage. "I am a passionate man."

Sage shook her head at the man's boldness, though she wasn't embarrassed or offended. She met the old man's stare with a teasing, flirty smile.

"Do you remember meeting Austin Gallager?"

"Yes," Sage said. "I met him at the Hammonds House a couple of weeks ago."

"He's one of my buyers. He told me you were looking for paintings by black artists after the Civil War."

"Yes!" she said enthusiastically, understanding for the first time why she had been summoned to see him. "He was very interesting to talk to, very knowledgeable about black art and artists, especially from around the turn of the century."

"That's why I hired him."

"I intend to, shall we say, enhance the art collection at the Governor's Mansion." She stopped and waited for the octogenarian to stop coughing. "Right now, there aren't any paintings by black artists or sculptures, not even books by blacks."

"I have an extensive collection of post-Civil War pieces. You'd be surprised at the technique and style of artists from that period."

Sage could barely contain her excitement. "I'd love to see your collection," she gushed.

"Jeb will show you. He'll take you to the library. You're welcome to take whatever you like."

Sage stepped back, stunned by the gentleman's generosity. "Thank you so much, Mr. Lincoln!" She was struck with the urge to kiss the old man and went with the feeling. She bent over and kissed him lightly on the lips.

The old man smiled, pleasure shining in his eyes.

"Mr. Lincoln, you need to rest now," the nurse said after Sage left.

She placed her hand around Lincoln's bony wrist to check his pulse, but he flung her hand away.

"Not now. Get Jeb up here. I want him to get Ted Davidson on the phone. He's with the FBI. I believe his number is 555-3298. Just in case I'm wrong, tell Jeb to get my phone book."

"Mr. Lincoln. It's time for your medicine," said the nurse, scowling her disapproval. "You really should rest."

"No, I want to know what they're doing about that bombing. They need to find the person or persons who would hurt someone like her."

Chapter XVIII

Staring at her engagement ring, Sage picked up the telephone to call the wedding consultant and cancel her wedding arrangements. She dialed the number and hung up after the first ring. "I'll do it later," she thought. She'd attempted to call the wedding consultant several times, but had always hung up before anyone answered. Even though she knew she would never forgive Ramion for sleeping with Edwinna, she wasn't ready to make the phone call that would unravel her life.

Sage avoided contact with Ramion. She refused to take his calls at work or at home. Ramion's voice made her heart tremble. She ignored the doorbell when he came to her house, refusing even to look out the window. She didn't want to see him; her eyes would mist and her stomach quiver. She didn't want to read his cards or letters; his words would sear her soul.

Breathing deeply, Sage forced herself to concentrate on preparations for an upcoming visit by a foreign ambassador. She was writing a note to herself to find a book on the country's customs when Marika entered her office, holding a vase filled with a dozen long-stemmed roses. "These flowers were just delivered," Marika said meekly.

Marika was concerned about Sage's distracted, erratic behavior of the past week. She'd surmised that Sage had broken up with Ramion, but they didn't discuss it. Marika was tempted to ask what happened, but it wasn't her place to pry.

"Send them back," Sage said, assuming the flowers had been sent by Ramion.

"I think you should read the card," Marika said.

"I'm in no mood for games," Sage said, irritation in her voice. She looked at Marika the way a mother looks at a child who has misbehaved. Sage snatched the card from the vase, but a faint smile curled her lip when she saw Enrique's name.

"I'll keep them."

Marika was intrigued and dying to know who they were from, though she didn't dare ask. "Should I bring the other ones in, too?"

"There are more?" Sage asked, her brows raised.

"Twelve dozen in all. I don't know where we're going to put them," Marika said, wondering if this explained Sage's breakup with Ramion.

"Excuse me," Ramion said, tapping lightly on the door.

Sage felt the blood in her heart coagulate. She looked guiltily at Ramion, as if he had caught her in bed with Enrique instead of holding a card.

"Marika, I'd like to talk to Sage alone," he said, his tone authoritative and commanding.

Marika left the flowers on the corner of Sage's desk and quickly moved out of the office. She resisted the temptation to stand by the door and listen to their conversation.

Ramion walked over to Sage's desk. The flowers stopped him from kissing her down to the floor and making love to her right in her office.

There was an uncomfortable silence as they stared at each other, waiting to see who would speak first.

Who sent those damned flowers, Ramion wondered.

Why'd you have to sleep with her, Sage thought. There's no way we can return to what we had.

Staring at the flowers, Ramion felt his emotions change from those of a man vindicated by truth to those of a man deceived by love. "It's only been two weeks and you already have someone?" Ramion asked.

"At least I haven't done anything under false pretenses. I didn't pretend one thing and do another."

"I wasn't unfaithful to you. I did not sleep with Edwinna."

She pierced him with her angry eyes. "A moving picture is worth a thousand stabs in my heart."

"She had the tape doctored," Ramion explained. "It wasn't an original tape."

With her palms flat against the desk, she leaned forward. "Why don't you admit that you went back to her to keep your political career on track? Don't play me crazy, Ramion, and try to convince me that I didn't see what I did. Cameras don't lie."

"They do if it's a fake."

"You expect me to believe that?"

"I would hope you'd trust me. I had the tape examined by experts. The same thing I would do for a client if I wanted to challenge the evidence. The lab report verifies my explanation—the tape was duplicated and recorded on a different date to create a new date stamp. Edwinna had it rerecorded."

"Let me see the report," Sage said skeptically.

Ramion reached inside his jacket pocket, retrieved the envelope, and placed the report on her desk. "Considering that you've found someone else, I guess it really doesn't matter now."

"It matters," Sage said, staring into the charcoal eyes that had penetrated her soul.

"When I was seeing Edwinna, she apparently had a video camera on one time when we were together." He lowered his voice, embarrassed to discuss his past sexual relationship with Edwinna. "I didn't realize it at first, but when I saw that the camera was on, I made her turn the damn thing off. I would never do anything like that. I know how easy it would be for it to get in the wrong hands and come back to haunt me."

"A week before an election." Sage quickly read through the report. Her heart soared after reading the first sentence about the duplication. Relief turned into anger when she thought about Edwinna's vicious machinations to stop them from getting married and then remembered her odd comments about last-minute wedding cancellations.

The door suddenly swung open and Enrique sauntered into Sage's office. "I see you got the flowers," he said, smiling seductively.

Never expecting to see him again, Sage was dumbfounded.

With confident grace, Enrique eased over to Sage's desk. "This is my way of letting you know how much I enjoyed our evening together."

"We had one drink in the hotel lobby," Sage said, catching Ramion's confused expression. "Let me introduce you to Ramion Sandidge. Ramion, this is Enrique Lopez."

"I'm her fiancé," Ramion said with a hostile look.

"Ah, the ex-fiancé."

Ramion's beeper sounded. "I'm late for court. That's probably Judge Perkins." He looked at the number displayed on the beeper and said, "I've got to go." He whisked past Enrique to stand next to Sage. "I'll talk to you tonight, baby," he said, softly kissing her on the lips. He whispered into her ear, "I love you."

Turning to Enrique, he said, "We *are* getting married."

＊ ＊ ＊ ＊ ＊ ＊ ＊ ＊ ＊ ＊ ＊ ＊ ＊

Sage sat on the bed reading a book, but the words were a hodge-podge of letters. The television was on, but she wasn't paying attention to the comedy show, although she could use some laughter. The television didn't capture her attention, nor did the legal thriller opened on her lap, her thoughts straying to Ramion. She wondered if the two weeks they'd been apart had damaged their relationship.

Hearing a car pull into the driveway, Sage peeked out the bedroom window and spotted the police car parked in front of her house, a few feet from Ramion's car. By the time he rang the doorbell, she had opened the door for him. He greeted her with a kiss, came into the house, and followed her into the kitchen.

"I'm glad the police are still watching over you. Any suspects?"

"No."

"Do they think whoever burned the flag is also responsible for the bombing?"

"The FBI thinks it was two different types of people. The profiles don't match."

She was about to open the refrigerator when Ramion pressed her against the door and kissed her again, though this time with the zeal and passion of a man denied too long.

"I'm sorry Edwinna hurt you. I went to see her and told her to leave you alone."

"I hate her, Ramion. I just want her to stay out of our lives. Why can't she move on?"

"I don't know. She knows now that whatever she thought we had was completely destroyed when she sent you that tape. I'm very sorry that you saw us like that." His hands on her cheeks, he said, "I want you to know I would never be unfaithful to you. I love you too much."

Ramion kept his arms around her, reveling in the closeness of her body, the scent of her perfume, her very presence.

"I love you, too," Sage said, gazing into his eyes, reassured by the familiar feelings that stirred with his touch. She hadn't realized how much she had missed him and how much she needed him to make love to her.

"Is Ava home?" Ramion asked, wanting to tear off her nightgown and make love to her right there on the kitchen floor.

"No."

"Sage, there is one thing I need to know. I haven't been unfaithful to you, but have you been faithful to me?"

"Of course," Sage answered, moving away from the refrigerator to stand next to the kitchen table.

"Why did he send you those flowers?"

"I suppose he wanted me."

"Why did you tell him you weren't engaged?"

"I wasn't at the time," Sage said pointedly.

"And you were ready to find someone else right away?"

"I was in a daze, Ramion," she said. "That damn tape kept replaying in my mind. But meeting someone was the last thing on my mind."

"So what happened?"

"We had a couple of drinks."

"And?"

"That's all there is to it."

"There must be more. Did you go out with him?"

"No."

"Did you have dinner with him?"

"No."

Ramion stared at her, his dark eyes questioning. "Why did he send all those flowers?"

Sage shrugged her shoulders and sat down at the kitchen table. "I already told you. I met him on the last day of the conference. We had some drinks, end of story."

"So how did he know where you were from? Where you worked?"

"He knew I worked for Governor Hudson," she said flippantly. "He knew who I was when he introduced himself to me."

"And did you know who he was?"

"Of course I did. It's my job to know who's who," she said, her tone impatient.

"What did you tell him after I left?"

"Stop drilling me. I told him we were going to work things out and he left. Now you know how I feel about Edwinna."

He crossed his arms over his chest. "That's different."

"Enrique is a stranger to me. But you were involved with Edwinna. You slept with her. You had feelings for her."

"The operative word is *had*."

She pointed her finger into his chest. "The point is, you're jealous."

He held up his hands in mock surrender. "Okay, I'll admit it. Guilty as charged," he said. "I'm jealous. I can't stand the thought of you with anybody else." He turned her chair around to face him. "Oh, how I've missed you." He slipped her nightgown off her shoulders, kissing her lips, neck, shoulders, breasts, stomach, until he worked his way down to her thighs. She reared back, her eyes closed, realizing just how much she missed this sensual feeling.

"Open them," he said.

She spread her legs, and Ramion buried his face.

* * * * * * * * * * * * *

Residents, community and religious leaders, and business owners convened at a high school gymnasium to hear Ramion officially announce his bid for the state senate seat. The media was on hand to report Ramion's foray into politics.

"In closing, I'd like to say that it's time, time that we empower our communities. To make them the thriving areas they once were, we must be environmentally conscious, economically responsible, and educationally responsive," Ramion said, speaking into the microphone. With his hands resting on the podium, he addressed the audience, "I stand before you committed to empowering your communities, to empowering your neighborhoods, your homes, and your lives. As state representative for this district, I will help you do that. That's my commitment to you."

Ramion's campaign commitment drew a boisterous response from the residents of District 11.

"Congratulations, son," Raymond said, affectionately patting Ramion on the back. "You gave a dynamite speech."

"Thanks, Pops." Ramion loosened the multistriped tie around his neck and said, "I thought those reporters were never going to leave."

"They like you. They respect you. It's good to have them on your side."

"For now they are. The moment something goes wrong, they'll go after me like sharks on a trail of blood."

"You have nothing to worry about."

"Just getting elected," Ramion said, with a light laugh.

"Boy, I've already told my golfing buddies about you. They promised to vote for you."

"Thanks, Pops."

Chapter XIX

"Ooh, it's gorgeous!" Ava shrieked excitedly when Sage emerged from the dressing room wearing her wedding gown.

Sage slowly turned around, careful to hold up the elaborately designed train.

"I mean, Sage, it's on. It's elegant and sophisticated." Giggling, she added, "It's crazysexycool."

"A TLC fan," Xavier said.

"Those are my girls!" Ava said.

Sage stood in front of the mirror, nervous with anticipation. When she put on the gown, the reality of her impending wedding hit her. She was going to marry Ramion Sandidge in the Governor's Mansion. Her stomach was suddenly jittery.

Now, standing before the mirror, she closed her eyes. She was suddenly afraid of being disappointed again. The last time she met with Xavier, she had regretted her decision to have a custom-designed gown. When Xavier saw Sage's face drop with disappointment like a wilted flower, he promised to redesign the gown.

Slowly she opened her eyes. This time, her face was as vibrant as a flower blooming in spring. A happy smile spread across her face when she saw the gown.

"It's beautiful," Sage uttered breathlessly. "This is it, Xavier."

With his hand draped across his forehead, Xavier said dramatically, "Sage, I'm so glad you like it. I was getting very worried. I didn't want you to be unhappy."

"You don't have to be worried about that now," Ava said, straddling a chair. "Look at her face. I've never seen her look so happy. I mean, she looks like she won the lottery or something."

"Oh, I won more than the lottery," Sage said, spinning around to get a side view in the three-way mirror. "I hit the jackpot when I met Ramion," Sage said, mostly to herself, thinking how she almost lost Ramion to Edwinna's devious play.

"Right," Ava said sarcastically, twisting her wrist. "Like you ever had a problem finding a man."

"It hasn't been easy, girl. It's hard finding a man you can love and who loves you back with the same depth."

"I just hope your luck rubs off on me. All the men in my life dogged me," Ava complained.

"I can't imagine that Ava," Xavier said. "They just don't know a treasure when they see one."

"That's sweet," Ava said with a pleased grin. "You're right, some men don't know a diamond from a cubic zirconia, and if they can't tell the difference, who needs them."

"That's the spirit," Xavier winked and turned back to Sage. "If this is really what you want, all I have to do is put on the finishing touches—hem the sleeves, sew on the pearls, stitch the bodice."

Her arms extended at her sides, Sage declared joyfully, "This is it!"

"Yeah, it's perfect," Ava agreed.

"I'm going to get out of it," Sage said, moving toward the dressing room. "I'll be right back."

"The wedding is going to be live, Xavier, so live," Ava said with the excitement of an expectant sister of the bride. "I can't wait."

* * * * * * * * * * * * *

Sage opened the door to her kitchen and was instantly overwhelmed by the smell of food cooking. "Ava?" she called out curiously. It was the first time she ever smelled anything cooking. Ava was the queen of fast food, never showing the faintest interest in cooking.

236

After placing her purse and briefcase on the kitchen table, Sage opened the pots and casserole dishes that were sitting on the stove: fried chicken, macaroni and cheese, cabbage, and candied yams. She peeked inside the oven and saw cornbread baking in a cast iron skillet. The sight and smell of a home-cooked meal made Sage's stomach growl.

"Ava!" she yelled up the stairs. "I know you didn't make this food."

Sage walked over to the kitchen desk and sorted through her mail. "Finally," she said, when she saw the letter from the Veteran's Administration. She tore open the envelope and read a customized form letter that told her no more than what she already knew. Her father was killed in action and, even though his body was never found, he wasn't considered missing.

Thanks for nothing, Sage thought, as she put the letter back into the envelope. "There's nothing more I can do," she said out loud to herself.

Sage looked up when she heard footsteps on the stairs. "I know you didn't cook this feast, Ava. You wouldn't know where to begin."

"You got that right! I didn't," Ava said as she reached the bottom of the steps. "But Mama did. Surprise!"

Audra came from behind Ava, her face a mixture of uncertainty and anticipation. She greeted Sage with a healthy hug. "Didn't expect to see me so soon?"

"No, Mama, I didn't." Sage was silent for a moment, staring dazedly at her mother looking so different from when she'd seen her at the funeral. Grief had settled into permanent sadness in her eyes.

"I made your favorite dinner," Audra said. "At least what you liked when you were a little girl."

"I still love fried chicken. I can't remember the last time I had some that wasn't from the store."

"It was my idea, Sage," Ava said.

"Dinner?"

"No. Mama," Ava said. "It was my idea to have Mama come down. She's been itching to visit you for years, so I said why not now. I had to talk her into it. She was very reluctant."

"I didn't want to intrude, Sage," Audra said hesitantly. She was casually dressed in a navy knit pants outfit. "I know you're busy planning your wedding and working for the governor."

"And they're looking for a house," Ava said. "You should see some of the places they've looked at. They're awesome! Jacuzzi, spiral staircase, the works."

"Speaking of Ramion," Audra said, moving past Sage to the stove. "Would you like to invite him over for dinner? I made plenty."

"Ramion's working late. He's starting a new trial tomorrow."

"I see. Well, I hope my being here isn't a problem," Audra said, sifting red pepper into the pot of cabbage. "I can help with your wedding plans."

Finding her mother in her house was as unexpected as a visit by the Publisher's Clearinghouse prize patrol. Not only was Sage surprised to see her mother, but she was surprised at her own reaction. Instead of anger, she felt the melodic peace of the ocean after a raging storm. "It's okay, Mama," Sage said, her smile warm. "You're welcome to stay."

Ava clapped her hands. "Goodie. I'm glad that's all worked out. I'm going to set the table," she said as she removed silverware from a drawer.

"I'm going to change clothes," Sage said and headed toward her bedroom, then she suddenly turned to face Audra.

"Mama, why didn't you ever tell me that Daddy's body was never found?"

Audra closed the lid on the pot. "You were too young at the time, and then it never seemed like the right time to bring it up. You grieved so hard for him. We both did. And when you seemed finally to be getting over it, I didn't want to open a wound."

"I never got over losing him, Mama," Sage said, her voice laced with hurt. "I thought about Daddy a lot, especially as a teenager. I wished he was around to protect me."

Audra knew what Sage meant by that comment, that if Satchel had lived she wouldn't have been raped. Audra busied herself at the kitchen stove, turning on the gas, opening the pots, stirring the food, adding seasoning, and tasting.

Sage pursued the topic. "I have a letter here from the VA."

The mention of the VA caught Audra's attention. She stopped stirring the cabbage and looked over at Sage. "Why would the VA write you?"

"I tried to find out if Daddy's body was ever found."

"Oh, they told me he was in a village that was bombed. The entire village was wiped out. There were few survivors. I always wondered why they would bomb a village with innocent women and children, but I never really questioned them. There were all kinds of tragic stories in that war."

"Who bombed whom? And why would the soldiers be in the village?" Sage probed.

"I don't know," Audra said, shrugging. "I really don't know."

"You don't remember them telling you anything about the circumstances surrounding his death. What if he really didn't die?"

"Come on, Sage," Ava interrupted. "If your father is alive, where has he been all these years? Why didn't he ever get in touch with his family?"

"They found his dog tags," Audra said.

"But not his body," Sage said.

"Sage, you tripping girl," Ava said. "He was killed in the war."

Sage was quiet for a few minutes. "You're right."

"Ava told me about some nut burning a flag in your yard," Audra said in a concerned voice. "Have they caught the person?"

"No," Sage said. She had quickly grown tired of having a bodyguard. "Not yet, anyway. They're seriously investigating it. They've got a lead from some of the neighbors."

"Do you still have protection?" Audra asked.

"Yes, the police officer is outside, but I can't wait until this is all over." Changing subjects, Sage asked Audra, "Did you see the painting Aunt Maddie sent me?"

"I remember that painting. Satchel was very good. I always thought he could have been a great painter," Audra said. "Your butterfly collection is beautiful. I've never seen so many different kinds of butterflies. I'm amazed that you remembered."

"That's all I really have of Daddy. Memories."

* * * * * * * * * * * * *

"Hello," Savannah said when she walked into Edwinna's office. "I was in . . ." Savannah stopped talking when she realized that Edwinna was on the phone and took a seat across from her friend's desk.

Edwinna nodded and held up a finger to indicate she would be off the phone shortly. Edwinna's office was ultra modern, with large contemporary paintings, rosewood furniture, and a round glass conference table.

Savannah picked up the *Wall Street Journal* sitting on the corner of Edwinna's desk and started reading the newspaper.

"What brings you downtown?" Edwinna said when she hung up the telephone five minutes later.

"Danielle had a dentist appointment."

"My godchild is here, and she hasn't come in to say hello?" Edwinna teased.

"I guess the fish are more important. She's in the waiting room, looking at the aquarium. She claims there are more fish in the tank. She says there were forty-eight fish the last time we were here."

Edwinna chuckled. "I wouldn't know. I take it you got my message."

"Yes, girl, you sounded like a mad woman," Savannah chided. "I should have made a copy and sent it to your clients."

Edwinna narrowed her eyes at Savannah, ignoring her smart remark. "I just couldn't believe that Ramion would announce his candidacy so soon. The election is still months away. He took everybody by surprise."

"Maybe that will be to his advantage."

"I have to admit it was a smart move." Edwinna picked up her onyx and pearl earring and clipped it onto her left earlobe.

Savannah arched an eyebrow. "Giving Ramion a compliment?"

"No! I'm just acknowledging that it was a good offensive move. Unusual because most lawyers think defensively."

"So are you going to run against him?" Savannah asked, crossing her legs.

"I'm going to do it," Edwinna said, pounding the desk with her fist. "I'm going to run for the state senate."

Savannah shook her head. "Don't do it. You'll hate it, Edwinna. You don't want to be in the spotlight. You have to watch everything you do."

"So?" Edwinna said nonchalantly.

"You know how the media is. They can destroy you. What if it comes out?"

"What?"

240

Savannah lowered her voice to a whisper. "About me and you."

"Nobody knows. I've never told anyone. Have you?"

"No, but . . ."

"We've always been careful. We've always had men in our lives."

Savannah shrugged her shoulders. "If you're not worried, then I'm not worried."

"No, I'm not worried about that. I'm just worried about beating Ramion."

"So how are you going to beat him?" Savannah asked. "He's already made a name for himself. Not to be insensitive, Edwinna, but nobody knows who the hell you are."

"By the time November rolls around they will," she said, leafing through a stack of legal-sized file folders.

"Tell me this, do you really want to win, or are you only aiming to screw up Ramion's chances of winning?"

"It won't hurt my career to hold public office. At first, I'll admit, I just wanted to run for the pleasure of defeating Ramion, to totally ruin his plans. But now that I've got my father involved and other supporters behind me, I'm taking it more seriously."

Savannah rolled her eyes in disbelief. "You suddenly care about the people who live there?"

"You've forgotten that I grew up there."

"But you moved away when you were a teenager." Savannah put the newspaper back on Edwinna's desk and said, "All I'm saying is don't do it just to get back at a man."

"It doesn't matter why I'm doing it. What matters is that I'm going to win. And I've got something on Ramion that will cost him votes."

"What is that?" Savannah asked with curious interest.

Edwinna opened her black Dooney Burke pocketbook and retrieved her key ring. She unlocked the file cabinet, opened the top drawer, and removed a red folder.

Her curiosity aroused, Savannah asked, "What is it?"

"Remember when Art Hinkle was accused of taking a bribe to get the stadium contract?"

"Yes. He ended up losing his seat on the city council."

"Ramion handled the case, and I think he was in on it."

"Get out of town," Savannah said.

"He represented Hinkle during contract negotiations."

"Are you sure about this?"

"Eighty percent. I'm going to talk to Selena Tucker. She's the law clerk who worked with Ramion on the case. I'm going to find out what she knows."

"Do you know her?"

"Not well. I heard she's working at another law firm. She's probably passed the bar by now. But I'm going to check into it."

"You might have something."

Edwinna released a long sad sigh. "Too bad I can't stop the wedding."

"Get over it, girl. He's a goner."

"Yeah, well I heard the wedding is going to be in the garden of the Governor's Mansion. I hope it rains like hell."

"We can get together that day. So you won't have to think about it."

"What are you going to do?" Edwinna asked, feeling a tingling sensation between her thighs.

Savannah licked her lips. "Make you come in my mouth."

* * * * * * * * * * * * *

Selena Tucker exited off the interstate onto Peachtree Corners, relieved to accelerate to more than forty miles an hour, instead of the stop-and-go pace of the congested interstate. She stopped at Kenny Roger's drive-through window for a chicken salad lunch and then headed to her apartment complex. She stopped at the leasing office and dropped her late rent check into the mail slot. She pretended not to notice a woman from the leasing office waving at her to come into the office and got back into her car and quickly drove away.

Selena rounded the corner from the leasing office, slowing down for speed bumps. She drove past the stream of furniture stacked near the dumpsters before she realized that the white-washed bedroom and living room furniture was hers. Without checking her rearview mirror, she put her car in reverse and backed up. Tears welled in her eyes when she saw everything she owned piled in a disheveled mess.

Her next door neighbor ran over to her car. "They wrong, girl, to throw us out of here like that. Without no kind of warning," Kiki said. "I had an agreement for my back payments, but some new company has taken over and they ain't studying our agreements."

"Another company bought out the complex?" Selena asked, stunned by the news.

"I don't know if a new company bought the complex or it's a new company that's managing the property, I just know they done thrown us out like we were dogs or something."

"Assholes!" Selena said, drying her eyes, anger replacing shock.

"I've been watching your stuff. You know people are like vultures. They walk off with your shit if you ain't watching."

"Thanks a lot, Kiki. I guess I'm going to have to move this stuff into my mother's house."

"You're a lawyer, Selena. Can't you do something about this?"

"I can try. But you know the legal system moves slow. Real slow," Selena said, loathe to admit that she had been behind on her rent.

Chapter XX

The tall police officer entered the room filled with twenty women laughing and talking, sharing stories about boyfriends, husbands, and lovers. With the snatches of laughter and a movie soundtrack playing loudly, Sage didn't notice the police officer approach her.

"Are you Sage Kennedy?" the officer asked in a gruff, unfriendly voice.

Sage gazed up at him, thinking he looked young enough to be in high school. He was so good-looking, Sage wondered why he'd chosen law enforcement instead of a career as a model or actor. With his muscular physique and Denzel Washington face, she thought, he could have gone straight to Hollywood and landed the lead role in an action flick.

"Yes, officer," Sage said, her eyebrows drawn together in a questioning gaze.

The officer held out an envelope. "I have something for you."

Sage stood up. "What is it?" she asked, staring into the officer's stony face. The serious crease in his brows and the tightness around his mouth belied the mirth in his eyes. When Sage extended her hand to take the papers, the police officer handcuffed his hand to hers.

"What the hell are you doing?" she demanded angrily. She didn't notice the flash of cameras as her picture was taken.

"Take these off!" she snapped. "I'm not going anywhere with you."

The laughter from the other women distracted her from her pique. "Why are you laughing? This isn't funny!" Then she heard the unmistakable beat of a rap song, a thumping party groove.

"Miss Kennedy," the police officer said, "I'm not taking you anywhere. But I do need your help."

Sage burst into laughter, realizing that the young brother she was handcuffed to was not a police officer at all, but a stripper or dancer. She narrowed her eyes at Tawny, "Whose bright idea was this?"

"Ava's," Tawny said.

The music thumped on the boom box, and the women started clapping.

"I need you to help me take my clothes off," the stripper said.

Her cheeks blushed in embarrassment. "I'm sure you can do it yourself."

"I only have one hand free," the police impostor taunted.

"I suppose the only way you're going to take these handcuffs off is for me to help you," Sage said.

"Exactly!" the stripper said, positioning his thumb and index finger like a gun.

With merriment in her eyes and a mischievous grin, Sage unbuttoned his shirt. And when she reached for his belt, some of her friends yelled, "Ooh, we didn't think you'd go there!"

Sage unzipped his pants as the agile dancer moved his body in erotic rhythm to the music, gyrating his hips and pressing against Sage.

"Pull them down! Pull them down!" Ava screamed.

Sage hesitated before pulling the officer's black pants from his hips. When Sage saw the red bikinis, she covered her face. "That's it! I can't do any more."

"You don't have to, Miss Kennedy." He unlocked the handcuffs. "Sit down. Watch and enjoy."

Addressing the group of sexually charged women, the stripper said, "I've got something to cool you off." Two young men came into the room, dressed as firemen in red raincoats and black hats, brandishing fire hoses.

To the beat of "Erotic City" by Prince, the three male dancers gyrated their hips and wiggled their behinds, removing their raincoats to reveal red bikinis. When they finished performing, each dancer presented Sage with a red rose.

Everyone clapped as the dancers left the room.

"Girlfriend, I'd love to take one of them home with me!"

"It's been so long since I had any, I don't know if I'd still know how."

"I'll take the tall one. I could teach him a few things. You know, ways to make a woman purr."

Laugher abounded as the women talked and joked about the strippers. Tawny stood in the center of the room and announced, "The party's not over yet. It's fantasy time." She walked over to Sage, who was sitting in a corner chair.

"Now what?" Sage asked.

"You get to read your friends' sexual fantasies." Tawny handed Sage a shoe box filled with folded sheets of paper. "You know, ideas for your honeymoon."

"Hmh," Sage said, a grin spreading across her face.

"We'll be here all night," someone complained. "I want to see her gifts."

"Okay, okay," Tawny said. "Just read three."

Sage reached into the box and pulled out a piece of paper. She quickly read the three paragraphs and said, "I see someone has a dirty mind. A very dirty mind," she repeated, wondering who wrote what she was about to read.

"I hear you, girl," Tawny said.

"Listen up," Sage said. "This is from . . ."

"Don't read the name," a high-pitched voice said.

Sage sipped her margarita and said, "Girlfriends, I hope you didn't write about anything you wouldn't want the rest of us to hear. You know, stuff about whips and chains and . . ."

"Go on, read one," Ava urged.

With an impish smile, Sage began to read the sexual fantasy. "I walk into a darkened room, and a deep, unfamiliar voice says, "Hello." I say, "hello," and he says, "I can't wait to lick you where you're hot. I'll slither my tongue around your tender spot . . ."

* * * * * * * * * * * * *

"Sage, there are some senior citizens here to see you," Marika said as she entered Sage's office.

Staring at her computer monitor, Sage didn't look up. Her fingers moving deftly over the keyboard, she asked, "What do they want to see me for?"

"They're from the Preserve the Mansion Committee," Marika said, placing a business card on Sage's desk.

"Damn," Sage muttered. "How did they find out about what we're doing?"

"I don't know. But they're some mean-looking old biddies. I'd be afraid to tell them you're busy, they might have me for lunch."

Sage leaned back in her chair and ran her hands through her hair. "How many are there?"

"Two."

Sage was quiet for a minute, deciding how to handle them. "Tell them to come in. But buzz me in ten minutes to say that the governor wants to see me." Sage stood up and walked over to the door. She put on her double-breasted navy suit jacket. "Thank goodness I dressed conservatively today."

"I'm so glad you didn't wear that black miniskirt," Marika teased.

A few minutes later, two elderly white women entered Sage's office.

"Welcome, ladies," Sage said, with a cheerful smile. She started to offer her hand, but remembered that the women were from a generation when women didn't shake hands. "I'm Sage Kennedy."

"Hello. I'm Lilah Chambers and this is Ethel Newman."

"It's a pleasure meeting you ladies. Won't you please take a seat?" Sage offered, leading the women to the conference table.

They sat down opposite Sage.

"Would you like something to drink?" Sage offered. "Coffee, tea, soda . . ."

"No, thank you. We aren't here to socialize. We've come to protest," Ms. Chambers said.

Sage raised her eyebrows. "I see."

"I've heard, from a very good source, that you plan to completely renovate the mansion and get rid of the beautiful artwork," Ms. Chambers said, her mouth tight.

"Yes, you're going to replace the beautiful paintings with works by blacks," Ms. Newman said. She coughed a bit and continued, "I mean, African-Americans. We don't think that is appropriate."

"First, let me assure you that we are not renovating the Mansion. We are, however, enhancing the Mansion to include creations by black artists. We feel that the Governor's Mansion should reflect the people who helped build this great state. Blacks have contributed to its growth and development in many ways. Right now, there isn't a single painting, sculpture, or book by a black artist anywhere in the Mansion."

"You may not know this, but some of the pieces are quite rare, Miss Kennedy," Ms. Chambers said. "They shouldn't be hidden away."

"Our plan is to donate any pieces that are replaced to a museum or art gallery. As a matter of fact, you might be able to help with that."

"How so?" Ms. Chambers asked, her lips pursed together in a curious expression.

"Perhaps you can help us find a new place for these works," Sage said, the idea of soliciting their help just occurring as she spoke the words.

"Are you going to sell them?" Ms. Norman asked.

"We hadn't considered that, but perhaps we could sell some and donate the proceeds to charity. Let me look into it but, in the meantime, would you be interested in helping us find a new home for the pieces?"

Ms. Chambers looked at Ms. Newman, who nodded with genteel grace. Ms. Chambers turned back to Sage. "Of course we'll help."

Sage escorted the women out of her office and then settled back at her desk. She was searching the computer for a presentation file when Marika knocked on her door.

"Don't get too comfortable," Marika said. "You've got more visitors."

"What's with all the walk-ins? Don't people make appointments?"

"I don't know," Marika said. "But I think you'll want to talk to these people."

Marika's insistent tone caught her attention. Sage asked, "Who are they?"

"The FBI."

"Oh, definitely," Sage said. "Show them in."

Agent Davis and Agent Bennett, the FBI agents who had visited her in the hospital after the bombing, walked into her office, their expressions unreadable as they approached her desk.

"How are you, Ms. Kennedy?" Agent Bennett asked.

"I'm just fine. Would you like to sit down?"

"No, thanks. We'll get right to the point."

"Please do," Sage said, anxious to find out the reason for their visit.

"We have the man who burned the flag in your yard," Agent Bennett said, standing directly in front of her desk.

"Great news!" Sage said and unconsciously clapped her hands. "What a relief. How did you find him so fast?"

"First, let me show you his picture," Agent Bennett said, placing a black and white photograph on her desk. "Do you recognize this man?"

Sage peered at the picture of a scruffy-looking white man in his early twenties. His grimacing stare sent a bone-deep chill through her body as she thought about him prowling around her house. "I've never seen him. I told you that I hadn't noticed anybody unusual by my house or here at work."

"Your neighbor did," Agent Davis said.

"Who? Mrs. Peterson?"

"Yes, she wrote down the license plate on his truck," Agent Davis said.

Sage creased her brows together in a curious frown. "How did she . . ."

"He apparently was stupid enough to case out your neighborhood in broad daylight, then he came back to perform his dastardly deed in the very same truck," Agent Bennett explained.

"Are you sure it's him?"

"There's no question he did it. He confessed, and he was stupid enough to brag to some of his buddies."

"He's not a bright fellow," Agent Davis concurred.

"Was anybody else involved?" Sage asked. "Is he responsible for the bombing too?"

"Whoever planted that bomb fits a different kind of profile. The device was fairly sophisticated." Pointing to the suspect's picture, Agent Bennett said, "He's not associated with any groups."

"It's scary to think there may be others . . ."

"No, he's a loner type," Agent Bennett said. "We're sure he acted alone. So you don't have to worry anymore."

* * * * * * * * * * * * *

"Wake up! I have a surprise for you," Sage said to Ramion lying on the couch.

Ramion stretched out his arms. "I must have dozed off. I hope it's more interesting than this case," he said, shuffling the legal papers from the floor to the table.

"Trust me," Sage said, with the proud smile of a child excitedly showing his mother a straight-A report card.

She inserted the tape into the VCR and turned up the volume on the television. Ramion appeared on the screen shaking hands with the kids at a high school. The two-minute commercial ended with the voice of a sports announcer saying, "A man who was born here rises to lead here."

"I told them to edit some of the scenes a bit," Sage said, pressing the rewind button on the VCR remote. She stopped the rewind action and froze the screen. "They're going to splice in a scene of you at the office here and rearrange some of the shots a bit." She pressed play and said, "But it's mostly finished."

"Baby, I love it," Ramion said excitedly. "I didn't think it was going to be ready until after we got back from our honeymoon."

Sage plopped down on the sofa. "That was the plan. But I decided not to wait until then. I wanted to make sure everything was done before we left so we can enjoy ourselves. And now that Edwinna has officially thrown her hat into the ring, we have to stay one step ahead of her."

"Her news conference was a sideshow," Ramion said, referring to Edwinna's press conference, which was as orchestrated as a presidential campaign. He put his arms around her shoulders, grazing her neck with soft kisses. "With you in my corner, I know I'm going to win."

She reached into the box on the floor and pulled out a brochure with Ramion's picture on it. "These brochures are all ready and the 'Vote for Ramion Sandidge' stickers are done. I already put one on my car, and you know how I hate stickers and stuff cluttering my windows." She patted his nose with her finger. "Only for you."

"Thank you, baby. For all you've done on my campaign. And for just being you." Ramion caressed her lips, slowly moving his tongue inside her mouth.

"Ramion," she said, "Remember, we're not . . ."

Sage fell back against the arm of the sofa, his kisses warming her body.

When Ramion's hands snaked inside her blouse, she blurted, "No sex until our wedding night."

"Oh, I forgot," Ramion said, moving off the sofa.

Sage narrowed her eyes. "Sure you forgot."

* * * * * * * * * * * * *

The governor of Georgia offered his deputy chief of staff his bowed arm. His eyes were filled with paternal pride because she held a special place in his heart reserved for family members. He smiled at Sage. "Are you ready?"

Sage closed her eyes for a moment, calming her emotions before responding with a simple nod. She was a vision of a fairy-tale fantasy, dressed in a beautiful silk, satin, and alencon lace off-the-shoulder wedding gown. Hand-embroidered palm leaves embossed with iris flowers made of nakar and mother-of-pearl dotted the sheath gown adorned by a long, cathedral-length train. A heart-shaped diamond pendant hung around her neck. Ramion had declared his love to Sage when he gave her the pendant after they had reclaimed their love from Edwinna's machinations.

The pianist announced the bride's presence with the first chords of "The Wedding March." Three hundred people stood as Cameron escorted Sage down the aisle of hand-draped gold lamé peppered with thousands of flowers—white and red roses, white Queen Anne's lace, pompons, carnations, and snapdragons. Her eyes shining as bright as a shooting star, Sage slowly eased down the aisle, step by step, closer and closer to the wedding party. Sage felt the eyes of family, friends, and relatives watch her every move, but she only had eyes for Ramion who was about to become her husband.

The wedding party watched as Sage approached them, their numbers resembling a group of Christmas carollers—five bridesmaids, five groomsmen, five ushers, five hostesses, a flower girl, a bell ringer, and a ring bearer. The bridesmaids were dressed in strapless teal gowns, the hostesses in purple ones, the men in white tuxedos, and the children wore miniature versions of the adults' attire.

Ramion nervously watched Sage and Cameron move toward him, seemingly in slow motion. As Sage neared the alter, Ramion took a few steps forward and reached out, as if magnetically drawn to his bride. Sage felt the pull of his attraction when he touched her hand.

The Reverend DuBois performed the ceremony in his typical enigmatic and eloquent style. He spoke about the sanctity of marriage and the commitment of love, quoting the meaning of love from scriptures in the Bible and reciting from sonnets and poems about the beauty of love. The ceremony included a tapestry of songs about everlasting love, weaving a magical feeling that escaped no one who witnessed the wedding.

Sage and Ramion repeated the vows they had chosen to represent their eternal love.

"I, Sage Kennedy, take you, Ramion Sandidge, to be my beloved husband, to give you, from this day forward, the gift of my tender love. To honor you with my body, to fill up the wounds in your heart. To sleep in your bed and stand at your side in good times and bad. When things go easy with us and when they are difficult.

"I give you my love, I give you my heart, I give you my hope. I give you my love for the rest of the days of my life. I promise to delight in your body, to nourish your mind; to be at home with your spirit the way a star is at home in the sky, to celebrate your whole being with joy as the sun emblazons the sky with its light, to know you, love you, hold you, warm you, through all the days of our lives."

With the exchange of vows and rings, Reverend DuBois pronounced them husband and wife. "You may now kiss your bride."

Ramion raised the tulle veil covering Sage's luminous face and pressed his lips against hers. Aware of the crowd watching them, Sage hadn't planned on a between-the-sheets kind of kiss. But she was overwhelmed by the moment—the vows they exchanged, the way his eyes caressed her soul, the way her heart felt enveloped by his love. She could not hold back her feelings and kissed him with the velocity of her love. It was a long, deep, soul-stirring kiss.

It was a kiss that marked their new beginning, a kiss that transformed them into husband and wife.

Chapter XXI

Sage tensed as she felt the airplane descend from the clouds. She peered out the window, the rooftops and trees looming larger and larger as the plane neared the ground. She tightened her seatbelt when the plane abruptly hit the ground, bouncing up and down a few times before the Boeing 747 hit the ground with the force of its massive tonnage. She heard the tires thump hard against the concrete, the brakes squeal, and the wings opening out against the wind. She closed her eyes and held onto the seat, waiting for the plane to come to a complete stop.

"That pilot needs lessons in landing," Sage complained to Ramion, who looked at her with a bemused expression.

"It wasn't that bad," Ramion said. "I've been in planes that seemed to be trying to land without brakes."

"I'm just glad to be on the ground. All that bouncing up and down like a seesaw. I didn't get seasick on the ship, but I feel pretty sick now."

They heard the high-pitched, two-toned signal indicating that passengers could begin disembarking the plane.

"I guess our honeymoon is officially over," Ramion said, kissing his bride on her orange-glossed lips that complimented her sun-kissed, golden-brown skin.

"What a blast!" Sage said, smiling at all the wonderful memories. "The sun, the water, the islands . . ."

"The sex," Ramion said.

"The shopping, the delicious food . . ."

"The sex," he repeated.

"Is that all you're going to remember about our honeymoon?"

"No, I'll remember how much money I lost gambling," Ramion said, with a twinge of regret. "Every time I thought I was ahead, I ended up further in the hole." He stood up and opened the overhead compartment.

"I warned you," Sage lightly chided as she unstrapped her seatbelt.

"Here's your hat," Ramion said, handing her a brown straw hat. He juggled two bags of duty-free liquor in his arms.

"I'll grab the other bag," Sage said, reaching into the overhead compartment and pulling down a brown and yellow Louis Vuitton garment bag.

Sage and Ramion filed off the plane, trailing behind the other passengers, and departing through the porthole into the terminal gate. Sage's wallet fell from her handbag, and Ramion bent down to pick it up. He slipped the wallet back into her handbag just as they stepped inside the airport. Suddenly camera lights flashed in their faces and reporters shouted questions.

"Did you do it, Ramion?"

"Are the woman's allegations true?"

"What do you have to say about your relationship?"

In the midst of the reporters, Sage saw Ava and Marika trying to make their way through the media crush. In the corner of her eye, she glimpsed Ramion's dumbfounded expression when a reporter pointed a microphone at him. Tape recorders and video cameras were positioned to record his response. They captured a flustered, almost angry look on Ramion's face. His jaw was thrust forward pugnaciously, and his eyes were wide with astonishment.

Sage adroitly stepped into the camera's view and said, "Mr. Sandidge has no comment at this time." Hearing Sage refer to him as Mr. Sandidge, Ramion recovered his composure, the expression of ambushed confusion metamorphosing into his more customary in-control demeanor. "Frankly, I have know no idea what this is all about. If allegations have, in fact, been levied against me, I'll confront the charges before I respond." He cleared his throat. "I can only say I'll make a statement within the next forty-eight hours."

Ava pushed through the paparazzi to Sage's side and whispered in her ear. "I tried to call you before you left the hotel, but you were gone. Then we tried the limo, but there was no way to reach you."

"What is it?" Sage asked anxiously, though dreading Ava's response at the same time.

"Selena Tucker, an intern that worked at Ramion's old law firm, has filed sexual harassment charges against him."

Sage's eyes widened as she covered her mouth with her hand. "Oh, no! This could cost him the election."

"If he didn't do it," Ava said, shrugging, "then it shouldn't make a difference."

"It may not matter if he's guilty or innocent. In politics, image is everything, and the election is only two months away," Sage said, thinking about the potential damage to Ramion's credibility and hoping it wouldn't be irreparable.

The newlyweds made their way to the baggage terminal, fully aware that their every movement was being watched as reporters lurked around, searching for a new angle to the story. They collected their luggage, checking their bags with security before leaving the baggage terminal.

"Our bags aren't going to fit," Ramion said, when he saw Marika's Ford Mustang parked in front of the airport. "Let's get a limo," he said, heading toward the ground transportation sign.

"I'll go with them," Ava said, trailing behind Ramion and Sage.

"Thanks for coming," Sage called to Marika. "I'll talk to you later."

After Ramion secured a limo, they climbed inside while the driver put their luggage into the trunk.

"What the hell is going on?" Ramion asked when the driver pulled away from the airport.

"A former intern at your old law firm is suing you for sexual harassment," Ava explained.

"What?" Ramion asked in an absurd tone of voice. He looked over at Sage, whose blissful expression had been transformed by shock and dismay. Ramion turned back to Ava. "Who made these ridiculous charges?"

"Selena Tucker," Ava answered, handing Ramion the morning newspaper with a blaring headline, "Student Levies Sexual Harassment Charge Against Candidate Ramion Sandidge." Ramion scanned through the article, shaking his head in disbelief. His future was slipping away like the grains of sand sliding through an hourglass. He was scowling by the time he finished the article. He racked his brain, trying to recall what he could have done to provoke her fantastic claim of sexual harassment.

Sage watched Ramion's reaction, studying his face, looking for a mirror of truth. She searched the subtle reflection in his eyes and the clenching of his jaws for a trace of guilt. But all she found was utter amazement and righteous anger.

"I don't understand why she would lie. It's absolutely not true," Ramion said. "She wasn't a great law clerk . . ."

"She failed the bar twice," Ava said.

"She did?" Sage queried.

"I don't know what this is about," Ramion said. "But I'll be damned if some lying, conniving law student is going to ruin my career."

The driver parked in front of Ramion's house, where they were going to live while their house was being built. They unloaded the luggage from the trunk, and Ramion paid the limo driver.

Sage hardly noticed the streamers and balloons decorating the door or the sign that read, "Welcome home Mr. and Mrs. Sandidge." She collapsed on the sofa and said, "Fill us in."

Ava was reluctant to tell them about the past two days. She hated ruining their homecoming.

"Well?" Ramion urged.

"Selena's lawyer, Cynthia Powers . . ."

"Not her," Ramion groaned, fear tightening in his stomach like a vise. "She's not a lawyer! She's a publicity monger!"

Silently agreeing with Ramion, Sage said, "She's also a well-known champion of women who are victimized by men. Palimony suits are her forte. If I remember correctly, she represented a woman suing a priest, claiming they had lived together in connubial bliss."

"That's her," Ramion said. He motioned with his hands for Ava to continue.

"She called a press conference yesterday and announced that Selena Tucker had filed a civil suit against you, alleging that you sexually harassed her when she was a clerk at Williamson—you know, your old law firm. Selena claims your harassment adversely affected her ability to pass the bar."

256

Ramion stood by the fireplace while listening to Ava. "She's full of shit."

"She fails her bar exam," Sage said, "and she wants to blame Ramion?" She leaned back against the sofa and massaged her temples. She suddenly felt exhausted from the busy honeymoon and the unexpected, and very unwelcome, media greeting.

"Was she there?" Ramion asked, speculating that Cynthia would use every opportunity to portray her client as a victim. He wasn't surprised when Ava nodded.

"She didn't say a whole lot. She read a prepared statement, something about Ramion destroying her dream. She looked very polished and professional in a business suit."

"And, of course, the public needed to know this right before the election," Sage cynically said, then stood up. "I'm exhausted. Let's talk about this in the morning and figure out what to do then. We have to hold a press conference by tomorrow evening. If we wait too long, it will look like you're guilty. Right now, I need some rest."

"I'm sorry you had to come home to this," Ava said, and hugged her sister. "Get some rest."

"I'll try," Sage said, knowing she would probably do more thinking than sleeping.

After Ava left, Sage took a hot shower, the pulsating water soothing her frazzled nerves. She brushed her teeth and tucked her hair into a ponytail. She slipped into a green satin nightgown, remembering the last seven days in Ramion's arms, when all she'd worn to bed were teddies and negligees or nothing at all. From passion to scandal, she thought, as she left the bathroom to enter their bedroom.

Ramion was sitting on the edge of the bed, going over the newspaper article again and again, his face a mask of worry. He reached for the glass on the nightstand and took a sip of bourbon on ice.

"This is crazy," he said angrily. He thumped his hand against the newspaper. "Lies! Lies! Lies!"

Sage slipped under the covers and sat upright against the headboard. "What happened? Did you do anything that . . ."

"Never! I was never out of line with her!" Ramion exploded. "I don't know why she would lie like this. The real truth is that she flirted with me. She asked me out on several occasions."

"Did you ever accept?"

Ramion shot Sage an exasperated glare. "We never even had lunch."

"Can anyone confirm that *she* asked you out?"

Ramion stood up and tossed the newspaper article on the floor. "I don't remember anybody ever being around. That was almost two years ago. She did some research for some of my cases. We worked late a couple of evenings. But I never so much as said 'That's a pretty dress' or 'You look nice.'"

"Were you attracted to her?"

"She's a pretty lady, but I only thought of her in professional terms. From time to time, she made suggestive remarks. I always ignored them, and I think it frustrated her that I didn't respond." He shrugged. "She's the type of woman that's used to men fawning over her. I didn't. Maybe that pissed her off."

"But why now, in the middle of your campaign?"

"I don't know, except we know who would benefit if I lose the election."

"Edwinna," Sage said, thinking she would do anything to hurt Ramion.

"But how could she talk Selena into doing this? Why would Selena lie and risk her career?"

"What career? She's failed the bar twice."

"She can take it again," Ramion said. "Anyway, whatever the reason, we have to deal with it."

"We're going to have to issue a statement tomorrow, or voters will think there's some truth in her lies," Sage said. "You have to deny the charges and quickly remind voters about your campaign commitment."

"I know. I know," he said, rubbing his forehead with his hand. "The problem is the court docket. I have to figure a way to get this into court and exonerate myself before the election."

"The election is only two months away. It could take you that long to get a court date."

"Especially in civil court," Ramion said in a defeated tone.

Sage leaned back against the pillow with a yawn. She closed her eyes for a moment, pondering the next two months.

"Get some sleep, Sage. I'm too wound up to go to bed right now." Ramion walked around to the other side of the bed. He kissed his wife on the forehead, then on her lips.

"What an ending to our honeymoon," she said, burrowing under the covers.

"I'm sorry, baby," Ramion said, holding her hand. "You do believe me, don't you? I absolutely did not harass that woman."

Grasping his hand tighter, she said firmly, "I believe you. I'm behind you one hundred percent."

* * * * * * * * * * * * *

Sage turned into a strip shopping mall that included a nail salon along with seven other small businesses. She parked in front of the salon and got out of her car. She saw a sign, "Closed . . . Family Emergency," posted on the door and peered through the window at the empty room.

Returning to her car, Sage started the engine and headed toward the end of the shopping center. She stopped at the cleaner's drive-through window, picked up her suits and dresses, and dropped off another bag of clothes to be dry cleaned. She turned onto Roswell Road, stopping for a red light. While waiting for the light to turn green, she spotted another nail salon in the shopping center across the street. She quickly changed lanes and steered her car into the recently built shopping center. She parked near the salon, then picked up the telephone to call Ramion. There was no answer, so she left a voice message telling him she wouldn't be home until after seven.

She passed a drugstore and a pet shop as she made her way to the NuYou Salon. She opened the door and was immediately greeted by a pretty chestnut-brown girl whose Asian and black mixture showed in her slanted eyes and black hair.

"I don't have an appointment," Sage said. "but I'd like to get my nails done. Can someone take me right away?"

"Acrylic or gel?" the girl asked.

"Acrylic. Just a fill-in," Sage said.

The receptionist picked up the phone, pressed an intercom button, and spoke in Vietnamese. She hung up and directed Sage to the counter containing bottles of nail polish. "Pick out a color. Someone will be with you shortly."

Sage scanned the shelves stocked with nail polish bottles in shades from pink to maroon and orange to red. She glanced around the salon,

259

appreciatively noticing the private booths instead of the typical long table of manicurists lined against a mirrored wall. Several black contemporary paintings caught her attention as she sat down in the waiting room.

"Ready?" a petite, pregnant Vietnamese woman asked.

Sage nodded.

"Come with me," the woman said.

Sage followed the woman into a small booth that reminded her of an office cubicle. Sage placed her hands flat on the table and spread her fingers apart.

"How are you?" the woman asked, dipping a cotton ball into a bowl of nail polish remover.

"Fine," Sage responded, watching the woman remove her bright red nail polish.

"Song be with you in a minute," the woman said after removing the polish on Sage's nails. "I go now."

Within seconds, an attractive, middle-aged Vietnamese woman with an ear-length bob and strong facial features entered the booth. "Hello," she said, greeting Sage with a friendly smile. "I am Song."

"Nice to meet you," Sage said.

Song stared at Sage for a long, uncomfortable minute, gazing into her eyes with a curious expression. "You have pretty eyes," the woman said suddenly, then sat down opposite Sage.

The woman named Song said very little at first as she examined Sage's nails, then proceeded to apply the acrylic—dipping a thin brush into a white powder and smoothing it on Sage's nails. When Song started buffing and filing her nails, she began telling Sage about her recent move from California and her plans to make the salon a big success.

After applying a top coat over the dark red polish, Song directed Sage into the drying room. Sage placed her hands under an electric hand dryer. She looked across the room and saw a picture hanging on the wall that reminded her of the painting she had bought from Tawny.

As she stared at the painting, its bright red and yellow hues swirling into a sea of purple and green, she had an inexplicable feeling, a sense of dèjá vu but she had never been in the salon before. She couldn't take her eyes off the painting, couldn't stop staring into the mysterious faces in the painting—faces that weren't faces at all, only eyes.

"I think I'm dry," Sage said, removing her hands from under the electric hand dryer.

"Let me spray you," Song said, shaking the tall can of instant dry and then spraying it over Sage's nails. "I hope you come again." Song fished in her pocket for a card and handed it to Sage. "Next time you come, you get twenty percent off our services. We do manicures and pedicures. We do facials, too. Would you be interested?"

"Sure."

"Great. Please sign our guest list. We call you to schedule your next appointment."

* * * * * * * * * * * * *

When the elevator doors opened on the first floor of the Fulton County Courthouse, Sage and Ramion were greeted by the media, ready to report the outcome of Ramion's request for a preliminary hearing.

Ramion smiled confidently into the cameras, not betraying the range of feelings he had just experienced: uncertainty about the case law supporting his argument, fear that the judge would automatically dismiss his request, and relief when the judge had ruled in his favor.

This time, when the media pounced on Ramion like a panther after his prey, he roared back.

"Judge Brackett granted my request for a preliminary hearing to investigate the charges made by Miss Selena Tucker," Ramion told the print and broadcast journalists. "He'll hear the case in two weeks and determine then whether there's enough evidence to warrant further investigation."

"So you're hoping to clear your name before the election?"

"Absolutely. I'd like to remind voters that I'm running for the State House because I want to improve the communities on the south side. Economic prosperity isn't just for the folks who live north of the perimeter. Environmental consciousness is not a black or white issue, it's a human issue that affects us all . . ."

Ramion's interview was cut short when his accuser, Selena Tucker, and her lawyer, Cynthia Powers, emerged from the elevator, their heels clicking against the polished linoleum floor. The reporters and cameramen directed their microphones and camcorders on the two women.

"Selena, how do you feel about today's ruling?" a reporter asked.

Selena opened her mouth, but Cynthia stepped forward, her stern eyes communicating an order to remain quiet. The usually cool and composed Cynthia Powers was as angry as a fire-breathing dragon. "I'm appalled that the justice system can be so easily circumvented to accommodate the whims and fancies of a privileged insider. It appears that my client will not be given due process, but rushed process . . ."

Ramion and Sage walked away, their adversary's ramblings fading into the distance.

Chapter XXII

The doorbell rang as Sage and Ramion worked at the kitchen table. Ramion's open briefcase lay on the floor next to his feet; he was bent over, reading a deposition. Sage's laptop computer was flipped open, and she leaned in, rapidly clicking on the keyboard, reading and responding to her electronic mail. The shrill sound of the doorbell broke their concentration.

"Expecting anybody?" Ramion asked when the doorbell rang for the second time.

Sage glanced at her watch and said, "Not this late."

"I'll see who it is," Ramion said, getting up from his chair.

Wearing jeans and a Falcons tee-shirt, Ramion strode down the hall and peeked through the window. "Hey, Drew," he said after opening the door. "What's going on, man?"

They shook hands. "Ain't much happening with me," Drew said. "Just thought I'd stop by and see what's going on here."

"Come on into the kitchen."

Drew followed Ramion around the corner into the kitchen. Pointing to the refrigerator, Ramion said, "Grab a beer."

"Drew?" Sage intoned, leaning back against the brewer-cane chair.

"Hello, Mrs. Sandidge," Drew said with smile, while opening the refrigerator door.

Sage chuckled, "Not too many people call me that."

Drew reached inside the refrigerator and removed a bottle of beer from the shelf on the door. He twisted off the bottle cap and drained some of the beer. He turned a kitchen chair toward him and straddled it. "What are you guys doing?"

"I'm reviewing some of the depositions from people at my old law firm for the hearing."

"Are they favorable?" Drew asked.

"Oh, yeah, everyone says basically the same thing: that I was always professional and never acted out of line with *any* woman. No one confirms Selena's allegation that I tapped her on the butt in a meeting."

"That's good," Drew said.

"I'm waiting to get the depositions from Cynthia. She's been stalling."

"That's because she has no case," Sage said. "I think this is all smoke, Ramion. It's the timing that is so incredible. She makes allegations against you, assuming that it wouldn't go to court until after the election. Even if she later drops the suit, you've lost the election."

"Cameron did me a big favor calling Judge Brackett. I owe him big time," Ramion said. "If he hadn't made that call, I might as well pull out of the race right now."

"What's the girl's motive?" Drew asked.

"I don't know," Ramion said, twirling a pen in his hand. "Unless Edwinna put her up to this."

"Edwinna?" Drew said, with a puzzled frown.

"Considering the trouble she went through to fake a tape, I think she would do anything," Ramion said. "The bitch is crazy, obsessed with destroying me."

Sage nodded. "You know how I feel about her. If it wasn't totally out of my character, I'd love to beat the crap out of her."

Ramion shrugged. "If not Edwinna, who?"

"My thing is, if the girl wants to be a lawyer and she goes public with a crazy story like this one, she ruins her chance of ever becoming a respected attorney," Drew said.

"Yeah, but she's failed the bar twice. At this point, why would she care? She's probably given up on becoming a lawyer," Sage said. "From what I heard, her real goal was to marry a lawyer. That's the reason she went to law school in the first place."

"Where'd you hear that?" Drew asked.

"From Tawny. She knows a girl who went to law school with Selena. She says Selena just barely got by. She was more interested in men than books," Sage said.

"That explains why she was so inept," Ramion said. "She did some research for me and always came back with the wrong cases. It wasn't complicated, but she was overwhelmed. After a month or so, I requested a new intern."

"Maybe that's it," Sage said.

Ramion and Drew stared at her, their expressions puzzled.

"Maybe she has a grudge against you because you offended her."

"That was never my intention. I asked for a different intern—and no, I didn't explain why—but frankly, no one ever asked," Ramion said. "She also worked for Edwinna."

"Maybe that's the connection," Drew said.

"I still can't understand why she would put herself on the line for Edwinna," Ramion said.

"Maybe Edwinna paid her," Sage suggested.

"That's possible," Drew said. "Anyway, can't you talk to her?"

"No, that would be unethical. I'd be digging my own grave. And to tell you the truth, I couldn't trust myself not to ring her neck."

"I just might check out what's going on with Selena," Drew said. "See if there's a connection with Edwinna, maybe find out more about the law firm she's working for."

"Now I know why she didn't want to say what firm she was with when we ran into her at the Fox," Sage said. "She didn't want you to know that she wasn't a lawyer."

"I was just making conversation with the woman," Ramion said.

"I remember she acted strange about it," Sage said.

"Maybe I'll find a new angle to the story or nothing at all, but something smells fishy," Drew said with a small laugh. "That's the reporter in me."

"Do your thing," Sage said. "Maybe you'll find something that will help us."

"Anyway, I came by to give you a heads-up." Drew paused before adding, "I'm afraid I've got some more bad news."

"What now?" Sage asked, rubbing her face with her hands. She was tired and planned to go to bed after responding to the more than one-hundred-plus electronic mail inquiries.

Drew took a swig of beer. "Ramion's behind in the polls. Edwinna's got a fifteen percent lead on him. It's going to be in the papers tomorrow."

"Damn!" Ramion uttered, banging his fist on the table.

"I'm not surprised," Sage said. Massaging her temples, she felt the onslaught of a migraine headache.

"That hearing can't come fast enough," Ramion said wearily.

"It's time to flip the script," Sage said. "You're going to have to debate Edwinna."

"This isn't the race for the U.S. senate or the governor," Drew said, his look patronizing.

"I know, but he may not have a choice. How else is Ramion going to redeem himself? It's the best way to show who he is, what he believes, and how he would vote on different issues. Edwinna will come across professional and polished, but she has no compassion for the people—and she won't be able to hide that."

"You have a point," Drew said. "She's haughty and doesn't hide it. Humility's a word she doesn't understand, and there's no way she'd come across as a servant to the people."

"She's only running because she wants me to lose," Ramion said. "But you're right, Sage. I'm going to challenge her to a debate." Ramion raised his bottle of beer. "I propose a toast—to my brilliant wife."

"Here, here," Drew said, clinking his bottle against Ramion's.

* * * * * * * * * * * * *

Oliver Lincoln rolled into the Governor's Mansion in a wheelchair, excited to attend the reception for the unveiling of new art for the Mansion. Attired in a black and white tuxedo with a little red bow at his neck, Mr. Lincoln had a smile on his face the size of Mount Rushmore. Escorted by his butler and private duty nurse, he was thrilled to be away from home, where he had become a prisoner to his failing health. He directed his butler to find Ms. Kennedy and waited in the foyer.

Sage was talking to the governor's wife when the butler patted her on the shoulder. "Excuse me, Miss Kennedy, but Mr. Lincoln asked me to let you know he's here."

"Mr. Lincoln's here?" Sage said with surprise.

"He's waiting in the foyer," the butler said before turning away.

"What did you do to him, Sage?" Sarah teased. "He donates original paintings, and now he comes to our reception. The man hasn't been seen in public in years."

Sage cocked an eyebrow, smiling impishly. "I don't know, Sarah. Maybe I just have the magic touch. Anyway, he's really a very sweet man."

"Before he became ill, he was ruthless. Tough as nails. People feared him."

"Well, he's not like that at all now," Sage said. "I'll see you later."

Sage went into the hall where she found Oliver Lincoln speaking with two members of the city council. When he spotted Sage, he abruptly ended his conversation, waving his hand and beckoning to her.

"Hello, Mr. Lincoln," Sage smiled brightly, holding out her hand.

He pushed her hand away, chuckling. "Come now, you know me better than that."

With a twinkle in her olive eyes, Sage bent over and kissed him, unintentionally flashing her cleavage in his face. She wore a black lace evening gown that dipped to a dramatically low décolletage, showcasing her ample cleavage. Diamonds dangled from her ears and sparkled around her neck.

"I'm so glad you could come," Sage said. "I feel very honored."

"No, it is you who honors me with your presence."

"I can't thank you enough for the paintings. They're so beautiful! They're the biggest hit of the reception. I still can't believe they were created by a black painter who studied in France after the Civil War. It's incredible."

"Many people in his circle of friends didn't know he was black until they saw his paintings. He painted about the suffering of his people, even though he was granted the privileges and lifestyle of a white man."

"He must have been very brave."

"It cost him his life in the end. A young white woman fell in love with him. They wanted to marry. But when her father found out he was a black man, he killed him," Mr. Lincoln said, breaking into a coughing spasm.

"Can I get you some water?" Sage offered.

He cleared his throat and shook his head. "I'm fine," he said in a scratchy voice. "His technique was very unusual for the late 1800s."

"Yes, it was," she said, nodding. "Would you like me to show you around?"

"I'd be delighted," the octogenarian said, his eyes glowing with his fervor for the subject at hand.

Sage wheeled him into the library, indicating all the new paintings and books. As they made their way through the Governor's Mansion, several people stopped them to speak with the distinguished gentleman.

"You've caused quite a stir," Sage said.

"I haven't been out of the house in five years."

"Oh, that's so sad. I'm sorry to hear that."

"If this old body was as strong as my mind, I'd still be running this town."

Sage chuckled. "I'm sure you would."

Ramion walked over to them.

"Mr. Lincoln," Sage said. "I'd like you to meet my husband, Ramion Sandidge. Ramion, this is Oliver Lincoln, the art collector."

"And founder of Lincoln Insurance Company and the Investment Fund," Ramion said, extending his hand. "It's an honor to meet you."

"You're a lucky young man. If I was a might younger myself, I'd have to take your girl from you."

Ramion laughed. "I'm afraid you'd have to fight for her."

"I'm pulling for you to win the election, Ramion. I know you've run into some trouble, but I have faith you can still win."

Ramion was taken aback, surprised the man knew so much about the election and shocked to have his support. "Why, thank you, sir. I appreciate that."

"I'm feeling tired," Mr. Lincoln said, suddenly.

"Okay," Sage said. "I'll take you back to the foyer."

"It was a pleasure meeting you, Mr. Lincoln," Ramion said, and walked away.

Sage wheeled the man into the elegant foyer, where the butler and nurse were waiting anxiously. She could tell by the concerned, angry flash in the nurse's eyes that her patient had probably overextended himself.

"Goodnight, Mr. Lincoln," Sage said, bending forward to brush her lips against his. This time she was fully aware her breasts were in his face. "Thank you for coming."

"I'm glad my paintings are here for others to enjoy." He squeezed her hand and whispered in her ear, "Be sure to watch the newspaper in the next few days. You might read some interesting developments."

Sage peered at him quizzically.

"I'm sure it'll make the front page," he said with a wink. "Goodnight."

* * * * * * * * * * * * *

"I told you not to call my office," Edwinna said to Selena, sliding into the booth at a near-empty Waffle House restaurant.

"I didn't leave a message. I just kept calling until you answered. It took two days to get through," Selena said.

"What's so damn urgent?"

"You never said anything about going to court. You said that by the time it came to trial I could drop the charges," Selena said, her high-pitched voice loud.

Edwinna shot her a piercing look. "Lower your voice!" she whispered between clenched teeth.

"Well, the hearing is next week, and I'm not going to lie to a judge."

"The judge isn't going to know you're lying," Edwinna said dismissively. "It would be your word against his."

"That's not the point," Selena said, leaning into the table. "We never talked about going to court. If I had known that, I wouldn't have agreed to do this."

"It's too late now. I didn't think it would go to court this fast. Ramion or Sage or somebody they know, probably the governor, pulled some strings and got it on the calendar."

"I'm not prepared to go to court. You never mentioned it, and neither did Cynthia, for that matter," Selena said.

"Would you like to order something?" interrupted a middle-aged waitress with crooked teeth and a blank expression. She placed a grease-stained menu in front of Edwinna.

Dressed in a fur jacket and matching hat, Edwinna glared at the woman with a you-must-be-kidding look.

"Suit yourself," the woman said and walked away.

Selena said, "If I go into the court . . ."

"Wait until she's gone," Edwinna said in an impatient whisper. When the waitress was out of hearing distance, she said, "Nothing much is going to happen. It's just a preliminary hearing. You're not going to have to testify."

Selena finished her coffee. "I have no intention of taking the stand," she said, staring impudently at Edwinna. She felt like she had walked onto the set of a soap opera but wasn't reading lines for the camera. Guilt had plagued her ever since she saw Ramion's shocked face on television.

"You won't have to. There won't be enough time. The judge will probably turn the case over and set a court date for months from now. By that time, the election will be over," Edwinna said, glancing at her watch.

"I don't know about this. I kind of liked Ramion."

"I don't want to hear that," Edwinna said forcefully. "We had an agreement."

"If I have to go to court, I want more."

From the moment Selena had called her unexpectedly at work, Edwinna became nervous about their affiliation. She glanced suspiciously around the restaurant and outside the window into the parking lot. "We agreed."

"We didn't agree that I would have to go to court."

Edwinna checked her watch, noting that she had been there for ten minutes. She stared at Selena for a minute before nodding. "I'll drop a cashier's check in your mother's mailbox. Don't deposit it in your account."

Selena studied Edwinna, intrigued by the woman's motive. She wondered whether Edwinna was desperate to beat Ramion in the election or was motivated by some sort of twisted revenge. She had never understood Edwinna, even during the two months she worked for her. Her own reason for perpetrating a lie was simple—survival. She needed the money to clear up some debts and move to her own place. She had given up her dream of becoming an attorney, and she still wasn't ready to admit to herself that working as a hairdresser in her mother's salon was an alternative way to make the kind of money that would support her lifestyle.

"How much?" she asked when Edwinna abruptly stood up.

"One thousand."

"Make it fifteen hundred, or I won't show up." Selena didn't waver under Edwinna's indignant stare. Her stubborn expression communicating that she had the upper hand, if only for the moment.

"Done," Edwinna said, then walked off.

Chapter XXIII

Selena Tucker appeared poised and confident in a black suit as she entered the courtroom with her attorney. Behind dark glasses, she glanced furtively at Ramion. She almost stumbled when she recognized several of the lawyers and staff members from Ramion's former law firm.

"I didn't know they were going to be here," Selena whispered anxiously to Cynthia Powers. She sat down next to her attorney, refusing to look at the team of attorneys flanking her adversary. His wife, parents, and sister were there to support him, but she had only Cynthia beside her.

"Neither did I," Cynthia said angrily, taking several file folders from her briefcase. "It's much too early for witnesses." She caught Ramion staring at her with the cockiness of a prize-winning rooster. "Whatever they're planning, I hope the judge doesn't buy into it. Take those sunglasses off. It makes you look like you're hiding behind them."

"Am I going to have to testify?" Selena asked, as she removed the designer shades. She felt unprotected without the dark glasses. She tilted her head to peek at Ramion, feeling even more nervous about the court proceedings that were closed to the public.

"You shouldn't have to. This is just a preliminary hearing."

Everyone stood up when Judge Brackett entered the courtroom. After the judge settled into his chair, the bailiff motioned with his hands to sit down.

Judge Brackett had a noble face—high forehead, furrowed from years of worry, lines deeply etched on his cheeks, a strong nose and chin. He might have been handsome as a young man, but at some point his features had settled into an expression of somber dignity that was now hardened like concrete, so that even a faint smile had a chilling effect. He motioned for the proceedings to begin.

Donald Moore, a partner from Ramion's law firm stood. "Good morning, Your Honor."

Judge Brackett acknowledged the distinguished-looking attorney with a slight nod.

"I would like to submit to the court depositions from people who worked with Mr. Sandidge at Williamson, Beckett, Evans, and Logan," Moore said. "Further, several of the witnesses are here in this courtroom and willing to testify on Mr. Sandidge's behalf. "

The judge nodded affirmatively.

Cynthia bolted from her chair. "I object, Your Honor. This is a hearing, not a trial. Any testimony at this time would be premature."

Selena stared at the judge, her stomach in knots. Suddenly the light breakfast she had eaten felt like a ton of bricks. She had an awful feeling the judge had already made up his mind and was not going to rule in her favor.

"We are here because of allegations levied by Ms. Tucker. She brings them with no corroborating evidence, so we have to rely solely on Ms. Tucker's testimony," Moore said.

"Corroborating evidence isn't a requirement of the suit," Ms. Powers snapped.

"A trial isn't necessary if there isn't any substance to Ms. Tucker's charges," Moore scoffed. He turned for a moment to look at Selena, his eyes communicating the rigors he intended to take her through. Turning back to the judge, he said, "Your Honor, we could simplify this whole matter by bringing Ms. Tucker to the stand right now. Let's find out here and now if there is any merit to Ms. Tucker's charges before we waste any more of the court's time and the taxpayers' money."

"Your concern has nothing to do with the taxpayers or the court,"

Cynthia railed. "This whole fishing expedition is intended only as a means to save Mr. Sandidge's political career."

"Exactly the point, Your Honor. Should my client's career be ruined if Ms. Tucker's suit proves frivolous? As I understand it, this isn't the first time Ms. Tucker has levied such charges."

"Your Honor, Mr. Moore is purposefully trying to prejudice the court by bringing up information that isn't relevant to this case," Cynthia said heatedly.

Speaking for the first time, Judge Bracket said, "I agree. Stick to the facts of this case, counselor."

Donald Moore turned toward the plaintiff, intimidating her with the menace of his expression. "I would like to call Ms. Tucker to the stand."

Selena's hands trembled, remembering Edwinna's promise that she wouldn't have to go to court. She wouldn't have agreed to the charade if she had known she would have to take the stand.

"I object, Your Honor," Cynthia said vehemently, striding from behind the table to stand directly in front of the judge.

His hands folded, Judge Brackett gave Cynthia an imperious look. "I agree with Mr. Moore. Let's find out from Ms. Tucker what she defines as sexual harassment."

"Your Honor, this is a civil case," Cynthia said. "I haven't had time to prepare my client."

Judge Brackett ignored the attorney, looking past her to Selena. "Ms. Tucker, please approach the bench."

Selena's eyes widened. She stood, her knees wobbling, her hands shaking, her stomach churning. Fear engulfed her, and she felt faint. Realizing that she was about to commit perjury, she fell back against the chair. I should have asked for more money, Selena thought.

"Your Honor," Ms. Powers said, "Please allow me time to confer with my client."

"Two minutes," Judge Brackett said crisply.

"Are you all right?" Cynthia whispered to Selena, noticing that she was trembling.

"I can't go up there," Selena whispered into her attorney's ear.

"You don't have a choice. That's what the judge wants."

"If I commit perjury, he can put me in jail, right?"

"Yes, but they'll have to prove intent, and . . ."

Selena interrupted her. "No! That judge looks mean enough to send me to prison. I'm not going to jail!"

"Don't let him get away with it. Don't crumble now."

Selena shook her head vigorously. "I'm not going up there. I can't."

"Are you recanting the charges?"

"Yes."

"What about what he did to you? The crude remarks, touching you on the butt, promising to help you study for the bar?"

Selena looked down at her feet.

"Don't let him get away with it," Cynthia insisted.

Selena kept her eyes glued to the floor.

For the first time, Cynthia began to doubt her client. "Did he or didn't he sexually harass you?"

Selena stared at her hands folded on her lap. She put on her sunglasses and looked at her attorney. "No," she said in a quiet, emotionless voice.

* * * * * * * * * * * *

"Son, I'm so glad the judge dismissed those darn charges," Linnell Sandidge said, affectionately patting Ramion on the back. "I've been praying for you. God works miracles. Yes, he does."

"Yes, he does," Ramion repeated, looking around his campaign headquarters, elated about his chances of winning the election now that his name was cleared. He waved at two women from his church stuffing envelopes.

"She's a wicked woman," Linnell said. "I don't understand how she could lie like that." She shook her head and repeated, "Wicked!"

"I've got a better word to describe her," Olivia said, standing next to her mother.

Mrs. Sandidge frowned reprovingly, "You know I don't curse."

"I just glad it worked out for you, big brother," Olivia said, spontaneously hugging Ramion.

Sage approached them with a stack of flyers in her hands. "The printer just dropped these off."

"Oh, how nice," Linnell said, clapping her hands. She took a flyer and read it out loud: "Vote for Ramion Sandidge."

"We've only five weeks to sway the voters," Sage said.

274

"I've recruited some more ladies from the church," Linnell said. "They're going to help stuff envelopes."

"What about passing out flyers at the malls and shopping centers?" Olivia questioned.

"We'll do that, too," Linnell said.

"Good, good," Sage said.

"Don't forget to put signs on the roads and close to businesses," Ramion said, his mind shifting into overdrive.

"I've hired some college kids to do that tomorrow," Sage said. "I'm working on the list of places where we want to post signs."

Olivia giggled with excitement. "I love it! What can I do?"

"Stuff envelopes or pass out flyers," Linnell said.

"I'll hand out the flyers. I want to tell people face-to-face to vote for my big brother."

"A film crew is coming tomorrow to shoot his new commercial," Sage said. "Ten days before the election we're going to do a full-scale media blitz. You'll see Ramion's face every commercial time we can get."

"Tell me what time to be here. I might want to be in the commercial," Olivia joked.

* * * * * * * * * * * *

Sage placed a plate filled with pancakes, bacon, and eggs on Ramion's side of the table. She returned to the sink, wiped off the counters, and put dirty dishes into the dishwasher. "Breakfast is ready," she called, then sat down at the table. She was pouring syrup over her pancakes when Ramion shuffled into the kitchen with a pleased grin.

"What are you all happy about this morning?" Sage asked, wondering what Ramion was hiding behind his back.

"Close your eyes," said Ramion, dressed in pajamas and a robe.

Sage looked at him quizzically for a second, then closed her eyes.

Ramion unfolded the newspaper, spread open the front page, and positioned it in front of Sage's face. "Open them."

Her eyes flashed open, and she leaned forward to read the bold face headline "CAMPAIGN BOMBING SUSPECT ARRESTED." "They caught them?"

Ramion handed her the newspaper. "They sure did. Apparently this white supremacist group that was run by a father-and-son team who didn't want Cameron governor. The FBI has known about them for a while, but they never had anything concrete on them."

Sage scanned through the article. "How do they know it's them?"

"A store owner identified the son as the person who bought items for a bomb. The son had been in the army and was dishonorably discharged. He knew about explosives."

"It doesn't say much more than that," Sage said, looking up from the newspaper.

"They probably don't want to give away their case."

"Mr. Lincoln told me to watch the newspaper," Sage said thoughtfully.

"What do you mean?" Ramion said, sitting at the table and buttering his pancakes.

"When he was getting ready to leave the reception, he told me to check the newspaper."

"How would he know?"

"That's a good question. But, he must have known something."

Shaking his head, Ramion said, "He must have. That old man still has clout."

"Isn't that something?" Sage ate some of her eggs and pancakes. "Remember we're supposed to meet with the builders."

"Today? It's Sunday."

"I want you to see the things I picked out. You know, the cabinets, wallpaper, lighting fixtures. Just to make sure you like them."

"If I don't," Ramion said with a slight smile, cocking his head.

"What do we do?" Sage lightly challenged.

"Baby, you have good taste. Whatever you choose will be fine."

"We'll be moving right after the election," Sage said. "Of course, you'll be State Senator Sandidge by then."

"Of course."

* * * * * * * * * * * *

Sage's handbag flipped open when she tucked it in her office desk drawer. She finished her telephone conversation and noticed the NuYou Salon card that had fallen from her purse. She picked up the card, remembering how the Vietnamese woman had stared at her. She couldn't explain it, but there was something in the woman's eyes that spoke to her.

Not really knowing why, Sage decided to make an appointment for a nail touch-up and pedicure. She scheduled the appointment for four o'clock.

Three hours later, Sage walked into the salon with a sense of anticipation, although she didn't know exactly what it was she expected.

She was greeted by the same friendly receptionist and was immediately escorted to a booth. She was given a touch-up and a manicure at the same time. After polish was applied to her nails, she was moved into the drying room. As soon as she walked into the room, she knew why she had come back to the salon. The eyes in the painting, the colors swirling around. It was the painting that beckoned her.

"You like?" a voice said from behind her.

Startled, Sage spun around and saw Song. "Yes, it reminds me of a painting I have."

"It does?"

"The broad strokes and the color palette are so similar . . ." Her voice trailed off. "Is this an original?"

"Oh yes, not a copy." Song stared at Sage, staring into her eyes. "Sorry for staring. Your face very familiar."

"How so?"

"My husband is an artist. He paints. He used to paint pictures of a little girl. He hasn't painted her for long time. Now he paints . . ."

Sage felt a strange sensation in her head. It was dizzying and frightening. In the echoes of her memory, she heard her father's laugher, raw and hearty.

"You have the eyes of the little girl in his paintings. That's why I stare. I never seen such eyes."

Could it be Daddy? Sage wondered. The more I look at this painting, the more it reminds me of his work. Out loud, Sage asked, "Did he paint this?"

"Yes. There are so many I couldn't decide which ones to hang here."

"Oh, is this painting for sale?"

Song shook her head.

"Are any of his paintings for sale? I collect artwork. I'd like to see some of his other work."

"He is not a popular commercial artist. He mostly paints for himself. Soothes his soul."

"What is his name? Perhaps I've heard of him."

"Shakura. He is not famous. We just moved here. He showed his art in small galleries in California."

"I would still like to see his work. I have friends who are art dealers and collectors. Who knows, maybe he'll get to do some showings here."

"He has studio at a place called the King Arts Plow Center."

* * * * * * * * * * * * *

"Congratulations, son, I think you just won the election," Raymond Sandidge said, his hand outstretched.

Ramion shook his father's hand and drew him in, patting him on the back as they hugged. "Thanks for the vote of confidence, Pop, but it's still too early to call."

"I'm telling you, son, Edwinna made a major mistake debating you. It was obvious she doesn't know the community she wants to represent."

Ramion wiped his sweating brow with a white handkerchief. "I'm glad the debate is over." Craning his neck, he added, "It looks like the reporters are gone. I'm tired of answering the same questions."

Sage and Olivia joined them, their faces as eager as two teenagers on their way to their first concert. "You're in there, big brother," Olivia said.

Sage kissed her husband. "You did a great job, honey. You were outstanding." Sage reached inside his jacket pocket for a handkerchief and blotted off the red lipstick she'd left on his lips.

"If this had been a boxing match," Olivia said, "I'd say you knocked Edwinna out in the third round."

Sage, Ramion, Raymond, and Olivia broke into laughter, the tension of the campaign disappearing from the moment.

"I like that analogy," Sage said, still laughing. "You know, a part of me really would like to knock her out."

"Now, now, Sage," Olivia said. "Ramion did it all with words."

"I just can't believe she didn't know anything about the landfill," Sage said.

"Folks have been dying over there," Raymond said. "Some of my co-workers lived there, and they used to complain about the smell and the high rate of cancer. People that live by that landfill are dying early."

"I don't understand how those companies can get away with it," Olivia said. "I mean, rates of people dying from cancer are sky-high in communities next to landfills. That's not a coincidence."

"Until it's scientifically proven, they will continue to deny responsibility," Ramion said. "This issue is much bigger than I expected."

"Excuse me," an unwelcome voice said.

They all turned and stared at Edwinna, their faces betraying a mixture of surprise, contempt, and displeasure.

Ramion's scowl turned into a cocky smile. "Hey, everyone, it's my opponent. Come over to congratulate me, have you?"

"I wouldn't count my chickens before they hatch. It's not over yet."

"Face it, Edwinna," Sage said. "He chewed you up and spit you out."

Edwinna glared at Sage. "Believe me, I have great support. People willing to put their money where there mouth is."

"So where were they today?" Ramion said. "And what about switching parties? You thought that was suddenly going to put you on easy street."

"You know, Ramion, it really doesn't matter to me one way or the other," Edwinna said, shrugging her shoulders. "I was just exercising my options."

"Oh, yeah, it matters," Ramion said. "You'll soon find out this has been an exercise in futility."

"Like I said, Que sera sera," Edwinna said. "Whoever wins, wins."

"Even your scheme with Selena couldn't help you win this one," Ramion said.

"I had nothing to do with that," Edwinna protested before stomping off.

"She doesn't care if she wins the election," Sage said. "But they have spent thousands of dollars on her campaign."

Drew joined them as Edwinna walked away. "She's got a lot of nerve."

Olivia said, "She just doesn't give a damn. I'm going to drive Mom and Dad home. See you later."

"Goodnight," Sage said, as Olivia and Raymond headed toward the door.

"I wanted to tell you that I found out some interesting information about Selena," Drew said to Sage and Ramion.

"Clue us in," Ramion said, moving closer to him.

"She flunked the bar *three* times. But, she likes to live like she's a lawyer with a high income. She was evicted from her apartment a couple of months ago."

"Hmm. Where is she living now?" Sage asked.

"She's staying with her mother."

"Where is she working? I can't imagine that a law firm would hire her. Not unless she's using an alias," Ramion said.

"She's a hairdresser, and she's working at her mother's salon in Decatur."

Sage shrugged her shoulders. "So what's so interesting?"

"She's been really broke, bouncing checks and not paying bills. Two weeks before she filed charges against you, a large deposit was made into her account."

"That should be easy to trace," Ramion said.

"It actually was transferred to her account," Drew said.

"Don't tell me it was transferred from Edwinna's account," Sage said suspiciously.

"I don't think she'd be that stupid," Ramion said. "Where'd the money come from?"

"Her mother's business account. I'm tracing the source of the deposit."

"It does sound fishy," Ramion said.

"Oh, I would love to expose her," Sage said strongly.

"I know it's probably too late to help, with the election three days from now, but you never know," Drew said, shrugging his shoulders.

"Let me know what you find out," Ramion said.

* * * * * * * * * * * *

The cork flew out of the dark green bottle, and champagne bubbled over the top of the bottle. "Give me your glass, give me your glass," Ramion urgently said, not wanting the entire contents of the bottle to spill onto the floor.

280

Sage tilted her glass as Ramion poured Dom Perigon into the gold-rimmed champagne glass. Laughter pealed from her mouth as the bubbles tickled her nose when she drank the champagne. "Ummh, delicious," she said.

She signaled with her glass for a refill.

"Already?" Ramion teased before filling up her glass.

"Congratulations, honey," Sage said, and spontaneously hugged her husband. "I'm so happy for you! I'm so proud of you!"

"Thanks to you, baby, I won," Ramion said.

"To Senator Sandidge," Sage said, clinking her glass against his.

They stood on the balcony, overlooking the hotel ballroom where family, voters, and supporters were celebrating Ramion's victory.

"It wasn't as close as I'd expected it to be. All that worrying for nothing," Sage said, her voice lilting with joy.

"It was the debate you talked me into. Good move." Ramion kissed her on the top of her head. "Now I know why you have that Maya Angelous poem on your office wall. You're a phenomenal woman, baby."

"That's my inspiration. But then again, you are too." She kissed him softly on the lips. "Do you think they'd miss us down there?"

"Hmmh," Ramion said, with a seductive smile. "What did you have in mind?"

"I happen to know that the penthouse suite is available. It has a heart-shaped bed, a Jacuzzi tub . . ."

"Say no more," Ramion said. "Let's go."

"On second thought, I don't have a change of clothes or . . ."

"No second thoughts allowed. All you need is what's under those clothes. Nothing more, and certainly nothing less."

Chapter XXIV

Ramion sat in the chair across from his mentor's desk. Looking around the office, he didn't notice anything different since the last time he'd been in the office a year ago. He glanced over at Sage, who was looking out the window, lost in thought. It was mid-afternoon, and the sky threatened rain.

They heard Edwin Williamson's distinctive voice as he approached the office. "Good to see you, Ramion," Edwin said when he came inside.

Ramion stood up and extended his hand to Edwin.

"Hello, Sage," Edwin said, nodding in her direction. "How are you?"

"Hello, Mr. Williamson," Sage said with a slight smile. "I'm doing fine."

"Call me Ed." He settled in his chair, and then said, "I was surprised by your call."

"I was surprised by what I found out about . . ."

"Winna. I know things have been awkward, but I do understand that you wanted to win on your own." Edwin leaned back comfortably in his massive desk chair. "And you did. Congratulations."

"Thanks," Ramion said. He cleared his throat before adding, "I'm here today on a very difficult matter."

"You know I'm a straight shooter. Let's be direct."

"I have a copy of a cashier's check drafted from Edwinna's account. It was deposited into Selena Tucker's mother's account. The money was then transferred to Selena's account."

Edwin studied Ramion for a minute. "That's a very serious accusation," he said somberly.

Ramion leaned across the desk and handed him the check. "I know Ed. That's why I'm here."

Edwin stared at the check, his expression unreadable. "Can anyone else confirm this information?"

"Actually, it was Drew Evans. He's a reporter for the *Atlanta Times*. He uncovered this information and brought it to us." Sage paused, and then added, "I went to college with him."

Edwin laid the copy of the check face down on his desk. "Why didn't you use this during the campaign?"

"We didn't find out about this until two days ago," Ramion explained.

"I see. What do you plan to do about it?"

"That's why we're here, Ed. You've opened many doors for me and helped me in countless other ways. I'm letting you decide how to handle it. My wife did not agree."

"Your daughter has done everything she could to destroy our relationship. She's lied, and she's falsified tapes," Sage said. "Believe me, I would love to expose her in the newspaper. But Ramion felt that you would want to handle it."

"And I will. I'm most grateful that you chose not to embarrass me. Not only could she be disbarred, but she'd surely face criminal charges."

"I'll be honest, Ed. I feel the same way as Sage. But out of respect for you, I didn't go public with it."

Edwin looked at them and humbly said, "Thank you both."

* * * * * * * * * * * * *

When Edwinna returned from court, she was surprised to find her father sitting behind her desk. She couldn't remember ever seeing him in her office.

"Hi, Daddy," she said with a bright smile, then kissed him on the top of his bald head.

283

Edwin stared at his only child for a long time. He didn't speak.

"What is it, Daddy?" Edwinna asked.

Edwin continued to quietly stare at her.

"Daddy, what's the matter?"

He pointed to the copy of the cashier's check on her desk. "Explain this," he said.

Edwinna's stomach took a nose-dive when she saw the signature on the check. She slumped into a chair, too embarrassed to return her father's piercing gaze. She wondered how he found out, but it didn't matter. He would always look at her without respect. His respect was the only thing that really mattered to her.

Edwin moved over to the conference table and sat beside her. "Why?"

"I don't know. I was just so angry that he left me."

"So you risked your career, your reputation, your freedom . . ."

"I wanted to win the election, Daddy! I wanted to prove to him that I was better than him, better than Sage," she said vehemently.

"Ramion brought me this check. He didn't have to. He could have destroyed you and really embarrassed me," Edwin spoke the words slowly, deliberately, as if he were giving a final summation to a jury. "But he chose not to."

Edwinna looked at her father for the first time, her expression puzzled. "Why didn't he? I certainly would have."

"It's obvious, my child, you wouldn't understand."

Edwinna sunk back in the chair. "What's going to happen to me?"

"If it doesn't get in the media's hands, hopefully nothing." Edwina stood. "But, I think you should leave Atlanta for a while. Perhaps you should consider working for one of our affiliate offices."

Edwinna raised her head and stared into her father's eyes. She saw reflections of disappointment and suppressed anger. She swallowed, and asked, "For how long?"

"I don't know, Winna." Her father moved toward the door, and then turned around. "Surely you understand that you will never be elected managing partner."

* * * * * * * * * * * * *

Sage knocked on the door when no one responded to the ringing doorbell. Her knocking pushed the door open. "Hello," she called out at the front of the door. When no one responded, Sage stepped inside the studio. She walked down a narrow hall and around a corner into a large open area that reminded her of a big warehouse.

"Hello," she repeated.

Bright sunlight beamed through the skylights into the studio. It was the only source of light for the high-ceiling loft with walls of brick. The building had been a manufacturing facility, but now served as a consortium for creativity, housing artists of all types.

She heard the unmistakable voice of Billie Holiday singing, "God Bless the Child." Sage remembered stacking the Billie Holiday albums on the record player, waiting for an album to fall down and the needle to drop on the edge of the album. She'd hear the popping, scratching noises of an album played too many times, then the infectious whine and seductive purr of Billie Holiday's voice.

This time Billie Holiday's sultry voice was loud and clear, with no crackling sounds or sudden skipping to the next verse in the middle of a lyric.

Sage felt the bottom of her feet tingling, shooting straight up to her shoulders, as if she had stepped into a puddle of cold water. Can it be Daddy? Sage wondered. Billie Holiday is playing, it has to be him.

If it is Daddy, she thought, what do I do? Maybe he doesn't want to know me. Maybe he doesn't care after all these years. Maybe he never did.

With her thoughts swirling around in her head, she felt dizzy with fear and trepidation. I wish Ramion was here, she thought. Maybe I should leave and come back with Ramion.

She turned toward the front door. Suddenly the music stopped, Billie Holiday's plaintive voice lost in the air. She heard something hit the floor. She took a deep breath and called out again, "Hello, I'm looking for Shakura."

"Over here."

Sage walked in the direction of the voice, a voice that was familiar, that traveled inside her ears to tap her subconcious and retrieve one special memory from her past. It's him, she thought. Oh my God, it's Daddy.

She heard water running and moved toward the sound. A large canvas was propped on an easel, and she could see feet underneath. She stopped in front of the easel and peered at a mural of people running around in circles, in bold vibrant colors. She stared at the painting, lost in the symposium of her memories. She heard her heart beat, louder and louder.

Sage sighed deeply and peeped around the mural painting. "Shakura," she whispered. She saw a man leaning over a sink, cleaning his brushes. He had a wild grey beard that seemed to cover his face She tiptoed closer. Her heartbeat and the running water were the only sounds she could hear.

"Shakura," she said in a quiet whisper.

"That's me." He tilted his head in her direction, but the glaring light from the skylight distorted his vision. He put his hand over his eyes to block out the sun.

He stared at Sage.

"Oh no," he cried, grabbing at his chest and falling back against the sink, knocking his paintbrushes to the ground.

Suddenly frightened, Sage stumbled over to help Shakura to the table.

"Are you all right?" she asked, looking into eyes that were the save olive green as hers. It's Daddy, she thought. It's *him!*

He shook his head and moved over to the small sofa and two chairs positioned in the corner. Crackers, cheese, and a decanter of red wine rested on the table. Shakura took a sip from the glass of wine.

With his eyes closed, he took long deep breaths.

"Should I call a doctor?" Sage asked. How do I explain who I am? she wondered. And what do I do if he denies me? She desperately wanted to touch him, to gently stroke the full grey beard framing his caramel brown face. She peered closer and saw brown freckles splattered across his cheeks. Tears puddled in her eyes. She had forgotten about his freckles.

He shook his head.

Sage didn't know what to say and resisted the urge to bolt out the door, to leave their lives intact. Because the moment he recognized her, their lives would be forever changed. And what if the past unraveled the present and destroyed the future? She stood up and said, "I'm sorry for disturbing you."

Sage took a few steps and stopped when she heard a voice from the past.

"I should know you—" Satchel said. Memories from his past life zoomed through his mind like a reel of film on fast forward. He closed his eyes to freeze a frame and catch a memory of the little girl from his dreams. But the memories, as always, were as elusive as a ray of sun.

She turned around slowly, her stomach churning with anticipation. Peering into her father's eyes, Sage saw his confusion as he struggled to grip reality. She walked over to him, her steps slow and deliberate.

"Who are you?" Satchel asked in a choked whisper.

"My name's Sage," she replied softly. She wasn't sure she should explain their relationship. Green eyes stared into green eyes, both lost in the prism of the past. Sage averted her gaze from her father's probing stare. She looked around the studio, a tender smile warming her face at the different paintings—some bright and literal, some colorful and abstract. She noticed a painting that was similar to the one she'd bought from Tawny.

A series of pictures hanging on the wall behind Shakura suddenly caught her attention, sending a jolt of excitment that vibrated from her heart to her stomach. Beautiful paintings of a little amber-colored girl with olive-green eyes.

"I'm . . . your . . ."

Satchel's eyes followed Sage's gaze. "You're the little girl I paint. You're the one I dream about."

Smiling at the man she never imagined ever seeing again, she softly said, "I'm your daughter."

A door was unlocked in Satchel's mind when Sage explained who she was, releasing a floodgate of memories.

"My, how you've grown," he said tenderly, then took the last step between them and hugged his daughter to him.

* * * * * * * * * * * * *

Boxes were scattered around Sage's bedroom in her new house. Some boxes were opened, but most were closed. The furniture was properly placed in new surroundings, but everything else still needed to be organized.

Instead of unpacking the boxes marked for the master bedroom closet, Sage sat on the bed staring at her father's painting of butterflies leaning against the wall. The excitement of moving into a brand new house was lost in the wonder of finding her father. Sage didn't notice

Ramion's quiet entrance. She didn't know he was in the room until she felt his lips graze her neck. "My father is alive," she said, repeating the words she had uttered a hundred times in the past twenty-four hours.

"Unbelievable," Ramion said, easing down on the bed.

"When I was little I used to fantasize that Daddy was lost in Vietnam, that he was a prisoner of war, and that one day he was going to return," Sage said.

"He was lost all right," Ramion said. "Losing his memory, not knowing who he was or where he came from."

"He still doesn't remember what happened to him. Doesn't know how he was injured. All he remembers is waking up and being cared for by a Vietnamese woman."

"Apparently she saved his life," Ramion said wryly.

"She took him home to her family, and they took care of him." She sighed, remembering her father's answers to the questions rolling around in her head. "When he got better, they kept him hidden for many years because they were afraid if they turned him in, he'd become a prisoner of war. I guess by that time he'd fallen in love with the woman's daughter, Song."

"But he never really forgot you, baby," Ramion said, massaging the tight muscles in her neck.

"I know. He painted what he remembered," she said wistfully. "But now we have so much to learn about each other."

"I'll be right here with you," Ramion said, then kissed the woman he never wanted to lose. "Right by your side."

About the Author

Robin Hampton Allen is also the author of *Breeze*. She has written articles for several national publications, including *Black Elegance, Today's
Black Woman,* and *Diversity Careers.* She grew up in Pittsburgh, PA,
and now lives in Atlanta, GA, with her husband and two daughters.
She is currently working on her third novel.

Robin loves to hear from readers. You may write her at:

P.O. Box 673634
Marietta, GA 30006

Other titles available from Genesis Press

Date	Title	Author
April 1997	*Reckless Surrender* (R) 1-885478-17-8 $6.95	Rochelle Alers
May 1997	*Yesterday Is Gone* (R) 1-885478-12-7 $10.95	Beverly Clark
June 1997	*Nowhere to Run* (R) 1-885478-13-5 $10.95	Gay G. Gunn
July 1997	*Love Always* (R) 1-885478-15-1 $10.95	Mildred E. Riley
September 1997	*Passion* (R) 1-885478-21-6 $10.95	T. T. Henderson
October 1997	*Glory of Love* (R) 1-885478-19-4 $10.95	Sinclair LeBeau
October 1997	*Lasting Valor* (Bio) History 1-885478-30-5 $29.95	Vernon J. Baker/ Ken Olsen
October 1997	*The Smoking Life* (Gift book) 1-885478-22-4 $29.95	Ilene Barth
November 1997	*Uncommon Prayer* (Rel) 1-885478-31-3 $9.95	Rev. Kenneth Swanson
November 1997	*Secret Obsession* (R) 1-885478-20-8 $10.95	Charlene Berry
January 1998	*Again, My Love* (R) 1-885478-23-2 $10.95	Kayla Perrin
January 1998	*Montgomery's Children* (GF) 1-885478-25-9 $14.95	Richard Perry
February 1998	*Gentle Yearning* (R) 1-885478-24-0 $10.95	Rochelle Alers
February 1998	*The Honey Dipper's Legacy* (GF) 1-885478-28-3 $14.95	Myra Pannell-Allen
March 1998	*Midnight Peril* (R) 1-885478-27-5 $10.95	Vicki Andrews
March 1998	*Quiet Storm* (R) 1-885478-29-1 $10.95	Donna Hill